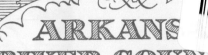

ARKANS
RIVER COUN
Based on Thos. Nuttall's Map
1819

O Z A R K

M T S.

BERRY CREEK

Dardanell

Che

JEAN CREEK

M T S.

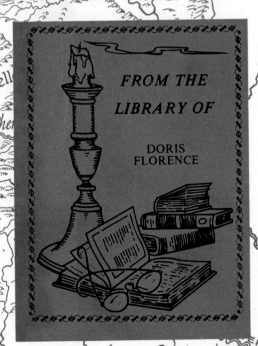

MISSISSIPPI RIVER

Post of Arkansas ★

Sam¹ H. Bryant

Much thanks
for all your love and
patience during our two
month stay — Sandy and Darrell
11/4/76

Johnny Osage

Books by Janice Holt Giles

JOHNNY OSAGE

by Janice Holt Giles

Houghton Mifflin Company Boston

Foreword

The reader of any historical novel is entitled to know who, among the characters, are real and who are fictional. The following people are real: Major William Bradford; Lieutenant Martin Scott; Colonel Matthew Arbuckle; Governor Miller; Nathaniel Pryor; Mark Bean; Joseph Revoir; Claymore, the Osage chief; all the people of Union Mission save Judith Lowell; the firms of Brand & Barbour and Chouteau. The others, as well as the establishment of Burke & Fowler, are fictional.

Scammon, or the Blade, stands in a category alone. He is not real but he is based on a composite of several such men.

The Cherokee-Osage wars of the early nineteenth century are a matter of record and I have not falsified the record. The historical events happened as related, and all letters and documents and speeches quoted are from the archives.

I have no personal bias for the Osage Indians as against any others, but if my characters, in their time and place, were to have any validity and integrity, they had to be prejudiced. At Three Forks, in 1821, this is the way it was.

I am grateful to the Oklahoma Historical Society for permission to make a transcript of part of the Union Mission Journal, and to Mrs. Dorothy Williams, librarian, for making it. I am also indebted to Mr. Paul Bruner of the Chamber of Commerce, Muskogee, Oklahoma, for directing me to various pamphlets and documents; to Miss Grace Upchurch of the Library of the University of Arkansas for interested and valuable help; to Mrs. N. F. Childress, Sallisaw, Oklahoma, for numerous clippings, booklets and pamphlets given freely from her collection.

I am especially grateful to Mr. John Joseph Mathews, the Blackjacks, Pawhuska, Oklahoma, for permission to use the ceremony of the dove as recounted in his own beautiful book about the Osages, *Wah'-Kon-Tah*. He also advised me on the use of Osage proper names.

Last, but not least, I wish to thank my sister, Mary Holt Sullivan, who drove with me to all the places and helped me map the country, who stood with me beside the grave of Epaphras Chapman, and who cheerfully faced the prairie heat with me that blazing summer of 1956.

J.H.G.

Spout Springs
Knifley, Kentucky

Chapter 1

He lay in the darkness of the lodge, warily alert, and tried to think what had awakened him. It was cold. No one was stirring. There was no movement among the blanket-wrapped forms all around him. But he had wakened as suddenly as if a voice had called him, or a hand had shaken his shoulder, wide awake, alert in a moment. He had a premonition of daylight coming, although there was no real fading of the dark yet. But he sensed, as he smelled the cold air, a lighter, thinner quality in it, as if the earth had accelerated a little, was spinning off the thick layers of night. He lay very still and listened with the nerves of his body, reached with them to feel whatever sound had broken his sleep.

There was an uneasiness in the earth beneath him, a small vibration as if buffalo, in a great herd, were running very far away. He felt it in his shoulders and thighs, not really a sound, no more than the quiver of a sound, felt rather than heard, a ripple of nerve ends disturbed. He felt it through the length of his body, as if the pulse of his blood had changed and had become more insistent, as if it ran its course more swiftly. And then, though he yet could not hear the sound, he knew what it was . . . drums. Drums outside the village were beating, softly yet, but like his pulse beat, rhythmic, unbroken, steady. Drums for the long day's ceremony beginning, sending along, muffled by distance, an insistent, urging throbbing which carried not so much on the air as through the earth, as if it sank and became the bloodstream of the earth, traveled through its veined layers.

As at a signal the sleeping Indians around him wakened. They lay still for a moment as he had done, then moved concertedly from their robes and blankets. They left the lodge and all around him the trader heard the soft slipping sounds as the entire village, wakened all at once, moved off into the woods. He waited for the first voice to be lifted in the morning chant. It would come when the first knife-edge of light slit the night around the horizon, separated the earth from the night sky by a narrow band of light. To Wah-kon-tah, then, the Great Mystery, the Osages would chant their rising prayer.

It came, a long-drawn sound — Ah, hooooooooooooo — lifted over the night-tented prairie, echoing from the blackjack hills, wailing into the river bottom. It was allowed to die away on a single sighing, lonely-falling note, then raised again it was taken up by hundreds of joining voices — Ah, hooooooooooooooo!

Each face was turned to the east, the place of mystery. Each soul sought the mystery, felt the mystery, sang to it with a sad loneliness of mystery, knowing the children of the earth could not penetrate it, loving it, fearing it, placating it, praying to it, absorbing it, voicing in concert but each alone, as do the wolves under the cold stars, the heart-penetration of mystery. Each throat trilled quaveringly the long, lonely song, lifting it, chanting it, crying it — needing the mystery, the miracle, the benevolence. The danger of the night was past; each man's soul which might have vanished in the dark had been returned to him; the evil spirits which haunted the darkness were vanquished for another night. Let Wah-kon-tah guard his children through the coming day. Let the mysteries be propitiated. Let the sun rise blessedly.

Johnny Fowler lay still and listened, haunted by the urgency of the morning chant, chained by its lonely beauty, penetrated himself by its necessity. It was a cry which echoed every lonely prayer which had ever risen from the solitary heart of man, uneasy in the presence of mystery, yearning for a sign that he was not alone.

Then, as suddenly as it had begun and again as if on signal, it ceased. Not one voice trailed on brokenly and alone. The morning prayers were over and Johnny Fowler arose, hearing the quick noises of the returning Indians, now calling to each other, laughing among themselves. There were the light, chittering voices of children, like little birds waked, threading their thin notes onto a string of rising and falling sound, crystal, brittle in the cold air. There were the quarreling, muttering voices of the women going for wood to bring to the lodges. There were the yelping snarls of the multitudinous dogs of the village. Only the voices of the men were absent. Men, in their dignity, kept silence in the awakening tumult.

He passed outside the lodge and walked down the street of the village to the river. The sky was milky with light now and there was a flushed look in the east. The air was brisk with frost and the edges of the river when he reached it were ribbed with thin, webby ice. He cracked the ice and washed. The back of winter was broken now. The ice was thinner and thinner each day. The iron-hardness of the ground was slowly thawing. The willows along the river were reddening down their trailing streamers and soon the small yellow threads of leaves would appear. He sniffed the smells which came to his nostrils — the acrid smell of the walnut and pecan trees, the sour smell of dead ironweeds, the tonic smell of sweet gum, the muddy, spongy smell of thawing ground and, from the lodges now, the smell of wood smoke. They were good smells. It was February, Mi-u-kon-dsi, the month of the solitary moon. Spring was on its way.

He returned to the lodge of Sho-mo-kah-se, "the Wolf," and took his place before the fire. He took the horn ladle handed him by one of the women and ate from the wooden family bowl of the boiled, pounded corn. There was no meat. There would be no meat until the spring hunt. But the pounded corn had cooked to a mush and it was good. He ate hungrily, then taking out his pipe he lit it, passed it to the Wolf who dipped it ceremoniously in the four directions, toward the earth and the sky, then took a deep breath of the smoke and handed the pipe back to Johnny Fowler.

When they had finished the pipe they rose and walked through the village, out onto the open prairie. They walked across the short, winter-dun grass, their moccasined feet leaving wet marks in the white frost. The trader's moccasins made a silky sound in the frosty grass. The Indian's, tied with small bells, tinkled silverily as he walked. Only a man who had killed his enemy could wear bells on his feet and carry the war hatchet. This man did both.

Long before they reached the little grove of shin-oaks which marked the place of the ritual they could hear the drums, the muffled note of the great, deep kettledrum joined by the lighter beat of the smaller ones. The beat was slow, regular, steady — an emphasis, then a lighter note — *dum*-dum, *dum*-dum, *dum*-dum. Because he once was a soldier and marching to drums came natural to him, Johnny Fowler found himself slowing his steps to keep the slow rhythm of the drums; but if the Osage beside him felt the rhythm he gave no sign of it. Tall, regal in his best shirt and leggins, a fine buffalo robe held loosely about his shoulders, his necklaces of bear claws and teeth swaying with his movements, his ear lobes heavy with their silver rings, he walked gravely and silently beside the trader. His roach bristled and from his two braids dangled and spun his red-painted eagle feathers. Only a man who had stolen horses could wear the eagle feather. This man was one who had done so many times.

Other Indians had gathered by the time they reached the grove of trees and were moving into places. In the center of the winter-stripped shin-oaks the drummers were stationed. As if in a trance they beat out the steady, unfaltering rhythm, paying no heed to the gathering throng. *Dum*-dum, *dum*-dum, *dum*-dum. The chanters were ringing themselves near the drums.

Seating himself with the Wolf and Handsome Bird and Big Striker, who joined them, Johnny Fowler watched intently what was going on. Apart from the other Indians were the Wah-kon-da-gis, the medicine men. Their faces were painted and each carried his sacred bundle, his wa-xo-be, a skin bag enclosing only each man knew what, the bones of some bird or animal, some sacred relic perhaps, some talisman which that particular man considered his own peculiar medicine. Some only carried rattles, dried bladders with small pebbles latched inside. Among the medicine men stood the man who was to be initiated, for the ritual of the dove was the initiation of a new medicine man.

The drums accelerated, changed their rhythm, and the singers began, their chant keeping the rhythm of the drums, reminding Wah-kon-tah that his children were gathered here for a grave purpose. With supplication they pleaded for attention. The song also reminded the initiate of the graveness of his intent.

To one side of the group a short post had been driven into the ground and tied upon it was a dove. It was not a live dove. No live dove would have been so large, for it had been made for the purpose, of parts of several doves. It faced east. Motionless, inscrutable, unblinking, it sat on its perch, a symbol of Johnny Fowler knew not what.

The drums continued, swelling to a great volume at times, dying softly away at other times, the voices of the chanters following the volume and the rhythm perfectly. The trader knew what patient practice it had required to achieve such perfection. Every intonation, every syllable, had its particular meaning and the discipline of the unison was difficult. It took years for a man to become a good singer.

The medicine men shook their rattles, joined in the chanting, then when it was thought Wah-kon-tah was listening, the group moved over to the post, the drums continuing to beat, the chanters continuing to sing. Johnny Fowler and the three Osages, having already good positions, remained where they were.

When the people had gathered again the medicine men took their places behind the drummers and among them now were the several witnesses of the man to be initiated. Gravely they took their seats and did certain things, observed certain traditional formalities. One by one, and slowly, the drums still beating the rhythm, each witness did with his hands what he was supposed to do, made supplication, or promise, or propitiating gesture.

The sun was high now, warming the earth and the prairie grass, melting the frost, sifting through the dark limbs of the shin-oaks. Johnny Fowler felt it good on his back and shoulders.

Suddenly the drums thrummed louder and one of the witnesses rose and walked toward the dove. In his hand he carried several little sticks. He approached the dove with slow, precise movements and stood for a moment before it. The chanters lowered their voices, and the witness addressed the dove in solemn, stylized speech. "Fly away. Fly away to Wah-kon-tah. Fly away and tell him this man is worthy. Tell him I know this man. Tell him this thing. Tell him I saw this man do good thing." There followed a slow, halting, stiff speech recounting the good deed, telling how the man had fed an old person all one winter, though the hunting was poor, meat was scarce, and his own family was often hungry. He had kept the old person all winter in his lodge and the old one had eaten as often as had the man's own children. "This was good. I know this thing which he did. Fly away to Wah-kon-tah and tell him."

The witness broke one of the sticks and flung it down beside the post on which the dove looked, sightlessly, to the east. The drums throbbed louder and louder and the chanters lifted their voices in swelled volume. Wah-kon-tah, they were pleading, hear what this man has done, heed him, he is a good man.

After an interval the witness began to tell of another deed. This man had taken the scalp of his enemy. He had taken it because his enemy had killed his uncle. Now his uncle's spirit could make its journey in peace to the Great Mystery, his soul restored to him by his enemy's scalp.

When the witness had told a good deed for each stick he carried he returned to his place among the medicine men. He was brought immediately a good, four-point blanket, a pair of new leggins, a beaded belt. These things were the gifts he received for being a witness. Sho-mo-kah-se poked Johnny in the side and hissed in his ear, "When I received my wa-xo-be it cost me forty ponies."

"Was it worth it?" Johnny said, grinning.

Shocked the old man rounded his eyes at the trader and lapsed into an affronted silence.

The next witness had approached the dove with his small bundle of sticks.

All day the ceremony went on. In the middle of the day it stopped long enough for the men to eat the food the women brought, but when everyone had eaten the ritual began again and it continued all during the afternoon. Without restlessness Johnny Fowler sat and watched it. If it grew tedious to him and he grew weary of the tedium, he did not show it. As grave as the Osages and as silently he watched each movement, listened to each speech. He listened with no sign of impatience, no slacking of interest or courtesy, to the long repetitive tales of good deeds, to the monotone of the chants, to the steady, unrelenting beat of the drums. He might have been an Osage himself so impassively did he sit, so silently did he listen.

The sun wheeled across the sky, dropped low in the west, reddened the clouds, and the prairie wind got up and skirled dry leaves among the Osages, ruffled their blankets, spun their eagle feathers like spinning wheels. The wind was cold, but no one noticed. The ritual proceeded. Then when the sun went down in a blaze of red, with no warning the drums stopped, the chanters hushed their song, and like the waters of a river flowing quietly, the people slipped away into the gathering gloom. The ritual of the dove was over. There was another Wah-kon-da-gi in the village.

Back at the Wolf's lodge, Johnny Fowler ate again and smoked a pipe with the old man once more. They took their places just inside the door of the lodge. In the masking twilight he listened to the softly quarreling voices of the women behind him. An Osage woman quarreled incessantly, grumbling against the perversity of all things. She scolded the wind which blew the fire and made it smoke; she scolded the fire for smoking; she scolded the roof which leaked and the rain which leaked through as well as the skins which got wet under the leak. These things were all personal affronts to her and she made her complaint directly to them. In the lodge she also quarreled at her husband. On the hunt, at war, men were the kings and women were servants. In the village, in the lodges, women spoke up.

In the lodge of the Wolf there were many women to quarrel. He had four wives, and in the good Osage way his daughters lived with him, with their husbands and children. The most complaining voice in his lodge was that of his eldest daughter whose husband was a fat, lazy, no-good man called One-Eye. Shrilly now her voice was raised in complaint against him. "You can never do anything right. No one but someone as lazy and no good as you would stumble over the kettle and spill the food!"

The man muttered in reply, something which Johnny Fowler and the Wolf could not hear. The woman's voice shrewed out at him. "Go away! Awkward, stupid man! Go away outside with your great clumsy feet. Go away before I hit you!"

Moving indolently but obediently One-Eye passed between the Wolf and Johnny. He cut a slantwise look from his good eye at the trader. "My old woman," he said, a chuckle of lazy good humor in his voice, "he knows how to scold good, ain't it?"

When he had passed, the Wolf said in a flat, even voice, "In that man's shoes I would lodgepole that woman. It would be a good thing. The scolding would cease for a while. But he is too lazy."

Johnny laughed but he made no reply. It was not good to venture opinions in family matters.

The silence deepened as the dark blotted out the village and as the Indians drifted quietly into their lodges for the night. Johnny Fowler waited. He had come here to talk to this old man, chief of the wolf band who, though not the principal chief of the village, was not only wise and intelligent but was as well very influential. Arriving on the eve of the dove ceremony he had, without mentioning his purpose, adjusted himself to the necessity of waiting until it was over. He had yet to wait a while. There could be no talk until the women were quiet, wrapped in their robes, lain down for the night. A woman, with her noise and her chatter, her quarrelings, kept a man's thoughts in turmoil. A man could not reflect with the noise of women in his ears.

When the sounds of the lodge were finally stilled, when the last soft muttering voice was quiet, Johnny Fowler began to speak in the soft, singing tongue of the Osages. "My friend," he said, "there is a thing I wish to talk about."

"My ears are open," the old man said courteously.

"I have heard," Johnny said, "that Osages will not go to the fort to council with the Cherokees."

"The wind carries many tales," the old man murmured.

"The wind carries many tales," Johnny agreed, "but I believe this thing is true." He waited, giving the old man time to sort out his thoughts, determine whether he would discuss this thing with this white man.

The Wolf took out his own pipe, lit it with a coal, passed it to the trader. When Johnny passed it back to him, the old man puffed thoughtfully, the smoke wreathing his head. "I think this thing you have heard," he said then, quietly, "is true."

"I would like to talk about why Osages will not go to this council," Johnny said. "The soldier chief at the fort has asked me to talk to Sho-mo-kah-se. He has told me to ask Sho-mo-kah-se to come to the fort and council. He has told me he thinks it will be a good thing."

"Sho-mo-kah-se is not the principal chief," the old Indian said. "Sho-mo-kah-se does not decide these things."

"But Sho-mo-kah-se," the trader said, "talks with Grah-moh and Grah-moh listens to him."

The old man grunted. There was a long silence and the deeper silence which lay over the village was felt more heavily. A man, Johnny Fowler thought, can make friends with the sounds of night, even the sounds of danger, but a silence in the

night is a burdensome thing, an unnatural and unfriendly thing.
He waited patiently.

Out of the silence, his voice somber and grave, the old Indian
spoke finally. "My friend," he said, "my mind is troubled. I do
not know about these things. I am an old man. I have lived
many years. For as long as I can remember Osages have lived
on this land, and for as long as my father before him and his father before him. This is the only thing I know, for how can a
man be wrong about his home? Within my memory there have
always been white men who told us many things. Osages have
believed some of these things. Osages believed when their friend
Chouteau told them the great chief across the water was their
father and their king. Osages let the French men live among
them because they believed they were their brothers."

Johnny Fowler settled himself more comfortably. The Wolf
was going back to the beginning. It would be a long speech. It
would require much patience.

"Then," the old man continued, "our friend Chouteau told us
that the king was no longer our great father and that our father
was now the Great White Father in Washington and that the
French were not our brothers now, but that our brothers were
the Americans. This thing we believed also, though our hearts
were sad because we liked our French brothers. Our French
brothers lived among us honoring our ways. Our French brothers did not want Osage land. Our French brothers did not put
up lodges which could not be moved. They did not build fences
around themselves. They did not tear up the land with pointed
irons. They hunted on the prairies with Osages and trapped the
rivers. They married our daughters and lived among us the way
Osages live.

"Our American brothers are different. They come here to our
land and they build lodges which cannot be moved. They put
fences about themselves. They dig up the earth with the pointed
irons. Osages do not like these things our American brothers
do. They believe this thing is bad, for our friend Chouteau said
the President in Washington would not let our American broth-

ers do these things. When the President in Washington did not stop our American brothers from doing these things, Osages believed they were not our brothers. They were our enemies and Osages took their horses and took their scalps. These things I saw, and these things I did, myself, many years ago."

The old man's voice continued, plaintive, puzzled, questioning. "Because Osages killed Americans the red-haired one in Chouteau's town called the chiefs together for a council. The white men held a council at Fire Prairie and they scolded the chiefs, the way a man's wife scolds him in his lodge, and they said, 'Because you have stolen this many horses and because you have killed this many white men, you owe this much money.' How can a man have a debt without knowing it? How can taking his enemies' horses mean he must pay? Osages have always taken the horses of their enemies. Osages have always taken the scalps of their enemies. Osages are men. They have those things which make men different from women. Osages know how to deal with their enemies." The slow, breathy voice, shaping the round vowels and the long, sibilant consonants, quickened and hardened. "What must a warrior do? Sit like an old woman before the door of his lodge and let his enemies take his land and his home? Osages are not weaklings. They know how to protect themselves."

Johnny Fowler waited, knowing the end had not come yet, until the old man sorted out his thoughts again. He was one of the greatest orators among the Osages. He did not speak hastily or thoughtlessly. He weighed each word carefully. "The red-haired one," he continued, "said 'You must not kill these people. You must be peaceful and the Great White Father will protect you.' He told us that the President would pay for the horses and for the scalps and he would also give the Osages many presents. He said we must make our marks on a paper and give up some of our land if the President did this thing.

"Osages thought about this for a long time. We did not know what to do. I saw this thing. My mind was troubled. Osages talked to their friend Chouteau and he said the land the President wanted was not worth much to Osages. He said it was where the Ni-shu-dse runs shallow and slow. The hunting is not good there. He said it would be a good thing if we gave this land to the President. He said if we gave this land to the President he would set up a place at Fire Prairie where Osages could take their furs and buy those things which they needed. He said no one would cross Osage land again. He said Americans would not build their lodges there and tear up the earth with their pointed irons. He said the President would give Osages many presents if they did this thing.

"Osages thought if no more Americans would come on their land it would be a good thing. The red-haired one was a man with a good heart, they believed. Osages counciled together and they said these things and they made their marks on the paper and gave the President the land."

Again the old man paused and when he resumed talking there was a certain weariness in his voice as if even to speak of these things tired him. "The red-haired one did not lie. The Great White Father built this place at Fire Prairie and he sent his soldiers there. Osages were given presents. For a little while there was this fort at Fire Prairie and then the Great White Father took his soldiers away and took his goods away also.

"For a long time there was no fort and no soldiers. The Americans kept coming. And now the Osages learned why the President wanted their land on the Ni-shu-dse. He moved the Cherokees there and they put up their lodges. The President told the Cherokees not to hunt on Osage land. He built the fort on the Ni-shu-dse and sent his soldiers there. But the soldiers do not protect the Osages.

"Cherokees look with longing on our hunting grounds. Cherokees make war upon our villages and send their hunting parties to our lands because they are not satisfied with the land the President gave them. Osages," here the old man's voice deepened with contempt, "have never made war on Cherokee villages. Osages do not want what Cherokees have. But when Cherokees hunt on Osage land, Osages know what to do." The old man was silent again. Johnny Fowler waited.

"My friend," the old man went on, after a time of pondering, "some Osage young men have killed some Cherokees who were hunting on Osage land. Cherokees now say they will go to war. Osages do not want war. Osages will live at peace with Cherokees, but Cherokees must not hunt on Osage land and Cherokees must not make war on Osage villages. Osages are tired of these things. Cherokees must return our people they have taken away. These things Osages know." He fell silent and then resumed sadly. "My mind is troubled. The man who is the soldier chief at the fort has sent for Osage chiefs to council. Osages cannot council with Cherokees as long as their hearts are bad. They have said many times they will return our people, but they do not. Let Cherokees do this thing they have said they will do. Let Cherokees show that their hearts are good, then Osages will council with them." His voice ended strongly, hung urgently between them, then fell in a final, dropping period. He had finished.

Johnny Fowler eased a bent knee and drew in his breath. "I will tell the soldier chief at the fort these things Sho-mo-kah-se has said."

"Tell him," the old man said, "Osages do not want war. Osages do not have guns and ammunition as many as Cherokees. But Osages have hearts and Grah-moh has many warriors to send against Cherokees if they make war."

"I will tell him."

The old man's head which had been held so proudly upright all during the talk drooped a little. "My friend," he said, "I do not know. My mind is troubled. Osages must protect their children and their wives and their old people. Like a place where there are too many tracks to follow, my mind goes in too many ways. I do not know. My friend, who can an Osage believe?"

The beautiful human dignity of the old Indian, the beautiful human pride, invaded Johnny Fowler with such strength and such passionate pity that he moved convulsively as if a pain had shot through his limbs. He felt a spasm of anger, but it was wasted anger and he pushed it down. "I do not know either," he said. "Osages are my friends. I do not like these things which are done against them, but I do not know how to council about them. I believe this thing is true, that Osages must protect their lodges and their women and children. The soldier chief says it is not a good thing when Osage young men become angry and kill Cherokees. He says Osages should tell him when Cherokees hunt on Osage land. He says he will make Cherokees go home."

"Are Osages children to bear tales?" The old man's voice was quick with contempt. "Where are the soldier chief's eyes that he must be told?"

"He is but one man," Johnny Fowler said quietly. "He cannot see all things. When Osage young men become angry and kill Cherokees, Osages must pay. Cherokees tell the soldier chief. Cherokees say Osages have killed this many men, have stolen this many horses. Cherokees say Osages must pay."

"This thing you say is true. Cherokees become angry. Osages must pay. Does my friend," he continued slowly, his eyes fixed on the trader's firelit face, "does my friend think it would be a good thing if Osage young men did not kill Cherokees?"

In the gloom Johnny Fowler's face twisted, his mouth drawing down bent and flat. A great sadness, heavy with old pain, touched him and he winced away from it. It lingered a moment, while he drew a tightened breath, flexed his hand, then deliberately he put it away. The Wolf was asking him if he, who had his own reasons for hating the Cherokees, believed what the soldier chief believed, was counciling as the soldier chief counciled, that Osages no longer fight their own wars but let the soldier chief fight them for them. Pushing down the sadness, and the quick anger the sadness aroused, Johnny Fowler said gravely, "My friend, Osages cannot continue to pay with their land. The land does not last forever. It will be eaten away and Osages will find themselves with no place to build their lodges, no place

where their women and children may sleep. Osages are men,
but the ways of the Americans are not the ways of Osages and
the Americans do not understand Osage ways." There was a
note of pleading in the trader's voice. "I believe," he said, "it
would be a good thing if Osages did not kill Cherokees. Osages
would not have to pay, then."

It was the voice of wisdom speaking. It was the mind control-
ling the heart. With as much hot, angry blood in him as in any
Osage young man he would rather have fought by their sides,
but it was not the wise thing to do. Will Bradford at Fort Smith
was right. Osages could not continue their lawless ways of taking revenge into their own hands. Whatever grievance any man
of them had must be put aside for the good of them all. Those
young men who had lost wives and children in the Cherokee
raid on the village must not honor the tradition of revenge and
retribution, or even the personal grief they bore. The larger
vision must prevail. The trader felt a clotted nausea at the hard
thing he must advise. His mouth was full of a sour, coppery saliva and he spat it out on the ground. "I believe it would be a
good thing."

The old man pondered for a long time what the trader had
said. Then he said, "I will think about this thing. I will tell
Grah-moh what Man-Not-Afraid-of-Pawnees has said."

Johnny sighed and silence fell between them. There was nothing more to say. It was growing late. The solitary moon had
risen and the village lay whitely under its light, asleep and quiet.
Nearby, in the horse corrals, a horse snorted, fanning his breath
out his mouth and nostrils, ridding himself of weed chaff and
dust. Like an epidemic it spread through the herd and there
were a dozen snuffles and sneezes, the stamping of hooves, the
whicker of a young colt. They were unalarmed, domestic
sounds, however. Nothing was bothering the horses.

Johnny Fowler listened. They were good sounds to him. The
ways of this Indian village were good ways to him. He saw beneath the surface disorder of the village down to its ordered cor-

rectness, all things dictated by tradition so that each member of each band of the village knew what was proper for him to do at what time and in what place, knew his own place in the order and knew his own worth and distinction. He thought of the deep and profound religion of these people, with their reverence for all things Wah-kon-tah had made and surrounded them with, the sun, the wind, the stars, the rain, summer heat and winter cold.

He thought of their courtesy to each other, their great dignity, their refusal to try to control the destinies of others. He thought of the way children were so loved by them, educated so properly at each stage of their growth, so cherished, so loved, brought up so correctly that when grown any young man so respected his elders that he was willing to die at the command of one. He thought of the way the old people were so revered, their wisdom so respected. He thought of the layers of organization which leveled down through Osage life, the principal chief in his hereditary position but with power limited so wisely. There was always the council of braves and elders which could overrule him. He thought of the requirements for men to become braves, warriors, chiefs, partisans, soldiers, medicine men — the traditions, the rituals, the proper things, the correct things. There were no uncertainties save the uncertainties, the vagaries, of Wah-kon-tah. It was as if, knowing no man could penetrate that mystery, Osages had made certain of all things human. Johnny Fowler liked these ways. He thought white men could take a valuable lesson from them. He stirred, broke off his long thoughts, broke the long silence. "The summer year is coming," he said. "Osages will be moving their lodges soon."

The old Indian grunted his agreement.

In the winter the village moved to the river bottom where there was wood, water, and better shelter from the winds. In the early spring they moved onto the prairie, away from the mosquitoes and insects which plagued the streams. Twice a year the Osages went on their long hunt onto the plains west of the Arkansas — in the summer year, and again in the winter year — but these things had no exact timing. The long hunts came when the weather broke in the spring, before the time of planting corn, and again in the autumn, when the women had gathered the corn, but before the village was moved to the timber stands. The spring hunt might occur as early as February or as late as May. The fall hunt might occur in September, or it might be delayed until November. So many things controlled the departure — the weather, omens and signs and dreams, the presence or absence of enemies.

"Is my friend going to hunt the buffalo with Osages?" the old man asked.

"I do not know," Johnny Fowler said. "It may be. There are many things to consider."

The old man nodded. It was wise to leave any decision thus. An Osage always knew there were many things to consider. He rose and with no further word went farther back into the interior of the lodge.

Johnny Fowler stood a moment longer at the door looking down the long, irregular street of the village. The moonlight was pale and milky and the frozen street was satiny with its glaze. Shadows from the lodges pitted the light with pockets of darkness, but on all the long street nothing moved. All was still, all was quiet.

He turned then and followed the Wolf and lay down in the place near the fire prepared for him. The sleeping members of the Indian's family lay all about, the wives, the children, the married daughters and their husbands and children. An Osage chief's lodge held many people.

The fires had gone out except for glowing embers and the lodge was almost dark. The moon slanted through the smoke holes in the roof, throwing bars of white light across the earth floor. A child murmured and stirred sleepily, was hushed by a soft voice, was still.

Johnny Fowler drew the buffalo robe close about his shoulders. He thought briefly of the talk with the old Indian. He had done what he had been asked to do. He had brought Major Bradford's message. He had a message to take back to the major. What the Osages would do rested with their elders now.

He blotted out the moon with a corner of his robe, closed his eyes, and went immediately to sleep.

Chapter 2

Aᴀ ʜᴇ ʜᴀᴅ ᴇᴀᴛᴇɴ the next morning, a young boy, a lad still in early adolescence, brought Johnny's horse to the door of the lodge.

The boy was a grandson of Sho-mo-kah-se. His grandmother was the oldest wife of the Wolf and though both she and the old man were full bloods, she had been loaned one time to a French trader. She had conceived and the boy's mother was therefore half French. In turn the daughter had married a halfbreed, Suard, so that the boy and her other children had a strong French bloodline. It was evident in the boy in lighter coloring and in a finer, smaller bone structure. He would not be, when grown, as tall a man as his grandfather.

This boy who, as yet, had only a tentative name, Little Feather, would never remember when he had learned to ride a horse, so young had he been when placed on the back of one. At his present age it was part of his training to help with the care of the animals the men of his family owned. It was a grave responsibility. Though Osages used their horses very hard, they took excellent care of them. They were hobbled in such a way that if danger alerted them in the night and they fled, the tether would give easily and allow them their freedom. They were taken to the river each day, washed down, fed, allowed to drink, and brought back to the horse corral. When new mustangs were brought in, wild, from the prairie, they were gentled in such a way that their spirits were not broken. Rather they were taught, by patient repetition, that their free days were over and that hereafter their lives would be burden-bearing. All of these things the young lad, Little Feather, was now learning.

The principal chief, Grah-moh, whose name meant Arrow-Going-Home, came himself to bid the trader goodbye. French traders had called the chief Clermont — Americans made it Claymore. He was one who had broken, to some extent, with the vast Chouteau empire and it was with his large village that the American traders at Three Forks had the most exchange. Because Suard, the Wolf's son-in-law, was a trapper and hunter for Johnny Fowler and his partner, Johnny had first been accepted by the village. He had come to be trusted and liked because of his own nature, because he both liked and trusted the Osages and because they saw in him the qualities they most admired — a steely courage in times of danger, a silent dignity to match their own, a courtesy as natural as theirs, and a sincerity which they could honor and believe. He had been on many hunts with them and had even gone with a war party against their traditional enemies, the Pawnees. The name they had given him, Man-Not-Afraid-of-Pawnees, was an indication of their respect for him and of their acceptance of him. Their principal chief and their wisest old man stood now, bidding him farewell. The young boy held the reins of the trader's horse, keeping him quiet and free of nervousness. Johnny Fowler shook hands with both Indians. "Next time," Grah-moh said, "you will stay in my lodge."

"Next time," Johnny agreed, "I will stay in your lodge." He spoke the word of farewell, which was also the word of greeting. "Hou." No white man knew how this word was spelled. He only knew how it sounded. It seemed to have no literal meaning. It was simply a sound of recognition, of attention given.

The Indians replied gravely and Johnny Fowler turned to his horse. He ran a quick eye over the bridle, the cinch, the stirrups. He spoke quietly to the boy. "You have done well."

Only a flash of quick delight in his black eyes indicated the boy's pleasure at the words of commendation. His face remained impassive and he narrowed his eyes immediately. He released the reins and stepped back, covering his mouth with his hand to hide his amusement as the trader mounted from what was to an Indian the wrong side. It was a matter of perennial astonishment to an Osage that a white man ever got onto a horse at all. He himself vaulted onto his horse from the other side. To watch the laborious efforts of the white man, placing his foot in his stirrup, pulling himself onto the animal, was always amusing.

Johnny's horse was a mustang that he himself had gentled. He was, like all mustangs, hardy and almost tireless, but he was young and full of tricks yet. He pitched a time or two, tried to swallow his head and kicked up a considerable amount of dust. The boy, who could no longer control his laughter, ducked his head and fled before he should disgrace himself and his grandfather. The two older Indians laughed quietly. "Ho, Johnny!" the Wolf called to the trader. "Much better you get yourself an Osage pony."

Johnny Fowler laughed also. He motioned with his hand to the two men, then giving the mustang his head, let him run. Dogs and children and women scattered before the flying pony and were left behind in a rising cloud of dust.

For two hours he rode steadily south across the prairie which here was bounded by the Neosho River on the east and the Verdigris on the west. This was a strip of land which gradually narrowed some twenty-five miles farther down to a point where the two rivers flowed into the Arkansas only three miles apart. At the point, Johnny Fowler and his brother-in-law, Stephen Burke, had their trading post. There were two others on the Verdigris River within a few miles of them and of each other, Brand & Barbour, and Pryor & Mundy. Over on the Neosho River and much farther upstream was the Chouteau establishment which was managed by one of their kinsmen, Joseph Revoir. At one time it was the only trading post in the Osage country. Before that the Osages had been served by itinerant traders who brought their loaded pirogues up the Arkansas from New Orleans, or who came overland with loaded horses from

St. Louis. The settlement of trading posts was, because of the confluence of the rivers, called Three Forks. In 1821 it was a little more than seven years old.

The men who operated the posts were traders licensed to do business with the Osage Indians. Their wives, with the exception of Stephen Burke's, were Osage women, and the rest of the population consisted of halfbreed hunters and trappers who worked for the posts. There were no other white people except a few illegal squatters who gave Major Bradford, at Fort Smith, farther down the Arkansas, considerable trouble. East of the Osage line, and south of the river, the land had been opened to settlers, but here at Three Forks, and between it and the fort, no white person could legally settle. They consistently tried, however, and presented the commandant at the fort with one of his major problems.

When Johnny Fowler reached the timber which began a few miles north of the trading posts, he pulled his horse up in a stand of blackjacks and rested him a little while. Facing north he looked back over the prairie, across the wide, rolling land.

If he had wanted, he thought, a lonely land, he had found it all right. Nothing could be lonelier than the prairie unrolling so long and so far before him. It was a land that had no bones, no discernible skeleton. It was as softly rounded as a woman. There was no sharpness on the prairie; no rocks heaved up to break its flatness, no hills to hug it close and crowd it together and make jagged lines against the sky. Everything, he thought, flows. Everything flows and curves. The land flows and curves and away off to the west the sky flows and curves down to meet the land. It is a lonely, grieving land . . . a sad, melancholy land. It is lonelier, he thought, than the sea — lonelier than the hills. It makes a man feel as small as a speck of dust, weighs him down, burdens him with weight, pushes him into the earth in his smallness. It was no wonder that the Osages felt Wahkon-tah all about them. They had to people that solitary, long-reaching, silent land with something or feel themselves intruders where nothing human was ever meant to live — where lost on

its featureless, monotonous expanse there was the grieving feeling of something lost forever. The sea was solitary and featureless, but you rode on its bosom in a ship. You took your home
with you across its deeps. The mountains were solitary, but
there was a majestic lack of symmetry about them and you went
up and down, the path never any two days the same. The prairie, these plains — it was as if nature had taken solitude and
fashioned it into something visible, carved out the silences into
distance, into short grass forever flowing and curving, a vast sky
forever pressing down, nothing changing, nothing but sameness,
day after day after day, as far as you could see, as far as you
could go. It was like the solitude of God — as awesome, and as
beautiful.

Often, riding for days over the prairie, Johnny Fowler came
to have a burdening heartache, a torturing sense of exile. He
came to feel, as did the Osages, that Wah-kon-tah was not
pleased with him for invading this mystery. Then, as the feeling grew, a cold wind blew over his soul and he was glad to
come back to the sound of human voices, to the green of the
blackjacks and to the sense of home in the log trading post. But
he could never stay away. He always went back to it and
penned too long in the stockade he felt suffocated for its distances, felt smothered for its long-blowing winds.

It had something to do with having been raised in hill country, he supposed — something to do with having been crowded
up all his life. When he rode out on the prairie he felt released
and free, the way he thought a man was meant to feel before he
chained himself to land and belongings. It pulled at him and
would not let him alone. And then it punished him and burdened and oppressed him. He looked out across the short, dun-
topped grass now, the tops rippling a little in the wind, the wind
flowing through it and bending and shaking it, giving it the look
of shallow, wind-driven waves, turning the prairie, under the
bright sun, into a sea of sun and winter-dried grass . . . as endless as the ocean, as featureless as the sky.

If you left it, he thought — if you went, say, back to Kentucky, you might forget the settlement of Three Forks. In time you could forget the settlement without too much trouble. You might forget the mixed bloods with their French verve and humor. You might forget the roached, blanketed full bloods, the tall, proud, eagle-feathered men. You would hope, he thought, to forget the ignorant, trashy, Indian-hating white people who were pushing illegally into the country. Maybe, in time, you could even forget your own trading store and your own partner. Enough, at least, that the memory would be very dim and faded.

Back in Kentucky, on the banks of the Hanging Fork, or the Green, or the Cumberland, a man might forget the way the Arkansas and the Salt Fork and the Cimarron flowed shallow and roily on top the ground, cutting hardly any banks for themselves, just shifting their sands, disappearing into the sand during the droughty season till there wasn't even a sight of water for long stretches of distance — making it so you had to dig for water to drink or to slake your animals.

You might forget the buffalo hunts with the Osages, the long wind blowing in your face as your pony raced across the plains, the smell of wood smoke and grease in the lodges at night, the soft quarreling voices of women around the fires. You might forget the sudden rapid pulse when you came across the track of a Pawnee out there on the plains. He didn't much think you could, but back among people of your own kind, among people you had grown up with, wed to a neighbor girl, with young ones tumbling about, you might. Enough, anyhow, that it would not be too troublesome to you.

But one thing was certain. You couldn't go far enough or live long enough once you had got the prairie in your blood to get away from it. Set yourself down anywhere, build you a house and call it home, fill it with young ones and kinfolks and neighbors, but any time you came across a long, broad look of land you would be right back here on the prairie, the wind on your face, and the feel of it and the smell of it and the look of it would ache in your bones like an ague. The prairie — the long-reaching land, the old sea-floor land, the crying, grieving, prairie land. Know it once, he thought, and you would die away from it in some fine essential part of yourself.

It was white with sun ahead of him. East, behind him, was the settlement and the canebrakes and the timber stand. The Verdigris and the Neosho were both clear-running, fast-water streams, rising in the north. They were beautiful rivers, both of them, but not western. He guessed the line divided right here. Because west of here lay the plains and beyond them were the big mountains. That was where the old Arkansas rose. The Arkansas was a true western river. It had its beginnings in the mountains and it cut a long, winding trail across the plains, picking up all their silt and sand and drift along the way. It was a muddy, flat river, sprawly and ungovernable.

He looked across the prairie thinking of the western rivers — the Cimarron, the Platte, the Missouri, the Yellowstone, the Arkansas. You could start from here, he thought, from this grove of blackjacks, and head into the setting sun, keep going, and you would see those rivers, cross them and recross them, see the big mountains and no telling what beyond. Nathaniel Pryor had seen it all, the time he was with Lewis and Clark, and when he told of it, Johnny always felt a tug to see it himself. It was a big land that lay out there ahead of him.

Slowly he became aware of sounds all around him. There was a squirrel barking, and a skein of crows, noisy as they strung off from the top of a post-oak, flew away in a thin black line. The rattle of the wind in the dried leaves made a clack in his ears, and the saddle leather under him creaked as the horse moved. Johnny Fowler grinned, remembering how strange this land had seemed to him when he had first come, and how in the middle of the strangeness he had been surprised to find squirrels and crows the same as at home.

He had come with three years of the army and the Battle of New Orleans behind him. He had first gone home, to the big farm on the Hanging Fork which his father, Tice Fowler, and his mother, Hannah Fowler, had claimed and wrested from the virgin forests of Kentucky. He had never had a thought except, when the war with Britain was over, to follow the ways his father had followed before him. His father was dead now, but he knew that his mother meant to give him, as she had given each of the sons, his own four hundred acres. He thought he would marry, in time, a girl of the neighborhood, and he would be settled for life. He would be a family man. There would be a house full of children and there would be fences and stock, a house and barns, land to plow and crops to raise. He had not ever expected to do any different.

But when he got home a restlessness such as he had never known set in. His older brother lived in the house with his mother, married now, and his wife and children seemed to fill the old home to overflowing. A settlement had grown up nearby, and on all sides there were neighboring farms, touching the land his father had staked out of a wild, thick forest. A slow distaste for all of it grew in him. He felt crowded and pinched in and he thought with unexpected dislike of the tedium of the seasons and the life. Every spring you plowed and planted. All summer you tended. In the fall you gathered, and in the winter you fenced, cut wood, mended and patched, and once in a while, when nothing else was pressing, you could take your gun and get out in the woods. That was about as much as time allowed you. Necessity tracked at your heels and at best you could only keep about one step ahead of him.

He had heard his father talk about the early days in the country — how a man depended on his gun for food, went where he pleased, did what he pleased, always with an eye out for the Shawnees, but otherwise as free as the wind that blew. He wondered how his father had borne being tamed and chained to land. He asked his mother. She was short with words in replying. "He had his time in the woods. I reckon he was glad enough to settle down."

It was she, however, a tall, quiet woman, who put her finger on what was the matter with him. "You need to be lonesome," she said, "real lonesome for a while before you settle down. You been with folks too long. You been hemmed up in the army, and you're feeling hemmed up here. Whyn't you go to St. Louis and see Johnny and Janie? Go on out to the Territory where Rebecca and Stephen live. Rove a little all by yourself."

Jane and Rebecca were his older sisters. Jane was married to Johnny Cooper, the son of a neighbor, but they had gone farther west and Johnny worked in St. Louis for the Chouteaus. Stephen Burke, Rebecca's husband, also worked for them, but he ran a trading post for them in Indian country.

It was fate, he thought, that he should arrive at Three Forks just as Stephen Burke was ready to quit the Chouteaus and set up his own establishment. Johnny, at peace with himself on a new frontier, had put up his own savings and gone into partnership with him. It had been very simple and he had never, in the seven years since, regretted it. His mother had sensibly written him, "You have got to make your own way, I reckon. Your pa did before you. Your four hundred acres will be here, if you ever want the land, but if you like where you are best, it won't be me that quarrels with you about it. A man has his own notions of what is best for him."

Hannah Fowler knew how to cut the binding strings quickly and cleanly. Whatever she felt at losing her children to the widening west, she kept it to herself. She had a plain and simple interpretation of freedom.

Early in the partnership the line of division in their responsibilities had become clear. Johnny was better with the Indians, Stephen, who was English by birth and a scholar, was better at keeping the accounts and running the post. Each man had thus suited his own temperament and the partnership had prospered. It had all proven better, twice better, he thought, than any of his hopes.

He blew out a gusty breath and stirred restlessly in the saddle. There was this uneasy threat to the peace now. With white settlers squatting illegally on Indian land, with the new-come Cherokees crowding from the east, with the time-old enemies, the Pawnees, limiting them on the west, the Osages were being squeezed

and pinched. They were bewildered, perplexed, and angry, as
Johnny Fowler felt they had every right to be. He was passionately on the side of the Osages and he, himself, felt confused
about their problem much of the time.

The government was determined to move the eastern Indians
west of the Mississippi. They had begun with a part of the great
Cherokee tribe. They were dickering now with the Choctaws
and Creeks, and it would only be a matter of time before they,
too, left their ancestral homes and came into this new country.
The government, Johnny thought, must be about as confused as
anyone as it struggled to try to make everyone happy — the
white men of the east, the eastern Indians, the plains Indians
whose homes were being disturbed, the settlers moving ever
westward. Out of this vast tract of land which Thomas Jefferson
had purchased from Napoleon there had been born the opportunity to cut a new territory and rid the east of the continual
bother of the eastern Indians, to free their lands for the use of
the white men. They would move them, the government said,
paying them for their land, west of the Mississippi onto that land
which was not occupied by white men and which, so far as they
could tell, ought never to be wanted by them. It was thought to
be wasteland, flat prairies not good for farming, good only
for what was already there, a rich, short grass excellent for grazing, and for the herds of buffalo which roamed over it and fed
upon it.

There were honorable men involved in all of it Johnny Fowler
knew, though he grew so helplessly angry at the thought of it.
There were men who did their best to see that justice was done
to everyone. Caught in the swarming flood of the white man's
land-hungry expansion, they did what they could. Such a man
was William Clark who had been the governor of the Missouri
Territory until Missouri's boundaries were established and it was
admitted into the Union as a state. What he promised the
Osages he promised in good faith. It was not his fault that the
promises were broken.

Major Bradford, at the fort, was another good man, doing

what he had been sent to do as best he could, trying to keep the peace between the Cherokees and Osages, trying to keep white men off the Indian lands. It was not his fault that he had been given an almost impossible job to do.

Nathaniel Pryor was another good man, acting as a buffer between the Osages and the government and the more and more often irate Cherokees. His heart was increasingly heavy at the way things were going. He had told Johnny Fowler of a visit Takatoka, the principal chief of the Cherokees, had paid to Claymore when the Cherokees had first moved west of the Mississippi. "He told old Claymore," Pryor had said, "that the Osages were fools — that Cherokees had great knowledge of the lies and deceptions of the Americans and though they had sold their land to the President they meant to rise against the Americans. He told of a confederation he was trying to bring about, and of a great sweep they meant to make, ridding the Arkansas and the White and the Red rivers of all white men. The country, he said, would then be free of Americans. He asked Claymore to take up the war hatchet with him."

"What did Claymore do?"

"He refused. He told Takatoka that he had taken the President by the hand and that he did not mean to turn loose of it. He said he believed the Americans would do what they said. My God, Johnny, when you think of the old man's integrity and then look at what is happening to his people, it's enough to make you despise your own race!"

Johnny Fowler could see all sides of the problem. He could even agree with his brother-in-law, who saw everything so objectively, that the Indian was a vanishing race, that in time he must be assimilated by the white people or perish. He could see it all, but he could feel only one side of it, the Osage side. With all his heart he did not wish the Osages to perish, and slowly and gradually Osage enemies had become his personal enemies. There was nothing with which the white man could replace the Osage way of life which was half as good, he thought.

The wind was blowing colder. Johnny Fowler looked up, surprised. The sky had clouded over. It's breeding weather, he thought. It's going to rain again. He shook out the reins, drew the mustang about and headed downstream again. Well — perhaps the major could persuade the Cherokees once more. He had done so often enough before.

Chapter 3

Rᴇʙᴇᴄᴄᴀ Bᴜʀᴋᴇ stood at the window and looked out. The wind was making a gray cauldron of the sky, churning and boiling the gathering clouds, seething them and driving them swiftly before its gale. How fast the weather shifted in this prairie country, she thought. Thirty minutes before there had been nothing to indicate a storm was brewing except a low violet haze against the northern horizon. It had come up like a giant rising from sleep — violent, shifting, throwing his shadow before him.

She was a woman in her late thirties, beginning to carry a little extra weight, to broaden in the hips and thicken in the waist. She was dark-skinned, almost swarthy, and her hair, which had been as black as a moonless night when she was younger, had gray wings along the temples now. She was a handsome woman, without being at all pretty.

A spatter of heat noisy drops hit the windowpane and splashed wetly, making swift rivers down the clear glass, blurring and drifting it over. "Beginning to rain," she said to her husband, and then, "There's Johnny. Just in time."

She watched her brother ride up to the corral, dismount, let down the bars, lead his horse through and free him of saddle and bridle. "He looks more like Pa every day," she said. "Mama would say he's the spitten image."

Stephen Burke looked up from his book and asked vaguely, "Who?"

"Noodlehead," Rebecca chided mildly. "You haven't heard a

word I've said. Nose always stuck in a book. Johnny, of course. He looks just like Pa."

Stephen Burke marked his place in the book with his finger and rose to join his wife at the window. "Was your father as tall as Johnny?"

"No. I don't believe he was — though he may have been stooped by the time I remember him. He wasn't any young man when he and Mama got married. Pushing forty, I've heard her say. He always looked old to me."

"Well, Johnny don't look old."

"I didn't mean that. He's put together the same way Pa was . . . loose-jointed, sort of. Kind of awkward, as if he'd never grown up. Walks just like him, easy and quiet. He's got the same shape of face — a little long and thin in the cheeks. Same hair. Sandy, and looking like thatch most of the time."

Stephen Burke ran his hand through his own hair. "I expect I look pretty thatched most of the time too."

Rebecca smiled at her husband. "Your hair is as soft and fine as a baby's even though you do let it grow too long. Pa's was like straw. So's Johnny's. Johnny was tow-headed when he was little, though he got fighting mad if you named it to him." Her voice, remembering, was fondly wistful. "He always wanted to be called Tice, like Pa, but Mama wouldn't have it. Said one Tice in the family was enough."

"Is Johnny's name Matthias?"

"John Matthias. He was named for Pa." She was reflective. "It somehow seems in keeping to me he should grow up to look so much like him. As if Pa had a living statue to his memory. Johnny's even got Pa's eyes. Like a blue dress that's been washed until it's all but faded out."

"Don't keep him from being a dead shot, though."

"No. Nor did Pa's. Till the day he died he could bark a squirrel at a hundred yards. Where's he been, Steve? The village?"

"Yes. Major Bradford wanted him to see what he could do about getting Claymore to come to the fort for a council with the Cherokees."

Rebecca turned from the window, shivering a little. "Must be getting cold out there. He's coming to the house now. I guess the major sent the right man. Johnny's got to where he's about three-quarters Indian. He ought to be able to talk with them all right."

Stephen Burke followed her back to the fire, thinking almost absently how as she grew older Rebecca talked more and more like the Kentucky people she had grown up among. He didn't know whether it was a homesick reaching for an older and more dear homeland, or whether it was the presence of her brother who had brought out the family way of speaking. She had had more schooling than most women of her time because her mother, Hannah Fowler, had had a quiet determination that her children should be properly educated and had for several years given room and board to a transient and indigent scholar in exchange for tutoring them.

When Stephen had first known Rebecca she was a member of a Shaker community in south Kentucky, the wife of another man. Stephen had been a teacher in the Shaker school, though not an adherent to the faith. Rebecca had been a profoundly unhappy woman, married to a man who had led her unwillingly into the Shaker faith and into the Shaker life which forbade the continuance of the marriage relationship. Assigned to teach in the school along with him, she had come to know Stephen well and in time they had learned to love each other. Rebecca had fought a long and bitter fight with herself before reaching the decision to leave not only the Shaker village but her husband as well. Realizing eventually that this way of life was a living death, she had been the first woman in Kentucky to obtain a divorce under the new legislative act making membership in the Shaker faith automatic grounds for a divorce. If her faith had been genuine, as was her husband's, she would never have done it, Stephen knew. Not for love. But she could not believe, and finally she had come to feel that the sacrifice of herself to something she did not believe was not required of her. It had taken great courage on her part, for divorces were frowned on, even with the excellent reasons Rebecca had, and a divorced woman was a disgraced woman. The circle of shame was completed when she married him. A divorced woman might live down the scandal in time if she did not remarry. But by that act she stamped herself, in the eyes of many, an adulteress.

It was partly for that reason, because he knew how difficult their life would be in the old neighborhood, that Stephen had brought her to this new country, the Arkansas Territory. It was a lonely life for her, for the only white people near them were the drifting, illegal white settlers who were constantly being moved on. The few who were allowed legally in the country lived far away, on land the government had opened up to them on the lower Arkansas. She went for months at a time without seeing a white woman. But if she had ever regretted what they had done she had never said so, nor given any sign of it. He had been glad, however, when Johnny had come to be his partner and to live with them. It rounded out Rebecca's life somehow and made it better. There was with her, now, someone from home, someone with many of the same memories. Johnny had brought with him a part of the old place on the Hanging Fork, a part of their mother, a coal from the hearth fire.

There was a gust of rain against the window, and at the same time they heard the door of the trading store open and close. Their living quarters were a part of the store, two big rooms with loft bedrooms overhead, built on at the back of the larger room which housed the goods of Burke & Fowler. "I'd better tell Johnny that Parley Wade is back," Stephen said.

Rebecca took up a basket of mending. "Go along then. Tell him there's a roast of beef if he's hungry."

"I'll tell him."

Though Johnny Fowler took his meals, when he was at home, with his sister and her husband it was the only time he intruded. He slept above the store in another loft room. He was stowing his saddle and bridle behind the trading counter when Stephen Burke came in. He looked up. "Hou, Steve?"

"Any luck?"

"No." Johnny took off his hat, shook the water from it and laid it on the counter. "They won't council until the Cherokees return the prisoners."

Stephen Burke took out his pipe, filled it and lit it. "Seems fair enough to me."

"The Cherokees want the men who killed their hunters."

"That's natural, too."

Johnny squinted at his brother-in-law through the pipe smoke. "Don't solve anything, though. Natural or not, I reckon the major is going to have to try to talk 'em out of their desires. Old Claymore is not going to budge this time."

"You talk to him?"

"No. Talked to the Wolf. The old man listens to him mostly. Didn't see any signs of giving over. They've about got a craw full, Steve."

Stephen Burke puffed reflectively on his pipe. "Yes. I can see how they would. But killing Cherokees is no way of handling the problem. They'll just get more claims laid up against them."

Johnny stirred up the fire, laid a fresh log on it and backed up to its warmth. "I told the Wolf the same thing. He said he'd tell the chief. Seemed right impressed, though you can't tell for sure."

"If they could control those young men . . ."

"It can't be done. You know that. They're bound to break loose once in a while." He grinned at his brother-in-law. "It's only natural."

Stephen Burke returned the grin. "You were gone longer than you meant — what happened?"

"They were having a ceremony when I got there so I had to wait until that was over. Had a long talk with the Wolf last night then. He did most of the talking. Went clear back to the beginning again."

"They're not children. They know what's happening to them." Stephen Burke lifted his face, blew a ring of smoke toward the ceiling. "Whether they accept it or not, they know. They know they've got no hope. They can hold on a little longer . . . another generation or two, at the most."

"You talk as if they were people in a book."

"I talk the way I see it, and the way the Osages know in their hearts it's going to be. Nothing, Johnny, nothing under heaven is going to stop your white people."

"Well, what are they going to do? Kill off the Osages?"

"No. They'll make treaties and more treaties. They'll move them farther and farther away. Finally the Osages will have to come to terms, accept white men's ways, become Americans, be absorbed by them."

"They'll never do it."

"Yes, they will. Not in our lifetime, maybe, but they will."

"I hope I don't live to see it."

"You won't. In your lifetime they'll keep on fighting."

Johnny Fowler rubbed his hand against the wet front of his buckskins. "Why can't they leave 'em alone? God, it's their land! Who's got a better right to it?"

"The American government . . . who paid fifteen million dollars for it. Johnny, don't you ever see this westward movement as a great river, breaking through the mountains to the east, spreading slowly, slowly, but inevitably, engulfing everything that lies before it, swallowing it up whole? Nothing can dam it, nothing can check it, nothing can stand in its way."

"No," Johnny Fowler said shortly. "All I can see is shame and injustice. The government," he growled, "ought to bar every white man from taking up land west of the Mississippi."

Stephen Burke chuckled.

"What's funny about it?"

"Your father fought the Indians in Kentucky. He was on the side of the white settler. It's a queer turn of events, to say the least, for his son to be fighting white men, on the side of the Indians."

"There's a difference."

"None at all, basically. Not in the principles involved. I suspect the difference lies in the fact that you learned to read."

"Pa was a smart man . . ."

"But elementary. That itinerant tutor of yours, Johnny, gave you Homer and Ovid and Shakespeare to read. Learning always complicates life, my son."

"Oh, hell, you always manage to twist things around. All I know is the way I feel."

"Then forget it. You'll be going to the fort, I suppose."

"Yes. The major will have to know."

"Parley Wade is back."

"He is? He bring the goods?"

"They're in the shed. I told him to unload and go on home and eat. Told him to come back when you got home."

"I didn't see him."

The wind rattled the windows. Both men turned to look. "Blowing hard out there," Stephen Burke said.

"Blowing a gale. And raining. Keeps this up the rivers will begin rising again. Parley leave the tally sheet?"

Stephen Burke indicated with his head. "On the shelf there. Before you start checking, Becky said there's a roast of beef."

"I'll eat when we get through. It won't take long."

"I'll help."

Johnny Fowler picked up the tally sheet from the shelf and and the two men went into the shed room built alongside the store. It smelled, as it always did, of furs and tallow, of smoke and grease, of earth and tobacco and Indians. Stephen Burke wrinkled his nose with distaste. Johnny breathed it in as unconsciously as he breathed the outer air. It was a smell he was used to and liked.

They were halfway through when a squat, burly man came in, his ancient fur cap streaming with rain, his mackinaw jacket dark with it. "Ain't done checkin' yet?"

"Not quite." Johnny was shifting the goods, arranging them in order on the shelves, as Stephen called off the list. "Sit down there, Parley, till we're through."

The man sat on an upturned keg, eyeing the piles of colored

cloth, the blankets, axes, beads, vermilion, the guns and gun-
powder, the little mirrors and glass trinkets and tools with which
the firm of Burke & Fowler did business with the Osages. "Pretty
good calico there," he said, "but them blankets ain't nothin'
extry. Couldn't git no Canadian blankets. Them's New York."

Johnny Fowler nodded. The tally was finished. "Where's the
money?"

Parley Wade pulled a buckskin pouch from his jacket pocket
and handed it over.

"Let's go in the store," Johnny said, "it's cold in here."

Parley Wade loosened his jacket and warmed his hands at the
fire. Stephen sat near the end of the counter on a bench against
the wall. He watched as Johnny emptied the pouch and counted
the money.

Johnny fingered it a moment with a big, bear's-paw hand, then
leaned lazily against the shelves behind him and stared idly out
the window. Parley Wade shifted from one foot to the other
and spat on the dirt floor. "Fire feels good," he said. "It's a raw
day out."

Neither looking at the man nor heeding him, Johnny Fowler
picked up the tally sheet again, ran his eye over it and thrust
his tongue experimentally in his cheek. "You're short some
piasters, aren't you, Parley?"

The man bunched his cap in his hands. "You was short a bale
of he-pelts, Johnny."

"Who said so?"

"The feller at the warehouse in St. Louis. Said you was one
bale shy of yer figgers."

Johnny looked at the stack of coins on the counter. He ran
one hand through them, riffled them, clinked them, then he
made a neat pile of them. Watching him, Parley Wade shifted
on his feet again. As soon as the pile had been finished, Johnny
knocked it down, spread it, began over again.

They were Spanish piasters. It was the policy of the trading
firm to keep on hand at all times a little hard money, and when
Parley Wade had been sent to St. Louis with a mid-season load

of pelts and tallow he had been instructed to take one-twentieth of the payment in silver, the balance in goods.

Johnny Fowler played with the coins, saying nothing, studying the nicked edges of the pieces, their tarnish, their battered surfaces, his face expressionless, even mild, his eyes half-shuttered by their crinkled, sun-squinted lids. Stephen Burke watched him and waited for the decision he knew was forming. Johnny's inscrutable look did not fool him and he didn't much think it was fooling Parley Wade. Plainly the man was uncomfortable. He puffed and grunted and shifted, took off his cap, put it back on, scratched an ear, cleared his throat, buttoned his jacket, unbuttoned it. Stephen Burke puffed on his pipe. Parley, he thought, interestedly, is going to bust something in about one more minute. He blew a smoke ring and waited. Parley was Johnny's business.

Johnny continued to play with the coins, ignoring the movements of the other man. He riffled the silver from one hand to the other, stacked it, spread the stacks, listened with his head cocked to their clink against each other. Suddenly he reached behind him, pulled the firm's ledger off the shelf and turning rapidly to one of its pages ran his eye over the amount totaled there. Satisfied, he closed the ledger, replaced it on the shelf, then he picked up a small handful of the coins and began stacking them to one side. One on top the other he laid them, slowly, almost absently, keeping their edges, however, neat and trim.

Parley Wade watched him, his lips moving as he counted, his breathing heavy and noisy. As Johnny added a coin, Parley's eyes followed the hand anxiously to see if it was going to reach for another. Sweat broke out on his face and he wiped it off with the back of his hand.

At the count of eight, Johnny leveled off the stack, leaned back against the shelves behind him and for the first time looked directly at the other man. "I wouldn't have thought you'd try that on me, Parley."

Parley Wade sputtered. "Try what?"

Johnny picked up a buckskin pouch and swept the small stack

of coins into it. Thoughtfully and without haste he tightened the thong about its neck. "There's your pay," he said, "taking out for one bale of he-pelts and what you've got on the books." With a quick motion he sent the bag flying bullet-hard at the man. It caught him full in the stomach and he grunted and bent, the wind whistling out of him. "And quit trying to skin me! Next time I'll cut your craw out!"

The man coughed and choked, then wheezed. "Damnation, Johnny! Don't a man git no thanks fer packin' a load of skins to St. Louis in the middle of the winter? An' fer lookin' after yer interests as best he can?"

"You get paid," Johnny said dryly. "And I don't know as any thanks are due. I'm not sure you look after my interests. What happened? You get in a game and lose the money?"

Parley Wade chuckled, picked up the bag of coins from the floor and jingled them against his ear. "Naw. Got drunk. Spent it. Don't rightly know just what did happen. I just come up short some piasters."

"Say so next time."

Parley Wade sighed and looked at Stephen. "How you git along with him, Steve? Partnerin' with him shore can't be no cinch fer you."

Stephen removed his pipe from his mouth. "I don't try to skin him."

"Ain't much use of it, fer a fact." Parley set his ragged and fur-balding old cap on his bristly black hair. "Well, I reckon I'll be gittin' on. My old woman all right?"

"Haven't you been to the cabin yet? Steve said he sent you home to eat."

The man grinned. "I been to LeClerc's."

"You better let that firewater alone. It'll put your eyes out. Far as I know Sukie's all right."

"She hadn't of been, you'd a knowed it. When did her an' the kids come in from the village?"

"About a week ago."

Parley nodded. "She figgered I was about due." He grinned again. "Wanted to git her hands on some of these piasters. I never seen nothin' like a Injun woman fer wheedlin' a man outen ever'thing he's got."

Johnny Fowler raked the rest of the silver into another pouch and tossed it to Stephen. "You come around by the fort?" he asked Parley.

"Yeah. Governor Miller had done left for the Post of Arkansas, but I talked a little with the major."

"What'd he say?"

"Said the governor had come up for a council betwixt the Cherokees and our Injuns but wouldn't none of ours come to the fort. Said it looked to him like they was nothin' for it but war this time. Said he'd held off the Cherokees about as long as he could. Looked mighty worried to me. What happened, Johnny? Old Claymore didn't let them young bucks go sashayin' off a purpose, did he? He's smarter'n that commonly."

Johnny Fowler lifted his shoulders. "A hunting party came down from Pa-hus-ka's village. Said they were going to hunt down on the Red. It was a mixed party, Big Soldier heading it up, and he had some warriors from the Gross Côte on the upper Verdigris. He rounded up a few more from Claymore's town. There were about seventy of 'em in all. They ran onto a party of Cherokees hunting on the Poteau and killed a few of 'em, stole all their horses and pelts, and then just for good measure they raided some settlers' cabins on the way back. Claymore didn't like it, but those young men get all het up and they've got to take some scalps. Best I understand it, the Cherokees killed Big Soldier's wife last year and he had to take some hair pretty soon."

Parley Wade shrugged. "Well, if they was on the Poteau they was out of bounds again. Looks like they'd learn to stay at home."

Johnny Fowler grunted.

"There's times," Wade continued, "when it looks to me like Scammon and some of them other half-whites amongst 'em don't keer if a few Cherokee bucks is kilt, long as it gives 'em a right to claim indemnities and the government pays 'em off with a little more land."

"There's times," Johnny said, "when I think you're right."

"Well, maybe it won't come to nothin'. They been makin' their threats an' shakin' their fists an' howlin' their heads off a right smart while. Maybe that's all they'll do this time. I misdoubt they will go to war. Old Claymore ain't no ordinary Injun. I reckon Osage roaches is safe enough. Ain't nobody, Cherokees nor nobody else, hankerin' real bad to try to take 'em."

"I hope that's the way of it. Any more news?"

"Them missionary boats was there at the fort. They left out ahead of me, so I reckon they'll be along here in a day or two."

Johnny Fowler's hand jerked. "Oh, God," he muttered. "Missionaries!"

Stephen Burke grinned. "Say unto the Lord," he murmured, "that righteousness reigneth."

"Shut up, Steve."

"They been ten months on the way," Parley said. "Had to lay over at Little Rock for more'n four months account of the river bein' so low last year. Had the fever, too. Ever' last manjack of 'em. Two of their women died of it. What got into Nathaniel Pryor to help 'em git located here, Johnny?"

"Some fool notion of his," Johnny growled. "Said the Osages ought to learn white folks' ways better. Said they'd get farther if they did. Said the Cherokees already knew how to plow and plant and tend their stock and their women can spin and weave and Osages ought to learn."

"He's right," Stephen said. "He's looking ahead."

Johnny Fowler moved restlessly. "Osages won't take to such ways. Anybody knows 'em knows that. They're plains Indians, not settlement Indians like the Cherokees."

"Where's the piece of land old Claymore give the missionaries?" Parley asked.

"Up the Neosho," Stephen said, "about thirty miles. There

have been three of their men up there all winter. Said they were
sent on ahead to begin building the station."

"And much good they've done," Johnny said contemptuously.
"They raised one cabin. Been sick ever since. They're going to
be a trouble and a bother to the whole country, wait and see.
Green as gourds. Not used to the country. New Englanders.
Come in here to preach hellfire and brimstone to people whose
religion would make cornshucks of theirs."

"Not many would see it that way, Johnny," Stephen said,
mildly.

"No. They've got the Osages pictured as savages and heathens. Mission to the Osages! Hell, any Osage has got more religion than most white men — and lives by it better, too." Neither
of the other two men made any reply. This was a sore spot with
Johnny Fowler which they respected. Parley Wade whistled
softly between his teeth and Stephen Burke smoked his pipe.
"How many of 'em in the party?" Johnny asked finally.

"The major said there was ten men, four children and five
women. Said they left New York with twenty-one in the party
— then they hired a millwright at Marietta on the way, but two
of the women died of the fever, so they've got twenty left,
and some hands to pole their boats for 'em." Parley Wade
laughed. "They been havin' a time keepin' their hands. Reckon
they practice their preachin' on 'em a mite too much. The
hands is always forsakin' 'em. They let their pilot go, too, at
Little Rock. Major said Preacher Chapman told him the feller
got into a scrape. Didn't say what kind, but I reckon it was lik-
ker and women."

"Who was their pilot?"

"Cap'n Boggs."

Johnny Fowler exchanged a slow delighted look with Parley
Wade and Stephen Burke laughed. "They had a wolf in their
fold, all right," he said.

Boggs was a good river pilot and he had been bringing keelboats up the Arkansas for several years. But he was a lusty man,

liking his whisky and women, and with an excellently colorful
and profane vocabulary — none of which missionaries would be
calculated to enjoy. "I wonder," Johnny said, "how he lasted to
Little Rock." He straightened, as if slipping off his shoulders all
missionaries, their women, their children, their pilot troubles.
"How'd you do on your own skins, Parley?"

"Middlin'. If Sukie could dress a skin decent I'd of done better. Only Osage woman I ever seen couldn't dress a skin worth
a farthin' an' I have to take up with her."

"Nothing wrong with the way Sukie dresses a skin," Johnny
laughed. "She does a good job on the sorry hides you bring in."

Parley grinned good-naturedly. "I take 'em as they come."

"And you won't spend any time going farther afield where
they're better. You going to trap any more this winter?"

"If it ain't too cold, I might." He stretched and yawned.
"Lord, I'm glad to git back. City life is kind of wearin' on a
body."

Johnny Fowler snorted. "It don't have to be if you don't go
helling around."

Parley lifted his shoulders. "Well, I don't git there but oncet
or twicet a year. I aim to git me as much pleasure as my skin'll
hold when I do git there. I'll be goin'."

He lifted the door latch, waved a hand backward over his
shoulder, and Johnny Fowler and Stephen Burke watched him
walk across the already muddy area in front of the trading post
and disappear down the path. Stephen knocked out his pipe.
"Why do you put up with him, Johnny?"

Johnny rubbed his chin, his eyes reflective. "I dunno. I sort
of like the old codger. And then, he's from Kentucky. I know
he's lazy and trifling, but in his own way he's a loyal old cuss.
He don't sell out to the Chouteaus, anyhow. And he always
brings back a good bunch of stuff. There's nothing shoddy about
what he buys. He's got a good eye for things like that, and he
buys shrewd. Reckon I'll go eat now, Steve."

"Good. I'll put this silver away."

He watched his brother-in-law go through the back door into the house. His buckskins were old, greasy and dirty. His sandy hair was tied on his neck with a thong as slick from grease as his buckskins and as he passed he left behind him a strong smell of wood smoke and rancid grease. Rebecca was right, Stephen thought wryly. Johnny had become three-quarters Indian. He even smelled like one.

Chapter 4

.THE RAIN CONTINUED.

For a week there was a lowering, pewter sky which constantly drizzled, frequently showered, and occasionally poured. Once in a while the rain would stop briefly, but the sun would not shine and after an hour or two the wet fall would begin again. The days were short and dark and the big log room of the trading store would have been gloomy except for the fire which the men kept going strongly. "You'd think," Rebecca said, late one afternoon, "there couldn't be another drop of water left to fall after a whole week of it."

Johnny was mending a broken bridle. He did not look up from his work. "Does keep on right steady, don't it?" he said.

Stephen Burke put down his pen and wiped the ink from his fingers. "That," he said dryly, "is the damndest understatement I ever heard. The heavens have opened all their floodgates and we are apt to need the ark which Noah built, every cubit of it, and the man says the rain keeps on right steady. An Englishman is garrulous beside your brother, my love." Briskly, then, he added, "I've got these accounts finished, Johnny. We look to be in good shape. We've got all the stock we need for the rest of the season, all debts paid, and a little profit."

"Good." Accounts were Steve's affair. Johnny never troubled his head about them. If Steve said they were behind, he humped himself to get in more pelts and trade. If Steve said they were ahead, he took it a little easier. It was that simple.

Stephen went to the door and threw it open. "It's stuffy in here." He stretched and breathed deeply. "I'm cramped from bending over that counter. The sun is setting clear. Maybe the rain is over. It's a good thing you decided not to go to the fort, Johnny, till the weather faired up. LeClerc says the Neosho is running bank full all the way down and is overflowing at the point. Every stream between here and Fort Smith would be out of its banks likely."

"Likely," Johnny agreed. "Wasn't any hurry about it. Not in this weather. Brad won't be expecting me."

Stephen Burke leaned against the doorframe looking out onto the small half-village which had grown up around the trading post. There was a blacksmith shop, a tool shed, several warehouses, a shed for Becky's cow, and the log houses of the men who worked for the firm and who preferred to live near the post. Some of the trappers and hunters, like Suard, were halfbreeds who lived in the Osage village. But some of them liked it better at the post. There were also two white men, Parley Wade, who did every sort of odd job for them, and Adam Trench, the blacksmith. Both men had taken Osage wives.

Around the entire small settlement was what remained of a stockade fence. It had been so long since the Osages had given any trouble to traders that the fence had fallen into bad repair and much of it had fallen down.

The houses which the employees of the firm had built were of log. Few of them were floored, all of them had their mud chinking missing in gaps, the roofs curled a little, and the doors, if they had doors instead of blankets, sagged. They ought, Stephen thought idly, to make the men mend their cabins. The place had a ragtag and bobtail look to it. Johnny rarely bothered about such things, though, and he himself knew it was hopeless. Osage women wouldn't keep things orderly and if the cabins were mended and cleaned out it would be no time before they fell into disorder again.

The short street in front of the cabins was knee-deep in mud and as Stephen watched, ruminating, a horde of children rode their horses wildly down it, splattering the mud in every direction. Dodging, Stephen grumbled, "It don't help for those kids to ride their mustangs right up to the door. Keeps the mud churned up."

"They would sink to their crotch if they tried to walk," Johnny said.

"Ever count the kids in this settlement?" Stephen asked, grinning.

Johnny shook his head. "You?"

"I make it fifty on those mustangs right now."

"Oh, Steve," Rebecca said, laughing, "there aren't fifty in the whole of Three Forks."

"Count 'em for yourself," her husband insisted.

She peered around his shoulder. "There aren't more than a dozen. My goodness," she said, laughing again, "there's young Steve and William and Samuel out there amongst 'em. They'll be soaking wet." She hurried off to get her shawl, bent on rescuing her three small sons.

Johnny looked reproachfully at Stephen. "Now you've done and spoilt their fun."

"Didn't notice 'em until too late," Stephen said, nodding ruefully. "Well, it's time they came in, I expect." He craned his neck suddenly, looking down the street toward the wide gap in the fence where the gate had once been. "Company coming, Johnny."

"Pryor, I expect."

"No. Strangers. Several of 'em. Walking."

Johnny threw down the bridle and rose quickly to join his brother-in-law. "Coming from the point?"

"Yes."

They watched as the small group of men made their way, sloshing, bent-headed, down the road. Johnny counted them audibly. "Two . . . three . . . four . . . Steve! It's them missionaries. That's Chapman in the lead."

"Give them my best regards," Stephen said, wheeling.

"Oh, no you don't," Johnny caught him. "You're going to stay right here and talk to 'em. 'Twouldn't be polite not to."

"If I remember the Reverend Chapman correctly," Stephen said, "he'll do most of the talking."

A year and a half before there had come to Three Forks this New England preacher, Epaphras Chapman, in the company of Nathaniel Pryor. He had originally been sent, he told Johnny and Stephen, to found a mission among the Cherokees, but another mission board had already established a station there. "We did not deem it felicitous," he had told them, "to claim the same location. Captain Pryor has kindly suggested we might find a mission site among the Osage Indians."

Recalling the long evening of conversation, which had become a monologue as the minister expounded his plans for letting a little light into the blighted night of these heathen people, Johnny groaned. "My ears," he said, "are tired already."

As they watched, the men reached the end of the street and Stephen chuckled as they sank over their boot tops in the deep mud and floundered, heaving to lift themselves step by step through the muck. "Had we known you were coming, gentlemen," he murmured, "we would have laid some planks down for you."

"Not me. I wouldn't of," Johnny denied quickly. "I wish they'd mire plumb down."

"Now, Johnny," Stephen reproached, then added, sniffing, "Johnny, you smell. Reverend Chapman is going to find that offensive."

"Which," Johnny retorted, "I hope will discourage him from lingering."

The men from the missionary boats were looking about at the settlement curiously, noticing the blanket-wrapped children on the mustangs, the unkempt Indian women bringing up wood on their backs, the bleak looking log houses. Epaphras Chapman waved a hand which took in, generally, the street, the children, the women, the entire settlement, and said something to his companions in a voice too low to hear. "He's telling 'em, I'd think," Johnny Fowler growled, "look at the pass these traders have come to. What a field for the gospel!"

"Sh-h-h-h," Stephen warned, and he went to meet the group with an outstretched hand. "Gentlemen, welcome to Burke & Fowler's. You have had a wet time of it lately, I gather."

Epaphras Chapman took the hand and spoke in a deep, rich voice. "We have, sir. We have been as near drowned as mortals can be and still survive. The weather has been for some time now extremely inclement. These gentlemen are members of our party, Mr. Burke — Dr. Palmer, who is our medical adviser, Mr. Requa, who is an agricultural specialist, and our pilot, Captain Douglas."

"Come in, come in," Stephen said heartily. "We can furnish you a fire to dry yourselves beside and my wife will be happy to feed you. This is my brother-in-law and partner, gentlemen, Johnny Fowler. You will remember him, Mr. Chapman."

"I do indeed, and I remember also your most gracious hospitality to me when I was here before. Ah, that fire gives out a welcome warmth."

Johnny hauled up kegs and a bench and the men divested themselves of their streaming hats and outer coats, seated themselves before the fire and held out their chilled hands to it.

They were an unlikely looking crew, Johnny thought, looking them over sharply. They were thinned down by the fever, all but the pilot, and pallid from long confinement on the boats. Epaphras Chapman was a man of middle height, thin, slope-shouldered, narrow-faced, with hot blue eyes of intense, fanatic concentration. The doctor was blocky in build, swarthy-skinned, with a shock of dark hair. Requa was a small, flat-featured man, with large, protruding ears. The pilot was a giant, with an undershot jaw and a square, cleft chin. Chapman and Requa still looked sick and Requa, Johnny thought, was twisted in the grip of a chill right now. He watched him set his teeth and shudder against the bone-shaking cold he was feeling. What he needed was about a pint of good hot whisky, but recalling the error he had made before when he offered the preacher a mug of hot rum and had been reprovingly told that as a man of God he never used spirituous liquors, he'd be blasted and damned if he would offer the sick man anything, Johnny thought. He took his stand behind the group, leaning against the counter.

As before, the preacher took the conversation over immediately, detailing at length the trials and tribulations of the party on their journey. "The Lord has humiliated us," he concluded piously, "for our many sins of pride. We have been made to suffer much. We lost two of our members by death from the fever. I am happy to say, however," he added, "they died in Christ and we were able to rejoice in the will of the Lord."

"Amen," one of the men murmured softly.

"But we have gained the day," Epaphras Chapman continued, "and have now reached the last stage of our perilous journey. We have come, sir," he addressed Stephen, "to ask help of you in ascending the Neosho. Our pilot does not know that river."

"Certainly, sir," Stephen said, "when the river goes down."

"We mean to continue our journey tomorrow, sir."

Stephen stared at him in amazement. "But the Neosho is in flood, sir. Surely you noticed that it is running very swift and full. One of our breeds tells us it is overflowing at the point."

"Yes, we noticed," the missionary said. "In fact we are tied up near the point. But we have sick men at the station waiting for us. They are badly in need of medicines and Dr. Palmer's attention. Our people on the boats are suffering from their long voyage and we are eager to get them ashore so they may mend more rapidly. We feel we cannot tarry. We have made our way up the Arkansas in flood and we think we can ascend the Neosho without undue danger."

Johnny spoke. "The Arkansas is a broad, slow river. The Neosho is in spate right now, deep and swift. You would do best to wait until it ebbs."

"We would be happy to have your womenfolk and children come to the post, sir," Stephen offered. "My wife could make them comfortable during the delay. She would rejoice in the presence of gentlefolk again."

The thin, gaunt-faced missionary stared into the fire for a long moment, then his mouth firmed. "I appreciate your generosity, sir. But we think we had best continue our journey. Our women would not, I'm afraid . . ." He did not finish, but the implication was plain. Missionary women and children must not be exposed to the venality of the settlement. There were halfbreeds here, there were white men living openly with Indian women, the consequences of their cohabitation plainly evident in the swarm of children in the street now. Men drank whisky here, used oaths. It was an immoral place which godly people needed to avoid. Stephen flushed. Johnny had moved, but Stephen gave him a warning look. "I don't quite know how," he said, "we can help you then."

"Sir, we have two keelboats. They are large, unwieldy craft with only six hands left of our crew. The fever has reduced the men of our party to a scant few who are fit to work. We hoped we could prevail on you to hire out to us some of your employees."

"I see." Stephen glanced at Johnny. "What do you think, Johnny?"

The refused hospitality rankled with him, especially when he thought how much Becky would have enjoyed the company of the mission women, and the arrogance of the request, in the face of the stiff-necked, pious refusal, astonished him. He could not bring himself to abide by the open-handed rule of the country.

Johnny's face was bland and innocent looking. He studied a bruise on his thumb, rubbed it thoughtfully, and took his time about answering. "I am afraid," he said finally, his voice slowed to the flat Kentucky drawl which augured ill for anyone when he used it, "I couldn't conscientiously order any of our men on such a dangerous venture, sir." His eyelids were heavy over his narrowed eyes, only an edge of white showing beneath them. "They are too valuable to risk losing. If you would care to wait until the river goes down . . ."

"That," the missionary said impatiently, "is out of the question."

"Well, Reverend," Johnny said, "you can risk the necks of your own people if you want to, including your women and children. It is certainly your own affair. But I wouldn't let a man of mine set his foot on those boats of yours as long as the river is in flood."

The missionary turned red. "We are wasting our time, then," he said, shortly.

Johnny still examined the bruised thumb. "I don't know as you are. I haven't said *I* wouldn't help you."

"I don't understand you, sir."

Johnny thrust his body away from the counter abruptly, standing straight and looking down at the seated man. "Risking my neck is my own business, Reverend, but risking the neck of our men is the company's business." He hesitated, then added with grave courtesy, "I will be glad to help you in any way that I can."

Stephen applauded the stinging rebuke silently. Epaphras Chapman inclined his head. He was not an old man. In fact he was very young, too young, Stephen thought, to be leading this party of missionaries. He was so young that he allowed his piety to sit in weighty dignity on him, where an older man might have been humbler. He was so young that he could not make the simplest statement without lending it a sonorous importance. He was so young that his personal obsession blazed like a flame within him and blinded him and made him uncharitable and stubborn. With unexpected lewdness Stephen wondered if, like other men, Epaphras Chapman made use of an outhouse. The reverend with bodily functions was somehow difficult to imagine. "It is kind of you," the fine, deep voice said. "Is Captain Pryor at his trading establishment, do you know?"

"I believe," Johnny said, "he is at the Indian village. His woman," he continued, adding one more twist to the knife-edge of rebuke, "is Osage, I expect you know." It was Nathaniel Pryor who had helped this man most.

"Yes. Well, there is no reason to visit him then. I had hoped we might be able to find him ready to help us also."

Stephen, his anger vanished, made one more effort to dissuade the missionary from attempting the journey immediately. "I wish you would reconsider, sir. The Neosho is a mean river in flood. I would advise you strongly to wait a few days."

"I thank you for your concern, sir," the man replied, standing and beginning to struggle into his wet coat, "but we deem it advisable to labor on."

"At least you will have a meal with us?"

"No, though it is kind of you to ask us. Food is waiting for us on the boats."

With new energy, Johnny flung the door open. "I take it you want to push on early in the morning — rain or shine?"

"Rain or shine, yes, sir. But I pray the Lord may bless our efforts with a clear sky."

"Yes, sir."

The men filed out, not a one of them but Epaphras Chapman having said a word except the piously murmured "Amen."

Johnny closed the door and leaned against it, looking at his brother-in-law. "There are your missionaries," he said, "I hope you are pleased with them."

"The man," Stephen said, "is a blithering idiot."

"The man," Johnny said bluntly, "is a damned fool." Bitterly, flatly, he added, "That's civilization come to Three Forks — civilization with God in one hand and self-righteousness in the other. Pah! It makes me want to puke!"

The boats were tied two miles above the mouth of the Neosho. The stream had overflowed the bottoms, however, until it was several miles wide, a sea of water swirling in slow eddies among the canebrakes, the banks gone, only a swift roiling down the middle to indicate where the main channel was. The sun was up clear, and it was a sparkling cold morning. Johnny Fowler and Stephen sat their horses in the shallows, measuring the water thoughtfully. Stephen eyed the top of the canes swishing lazily in the water around the boats a hundred yards away. "About ten feet there, I'd say."

"About," Johnny agreed.

"It's going to be too deep for poles after you get out of the overflow, Johnny."

Johnny continued to study the water. "Yes." Coming to some decision, then, he dismounted and spoke more briskly. "Well, I'd best get on with it."

Stephen caught the reins he tossed to him. "You ought to let me come too, Johnny."

"No. You're not over that spell of lung fever too good yet."

"Well, don't take any chances."

"No more than I have to." He cupped his hands and shouted to the boats.

The pilot answered and immediately put a skiff over the side to fetch him.

The two boats were tied alongside and were lashed together. They were close to seventy-five feet long, but narrow, not more than twelve feet wide. Cabins were raised on the stern decks, and each boat boasted a mast in the center, the sails furled now. Johnny examined them as the skiff drew alongside. They were good boats, well built, stout, shallow-drawing. Whoever had built them, he thought, knew his business.

Epaphras Chapman hurried to meet him. "Ah," he said, "well, now that you have come, sir, we can cast off. Our people are ready."

"Who built your boats?" Johnny asked.

"Why, they were built for us in Pittsburgh. They have served us well, but we shall be glad to see the last of them."

"You own 'em outright?"

"The mission board owns them, yes."

"Aiming to keep both of them?"

"No. We mean to keep only one. We have orders to sell the other if possible."

"It's sold," Johnny said. "I'll take it."

"Do you always," the missionary asked, his face reflecting his astonishment, "do business so quickly, Mr. Fowler? You have not yet discovered the price."

"I don't figure you would try to cheat me, Reverend," Johnny said laconically.

"No, of course not. Shall we cast off now, sir?"

"If you don't mind I'd like to talk to the pilot first. And I think you'll want to hear what I've got to say."

"Fine." Epaphras Chapman beckoned for the pilot to join them. "Mr. Fowler has some counsel to give us," he said, when the man reached them.

Johnny rubbed his chin reflectively. "I don't want to appear to be taking over your business," he said, "but I know this river pretty well. How have you got the boats loaded, Reverend?"

"About evenly, wouldn't you say, Captain Douglas?"

"About," the pilot agreed.

"The captain here can only be on one boat at a time," Johnny continued. "Who is in charge of the other one?"

"I am," Epaphras Chapman said.

"Just wanted to know. I'll work with you then. The way I'd handle this," he continued, "is to use the poles as long as we're in the overflow here at the point. It's not too deep for 'em. About three miles upstream there is a spit of land that rises high and pokes out in a bluff into the river. The river will be in its banks there because the land is high. At that place I'd tack across to the other side."

The pilot nodded, understanding. "Take to the ropes then?"

"For as long as we can. There'll be too much overflow to use the ropes much. We'll likely have to bushwhack."

The pilot groaned. "I was afraid of that."

"Bushwhack?" the missionary said, curious.

"Means we'll have to grab the bushes from the boats, hang on, and pull the boat along by hand," Johnny explained.

"Won't that be slow hard work?"

"Don't know of anything that's slower, or harder. And it don't always work, either. A boat can get out of hand mighty quick. I'd like to warn you again that it would be best if you would lay over."

The missionary looked at the sea of water all around them. "How long will it take this flood to subside?"

"A week maybe — maybe two if it keeps on raining." Johnny squinted at the sky. "And it's clouding up again right now."

"Then we'll have to risk it, sir. We cannot linger here."

Johnny bunched his shoulders. "Just as you say." He wheeled on his heel. "Cap'n Douglas, we'll take this boat first. You follow. Keep at least a hundred yards behind so we'll have a little room. Reverend, how many men have you got fit to work?"

"Six hands and four men of our own party."

"Split 'em half and half."

The river pilot nodded and the missionary hurried away to make the arrangements. "No trouble, Cap'n," Johnny said, "till you get to the bluff. Use your sail, then."

He crossed the short gangplank to the next boat.

The men took up their poles and at Johnny's signal felt for the bottom and warped the boat away from the trees. Slowly it moved forward as the men fell into a sort of ragged rhythm of walking and hauling. When they had made a hundred yards of progress Johnny waved to the captain on the waiting boat.

It took them three hours to reach the bluff — three miles in three hours which, Johnny considered, was as good as they had any right to expect. A stiff breeze had sprung up, however, and the sun was hazed over now and a livid, purplish cloud was forming in the west. It was going to blow, Johnny thought, and he watched the cloud, weighing the speed of its wind against the chances of getting both boats across the river before the squall hit. They could make it, he decided, and he signaled the hands, who ran up the sail. The boat quartered across the stream, roughed up considerably by the current, but keeping her head, held steady by the strong wind, riding like a cork and answering to the tiller. Across, the men grabbed bushes to hold the boat and the sail was lowered. There was no bottom for their poles. Slowly they inched along, grabbing, pulling, turning loose to grab and pull again. Johnny went to the stern to watch the other boat make the crossing.

There was some delay. Anxiously Johnny watched the black cloud which was moving fast now. He cursed. If the captain didn't start he was going to lose his chance. Epaphras Chapman joined him. "Are they having difficulty?"

A man had swarmed up the mast. "Looks like a fouled line. Can't haul up the sail."

"I don't like the looks of that cloud, Mr. Fowler. And this wind is quickening sharply."

"I don't like the looks of the cloud, either, Reverend. And if the captain don't hurry he's going to be caught midstream."

The sail went up suddenly, but half of the ropes must have been still fouled, for it went up lopsided. Johnny cupped his hands and yelled at the pilot. "It's too late, Cap'n. Hold over on that side!"

But his voice was blown back to him. The wind caught the sail in that instant and careened the boat around. In another second the current was spinning her around and downstream, entirely out of control. At the same moment the full force of the squall hit with a blasting mast-bending wind and rain of such density it made an opaque curtain over the river. "Merciful God!" Epaphras Chapman cried, "they will be dashed to pieces!"

But their own boat was in danger now and Johnny ran to the bow. "Hang on," he yelled to the men as he passed them, "I'll try to get a line around a tree."

As the wind buffeted them and the rain fell in sheets the men were hard put to it to hang onto the bushes. They strained, blinded and gasping in the downpour, holding, now pulled by the wind and current out to a full arm's length, then shoved hard against the bank. "Hell of a way to get a boat upstream," a hand shouted to Johnny. "My arms are pulling out of their sockets."

"Save your breath," Johnny ordered curtly.

Epaphras Chapman reached him then, his head lowered against the driving rain. "What shall we do, Mr. Fowler?"

"I'm going to try to get a line around a tree," Johnny said. "Take a little of the strain off the men."

"About the other boat, I mean."

"Nothing we *can* do for that boat, Reverend," Johnny said. "We'll be lucky if we don't join them."

He wasted no more time talking. The din of the storm was

too great to be heard above even if there had been anything more
to say, and their own danger was too acute. Johnny unwound
rope from the stanchion, coiling it loosely in his hand. When he
had enough, he tied the end about his waist and waited until the
boat surged into the bank again. Then he jumped. Both hands
free he clutched at the bushes, slid back into the water, but kept
his hold and slowly, painfully, pulled himself up onto the bank.
Once there he quickly made the rope fast around a great cottonwood, then leaned against it, almost drowned, ducking his
head against the solid sheet of rain which made it difficult to get
a good breath. If the rope held, he thought, they would make
it.

For ten minutes more the rain poured, and then suddenly it
became hail and great stones the size of partridge eggs pelted
down. Johnny, holding to the rope, jumped aboard. The men
were bowed beneath the hail, grunting when hit on the face by
the sharp edges. He went among them, yelling encouragement.
"It'll be over soon, now. It won't last much longer now that the
hail's come."

The white ice piled up on the deck but Johnny was right and
as the hail passed on in a slashing white drift, the wind slowed,
eased off and died away. The sun came out then and shone brilliantly on the glazed deck of the boat. "God," said one of the
hands, "I thought we was done for. I'm quittin' this boat today.
I ain't goin' one step further."

"You'll go as far as the boat goes," Johnny told him. "You quit
today and I'll guarantee you'll never get out of this country."

"What business is it of yours, mister?"

"I don't like rats."

Johnny slipped and slid along the deck to the stern where
the missionary was standing, looking downstream. "There are
women and children on that boat, Mr. Fowler."

For the first time Johnny felt some sympathy for the man. His
own blind stubbornness had been the indirect cause of the trouble, but Johnny guessed that Epaphras Chapman's own young
wife was on the boat. "I misdoubt she's come to grief, Rever-

end," he said. "I'd think she's been carried back into the over-flow. The way this river is spread out at the mouth she'll eddy into the backwater and likely come to rest with no great harm done."

"I pray you are right, sir. If there was only some way we could help. If we only had the skiff on this boat." The man's face was twisted with his great anxiety and it somehow had lost its look of stern determination. It looked what it was, young, troubled, indecisive. He's just a kid after all, Johnny thought. A scared kid that has got an awfully big load to carry. He had been taught certain things, certain conventions that had been grained into him until he couldn't turn loose of them and there was no give and take in him. God was God, and never Wah-kon-tah; salvation was real and there was only one road to it; sin was sin and there were no shades and degrees of it. A man couldn't help his raising, Johnny thought, and maybe he couldn't help the turn of his mind, either. This man had grown up in Connecticut, in a cold and bigoted faith. For that faith he would drive himself and those he was leading to their deaths, if necessary. He would always comprehend the full meaning of the word justice, but maybe it was too much to expect that he would also know the meaning of the word charity. "Captain Douglas," Johnny said, "is a resourceful man, sir. If the boat has come to no harm he will get her warped back upstream now. The storm has passed over."

Something of the anxiety he was feeling left the missionary's eyes. His twisted, tightened mouth loosened a little. The young, scared look smoothed out. "Yes. Yes, of course. The storm has passed over. How wonderful, Mr. Fowler, that the storm always does pass — that God in His merciful kindness does always make the sun to shine again. O, ye of little faith! I shall go to my cabin, sir, to pray for forgiveness for my doubts."

Johnny's moment of liking passed as the storm had done. "I expect it would be a good idea, Reverend."

"Brother Chapman?"

The missionary wheeled about quickly. Less surprised, not

knowing the arrangements Epaphras Chapman had made for his passengers, Johnny turned more slowly. "Sister Lowell!" the missionary cried. "The women are on the other boat!"

"Yes," the young woman said, "but I was tending to Brother Requa, sir. He was very low this morning. I have remembered your injunction, however, and have stayed in the cabin." She smiled. "There is a pot of broth I brought to feed him, sir. It occurred to me that after their hard labor the men must be exhausted and there is a cupful each, I think. It isn't very hot, but it might be strengthening."

"An excellent idea. An excellent idea."

The young woman stood facing the two men, her face framed by the hood of the long cloak she wore, the sun shining full on her clear white skin, making her blink a little against its light. From her there came over to Johnny a trace of an odor — a faint, slightly pungent smell which made him widen his nostrils in an effort to absorb and place it. It was dry and tonic and clean smelling. He kept trying to think where he had smelled it before. He searched his memories. His mind went back to his childhood to which the odor was somehow connected. Home? His mother? The attic! Herbs . . . rows and rows and rows of them strung up to the rafters — ginseng, sweet basil, goldenseal, bloodroot, St. John's-wort, dill. The attic had always been full of the hanging, drying herbs, and the winter bedding, put away there in the summer, had always smelled of their fragrance when got out again for use in the fall. He had slept with that fragrance all his boyhood.

The girl put up a hand to shield her eyes and looked from the missionary to Johnny Fowler. Epaphras Chapman spoke. "This is Mr. Fowler, a trader at Three Forks. He is being good enough to assist us up the river. Sister Lowell," he said to Johnny, "is one of the young women of our party who expects to help us in our school when we are established. She is also an excellent nurse and I regret that she has had so much opportunity to be employed at it on this journey." He smiled gently at the girl.

She was, Johnny thought, as he made a slight bow and murmured a pleased-to-meet-you ma'am, uncommonly calm to have been so roughly buffeted about in the past hour. She gave him a frank, friendly smile. "It is very good of you to help us, sir."

"You had better wait with your thanks, ma'am, till we get to the station," he said, returning her smile. "We'll know better then whether I have been of any real help."

Her look lingered a moment on his weather-seasoned face, then she turned back to the missionary. "I have two cups, Brother Chapman. If you will send the men two at a time into the cabin, I'll give them the soup."

"Yes. They will welcome it, I'm sure. I'll go immediately to tell them."

The girl went back to the cabin. She stopped in the door. "Mr. Fowler? You'll have a cup?"

"Thank you, ma'am," Johnny said, "I'll be glad to."

Chapter 5

I<small>T WAS</small> the middle of the afternoon when the lost boat came crimping into sight along the far bank. "There she is!" a man cried, and a cheer went up from all the others.

"Thank God," Epaphras Chapman said prayerfully. "Can she make the crossing all right now, Mr. Fowler?"

"Oh, yes. There's a good breeze."

Nevertheless all eyes were fixed anxiously on the boat until it had safely crossed. As soon as it was tied up and the plank laid between them, the missionary strode across. The pilot, testing the lashings, came up to Johnny. He grimaced wryly. "I thought," he admitted, "for a time there, we might come to grief. I didn't know but what she'd pile up in the willows on that island in the Arkansas, but she got caught in the eddies at the point and was drifted into the shallows."

"I figured as much," Johnny said. "Any damage?"

"None — save we got shook up a right smart. And one of the women had a nervous prostration, but then Miss Eliza Cleaver's not been quite right in the head since she had the fever." He grinned. "She's not likely to improve much if this keeps up, either."

"I wouldn't think it."

"We going any further today?"

"No. The reverend says it's too late."

"I'm glad of that. He ought to've took your advice to begin

with." The captain sighed. "He's not got too much judgment, the reverend, but there is one thing he *has* got — the stubbornest mind a man was ever blessed with. I was afeared he had made it up to go on till night."

"I've noticed he's a right determined man."

The captain gazed at the swift water. "I don't much like the man. Never did care much for that pious kind of talk. But the reverend's got guts and you've got to admire that in any man. He's aiming to get these boats to the mission station and he'll get 'em there one way or another. There's been times when I thought he was going to pack 'em on his back if there wasn't no other way. Don't nothing discourage him for long, not even when he's half dead with the fever."

"No. I'd reckon not."

"He don't scare easy, either. When he found out there was liable to be war betwixt the Cherokees and Osages all he said was 'The Lord takes care of his own. We'll push on.' There's many would have turned back right then. But not him. I don't mind admitting, though, I'll be glad to get 'em to the station, done and over with."

Johnny nodded. "I'd like to borrow your skiff."

"Sure. Welcome to it. Going back to the post for the night?"

"Yes. It's a little crowded here."

The captain laughed. "You never said a truer word, friend."

"Tell the reverend," Johnny motioned with his head, "I'll be back first thing in the morning."

At the post he changed into dry clothing and ate a hot meal, telling the day's events as he ate. "Run it a mite close there at the crossing, I reckon," he confessed to Stephen, "but they would have made it if the sail hadn't been fouled."

"Captain's fault, looks to me," Stephen said.

"No. A man can't see to everything. He was short-handed."

"What are they like?" Rebecca asked, sitting at the table across from him when she had finished setting food before him. "The women, I mean."

"I didn't see but one. The others were on the boat that went adrift."

"Well, what was *she* like?"

"Like a woman." Johnny shrugged. He frowned, trying to remember. "Sort of thin and not very big. Pale, like she might have had the fever lately."

"What was her name?"

"Lowell."

"What was her first name?"

"I didn't ask."

"Is she married?"

"I didn't ask that either."

"How old was she?"

"I wouldn't have any idea."

Rebecca gazed at him in exasperation. "Johnny, don't you ever have any curiosity? Don't you ever notice anything?"

Johnny poked a forkful of food into his mouth and chewed slowly. "If she'd been a pony I could tell you. But how can you tell about a woman? She looked to be young. Her face wasn't all lined, anyhow. I'd guess she was twenty or so."

"That young? I wonder what she's doing with them?"

"The reverend said she was going to teach in their school. One thing I did notice about her. She smells herby."

"Herby?"

"He said she nurses some too. Reckon she makes her own tinctures the way Mama used to."

"Well." Rebecca pondered the information. "Well. I wonder if her folks are along. If they aren't, they were foolish to let her come away out here alone."

Mildly Johnny said, "She's not alone. There are twenty of 'em in the party."

"Oh, Johnny, you know what I mean. I don't care how many are in the party. If she's not got someone of her own, she's alone. Why wasn't she on the boat with the other women?"

"Lord, Becky, you can ask more questions! She said she was

minding a sick man. That one that was here yesterday, Steve, and was chilling. She had brought him some stew, she said. Reckon she got caught on the boat when we shoved off and just stayed in the cabin the way she had been told."

"What kind of stew was it?"

Stephen chuckled. "I hope you tasted the stew, Johnny."

"Happens I did. It was venison."

"You suppose they've just got game to eat?" Rebecca said. "You'd think they would be well provisioned."

"Been journeying nearly a year, Becky. Likely they've used 'em all up."

Rebecca rose purposefully. "Well, I'm going to make 'em up a kettle of beef stew and you can take it along with you in the morning. If they've been eating game very long they're sick and tired of it, and a change will do their sick folks good, too. I'll put it on to simmer right now."

When she had gone Johnny looked across at Stephen. "She gets lonesome for white women, don't she?"

"Yes. I wish they had stopped over. It would have meant a lot to her."

"They'll not be very far away. You can take her up to the station when they get settled in."

"I mean to. She's been pretty excited about having those missionaries close by."

"She's the only one, then." Johnny shoved his plate back, stood up, went to the door and stepped outside. He called back over his shoulder, "Stars are out. It'll be fair tomorrow."

It took a full week to bushwhack the mission boats the thirty miles up the Neosho to the station. On a good day they made six or seven miles, usually with the help of the sail. On a bad one they had to be content with three or four. On a Sunday, February 18, 1821, at ten o'clock in the morning they arrived. The people streamed ashore, weeping and giving thanks for the safe ending of their long, long journey.

It was a pretty place Claymore had given them. The land lay flat and level for a quarter of a mile back from the river and the men sent ahead had cleared several acres of it. They had then built one small cabin. On a rise of land farther back in the timber they had begun three more dwellings, but all three men had been plagued with the intermittent fever and the houses meant to be permanent homes stood without roofs, chinking, or flooring, and were uninhabitable.

Seeing the condition of the station Johnny sought out the missionary and offered to leave the boat he had bought until more houses could be finished. "You'll need it," he said, "for your people to live in a while longer."

"No," Epaphras Chapman told him, "a bargain is a bargain, sir. We have sold you the boat and it is your property. We will move our sick into the cabin ashore and the rest of us will live on the boat that still belongs to us. Missionaries," he added sternly, "must accustom themselves to hardship."

"I should think," Johnny said, provoked by the hair-shirt stubbornness of the man, "they had plenty of them already. I won't be needing the boat until April."

But the missionary refused. Johnny did not know whether it was because he did not want to be further beholden to him, or whether he actually did have so inflexible a sense of duty. Having made his offer, however, he said no more. If the man wanted to crowd all his sick people into the little, already stale and musty cabin on the riverbank, it was none of his affair. You could lead a horse to water but nothing under heaven could make him drink but his own thirst.

He set to work to help the hands and the men of the mission party unload the boat he had bought. The flour, he noticed, was moldy; the meal was mildewed; and the small amount of cured meat that was left was wormy. All the stores, he guessed, had been wet again and again and without proper facilities for drying they had been damaged considerably. "He's got a cargo of provisions he thinks might be waiting down at the Post of

Arkansas for him now," the captain told Johnny. "Said it was to be sent along early this year. I reckon that will be my next job, to drop down there and pick 'em up for him."

"He needs 'em," Johnny said shortly. "There's a sea chest in that forward cabin. You know who it belongs to?"

"No, but I'll ask."

He went ashore and Johnny saw him talking to two women who were helping to sort the stores. One of them was the girl he had seen the day of the storm, the other was an older woman. He had not talked to the girl again, nor seen her except at a distance, for she had rejoined the women on the other boat when it had caught up that first night.

The conference with the captain was brief and then the girl came toward the boat. She did not wear the long cloak today. It was sunny and mild, almost warm, and she had only a short shawl about her shoulders. Her head was bare. She came up to Johnny. "Captain Douglas says there is a sea chest in one of the cabins. It must be Dr. Palmer's. He has come down with the intermittent and can't see to it himself. Would you be good enough to set it ashore for him?"

"Be glad to. I didn't know but what it belonged to one of the hands that is going downstream with me."

"Are they leaving?" The girl seemed surprised. "I thought Brother Chapman meant to keep them on."

"Wouldn't but one of them stay. I'll get the chest."

The girl watched him set it ashore. "Thank you," she said. "Just leave it there. One of our men will pick it up." A quick, whirling breeze blew down on the clearing from the timber stand and set the girl's shawl whipping about her. She caught it with one hand and held it more closely. "Does the wind blow here all the time?"

"Mostly. It's a windy country, generally. Comes in off the prairie. Why? Don't you like wind?"

He didn't hear her reply. Remembering Rebecca's questions he was studying the girl more carefully. Her hair was the light,

reddish brown of a wren's wing, he thought, and smooth and
shining. It was combed back in a plain way and knotted on the
nape of her neck. Her eyes were brown, too, but they were
darker than her hair. They were large and round, the irises very
clear. She hadn't had the fever, then. They would be muddy
if she had. He guessed that she must naturally be pale, or else
it was the same boat pallor as the men. She was smaller than he
had first thought, but she didn't look frail. There was flesh on
her bones. Johnny approved of that. He had never seen a
woman yet that gauntness improved. Whatever flaws they had,
a little flesh was apt to hide.

"How far is it to the prairie?" the girl asked unexpectedly.
"Which way is it?"

Johnny motioned. "West. It's not more than a few miles."

"The Osage village is there, isn't it?"

"Yes."

"Brother Chapman means to go there tomorrow. He wishes to
hire an interpreter. We are greatly handicapped by not knowing
the tongue."

Johnny picked up a spiny twig of locust and began absently
to pick at its scaly bark. "Yes, I'd think it."

"He means to present our credentials to the chief, also."

Head bent, hands still busy with the twig, Johnny smiled.
"Old Claymore," he said, "wouldn't know a credential if he saw
one."

"Brother Chapman wants everything done properly."

"Yes. I can see he would."

A silence grew between them. Johnny ventured a look at the
girl and she smiled at him. He noticed that when she smiled her
eyes folded a little at the corners. He noticed, also, that she had
one slightly crooked tooth, perfectly white like the others, but
overlapping a little the one next to it. The small irregularity
was attractive. "What does the Osage village look like?" she
asked. "You have been there many times, haven't you?"

"Yes, ma'am. It looks like any other Indian village, I guess."

"I've never seen an Indian village at all," she reminded him.

"Why, no," he admitted, "I don't suppose you have. What was it you wanted to know, ma'am?"

"Well. How are the houses built? How many are there? What are the people like?"

Johnny grinned. She reminded him of Rebecca with her questions. He supposed all females must be curious. "The houses," he said, "are built long, about as long as these boats, I'd say. They're sided up with palings and roofed over with thatch the women make from canes and reeds. They've got dirt floors and fire holes. They don't build chimneys. They dig shallow holes in the floor, several to a lodge, depending on how big the family is, and leave smoke holes in the roof."

"Why? Why do they build that way?"

"Well, they move about considerably and they couldn't very well build their houses the way we do. Osages depend on hunting mostly for their food, and they take down their lodges when they move."

"We hope," the girl said, "to teach them to raise more of their food. To farm, like white men."

Johnny studied the twig in his hand. "Yes, ma'am."

"Go ahead. How many lodges are there in the village?"

"Around three hundred in the main village, I reckon."

"And how many people?"

"I believe Claymore reckons it at about twenty-five hundred."

"So many? I wouldn't have thought it. Are there many children?"

Johnny laughed. "There's always a lot of children in an Indian village. They're crazy about 'em. Every lodge is full of 'em. They are all over the place, like puppies."

"Brother Chapman hopes to start our school as soon as possible — as soon as we have a building."

"I wouldn't count on it, ma'am," Johnny said slowly, "not right now."

"Why?"

"With a war threatening they'll not let their kids go away from

them. If this mess with the Cherokees can be straightened out,
there might be a few come."

"Only a few, Mr. Fowler? You haven't much faith in us. We
hope . . ."

"Yes, ma'am, I know what you hope. You hope the whole tribe
will send their children. They won't. You don't know the Osages.
To ask them to send their children to you is like asking them to
cut out their hearts and give them to you. Indians love their
children more than any people you ever saw, and they bring
them up the proper way. They wouldn't be sure you folks would
do that."

The girl gazed at him, her round brown eyes full of question.
"You mean they would distrust us? They would be afraid we
wouldn't teach them properly?"

"According to Osage ways, ma'am, you wouldn't. There are
things a kid is taught every day, every week, every month of his
life. At the right time he is taught what he is supposed to know
and do. And they know when the right time is. How would
you, strangers to them and to their ways, know that, ma'am?"

"Oh, stop calling me ma'am! My name is Judith Lowell."

"Yes, ma'am," Johnny said meekly.

She looked at him suspiciously, but his face showed no hint
of laughter. "We don't need to know *their* ways," she continued,
after a moment. "In fact, we mean to change their ways. We
mean to educate the children differently, teach them more profitable things, train them up in the ways of the Lord."

"Which would be foreign to them. They have got their own
religion, and it serves them right well."

"But it's a savage, heathen religion. It is full of superstition."

"Not," Johnny said quietly, "any more than any other religion,
I'd say."

"Oh," the girl caught her breath. "Are you not a religious man,
Mr. Fowler?"

"Yes, ma'am. I think I am. But *you* might not think so. What
I mean by superstition — you pray, don't you? So does an Osage.

You take communion and you are baptized. They have their
rites and ceremonies. You have God — they have Wah-kon-tah.
Which is right, and where does the difference lie? So long as
you believe, so long as your life is directed by what you believe,
so long as it is good for you . . ."

"But there is only one true God!"

"The Osages are kinder. They say that all things are Wah-
kon-tah." Johnny suddenly broke the twig in two.

The wind blew the girl's shawl loose and it whipped about
her. Impatiently she clutched at it. Johnny grinned at her.
"Here's a thorn, ma'am. They make right good pins."

The girl stared at it, looked up at him angrily, then laughed
and took the sharp-pointed thorn. She pinned the short shawl
together with it. "I have pins," she said, "but I have misplaced
them in all this confusion."

"Yes, ma'am."

"It was good of your sister," the girl said then, deliberately
changing the subject Johnny thought, "to send us the kettle of
stew. And such a big kettle of it. I don't think I ever tasted anything so fine. We were so tired of game."

"She thought you would be."

Again silence grew between them and lengthened. It wasn't
polite to leave the girl standing there, but Johnny was weary of
all this talk. It got nowhere and it had been foolish of him to
say what he thought. They were half a world apart in their way
of thinking and there was no use troubling waters that couldn't
be stilled. "Well, ma'am . . ." he said, dropping the broken
pieces of the twig.

Hastily the girl spoke. "I'm delaying you, am I not? And there
are a thousand things I should be doing myself. You'll be leaving soon?"

"As soon as I can round up those men that are going with me.
Everything is unloaded now."

"What do you mean to do with the boat?"

"Haul pelts downriver to New Orleans."

"I see. Well," she continued more briskly, "I can't say I'm not glad to see the last of the pesky things. The voyage out to this country was a little more than I'd bargained for."

Johnny hesitated, then plunged. "If you'll excuse me, ma'am, are any of your folks with the party?"

"No. I have no people. No close relatives, that is. Both my parents have been dead since I was a child. I was reared by a brother."

"What did you come out here for?" Johnny asked then, bluntly.

"Why, that should be obvious, Mr. Fowler. I came to teach Osage children."

"It's a little puzzling to me how you're going to teach people that have got more courtesy and courage, that are more honest and generous, than white folks. The Osages have already got all the virtues your religion professes to admire. Looks to me as if it might be a little embarrassing and I wouldn't know where you could make a start."

"They haven't got God, Mr. Fowler."

"I think they have, though they don't call him by the same name. Doesn't it strike you as kind of sinful to try to change them?"

"*Sinful?*" She was appalled.

"Seems to me arrogance is always sinful and I don't know of anything more arrogant than coming in and saying to people that have got a perfectly good religion that their religion is wrong. Beats me how you can be so sure you're right."

"But the Bible — " she sputtered.

"The Bible gives one religion, and a good one. But there's so many good ones, each one good for the people who believe it."

Speechless for a moment, she glared at him. "I take it you think we are wasting our time," she said, then.

"No, ma'am. It would be doing the Osages a favor if you teach them some things they have got to learn sooner or later. Things like farming and being a little thriftier, and if they would learn to read and write English they might not be cheated so often in their dealings with the whites. If you'd leave their religion alone, I'd say you could do them a great deal of good."

"I see. But the Lord says go into all the world and proclaim His word. Wouldn't you be inclined to give Him a little credit for calling us to proclaim it?"

"I'd be more inclined," Johnny said shortly, "to give the reverend credit."

The girl's eyes widened. "Perhaps," she said tartly, "you had better listen to some of Brother Chapman's sermons, also, Mr. Fowler. You seem about as savage and heathen as your Osages to me. Good day, sir."

She swept away, her long, full skirt swishing angrily against the brittle grass, her shoulders squared, her head held up proudly. As angry as she was she walked as if the upper part of her body were nearly weightless, as if it exerted no pressure on her hips. It was a very graceful walk.

Johnny watched her go, chuckling at her outrage. He called to her. "Tell the reverend that Le Chapeau is the best interpreter, if he can get him."

The girl hesitated, stood a moment with her head bent, then she wheeled about. "Thank you, Mr. Fowler." She smiled at him. "I will tell him."

Chapter 6

I⟨T WASN'T MUCH⟩ of a fort, Johnny thought, this log stockade Major William Bradford had built at the Belle Point on the Arkansas. "But hell's fire, Johnny," the major had told him once, "what is a man to do? I had eighty-two men, raw recruits every one of them, and thirty of them sick with the fever. Orders! You know what the army's like. I was sitting there in St. Louis — best duty a man can draw — when like a bolt of lightning the orders came. Changed," he added plaintively, "my life forever."

"He whom the Lord loveth," Johnny said, laughing, "He chasteneth."

Johnny liked Will Bradford. He was a big, heavy man, round-shouldered, with a red, ugly, big-featured face and thinning mole-colored hair. He was the kind of man upon whom, no matter how much care he took, clothing never did sit neatly. His uniform coat rode up on his neck, his shirt front twisted, his trousers wrinkled. He sat loosely most of the time, half lounging in a chair, his boots cocked up on the nearest prop. He had the light blue eyes which seemed to be the mark of every good rifleman Johnny had ever known, a little faded in color but extremely sharp in sight. He had put on a little weight since Johnny first knew him and he was beginning to get a small paunch, but he was still well muscled and tightly boned. Mostly he seemed easygoing, but of late his face had begun to wear a worried, strained look.

He was another Kentuckian, who also had served in the War

of 1812, the Battle of New Orleans, and was one of Andrew
Jackson's men. He was a bluff, hearty man, with more patience,
Johnny thought, than any army man he had ever known. He
had a reasonable mind and a fine sense of duty. He was an excellent choice for this post, one of those random hits the army
occasionally made.

"I don't know about the loving," he had retorted, "but I have
surely been chastened. All I need is Job's boils. The post is unhealthy, the climate is vile and the loneliness is enough to make
a lunatic of the most sensible man. I don't know as the worst
criminal would have deserved such punishment. I didn't expect,"
he continued mournfully, "to be lucky enough to be posted to
Jefferson Barracks forever, but I was amazed to draw this duty.
I was so astounded I can still remember every word of those
orders. '15, September, 1817. You will proceed with Major
Stephen H. Long,'" he intoned hollowly, "'to descend the Mississippi River to its confluence with the Ohio, there to assume
command of a detachment of recruits for the Rifle Regiment.
With them you will ascend the Arkansas River to the point where
it is intersected by the Osage line. With the advice of Major
Long you will select the best site to be found upon it near to
that line and there erect as expeditiously as circumstance will
permit, a Stockade most sufficient for the comfortable accommodation of one company, with necessary quarters, Barracks,
Storehouses, Shops, Magazines and Hospital, conformable to
the plan furnished by Major Long, which he will adapt to the
nature of the position.' Nature of the position, hell! I never even
saw it. I 'proceeded' up the Arkansas exactly as far as Arkansas
Post and was lucky to get that far with an outfit of green recruits. I had to wet-nurse 'em there for two mortally long
months."

"But you built expeditiously when you got here, I recollect,"
Johnny reminded him, grinning.

"Oh, my, yes — damned expeditiously, and most sufficient for
the comfortable accommodation of one company. We cut down
trees, threw up log huts, got the sick men under shelter, and

reported to Colonel Smith on 1, Jany. 1818, 'Sir: I have the honor to report, et cetera, et cetera.'"

"Cantonment Smith, garrisoned and provisioned, the situation well in hand."

"Not so all-fired well in hand that first year, but we have not done too bad since."

All things considered Will Bradford had done pretty well in the three years since the garrison was constructed. The site selected by Major Long of the Topographical Engineers was a pretty place — a bluff of land overlooking a slow bend in the river, well timbered, with plenty of water. The French had called the place Belle Point because of its beauty. The face of the bluff was banked with ferns and wild grapes, and in the fertile bottoms of the Poteau, which emptied into the Arkansas at that point, was a beautiful park-like forest of tall trees, wide spaces between them as if they had been arranged and planted by hand. Here grew the lacy pecan trees, the tall aromatic sweet gums, the great, white-barked cottonwoods, the scaly hackberries, the ancient, roomy elms and oaks. Behind the bluff stretched a long undulating prairie, some two miles wide and over seven miles long.

The fort had been constructed atop the bluff. It was built in a hollow square, fenced with a ten-foot palisade. Two rows of hewn-log cabins faced across the square and a blockhouse towered at two opposing corners, one looking out over the river, the other facing the prairie to the rear. A squatty cannon, its snout pointing toward the gate, was planted square in the middle of the stockade. Company "A" of the Rifle Regiment, Major William Bradford commanding, garrisoned the post.

Outside the fence the men cultivated a considerable acreage planted in corn and garden truck. The grass of the prairie provided pasturage for the stock belonging to the garrison. With game plentiful all about, it was a self-contained stockade as far as provisions went. Bradford had a practical head on his shoulders and because duty in this first government post west of the Mississippi required very little soldiering, he kept his men busy farming.

The flaw which cracked all of his work right down the center was the intermittent fever. Because of its prevalence Bradford growled continually that the fort was situated in an unhealthy location. In three years he had lost too many of his original contingent of ninety men. The garrison now numbered seventy and the sick list was always long. The stockade, Bradford complained, made more use of the hospital than any other building within its confines. "It may be a pretty place," he grumbled often, "and the game may be plentiful and the land rich, but any place that keeps half your men on the sick list all the time is no place for a military post."

The necessity for this fort had arisen out of the situation which began slowly to develop when the government had moved the western Cherokees onto the lower Arkansas. The fort was built not, as forts and stockades in the east had been built, to protect the Americans, but to maintain a garrison whose principal duty would be to prevent conflict between the Indians, and to keep illegal squatters off the Indian lands.

Major Lovely, the first agent appointed to the western Cherokees, had felt helplessly exposed on this extreme frontier. As early as 1814, writing from his agency home on the lower Arkansas to Governor William Clark in St. Louis, he had pleaded, "It is in my opinion absolutely necessary that there should be two companys of troops stationed here. I beg therefore that if they can possibly be spared that you will send two companys to the place, or one at least as there are some white of the worst character in this country whose influence with the Indians is dangerous to the peace of the same."

It was not, however, until 1816, when the western Cherokees, augmented by their relatives in the east and recruits from the Koasati, Tonkawa and Comanche tribes, and eleven white men, to the number of six hundred warriors, marched into Osage country and fell upon Claymore's village in a raid which turned into a massacre, that the government acted. Almost the first duty Major Bradford found facing him was that of making a study of this raid and trying to excerpt from the various stories about it the truth. Eventually he could write to Governor Clark: "The friendly letter they wrote to the Osages when they got near their town, inviting them to come to the lick (to make a treaty assuring them only ten or fifteen of them had come to make a treaty of peace) was most dastardly. After getting an Osage chief to come down and smoke with them in friendship, to fall on him a lone man, and murder him is a species of barbarity and treachery unknown among Indians of the most uncivilized kind; this also under the eye of their chiefs Tulentuskey & Tuckatochee, the Black Fox and Bowls — the latter gave him the first stroke, immediately aided by several whites, Isaacs, the Chissoms and Williams. Isaacs and King, the whites among them, is more savage than the Cherokees themselves. The Choctaws and Chickasaws that is incorporated with the Cherokees together with the whites that live among them is a set of the most abandoned characters ever disgraced a gallows."

Claymore and the Osage warriors were away on a hunting trip. The Cherokees made certain of this, seized the opportunity and with their great attacking force fell with savagery upon the Osage village occupied by a defenseless group of women, children, and old men who had been left at home. The Osages had lost fourteen men killed, sixty-nine boys, women, and children needlessly and brutally slaughtered, several wounded as they retreated into the hills, and over a hundred made prisoners. The town was burned and the crops destroyed. There was a general feeling that the Osages had good cause to hate the Cherokees forever and to distrust the government that had brought the Cherokees to this land. But the raid had made the government take action at last and Fort Smith was the result.

Johnny Fowler sat now in the major's quarters. This was the second time this spring he had ridden over to the fort. Soon after he had helped the mission boats up the Neosho he had reported the results of his conversation with the Wolf. Now, in the second week of April, Bradford had sent for him. He came, willing enough to do what he could in this stalemated war, but wishing he need not. The prairie was turning green, starred with the earliest spring flowers. The willow thickets on the sand islands were furry with little trusting leaves. The skies were luminous and tender, the wind gentle and warm. Johnny wanted to be riding west, not eastward to the fort. The buffalo were beginning to move, to shift in their vast herds to the new spring grass. Soon they would be thick on the upper plains. On the Canadian's red, silty waters the white wings of wild geese would be flashing; the sandhill cranes would be standing in the shallows. Across the plains would be sounding the cry of plovers and curlews, and the wild turkeys would be thick in the cross timbers. Prairie hens would be scuttling over the rounding, wavelike undulations, and bands of mustangs, wild and free, would be shedding their rough winter coats. It was time for the spring hunt. But all things were disrupted by this threatening war.

Gloomily, Bradford surveyed him. Johnny tilted his hickory-splint chair onto its back legs and rested his head against the log wall. "What's it this time, Brad?"

"Read that." Bradford tossed a note to Johnny who caught it, spread it open and saw that it was a message from the Cherokee council, dated March 12. "We expect to have to go to war with our neighbors," they wrote, "in a very short time and there is a good many of your people in our way. We do not wish to injure the persons or property of any Citizen of the United States and for that reason we wish them out of the way; you know very well that it is difficult to control an army, there is wild young men among our people that is hard to govern which it is the case in all other armies . . ." Johnny read no further. He folded the note and laid it back on Bradford's table. "One of the whites writing for them," he said, "and not too well."

"Well enough," Bradford growled. "He gets the idea across."

"You think they mean it?"

"I don't know. They appear to. And the Governor has told them he won't stand in their way."

Governor Miller was a New Hampshire man. His appointment as governor of the newly created Arkansas Territory was a political appointment, and while he was a man of rectitude and personal courage the government could not have chosen a man more alien to the ways of the frontier. He was handicapped, also, by his knowledge that the government was very eager that the western Cherokees be satisfied in their new home so the remainder of the tribe, still living in the east, would be more easily removed.

It had never sweetened Johnny's disposition toward the Cherokees to know, as he did know through his brother-in-law connected with the Chouteaus in St. Louis, that the Arkansas Cherokees had been zealous to sign the treaty in 1817 which would bring the remainder of the tribe west of the Mississippi. He considered that the leaders of the Arkansas Cherokees had no right to sign the treaty. His brother-in-law had told him, "Old Andrew Jackson is a shrewd one, all right. Your Arkansas Cherokees haven't been getting any of the annuities. The eastern half of the tribe has been getting all of it. Chief Pathkiller has claimed that those who went west expatriated themselves and weren't entitled to a share. So, all Jackson had to do was hold a council when old Pathkiller was sick and ram through a treaty signed mostly by Arkansas Cherokees and send it through as a valid treaty to Calhoun. There wasn't a handful of eastern Cherokees there. But John Chisholm and James Rogers were there for the Arkansas Cherokees. Auguste Chouteau saw a letter that Jackson wrote to Calhoun which said they had paid Chisholm a thousand dollars 'To stop his mouth & obtain his consent.' Said they couldn't have got the relinquishment without it and Colonel Meigs was drawn on for the sum. Chouteau also said they paid every chief from Arkansas a hundred dollars. No real treaty at all, but the government will make it stick, with guns if necessary."

But that was all in the past.

"What do you aim to do?" Johnny asked Bradford, now.

"Well, I don't aim to sit here and let them go to war! If they do, it will be against the army's wishes and they will know it. I was sent here, Governor Miller or no Governor Miller, to prevent war and I am going to do it as long as I can."

Johnny reflected and then spoke, sourly. "They mean to drive the Osages out of the country, by hook or by crook. They are aiming to get this land as sure as shooting."

"Well, they have got one thing on their side, Johnny. The President did promise them an outlet to the west so they could hunt. The Osages stand square in the way of that outlet. I reckon the President didn't count on the Osages being so stubborn."

"Never counted on the Osages at all. Just figured they would shove and push them around to suit themselves."

Bradford laughed shortly.

"Why aren't they satisfied with the Lovely Purchase?" Johnny asked. "There is game there."

As indemnity for depredations, the now-dead Major Lovely had been able several years before to persuade the Osages into releasing hunting rights on a strip of land far to the west of the original Cherokee lands. It lay north of the Arkansas, to the boundary of the Verdigris, and then angled sharply northeastward.

"It is not an outlet," the major said. "There is game on that strip but no buffalo. They want to get onto the plains."

"*They* want! *They* want!" Johnny exploded. "Isn't what the Osages want ever to be considered? Osages want to quit being shoved and pushed around. They want a few promises kept. They want to be left alone on their own land."

Bradford tapped a finger against the table and studied the folded note before him. Then he shrugged. "I do the best I can, Johnny. I don't make policies and I can't take sides between them. My job is simply to try to keep the peace."

Johnny thrust his old hat back impatiently. "Hell, I know it, Brad. I'm not blaming you. But it's hard to reconcile to the stupidity of that bunch down in Washington."

"What I sent for you, Johnny," the major said, "is, I have had word that the Mad Buffalo is heading up a war party of around four hundred warriors and he has boasted he means to raid the Cherokee villages like they did Claymore's town."

"I wish that Indian would stay up north where he belongs,"

Johnny growled. "Every time he comes through the country he brings trouble."

There were several Osage villages on the Osage River, or near it, in Missouri. The great chief of all the Osages, White Hair, or Pa-hus-ka, lived there. Over the young men from those northern villages Claymore had no control. Mad Buffalo, or Skitok, came from there. "This is none of Claymore's doing, Brad," Johnny added.

"I didn't think it."

"Who brought you the word?"

"A man from that new mission station. Said Claymore himself came to see them and warned them not to let their stock stray. Told 'em the Mad Buffalo meant to hunt on the Neosho, then cross over and march down to the Cherokee Nation and attack. This fellow said Claymore was afraid because so many of the warriors were from the villages up north and he had no control over them. Know anything about it, Johnny?"

Johnny shook his head. "Old Claymore warned 'em, did he? That proves he didn't have anything to do with it. When did you get this word?"

"Yesterday. Man's name was Ransom. Said he was the mill-wright at the mission. Said he was looking for hands to hire."

"They must still be short-handed then."

"He said they were."

"He come clean down here to the fort?"

"No. I was over on the Sallisaw yesterday. Run up on him there. He had found three men willing to go to work for them but that was all. Said everybody was afraid to go into Osage country right now."

"When did Claymore warn the mission?"

"Ransom said it was four days ago."

Johnny frowned. "This is the ninth, isn't it? They're taking their time, aren't they?"

"You think there's any chance it's just a hunting party?"

"Not with four hundred warriors. And if Claymore warned the mission what he told them is likely true. Reason I've not heard of it, Brad, is I've not been at home lately. I've been over at Mark Bean's salt works the past week. We had run short. I reckon you want me to find Skitok and talk to him."

"I was hoping you would," Bradford admitted.

"It won't do any good. But I'll try. Maybe somebody has had a bad dream by now and they have given up the notion. But when they won't listen to their own old men they have worked themselves up into a state where they won't listen to anybody."

"Well, do what you can. If they make a raid on the Cherokee towns it will look pretty bad for them."

"A lot worse, I reckon," Johnny said with heavy sarcasm, and rising, "than the Cherokee raid on their town looked."

"Now, Johnny — "

"All right, all right. I'll do what I can."

Bradford rose also. "I would appreciate it, Johnny. I guess they are north of the river yet. Don't believe they would cross until they get lower down — past the fort."

Outside, the sun was streaming into the square warm and bright, and the muddy, grass-bare earth was drying out in its heat. There was so little wind, and it was so lazy, that the flag on its pole hung almost limp, only a wandering, light-fingered breeze fluttering its folds occasionally. For once the stocks were empty of offenders and the square was deserted of men. The silence was unreal, as if they two were the only inhabitants of the fort. Johnny tilted his face to the sun and sniffed the air. "This place," he said, wrinkling his nose, "smells like dung."

"It smells sick," Bradford retorted, "smells like fever. There is five men lying over there in the hospital right now. But your place," he added, "smells like hides and old tallow. Don't know as there is much difference as far as the nose goes."

"Heap of difference," Johnny laughed, "to me."

The major grunted. "You're half Injun and used to bad smells."

Lazy in the sun, reluctant to go yet, Johnny stood a while longer and the two men leaned against the iron of the squatty cannon and talked idly of things remote from the present situation: of a new horse the major had acquired; of the way the river was falling so rapidly; of the boat Johnny had bought from the missionaries; of the quality of the winter pelts the trappers had brought in. It was a peaceful conversation, like the washday gossip of women over their backyard fences. The day was so still, the sun so warm, both men felt lulled and lethargic, and the time passed gently.

The peace and the laziness were broken when a young officer burst out of the door of the west blockhouse. Running toward the major's quarters, he saw him with Johnny near the cannon and veered in that direction, slowing to a brisk walk. Coming up, he saluted and said, "There is a big party of Osages across the river, sir." His excitement was ill concealed.

Bradford stiffened. "What the hell — "

"Skitok!" Johnny snapped. He broke into a run heading for the blockhouse, the major and the young lieutenant on his heels. They climbed the stairs and peered out the loopholes. Across the river, it looked to Johnny as if all the Osages on the prairie had gathered together. The whole far shore was thick with Indians, most of them mounted, but groups on foot were huddled together near the water's edge. "God," Johnny said slowly, "if there's just four hundred of them they make an almighty show, don't they?"

Bradford looked thoughtful. "They're painted, Johnny."

"Yeah. It's a war party. That's Skitok on that hummock to the left there. Haranguing the rest of 'em."

The major had his telescope to his eye. "They're milling over there like ants on a hill. Reckon what's in their minds."

Poverty-stricken, as the Osages always were, in guns and powder, Johnny thought he knew but he said nothing. Brad knew, too. There was no lack of either guns or ammunition in the fort's magazine. Both men continued to watch the activities across the river silently. At the end of perhaps fifteen minutes Johnny said, "They're making a raft."

Bradford instantly snapped an order at the lieutenant. "Send an armed detail down to the landing. If they send over more than one raft, let only one land and have the detail escort them to my quarters."

"Yes, sir." Martin Scott, the young lieutenant, saluted briskly and turned on his heel and trotted to the stairs.

Johnny and Bradford continued to keep an eye on the Indians. They watched as the raft was constructed and waited until it had been loaded and shoved into the river. "Skitok is not coming himself," the major observed.

"No. He wouldn't. It would be a lowering of his position to have talk with you."

"You know any of those men on the raft?"

Johnny studied them carefully through the telescope. "No. None of them is from Claymore's village. They are Skitok's men, I expect."

Bradford showed his disappointment. "I was hoping you would know some of them and could talk to 'em."

When the raft neared the landing the two men went downstairs and Bradford led the way across the square to his quarters.

The detail of men who met the Indians at the landing escorted them to the stockade and brought them to Bradford's quarters. The major rose, extended his hand and made a little set speech of welcome. There were a dozen of the Indians, all painted and bedecked with every ornament they possessed. They folded their blankets about them and pretended not to see the hand Bradford held out to them. Flushing, he muttered to Johnny, "Damned insolent sons-of-barley-corn!" But he throttled his anger and courteously asked the Indians if they would eat, if they were thirsty. if they would smoke. Impassively the dozen men refused, shaking their heads, refusing even to make talk. They would not sit. They stood in a row, their heads rigid, eyes unblinking, their faces stony. Johnny sat in his former seat, his chair tilted back against the wall as before, studying the behavior of the Indians. Bradford's competence with the Osage tongue was limited to the courtesies and he floundered even there. Johnny warned him in English. "Don't talk so much, Brad. You've observed the rules. Let 'em sweat a while."

Bradford took his seat behind the table which served him as a desk. He lit a pipe and turned toward Johnny and deliberately began talking to him. From the corner of his eye Johnny watched for the effect this ignoring of them would have. The body of Indians remained as impassive as before, but one of them, evidently assigned to be the spokesman, moved, stirred an arm under his blanket. "Let him speak first," Johnny advised. "Go on talking to me as if they weren't here." Johnny pulled out his own pipe and lit it. The two men conversed casually in English, both of them guessing that none of the Indians could understand more than a word or two.

After ten minutes of this, the major swung about to face the Indians, but he still said nothing. He simply faced them, resting his eyes on them, his own face remaining composed and undisturbed. The spokesman for the Osages stepped forward. They had come, he said, to ask the soldier chief of the fort to allow them to cross the Ni-shu-dse. Skitok, he said, was the partisan of a great hunt which they wished to make on this side of the river. They had already been hunting, he continued, down the Neosho, but game was scarce there this year and they had heard that it was plentiful on the Ni-shu-dse. The spokesman talked for perhaps five minutes, carefully giving the impression that asking for permission was simply a courtesy, it was in no way a recognition of the power of the soldier chief. If Skitok desired it, this band of warriors could cross where they pleased, hunt where they pleased, but they wanted to do the proper thing, they wanted to observe the courtesies due the soldier chief.

Bradford listened thoughtfully, allowing his face to show nothing of what he was thinking. He waited until the spokesman had quite finished and had folded his hands again in his blanket and stepped back into the line of Indians. He rose, then, and stood as erectly as any Osage in the group. In the uniform of the United States Army, he was impressive. "Tell your partisan," he said, firmly but quietly, "that the soldier chief regrets that he cannot give him this permission. Osages may not hunt on this side of the river. This side of the river is not Osage land and the President does not want Osages to cross." He added nothing more to the refusal. It did not need amplifying. The Osages knew that permission would not be granted. Their faces did not show by any flicker of emotion their thoughts as the major finished. But once more the spokesman stepped forward. They would like, he said, to see the fort. They had never been inside a fort before. Would the soldier chief allow them to examine it?

"Let 'em look," Johnny interposed hastily. "Make sure they are shown the magazine and all the guns and the powder. Let 'em stay one hour and then get 'em out."

Bradford lifted one hand helplessly. "You tell 'em," he said.

Johnny spoke carefully and distinctly. "The soldier chief is happy to show the fort to Osages. He says Osages may look where they please. He has nothing to hide. But Osages must cross to other side of river before the sun sets."

The spokesman for the Indians grunted and the major ordered the detail of soldiers to take them around the fort. "Let them see everything," he said, "but watch 'em. Don't let 'em steal anything and get 'em out of here inside an hour's time."

When the Osages and the detail had left, Bradford sank into his chair. "They are wanting ammunition, I suppose."

"Sure," Johnny said, "they are always short. How much have you got?"

"Better than a hundred kegs of powder."

"Ought to be right impressive," Johnny grinned.

"Ought to be enough to make 'em storm the fort," Bradford growled. "You sure it was a good idea to let 'em see it?"

Johnny shrugged. "It's a gamble. But if they're aiming to storm the fort it may make 'em think twice before trying it."

"Wish we had more men," Bradford said. "There is nothing impressive about the handful we've got. He will know he has got us outnumbered ten to one."

"But you're behind walls and you've got artillery and all that powder. He won't try to storm the fort, in my opinion. A show of arms and he will think better of it."

When the detail reported that the Indians had gone back across the river, Bradford and Johnny went back to the west blockhouse to watch what happened on their return.

There was a short huddling conference and then a scattering of Indians in all directions. Soon it became evident that they meant to build a large number of rafts, for all were dragging timber down to the river's edge. "They're aiming to try," Bradford said, sighing. "Well, I'll post the men." He turned to the young lieutenant. "Bring everybody inside the stockade. Close the gate. Issue ammunition. Post men at every loophole. Send runners to Billingsley's settlement and tell them to prepare their defenses or to come into the fort. Post the gunners at the two six-pounders. Tell them to have their matches ready to light." The orders were crisp and succinct.

"Yes, sir."

The first rafts were in the water shortly, well above the fort however. "They're heading for those canebrakes between the Poteau and the Arkansas," Johnny said.

"We can't keep them from crossing anywhere but immediately in front of the stockade," Bradford said gloomily. "Vaugine has a hut over in those bottoms. I hope to hell he's not there."

Etienne Vaugine was a hunter for the fort. "He got any breeds working for him?" Johnny asked.

"Three Quapaws."

"Well," Johnny said dryly, "if they show their noses there's liable to be some Quapaw hair missing."

In silence, then, the two men watched as the rafts were hurriedly tied together, floated tipsily into the current and angled across toward the canebrakes. "I'm going out on the parapet," Bradford said.

Johnny accompanied him. Here, on the shelf built inside the stockade fence, the two six-pounders were fixed. The gunners had soaked their matches and stood quietly waiting. Bradford examined the guns and grunted with satisfaction when he had finished. He took up a position near one of the gunners where he could peer out a loophole. Johnny crossed behind him and took his stand at the next hole. "Seen that bustling around up above the bend?" he asked casually.

"I've seen it," Bradford said. "If they shove off from there the current will just about bring them to the stockade landing."

"Can't tell yet," Johnny said.

Ten minutes later it was obvious. The Osages meant to attempt a landing at the foot of the bluff. "Lieutenant Scott!" Bradford said, "when those rafts near the landing, have your men light their matches."

"Yes, sir."

There was not a sound on the parapet as the men watched the rafts enter the water, float out into the current, and begin their angling way across the river. Quietly every eye watched. Men posted at their stations along the fence handled their guns without noise, stood easily, waiting.

Twenty rafts were headed for the landing, each raft loaded full with painted Osages. The Indians were themselves remarkably quiet. This was not a charge on their swift little mustangs, when they would have been yelling and whooping. This was a crossing, in full daylight, in unusual and unfamiliar circumstances. Only a few of them had guns and Johnny suspected many of the guns had no ammunition. What orders they had been given no one could know. It was likely, Johnny thought, they had been told to land and to deploy into the surrounding country. He said so to Bradford. "They will not set foot on government land," the major replied flatly. "I'll fire on the first Indian that tries it."

Three rafts neared the landing simultaneously. Martin Scott, the young lieutenant, barked an order and the gunners lit their matches. They held them high so their flames could be seen above the fence. At the same time the ugly snouts of the six-pounders were elevated into firing position, thrust through the gun-holes.

The Indians saw the guns immediately and began gabbling together, pointing at the guns, their high, excited voices reaching up from the landing to the parapet. "Tell 'em, Johnny," Bradford said tersely, "that when the first man puts his foot on that landing, these guns will fire into them and blow the everlasting hell out of 'em."

Johnny cupped his hands and bellowed the message down. The Osages, their faces lifted toward the parapet, heard and the gabble of their voices began again. Uncertain now, the rafts held off from the landing revolving slowly with the wash of their own waves, the Indians talked. Tense, waiting, Johnny gripped a post hard. He didn't much think the Osages would try — he thought the bluff would work — but if it didn't, those two sixpounders would belch and Indians would be blown to smithereens. Not since this fort had been built had it had to fire its guns, but he knew Bradford meant what he said and knew, further, he had to mean it. They might as well pack up their things and leave the country as to let any band of Indians intimidate them.

The rafts swung lazily, came together in a huddle, held by the Osages as they talked together, as they looked up at the cannons and looked long at the blazing matches. They hung about and talked for an eternally long fifteen minutes, then they cast loose and paddled swiftly out into the stream and let their rafts float down toward the canebrakes. Johnny let out his breath gustily and the major sighed. "It worked, Brad," Johnny said.

"For now," Bradford said. "Don't relax the guard, Lieutenant. They may try again later."

"No, sir — yes, sir." Martin Scott was excited and he spluttered trying to answer. Glancing at him, Johnny thought it was probably the first threat of action he had ever seen. He expected the young lieutenant would have enjoyed giving the order to touch off the guns.

The rest of the afternoon the fort stood guard.

Twice more the Osages paddled across to the landing and stood on their rafts and harangued the major and the fort. They taunted him with cowardice in hiding behind walls and invited him to come forth and fight. Each time Bradford had the matches lit again and the cannon muzzles elevated. But it was simply a show. Neither he nor Johnny now feared any attack. The Osages were taking out their spleen in angry talk. They would do nothing more. In fact, many of them scattered.

A few families of white settlers battered at the gates and were admitted and given shelter. There was a stir of excitement just as the sun went down when Etienne Vaugine came paddling a pirogue around the bend of the Poteau River with several rafts of Osages trying to intercept him. They could see the halfbreed hunter bent over his paddle looking back over his shoulder, desperately trying to outrun the Indians. Bradford ordered the matches lit again and the six-pounders swiveled to cover the man. The Osages yelled and shrieked contemptuously but they gave over the chase.

Vaugine was admitted to the fort. He was part Osage himself. Still so scared he was pale, out of breath and shaking, he told the major his Quapaw hunters had been killed and mangled and that he himself had escaped only by hiding until he could reach his pirogue.

"They will loot and raid every house in the area," Bradford said.

Few of the settlers came to the fort. Feeling that the stockade was the object of the Osages' anger most of them fled downstream and they spread fear and consternation with them. The story grew in the telling. Isaac Jessop, electing to come to the fort, told the tale as he heard it. "Said there was over eight hundred of the Osages on the warpath. Said they was divided into three gangs and was raiding on the south side of the river, and another gang was coming down on the mountains back of the settlements lower down, and the third was killing and driving all before them in the settled country. I heard Mark Bean's salt works was raided. Heard William Murphy had lost all his horses and his merchandise and tools. Heard that Reuben Landers was robbed of his corn and bacon and horses. They took all the horses of William McMurtrey, too, and Samuel Guthrey, and Missus Guthrey's pewter plates and four stands of bees."

"Wish they'd sting the damned varmints to death," Bradford grumbled. "That's your Osages for you," he snapped at Johnny. Then back to Isaac Jessop. "You hear anything from the Cherokees?"

"Heard Rogers had the Spadra Bluff Cherokees on the road and had reached Mulberry Creek. It's claimed the Maw has got another party of warriors there, and there's some from the Illinois Bayou and Piney Creek. They're said to be heading this way."

"Good God! The whole country will be up in arms!"

"Wait and see," Johnny advised laconically. "If those Cherokees show, it sure will surprise me."

As night fell the fort settled into a state of armed readiness, quiet but determined. Bradford took Johnny into his own quarters. "I guess we had better get a little sleep the first part of the night," he said. "If there's going to be any excitement it won't come before daylight."

"It won't come," Johnny said, pulling off his shoes and laying aside his old hat. "It's all over."

"What makes you think so?"

Johnny sat on the side of the bed. "You can't keep a bunch up to such a big pitch for very long. And they've taken hair. The most of them will be wanting to go home in the morning."

"They gave up pretty easy on that landing." The major was undressing, as much as he meant to undress that night, taking off his coat and shoes, leaving on his trousers and shirt.

"An Indian always weighs the chances of success before he acts. They don't like to lose men."

The major mused, rubbing a knuckle he had skinned on the rough bark of the fence. "I figured they would risk it."

"I didn't. Not when you lit those matches and heaved those guns into position. Some of them have seen cannon fired. They know what they will do." He lay down and pulled a blanket over him. "Those six-pounders are right powerful persuaders."

"Thank God," Bradford said, lying down on the bed across

the room. He folded his arms under his head. "Makes me shiver, though."

"It's all over," Johnny said, yawning. "Won't be an Osage show his face tomorrow. They're palavering right now about going home."

"Maybe you're right. Now I'll have to try to get those horses and things back from 'em and parley with old Claymore and try to make some kind of restitution. I just hope they don't go clean wild and kill some white man and his family."

"I don't think it. The Quapaws will satisfy 'em."

To the major's intense relief Johnny Fowler was right and there was no sign of an Indian in the morning. He sent armed details out to make inquiries, however, and to search. They had gone. The remains of the murdered Quapaws were found and buried, and the detail visited the white settlements, then, taking the news that the Osages had gone.

Bradford sent a detail down to the Cherokee towns and when it returned Johnny roared with ribald laughter at the report. The Cherokees, the sergeant told Bradford, had met at Mulberry Creek as reported, and there had been a sizable number of them. But they had hung around all the rest of the day, unable to decide whether they should proceed or not, and had finally come to the conclusion the whole thing was a false alarm and returned to their homes. "That's your damned Cherokees, Major," Johnny said. "They're not hankering for any Osage hair, unless it's women and children." He swung on his heel. "I'm going home. You need me to get those horses back, let me know."

He left the major swearing lustily.

Chapter 7

JOHNNY DID NOT go home.

He had no intention of going home when he left the fort. Instead, with a great sense of urgency, he knew he must get to the Indian village quickly, before the Osage raiders returned if possible.

He rode the old trail north of the river which led by Mark Bean's salt works on the Illinois. Mark was still angry over the raid, still grumbling and fuming. "Goddamned heathens," he growled to Johnny, "overturned and smashed my kettles and made off with about fifty bushels of salt. And I was just getting a good start, too. I've not been in business long enough to get ahead yet, and here come them thieving varmints and overset my furnaces."

"You're lucky," Johnny told him, "that they had already taken Quapaw hair. You might have lost more than your kettles and salt."

"I'd of took," Mark said gloweringly, "two or three of them young bucks with me."

Johnny laughed. "They leave you any horses?"

"By good luck, yes. I had half a dozen pastured out beyond the timber, which they didn't find. They took all the others."

"I was afraid they might have got 'em all. Let me have one, Mark. I'll return him on my way back to the fort."

"You heading for the village?"

Johnny nodded. "And in a hurry, too. I think you'll get your salt and horses back, Mark."

"Yeah," the man said dryly, "I figured you Osage lovers would see to that. But what about my furnaces and kettles?"

Johnny spread his hands. "The kettles are brass and I guess you can pound 'em out. Bring 'em over to my blacksmith if you want and he'll do it for you. Only thing to do about your furnaces is rebuild, I guess."

"I ain't sure I want to. It's a big loss to me and I'm not certain it would be profitable."

Johnny mounted his horse. "I'll have to be moving on."

"Little horse with a star on his forehead is the fastest, Johnny. Just turn yours loose up there. He'll be all right — if them Osage friends of yours don't take him off."

"Thanks."

He went first to the place of encampment in the timber on the Verdigris, but whether because it was the time to move or because in his shrewd and crafty way old Claymore had thought his people would be safer should the Cherokees attack, the village had been moved onto the prairie.

Letting Mark Bean's tough little mustang drink in the river, resting him a while and letting him pick at the new grass, Johnny looked around him at the abandoned camp. He thought again, as he had done hundreds of times before, how few traces an Indian left of himself when he moved on. Very lightly did he scar the face of nature with his living. He took the earth as he did the sun and the wind and the rain, as a gift of Wah-kon-tah, not belonging to himself, to be used in a friendly way as a thing on which his feet must travel, his body lie, his lodges shelter, but in no way becoming personally his own. All of his belongings movable, he left no clutter when he changed his dwelling place. He left no stench and foulness behind him. Poverty-stricken in these latter days, he had nothing to discard, not even the broken bits of a cooking pot. There were left here in the clearing only the fire pits of the lodges and a few unwanted poles. Johnny surveyed them thoughtfully, then he mounted his horse again, turned him westward and left behind him the black-jack timberland.

All before him stretched the great sun-flooded, golden-hazed prairie, a floor of green carpet disappearing in slight swells into the pale, cloudless hood of the sky. It was greener than any green of leaf or cloth, the bright, rich green of new grass thickening under the warm sun, growing so fast the eye could almost see it and the ear almost hear it, the good, grazing grass of the prairie.

Like small, irregular lakes of blue water the tiny, short-stemmed johnny-jump-ups and spring beauties flowered in patches, patterning the great green rug with their soft, but intense, blue. There were also patches of prickly pears. They were a paler, more yellowish green than the grass and their flat ears were studded over with sharp spines. As summer came on they would turn dry and sandy, with very little green left around their edges, but their thorns would remain just as treacherous. There was a saying among the Indians: Leave a prickly pear spine in your foot and it would work itself clear through to the other side. Johnny didn't know. He never left one imbedded.

Mullein grew in small clumps here and there, the fuzzy, white-green leaves pointing upward for sun and air, and all over, but not clumped for company, were the creamy little cat-bells which drooped on their slender stalks, swaying soundlessly in each gentle puff of breeze, silent as if their graceful little bells were too delicate to give forth sound.

The muffled sound of his mustang's feet on the padded earth stirred up a whir of wings once as a covey of partridge, alarmed, took to the air, and now and then as they passed a prairie dog village there came the shrill, quarreling bark of the inhabitants, angry over the disturbance, defensive at once. Johnny grinned. If he should stop and dismount, every quarreling, angry little animal would scurry into his hole. Brave, empty sounds they made, retreating instantly when real danger threatened. Some people, he thought, were like that. All talk and no do.

Johnny let the mustang go along easily at a comfortable lope. The horse could go all day like that without tiring. He pushed his hat back and rested in the saddle, loosening one foot from its stirrup. His eye took in the broad sweep all around him, the sun was warm on his back, and he felt pretty good.

He slept that night on the prairie only a few miles from the village. He might have gone on in, but he preferred not to arrive after nightfall. A million stars made the night light. His bed was a pallet of crushed flowers. His saddle was his pillow.

Tired, he slept deeply for a while, then he woke suddenly, listening. Identifying the sound which had wakened him, he smiled. A lovesick young man was not far away. On a swell of land perhaps, in a clump of the bushy little shin-oak trees, he serenaded his love with his eagle-wing flute, making a crying, yearning little song which rose and fell sadly, sweetly, like the song of the wood thrush in the timberstands. Under the stars on the great spreading prairie he blew on his flute, telling his love, pleading it, asking that it be heard. Johnny turned over, grinning. Horses will talk louder than the flute, my friend. If you want to throw your blanket around her, take horses to her father's lodge. But it was sweet music the young man made, tender and soft and clear. She would be very hardhearted not to slip away and join the sweet singer. He fell asleep again with the young, sad song rising and falling in his ears.

The same young boy, Little Feather, took his horse when he arrived, and made as if to lead him away. Johnny touched his arm. "Your grandfather. He is in his lodge?"

"He watches the mourning dance." The Indian boy drew himself up proudly. "I will have my sisters and my mother prepare our friend food."

"I am not hungry," Johnny told the boy, smiling at his young male pride. "I will watch the dance also and I will return with Sho-mo-kah-se."

"It will be as our friend wishes," the boy said gravely, taking the horse away.

Johnny went to the place of the dance, a little apart from the village. He saw the Wolf at once and knew the old man saw him, but only their eyes gave recognition. Johnny did not at-

tempt to join him. He folded his legs under him and sat where
he was, apart from the Indians and farther back. The Wolf was
not painted in mourning colors. He was glad. He had been
afraid the wolf band was involved.

The dancers were circling, bending forward very low to the
ground, as if seeking a trail, then straightening, looking at the
sky. The drums were beating heavily and slowly and the singers were beseeching Wah-kon-tah to hear them. The dancers
were painted red and yellow and black on their faces and chests.
Many of them wore eagle feathers in their hair which were set
spinning by their bending and straightening movements. Some
wore heavy silver ornaments, bands on their arms, rings in their
ears, and some wore the beautiful breastplate edged with wam-
pum. They danced in a slow circle, round and round, bending,
seeking a trail, straightening, bending far back to look at the
sky, looking for a sign, an omen that Wah-kon-tah heard, that
the enemy would be sighted, be killed.

Around the dancers was a huddle of other Indians, all painted
as the dancers were. The women had mourning ashes in their
hair and smeared over their faces. They were chanting with the
singers, pleading that the trail of the enemy might be found, that
he might be killed so that this one, this one they mourned could
go in peace to the Great Mystery.

Johnny saw with relief that the ceremony was contained
within one band, the eagle band. He saw the totem of no other
band. The raiding young men, then, were not scattered through
the entire village. He had not expected them to be, but there
was an easing of anxiety in the recognition that Claymore and
the Wolf had been able to keep control so largely.

The dancers shifted, then, and moved into another stage of
the dance. Now they began backing away from the drums which
were centered in the circle, backing far away but keeping their
circle formed, then dancing slowly in to meet, touch hands, bend
low, then back, still bent, away again.

Johnny studied the movements trying to read in them the
message they were telling. Someone was dead. Someone had

been killed. Someone was restless, walking the face of the earth unrevenged, unable to enter the Great Mystery, a homeless shade, unhappy, unknown to Wah-kon-tah and unrecognized by him. The dancers made their slow or rapid movements, sought the plain and open trail which Wah-kon-tah meant the soul to take, raised their eyes to the skies, moved forward, moved backward, shook their eagle-feathered bows to show Wah-kon-tah they had sent their young men to find the enemy, they would leave nothing undone that should be done to honor Wah-kon-tah, to make known to him the honor of this dead and restless soul.

From the trodden grass in the circle Johnny knew the dance had been going on for several days, the dancers being refreshed by new dancers as they tired, all of them fasting, the drums never stopping. He knew also that it was the high-pitched frenzy of the dance, accompanied by its fasting, which sent young men into light-headed visionary states of mind, which had urged them into joining the Mad Buffalo on this raid. He tried to think whether Skitok belonged to the same clan and could not remember. But he probably did or he would not have been able to influence them into holding this mourning dance from which the young men had broken angry and uncontrollable.

All morning the dance continued, the dust rising now beneath the feet of the dancers, the wails of the women and the mourners hoarse and harsh, the long-drawn howls of the village curs lifting in reply. It sounded like hell, Johnny thought. But he knew how serious and grave the whole thing was. He felt his stomach gnawing and hoped the Wolf had not planned to spend the entire day watching. The sun was hot overhead, the shadows short, and the drumbeats were like his own pulse in his head, which was beginning to ache a little from hunger and the harsh mourning cries and the throb of the drums.

Apart from the Indians, on the fringe of the circle, he saw the Wolf rise finally, and he heard at almost the same time the swift drumming of a horse on the grass-carpeted ground. Johnny stood also and turned in the direction of the sound. A lone rider, coming in a zigzag across the prairie, rode his mustang toward the village at a dead run. The sudden pound of his heart abated in Johnny's chest. It was not the Cherokees then. The scout brought good news. Had it been bad news, the scout's course would have been a straight, direct line.

The scout came on, not checking his horse at the village, running it hard past the lodges and on to the circle of dancers. It looked as if he meant to ride the dancers down, but suddenly he pulled the mustang up in a quick slide of grass and dust, shouted his message, and turned his horse immediately to ride back to his station. "They come," he had said. "They come with the enemy's hair."

The dancers had not faltered, but the movement of the dance now shifted again and quickened, became instead of a mourning dance a ceremony of celebration. The cries of the mourners changed, became instead of the long, harsh, heartbroken wails, the quick, yelping cries of victory, the exultant barking notes of triumph. The drumbeats hurried now, beat out the news so all the village could hear, beat out a triple note of victory. Wah-kon-tah had heard. Wah-kon-tah had heeded. The soul that had wandered could now find its way home.

Over the slight rise of land which sheltered the village there now rode in massed and jubilant array the returning warriors. Quickly Johnny estimated the number at something less than thirty. Not more than that, he thought, perhaps two dozen in all. Skitok's men were on their way north, then. These were members of the eagle band of Claymore's village. They came pouring down the slope, their eagle-feathered bows held aloft, yelping their victory cries, their heels drumming their mustangs to a final, swifter flight. From the high-held bows of the three leading warriors streamed black hair. Anxiously Johnny looked for lighter hair — red, or brown, or sandy. There was none. Only the three black scalps decorated the long, strong, eagle-feathered bows. Etienne Vaugine's Quapaws had sufficed to send the homeless soul to Wah-kon-tah.

The earth trembling with hoofbeats, the horde of warriors rode straight to the mourning circle, rode triumphantly three times around it, brandishing the black-streaming bows, dragging them in the dust at the feet of the dancers. So, Johnny thought, had Achilles dragged Hector thrice around Troy.

As if signaled, then, the young men threw themselves off their horses and sank exhausted to the ground. The dancers dispersed and flung themselves to the ground beside them, and the women disappeared, already beginning to wipe off the ashes from their faces. Food would now be brought. The days of fasting were over. The days of mourning finished. The enemy had been found, had been struck, had been killed.

The Wolf gathered his fine blanket about him and turned to walk away. Johnny followed him, joining him as they left the celebrating band behind.

When they reached the Indian's lodge food was given to them and they ate. The coolness of the dim lodge was welcome after the morning and afternoon in the glare of the sun and Johnny ate with excellent appetite. There was meat this time, although the village had not yet been on the spring hunt. Someone, Suard likely, he thought, had brought in game. It had cooked until the marrow was leaking from the bones and the stew was rich with grease. Great chunks of tender flesh coated with pounded corn filled his spoon each time he dipped it into the big wooden bowl and Johnny gulped them down gratefully. When he had finished, when his stomach was stretched tight, he wiped his fingers down his buckskins, leaned back against the lodgepole and filled his pipe. "Good," he told the Wolf. "Your woman cooks good."

The old man laughed silently, his shoulders and belly shaking. "My old woman not cook good I beat him," he said. "He not like beating. He cook good." When the Wolf ventured into English, which he occasionally and proudly did, he still did not recognize a feminine pronoun. All things in the Indian world were he or it. A woman was a woman, but there was no word for "she."

A young girl took the big wooden bowl away. Johnny watched her move toward the back of the lodge with it. He did not recall having seen her about the Wolf's lodge before. Did the old man have a new wife? She was slimmer than most Osage girls, not so broad and squatty. It was an unfortunate fact that while Osage men were, he thought, the most magnificent men in the world, their women were not so handsome. Most of them were heavily built, low to the ground, with short, chunky legs, broad faces with fleshy, heavy noses and wide, full-lipped mouths. Occasionally there was one with some French blood in her who was lighter in color, with a neater bone structure and finer features. This girl taking away the family bowl was no darker than one of Rebecca's biscuits, baked to an even honey color all over, and she had small feet and trim ankles. She wore a wide, bright blue skirt with a red band about the edge and it swung as she moved in the slight pigeon-toed walk characteristic of her people. Her black braids were coiled over her ears, tied with small red bows, to indicate she was not married. He had missed that, Johnny thought, noticing now.

As she passed the Wolf's oldest wife the old woman growled at her and then suddenly there was the crack of her hand against the girl's blue-skirted thigh. Johnny jumped. Though watching, it had taken him by surprise. But the girl did not wail. Instead, she giggled, a sort of chuckling, water-over-stones sound which made both Johnny and the Wolf laugh. "He Suard's girl," the Wolf said. "He come from St. Louis. He go to school in St. Louis. Suard say bring him home now." The old man added, nudging him in the ribs slyly, "You like him?"

Broodingly Johnny watched the girl seat herself on a pile of pelts and begin to eat her own supper, her soft giggles higher and clearer than the low murmuring talk of the women. He would not have known her, he thought. When he had last seen her she was only a child. Suard had sent her away, he recalled now, after the Cherokee raid. His face, dark already in the shadowed lodge, went darker still suddenly, as if the sight of the girl bleakened and soured him. The cords of his neck tautened and his mouth became flat. "No," he jerked out, angry that the old man had offered him the girl. But the Wolf belched just then, belched profoundly and deeply and satisfyingly and Johnny's anger fled. He loosened his muscles and grinned at the old man, said in English, "No, I don't want the girl and you're a goddamned old son-of-a-bitch to offer her."

The old Indian grinned broadly, delighting in the profanity. He nodded wisely, covered his laughter with his hand and made the sound of amusement and astonishment, "Hoo-ooo."

"Hoo-ooo yourself," Johnny said. There was a comfortable understanding between the two men. An offer had been made. Inexplicably to the old man, the offer had been declined. No hard feelings.

There was an eruption of quarreling between One-Eye, the lazy son-in-law, and his woman. This was so constant a thing that no one heeded it. It was only one more noise added to the others. The woman, herself stringy and gaunt, was scolding because he had eaten too much. There was nothing, she said loudly and shrilly, left for her. "You might have considered somebody else," she screeched at him. "Fill your own belly and leave mine lank! You do nothing but lie in the sun all day! How can you be so hungry! I work all day. My shanks are thin. I need good food. You leave me an empty spoon!"

Johnny grinned. One-Eye, he thought, had to put up with much, but if he were not so lazy he need not have. All he had to do to escape it was to leave the lodge. The Wolf would return the same number of horses he had paid for the woman. He could be free of her eternal nagging. But everyone knew that One-Eye would never do that. Life was too easy in the lodge of the Wolf. It was worth hearing a woman's tongue clatter to be able to lie about in the sun and do nothing, eat well, sleep on a fine robe and keep warm by good wood fires. Life in the Wolf's lodge was good, and there was no danger that One-Eye would ever leave it.

The voices quieted and the Wolf and Johnny smoked. Johnny let a little time go by before bringing up the unpleasant subject he must discuss with the old man. Then slowly, careful of his words, measuring them, thinking of their effect, appearing casual and unworried, he recounted what he had seen at the fort.

"I saw this thing myself," he concluded. "I was there. I saw the Osages do this thing. The wind did not carry this tale to my ears. I was present and I saw the Osages try to cross the Ni-shu-dse at the foot of the fort. I myself saw the soldier chief lock the gates and give the order to point the big guns at the Osages. My heart was sad when I saw this thing which Mad Buffalo did against the white soldiers. The soldier chief was very angry. This was not a good thing, my friend."

The Wolf rose and adjusted his blanket. "I will take my friend to Grah-moh so he may tell the principal chief these things he has seen. I myself," he pointed to his chest, "am but the chief of the wolf band. I do not decide these things. These are matters which the principal chief must decide."

Johnny got to his feet and the two men walked silently down the village street to the big lodge which stood at its end. In the sun before it sat Claymore. It had come to the chief's ears, Johnny knew, that he was in the village. But it had been a courtesy to leave him to watch the mourning dance if he pleased and to wait for him at the door of his home, there to proffer him a pipe. In silence, not hurrying, Johnny smoked it. When he had finished, the Wolf said to the chief, "Man-Not-Afraid-of-Pawnees has something he wishes to talk about."

"My ears are open," the chief murmured, and Johnny told his story again.

Claymore was a fine looking man — big, tall, roached, beak-nosed, full-lipped, his chest broad and smooth, coppery in the sunlight, the great muscles of his upper arms banded with silver and bulging under the silky skin. He was one of the handsomest of the Osages and because of his intelligence, his wisdom, his honest efforts to control his people, he had the respect of every trader at Three Forks, of Major Bradford, and of the government generally. He had been often to St. Louis and once to Washington. He was, everyone knew, a man of his word inasmuch as it was allowed him to be. He was slow to reply to Johnny, and as careful as Johnny had been. "I did not wish this thing," he said, without haste. "I did not send my young men to behave so against the Americans. My heart is sad that they went. I do not wish always to have my hand on the trigger of a gun."

"The soldier chief knows this," Johnny said.

Claymore looked unwaveringly at him. "My friend knows this also."

"I know it also," Johnny agreed. "I did not think Claymore had sent his young men to conduct themselves so."

Claymore looked away from Johnny, across the street and into the blue, hazy distances. "I cannot control the young men from other villages. I cannot control all the bands in my own village sometimes." He set about telling what had happened, carefully, almost apologetically, glancing often at Johnny. "When the Cherokees made war against this town they killed the wife of Moi-neh-per-sha, a young chief of the eagle band. Moi-neh-per-sha was made sad because of this. He has not taken another wife because his heart was on the ground and his flesh goes away from him and he sits apart and mourns. He does not sing the good songs and he does not dance the young men dances.

"Not long ago he dreamed a dream that his wife was walking the face of the earth and that he was not known to Wah-kon-tah because there had been no mourning dance and no hair had been taken to rest his soul. Moi-neh-per-sha told the people of his band of his dream and they said it would be a good thing to have a mourning dance. Skitok came. He danced with the young men and it was revealed to Skitok in a sign that Moi-neh-per-sha must find and kill an enemy before the soul of his wife would enter the Great Mystery. The young men of the eagle band fasted and danced for two days and then they went away with Skitok." He paused, then added softly, "My friend, one does not prevent a mourning dance."

The old, flat, coppery taste had risen in Johnny's mouth as the Indian told the story. One did not, indeed, prevent a mourning dance. The memory of what he had seen five years ago, and had been trying ever since to forget, was clear again before his eyes — the charred remains of the lodges, the burnt-flesh smell still in the air when he reached the village, the torn, mutilated bodies of more than sixty women and children, the loose face muscles of the scalped old men, the castrated bodies of the young boys. Claymore's words echoed in his mind. "His heart was on the ground . . . his flesh goes away from him . . . he sits apart and mourns . . . he does not sing the good songs . . ." Johnny scrubbed his face with his hands to make the memory go away. But he said nothing. He dropped his hands and met the Indian's eyes, which held no blame, held only pain, and nodded, "One does not," he murmured.

They sat in silence then.

The slow-moving sun streamed hotly on them and Johnny narrowed his eyes against its glare, pulled his hat brim down to protect them. Slowly the warmth invaded him, made him feel loose and easy, banished the old and painful memories, drugged him with comfort and made him sleepy. He dozed a little, jerking his head up again from time to time. Beside him the principal chief sat, his great chest bared to the sun, his eagle feathers lifting in the soft-stirring breeze.

When the lodge made a shade that encompassed them the air cooled and Johnny roused. He dug at his eyes and grinned at Claymore whose face, not now so sober, not now so remembering, twitched with amusement. "Man-Not-Afraid-of-Pawnees has slept, I think," he said.

"I think he has too," Johnny said. He rubbed his foot, which had become numb, kicked it against the lodgepole to bring it back to life. "Getting old," he muttered to himself. "Danged joints as stiff as an old dog's."

Food was brought and they ate, then, smoking again, the principal chief outlined what he had been thinking and planning as Johnny dozed. "Tell the soldier chief," he said, "that Osages do not want the horses these young men have taken. Osages do not want the kettles and goods and salt and leather saddles and things. Tell him the people to whom they belong may come and receive them back. Grah-moh says this thing and it will be done. Only those things which the young men have destroyed or harmed will not be returned. The council of the elders will keep the horses apart so that no harm may be done to them, and they will take into their own lodges the other things to keep them safe."

"Can the council of elders do this thing? Will the young men of the eagle band give up these things?"

The principal chief looked straight into Johnny's eyes. "Grah-moh has said it will be done."

"Good."

The chief's eyes fixed themselves on the ground again. "Tell the soldier chief also that the young chief Moi-neh-per-sha will be sent away. He will go with his friends from Pa-hus-ka's village. He will no longer remain in this village. Tell the soldier chief he will not make trouble again."

Johnny hesitated. Then he said, "I will tell him."

They were wise things Claymore meant to do. They would go a long way toward mollifying the injured white people. They were the best the old man could do. Three Quapaws had been killed and no restitution could be made for them, but no settlers had been hurt or killed. The restoration of their stock and goods, made voluntarily, was in the nature of an apology to them and was, further, an affirmation of Claymore's intention to keep, as best he could, his word to the President.

Claymore had not finished. "Tell the Blade," he said slowly, contempt in his voice now, "tell the Blade that Grah-moh desires peace, that he is tired of war and wishes it to end. Tell him that Osages do not wish to injure the white people who live between them and the Cherokees. Tell him to send a man to talk with Osages and we will make a peace and that if we make a peace if any of my people break it Grah-moh will himself see that they are punished. Tell him that Osages will keep the peace for three months so that he may think about these things. If he will send a man to talk, a peace for three months can be made and he can think whether he wants to go to war or not. If the Blade wants a peace that will stand, he has only to say so and it will be made. But Osages will make a peace for three months

and he can think about it. Tell him that Grah-moh does not beg
for peace. He wishes it, but he does not beg, for he has a thousand warriors to send against the Blade if he desires to go to war
when the three months are passed. Tell him these things, my
friend."

At the mention of the Cherokee's name, Johnny's mouth tightened. He glanced at the Wolf and saw that his face had a set
look on it, as if a door had been closed. The Wolf did not look
at Johnny. Obsidian, inscrutable, his eyes were fixed on a point
a little above the head of Claymore. Johnny wiped his hand
against his thigh and lowered his own eyes. By his foot a large
red ant was struggling to pull along a small veined leaf, many
times larger than himself. The ant was trying to haul the leaf
over the obstacle of a stone. He pulled and tugged, but a horn
of the leaf, caught on the lip of the stone, always frustrated
him. He tried again and again, maneuvering the leaf into different positions, trying first one end of the stone, then shifting
the leaf and trying the other end of it. He pulled on the leaf,
then turned it loose, fled rapidly to the stalk end of it and
pushed. Nothing availed him. I don't know what you want with
it, bucko, Johnny told him silently, but you've just picked yourself out too big a job. Slowly and gently he reached out a big
finger, lifted the leaf as the ant hauled once more, gave it a small
push, and the leaf was over the stone. The ant did not pause.
Doggedly he began dragging the leaf across the smooth ground.
Johnny's mouth widened. Doubtless the ant thought he had
done it all himself. Claymore had finished. Johnny nodded. "I
will tell the soldier chief all these things."

Claymore drew his blanket over his chest, grunted to indicate
the conversation was finished, rose to his feet and went into his
lodge. The Wolf and Johnny went back down the street, the
multitude of dogs, lean and hungry curs, yelping at them and
nipping at their heels. It was the only thing about an Indian
village Johnny detested — the hordes of dogs which made every
step a hazard and filled the air with their everlasting yips and
yelps. He kicked at one who nipped too close. "Git!"

When they came to the Wolf's lodge Johnny looked back up the street. "He is considerable of a man, that Grah-moh," he said, thoughtfully.

The Wolf looked back up the street also, then slewing his eyes at Johnny he laughed quietly and said, in English, "Sommabitch got guts, ain't it?"

Johnny's laughter roared down the street. "You're damned right he's got guts, and plenty of 'em. Now," he added, "I'd like my horse, my friend."

Lapsing into Osage the Wolf asked in surprise, "My friend does not stay in my lodge tonight?"

"Not tonight. I must take these words to the soldier chief."

He was on his horse before he remembered that Rebecca had asked him to bring her some moccasins the next time he was in the village. She liked to wear them in the house. Johnny asked the Wolf if one of his wives had some. In reply, the Wolf sent for his oldest wife. She came with her arms laden — three pairs of moccasins, a reed basket, a reed mat, filling them. Johnny bargained with her for the moccasins, promising her a cake of vermilion, a package of needles, a handful of beads. The old woman was gleeful over the trade and Johnny stuffed the moccasins in his blanket roll behind his saddle.

Night caught him at the place of the winter encampment of the Osages in the timberstand. Against the night chill and mist of the river he built a big fire in one of the old fire pits. He shot a young buck for food and lay down later with a full belly.

Before he went to sleep, however, lying on his side staring into the flames of the fire, it occurred to him to ride by the mission the next day and tell them the danger was over. It wouldn't be much out of his way and it was tedious keeping stock penned up and having to feed, especially when the grass was rich for grazing. It would be a kindness to them to let them know it was no longer necessary.

Chapter 8

IT HAD BEEN two months since he had weighed the anchor of the big keelboat he bought from the missionaries and let the current swing its bow into midstream, drifted down and out of sight of the single fever-plagued cabin standing so solitarily in the clearing on the shore.

Occasionally Johnny had thought of these people and wondered a little, but only a little, how they were getting on. Usually it was when they were mentioned by someone else, and usually his thoughts lingered only as long as the conversation lasted. Like most of the other traders and the government people he had no idea they would get on well at all. They were considered a mis-sent, inept bunch of greenhorns, pious intruders where they had no business coming, and every mistake they made was greeted with hilarious contempt. "You hear what them missionaries has done now? Tried to raft a bunch of pine poles down the river on a tide."

"What happened?"

"Raft broke up — what'd you expect? Likely they didn't know how to bind it strong. Heard several of the men like to drowned trying to rescue them poles."

"What did they want 'em for?"

"Building. They're short of building timber, way I hear it. Nothing much but blackjack on them hills up that way."

"Reckon old Claymore didn't mean for 'em to stay when he let 'em have that land."

"No," Johnny spoke up, "he gave them what they wanted. He let them take their pick. Nathaniel Pryor told me the reverend knew what he wanted."

"Why'd he pick off up there?"

"He wanted as close to the village as he could get without going on the prairie, and he wanted as far away from the settlement at Three Forks as he could get."

"Looks like he'd of wanted close to the settlement."

To his surprise Johnny felt an impulse to be just to the missionaries. "It wouldn't be a very good place for a mission. They have to have their own place, same as anybody. They have got to have room to farm, and they mean to build a school and I guess a church. Nathaniel said the reverend wanted on the river because of the boat, and he wanted near a salt spring."

"Hey, Johnny! They converted you?"

"No. But every man's got his due."

"There's plenty of timber up there if they knew how to use it," someone else said. "It's their own ignorance making 'em raft pine poles down the river. You hear about 'em getting some of their kettles stolen, Johnny?"

"No."

"Well, there was a party of Osages had some tallow to trade and they went over to the mission with it. My opinion, it was mostly put on just to look over them people. Well, the reverend let 'em look all they wanted, then he took out his Bible and commenced reading to 'em. One of 'em kept him busy reading and asking him questions, whilst the rest of 'em took what they wanted."

"What did they get?"

"Some knives and kettles. Mission folks never even missed 'em for several hours, way I heard it."

"Must have been the Hat egging the reverend on," someone said.

"It was. Said he asked the reverend what was the book he was reading out of and the reverend told him it was the Bible. The Hat asked what the Bible was and the reverend told him it was the book of the white man's religion. The Hat bugged his eyes out the way he does and asked him what the book said. The reverend said it told how Jesus had come down from Heaven to live on the earth and how He had gone about doing good and making miracles. The Hat said if that was true why didn't He come down and make some miracles now. The reverend said the world was too wicked now."

"What'd the Hat say to that?"

"Said the book might say so but he didn't believe it. Said Indians didn't believe the world was wicked. Said Indian world was a good world."

Laughter rippled through the crowd of men. "Reckon the reverend has got his work cut out for him, all right."

"They'll never convert an Osage."

"Who wants 'em to?"

Johnny Fowler was surprised, therefore, to discover upon riding into the clearing that the three permanent houses, only just begun two months earlier, had been completed and were now occupied. Nor were they shacks. They were good, stout, double log houses, two-story, with a dog-trot between the halves of the lower floors. Eyeing them carefully as he came nearer he saw that they had been finished off well, better than most such houses in this country. Where, he wondered, had a New England carpenter learned to lock-notch the corners so trimly? A good joiner back east would know how to go about putting together lumber that had been sawed or planed, but his experience could hardly have included these great axe-hewn logs. The chimneys, too, he saw, were nicely trimmed and squared. And the roofs were three-ply against wind and rain, tiered neatly and evenly. They had done a good job on those houses.

A blacksmith shop had been set up, also, a less ambitious structure, plainly temporary, but the blacksmith was busy inside and Johnny could hear the ring of his hammer on the anvil. A little to one side another building was going up. From the size of it he thought it might be either the school or the church.

The rise of land on which the community was being built was the flank of a low hill which continued to rise behind it. Johnny rode down the slow ramp, his borrowed mustang's hooves striking fire from the flinty rocks which graveled the ground. Traveling his eyes over the flat land near the river he saw that they had cleared an extensive area both up and down the stream and he saw a group of men laying a rail fence at the upper end of it. They had not been idle, he admitted, in spite of greenness and the intermittent.

He guided his horse to the blacksmith shop, dismounted, hitched the mustang to the tie rail and entered the wide door. The blacksmith looked up, nodded glumly and continued to pound the white-hot metal under his hammer until he had shaped it. He plunged it hissing and steaming into a trough of water. Not until then did he speak. "You want something?"

He was a beefy, hefty man, the skin of his face permanently toughened from the fires of his forge, his eyes squinted from its smoke, his hands black from its soot. Johnny had not seen him before. He guessed he was one of the three men the missionary had sent ahead and who had been lying sick in the cabin when the boats arrived. "I'm Johnny Fowler," he said. "Trader. From Three Forks. Reverend Chapman here?"

"No."

"Can you tell me where he is?"

"Gone to the Indian town."

"When?"

"This morning."

"Mr. Vaill go with him?" William Vaill was Mr. Chapman's assistant. Johnny had met him when he assisted the boats up the Neosho in the spring.

"No."

"Is he where he can be reached?"

"He's down helping with the fence. Guess he c'n be reached if you're a mind to reach."

Johnny looked at the man sharply. He was a surly sorehead. Getting information from him was like drawing teeth. Then he noticed the sweat on the man's face and the yellow color of his eyes. "You're sick, aren't you?"

"The fever," the man said. "It's the day for a chill."

"Peruvian bark will help," Johnny said

"We've run out."

"Doctor ought to have brought in plenty."

"Brought in enough to dose all of New York state," the man said. "Half of us has been sick one time or another." He burst out explosively, "This is the worst country ever I saw for sickness!"

Mildly Johnny agreed. "It hits the hardest when you're new to it. After a few years you'll get hardened to it and it won't bother you."

"If there is any of us left by then," the man muttered.

Johnny laughed. "All right if I leave my horse here?"

The man's only answer was a tight nod. He took his tongs and picked the ring of iron out of the trough, plunged it into the forge, seized the handle of his bellows and began to work it vigorously. The conversation was over. Between a natural taciturnity and the misery of the fever, talk, Johnny thought, must come hard to him. He swung about and strode rapidly down the rise to the men laying the fence.

Here he talked with Mr. Vaill and gave him the latest news on the war development. He assured the missionary it was safe now to turn the stock loose and spoke to him of the hope of an armistice. In turn he heard the news of the settlement. They had saved most of the pine poles which had broken loose from the raft. Captain Douglas was on his way back up the Arkansas with a boatload of stores. Their money was running low but they had a credit balance in the east and Mr. Chapman meant to draw a draft as soon as he could get down to the Post of Arkansas. One bit of news was surprising. There had lately been a wedding — the carpenter, Abraham Redfield, and Miss Phoebe Beach. "They were affianced before leaving the east," Mr. Vaill said, "and they wished to be married as soon as permanent dwellings made it possible."

"It is likely," Johnny said, reflectively, "that they are the first white people to get married in this country."

"We thought they might be." The missionary laughed ruefully. "If Union Mission doesn't go down in history for any mightier achievement at least it can lay claim to having performed the first marriage ceremony between white people within the bounds of this Indian land."

"Which is not," Johnny chuckled, "a small thing."

"Well, it's a civilizing thing," the missionary agreed. He nodded his head vigorously. "Another romance is blossoming also, though it has not yet come to a wedding. We are happy to see these young men and women taking these steps. As our people are forged into strong family ties they will be strengthened in the Lord."

Johnny wondered if the romance mentioned concerned Judith Lowell. "To say nothing," he murmured, "of Paul's advice about it being better to marry than to burn."

The missionary looked startled. "Oh, there is nothing of that sort among our people."

"No. I wouldn't think it. Well, Reverend, I just stopped by to tell you there will likely be peace for the rest of the summer and it will be safe for your people to go about. And you can turn your stock loose on the prairie again."

"We are grateful to you, sir, for troubling yourself. Brother Chapman has been under so great a weight of anxiety concern·ing this war that he determined to ride over to the village himself and learn the precise state of things. I wonder that you did not meet up with him."

"There are several trails to the village, and the prairie is wide, sir. Did you ever get your interpreter, Reverend?"

"No. The man you recommended was not agreeable to coming. We had the promise of another, who said he would bring his wife and child with him and live among us. We thought the matter had been closed with him, his pay determined, and so forth. But he never did come. Brother Chapman was grieved because he had given the man some presents as an earnest of

our intention. They seem to have very little sense of responsibility." This last was said a little sadly.

"Why, Reverend," Johnny looked at the man quizzically, "they
have got a wonderful sense of responsibility for the things they
feel responsible about. It just don't happen to be the same as
what a white man feels responsible for."

"I don't know, Mr. Fowler. They break their word, they steal,
they are always expecting presents . . ."

"They don't break their word if they really commit themselves,
sir. Claymore didn't break his word about this land, did he?
I expect that all your interpreter said was *maybe* he would
come."

"But he took the presents."

"Sure, he took them. But he didn't think that obligated him.
Indians are generous themselves. Admire something that belongs to an Indian and he'll make you a present of it, like as
not. Like as not that Indian has been going around praising the
reverend for his generosity."

The missionary shook his head. "Brother Chapman understood that a transaction had been concluded and that the man
and his family would arrive here on a certain date."

"It's not very wise to try to pin them down to a definite date,
sir. Their sense of time is not like ours. They are very polite and
they will agree because it would not be courteous not to, but
they would expect you to understand that many things might
come up to keep them from doing what they have agreed to do.
Maybe they'll have a dream which they think means they
shouldn't do it. A dozen things could have made your man
change his mind, things which make perfectly good sense to
him. Or he may simply be delayed. He may still show up.
This threat of war with the Cherokees is enough to keep every
Osage man upset and troubled, and this raid against the fort
could have swept every thought your interpreter had of coming
here out of his mind."

Puzzled, the missionary said slowly, "We must teach them to
be more honest. We must teach them not to give their word un-

less they mean to keep it, and we must teach them not to steal."

"Stealing," Johnny said, "is an art to them. They don't steal from each other in the village. That would not be honorable. But anyone else is fair game. And it is your responsibility to guard your possessions. To an Indian it is not wrong to steal from you. It's clever. *You* are the responsible one. It is up to you not to let your things be stolen. You are a foolish person if you allow your things to be stolen."

The missionary's face now showed complete bewilderment. "We have much to learn, I fear."

Johnny was facing the community of houses on the rise of land. He saw, now, several children come from one of the houses, attended by a woman, and go running down the slope onto the flats which, green with new grass, had become a fine meadow. Curious, he watched them form themselves into a sort of ring, and begin to play some kind of game. Absently, he replied to the missionary, "A lifetime is too short to learn, Reverend. A white man's mind and an Indian's just don't work alike."

The preacher continued to talk. Johnny thought the young woman was Judith Lowell. Something about the way she ran so lightly among the children made him think so. And he thought her dress was the same blue dress she had worn the last time he had seen her. He caught the last words Mr. Vaill had said, ". . . and he means to visit the village frequently and learn their language himself so we shan't have need of an interpreter."

"Quite right, sir," Johnny said. His interest in the conversation was lagging.

"Brother Chapman thinks much is lost in interpretation . . ." the man wandered on.

Politely Johnny stood on. They were playing blind man's buff, he decided. He could see the white bandage about the tallest boy's eyes now, and he could tell from the groping way the youngster felt about that he was trying to capture one of the others. "Yes, sir," he agreed, and when there was a break in the monologue he seized the opportunity and said, "Well, sir, it's time I was moving along."

"You will stay to dinner, sir? One of our men killed an elk this morning."

"I thank you, but another time perhaps, Reverend. I have a message for Major Bradford at the fort now."

There was a repetition of the expressions of gratitude from Mr. Vaill, a dismissal of them from Johnny, then he was free.

He walked the long way around to pass by the group of playing children. As he had thought, the woman was Judith, and it was her turn to be blindfolded. She stood in the center of the meager little circle, her breath coming short from the exertions of the game, as the largest boy tied the white kerchief about her eyes. "Not too tight, Willie," she cautioned.

"Can you see? Can you see?" the other children chanted, ringing about her.

"I can't see," she assured them, "I can't see a thing." Her hair was a little wind-blown, a few strands at the sides loose from their pins. Her face was flushed and she was laughing.

Coming up quietly, the soft grass padding the sound of his feet, Johnny stood to one side. Astonished, the children stared at him, but he put a finger to his mouth and, understanding, they accepted him, giggling, and began their circling, running movement. "This way, Judith! Over here!"

With her hands stretched before her, feeling, groping, the girl laughed too. "Willie, I'm as blind as a bat."

"You're supposed to be! If you can see daylight, it's no fair."

The children milled around her, shrieking at her, and she turned and whirled as their voices came from different directions all about her. Occasionally they darted in very near, daringly, so that almost, but not quite, she could lay hands on one of them. Johnny stood where he was, not too far away, but not too close. It was like watching someone asleep, he thought, a little ashamed of this spying. She had no idea another adult was anywhere near. She was as much a child as any of the children around her, unself-conscious, laughing, hitching up her skirts to keep from stumbling, showing without fear a trim ankle and even, at times, a shapely calf which a thick black stocking could

not deform. The blue dress was without collar today, the upper edges turned in so that the white throat plunged visibly
lower, a little swollen where the tight bodice pushed the bosom
up.

She had been dashing about quite a while now, and was
becoming breathless. Funny, Johnny thought, he hadn't noticed
before that she was a real pretty girl. The sun had burned her a
little so that she wasn't as pale as she had been in February,
and her nose was peppered with a few light gold freckles. Once
when she whirled close to him, laughter widening her mouth, he
saw the crooked tooth plain. It gave her the look of a child, a
young, tender, innocent look. You would think a crooked tooth
would be a flaw, he thought, but on her it somehow wasn't. It
was a kind of cap of perfection.

Feeling increasingly guilty about being there, Johnny turned
to go. The children were hilarious, screaming in glee at her in-
ability to catch them and they trooped about her, teasing, taunt-
ing her for being able so easily to escape her. Suddenly the
oldest boy, with some impulse he probably did not recognize
himself, merely the whim, the quick instinct to shove, gave
Johnny a hard push which caught him off balance and threw
him into the ring against Judith. She stumbled and caught at
him, then fell against him, both of them going to their knees on
the ground, Johnny with an arm around her waist, Judith clutching at his arms, laughing and crying out, "I've got you! It's Willie. I've caught you now!"

Without rising, facing him on the ground, she swiftly ran her
hands up his arms. They slowed, patted his shoulder, found his
face and very lightly touched his mouth. For a moment longer
she knelt, motionless, as if frozen in that position. Johnny stayed
very still. Then she tore the kerchief from her eyes and stared,
unbelievingly, at him.

The children danced about them yelling. "No fair," they
screamed, jerking at Judith, "no fair, Judith, you didn't guess
who he was. You thought it was Willie. It's Mr. Fowler, Judith,
and you didn't guess who he was and you didn't know him. No

fair. You pulled the blindfold off and you lost the game, Judith. You'll have to be It again."

Judith moved stiffly, releasing herself, getting to her feet. Dryly she said, "I didn't know Mr. Fowler was playing."

Johnny scrambled to his feet hurriedly and stood back, embarrassed. He recovered his hat which had been knocked to the ground. He held it, rubbing its brim, and mumbled, "I'm sorry." He discovered that his words, queerly, came very thick as if pushed out of his throat over some obstacle.

"You should be," she said tautly. She smoothed her hair, pulled at the neck of her dress, shook out her skirt, went, had Johnny known it, through all the motions a woman makes when she is a little confused and nervous and wants to gain time—a necessity for setting herself to rights before she sets a man in his place. All Johnny saw was a remarkably composed young woman whose voice was cool, whose eyes were hot, and whose mouth no longer laughed.

He tried to think of something to say, to find an excuse for his presence, for his intrusion. There seemed to be nothing that would not make matters worse, so he said nothing. He simply stood awkwardly before her, turning his hat round and round, carefully keeping his face composed, knowing, somehow, that to laugh, to stammer, to utter some inanity, would only be to incur her swift wrath and bring it down on his head. It was easy to tell she was seething, that all she needed was his first word to start boiling over. Meekly he stood and waited, looking anywhere but at her — at his hat, at his feet, at the children, up the slope to the houses. The only other time he had ever felt so foolish in his life was, he thought, when his mother had caught him stealing sweet cakes once and had punished him by standing him in a corner. He wished he had a corner to face now instead of this angry girl.

The children, sensing the tension, uncertain now and a little fearful of being involved, looked on unhappily and silent. "Go to the house," Judith told them. "The game is over. I shall come presently and we will resume our lessons."

"Aw, Judith —"

"No arguments," she said sternly. "We have had a nice recess. Run along, now."

Seeing her immovable, they ran obediently away.

Watching them, Johnny said wryly, "I spoiled their fun, didn't I?"

She took no pity on him. "Yes."

"I ought to have minded my own business."

"I think you should have too. Whatever possessed you? One does not like to be spied on, Mr. Fowler. Nor, I might add, thrown to the ground." She added heatedly, "I might have been hurt."

Feeling better, Johnny's mouth quirked. "I don't think there was much danger of that. I am the one that might have been hurt. You would have fallen on me." Indignantly she glared at him and Johnny interposed swiftly, "Would you believe me, Miss Lowell, if I said I had no intention of joining your game? If I said I stopped to watch mostly because you seemed to be having such a lot of fun?"

"Is that a good reason for interrupting us?"

"That was unintentional, ma'am." He protected the boy who had shoved him. "One of the children ran into me and I stumbled." He grinned at her hopefully, not knowing how winsome the ragged, uncertain, one-sided smile on his face was. But he saw her mouth soften and twitch a little as if she might be trying to keep from smiling herself. "No harm done, Miss Lowell, far as I can see, except," taking courage from her silence, from the softened look of her eyes and mouth, he continued, "except I forgot to turn loose of you right quick, and," he ventured to add boldly, "I don't know as a man could be blamed for that."

But he presumed too much. The chill returned. "That will do, Mr. Fowler. We will not discuss it further."

"No, ma'am."

Folding the kerchief into a neat square, she said, formally, "I hope your sister is well, sir."

"She was when I last saw her, ma'am. I have not been at home these past weeks." Finding, with relief, a subject he could talk about safely he told her of his late activities. Seeing he had her attention he went into some detail, giving her a good account of the attempt of the Osages to cross the river at the fort. The result was what he hoped it would be. Everything else was driven from her mind. Her interest and her concern were immediately centered on what Johnny related to her. "Poor, poor misguided creatures," she said. "Oh, dear. The principal chief was dreadfully concerned when he was here lest they do harm to some of the white people. I am so glad they murdered none, though their stealing was bad enough. This was very wrong of them, Mr. Fowler."

Aimlessly, as if not knowing what she did, she wandered a little away to a stump left from the clearing of the forest. It had been a tree of tremendous girth and its stump was as wide and as round as a table. She folded her arms upon it and leaned against it. Following, Johnny crossed around and leaned his own arms on the tall stump.

"Why?" she asked, "don't they learn to live in peace with each other? How dreadful it would have been had they succeeded in raiding the Cherokee towns." She shuddered slightly. "Why can they not learn that war is a terrible way to settle their difficulties?"

"Indians," Johnny reminded her gently, "are not alone in making war to solve their troubles, Miss Lowell. It seems to be a common trait of all mankind. We have but lately concluded our own war with Britain."

"But Indians make it such a thing of glory! From all I can learn, Mr. Fowler, their greatest men are their greatest warriors. They make war a noble thing, a thing of honor among themselves."

"'For freedom, sons of Greece, freedom for country, wives, freedom for worship, for our fathers' graves,'" Johnny quoted, and added, "In all times, ma'am, men have glorified war."

Her eyes flashing Judith Lowell cried, "But women have not!

'Women know whom they sent forth,
    but instead of the living,
    back there comes to every house
    armor and dust from the burning.
And war who trades
    men for gold,
    living for dead,
    and holds his scales
Where the spear-points meet and clash,
    to their beloved,
    back from Troy
    he sends them dust
    from the flame,
    heavy dust,
    dust wet with tears,
    filling urns in seemly wise,
    freight well-stowed, the dust of men.' "

Beautifully, ringingly, the words hung between them. Johnny lowered his head. "The *Agamemnon* puts it nobly, ma'am — but I do not think any woman would want her man to be a coward. I do not see how she could love a man not willing to play his part."

"A woman wants her man alive," she retorted, "and it would be a nobler part if he tried to bring about peace instead of going to war."

Foolishness, he thought instantly. Pure foolishness trying to talk to any of these people. "We are trying, ma'am," he said. He shifted his position, pushed himself away from the stump with the flat of his hands, dusted them together. "I must be going." Another thought occurred to him. "The Osage women make right pretty moccasins, Miss Lowell. I am taking some back to the post with me. Would you like to see them?"

"Oh, I would." She fell into step beside him and they started up the hill. "Do they do any weaving? Or pottery work?" Giving him no time to reply she began to chatter. "As we came up the Arkansas last year we stopped by the Cherokee towns at

Dardanelle. Some of the Cherokees, you know, live quite as well
as white people do." Innocently her light, clear young voice
babbled on. "There were several very nice homes. They have
taken up agriculture and are succeeding in becoming farmers.
They have cattle and pigs and chickens, and one of their chiefs,
a Mr. Scammon, who I understand is part white, seemed to be
quite wealthy. He had several Negro slaves. Our men stayed
with him and they reported that he entertained them lavishly.
They were most impressed, also, by the skill of the Cherokee
women at weaving. They have been well taught and they do
very pretty work. The Cherokees, Mr. Fowler, seem to be well
on the road to becoming civilized."

"Yes, ma'am."

"Don't the Osage women weave at all?"

"Not in the way you mean. They do weaving of sorts, though.
They make some handsome rugs and mats."

"Oh. Of wool?"

"No. Of reeds and willow rushes."

Eyes rounded she looked at him. "How do they do it?"

"They use the tender young shoots. They take four sticks and
stand them in the ground and — I don't know, Miss Lowell.
They make strips of the reeds and in some fashion weave them.
They make a pretty diagonal pattern of dark and light stripes,
and things," he finished lamely.

"I would like to see them. There are times," she said laughing,
"when I envy men. I would not be a man," she continued, "for
all the world, but I do, occasionally, envy a man his freedom. I
wish so much I could visit the village. Our men have told us
how interesting it is."

Yes, Johnny thought, I'll bet they have told you all about how
dirty and filthy the Osages are, and how uncivilized and heathen
they are. "Yes, ma'am."

"What do they use these mats and rugs for? Do you buy them?"

"No. They make them for their lodges. They line the walls
with them, and they use them to sit on and to make their beds
on. They make baskets of reeds, too, and satchels to carry things

in. There are all sorts of uses for them. Most of the handsomest ones," he added, "were burned up when the Cherokees raided Claymore's town several years back."

Judith caught her lip between her teeth and shook her head. "That must have been a terrible thing. Mr. Pryor told Brother Chapman about it when he came into the country the first time. He said they were left destitute. That is another reason they should never go to war."

Johnny's restraint snapped. "Don't be so noble! That was one of the civilized ideas of Mr. Scammon whom you admire so much."

Judith Lowell stopped, her eyes widening, searching his face. "Mr. Scammon?" she said.

"We call him the Blade, Miss Lowell."

"Oh, no," she said, firmly, "it couldn't be the Mr. Scammon I was talking about. I have heard of the Blade. He is a savage — a treacherous, cruel savage. Mr. Scammon is . . ."

"Do you think we who have lived in this country don't know, Miss Lowell? They are the same man, identically the same man. We have good reason to know that."

She stared at Johnny who met her look grimly. Color flamed in her face, turned her scarlet. "I see. I see. Of course you would know. I had no idea they were the same — I have heard of the Blade . . . you must think me very foolish, Mr. Fowler, babbling on about something I knew nothing about. I quite forgot you know so much more — that we are so likely to judge by first impressions. I am afraid I will never understand."

Suddenly impatient with himself, not knowing why he had been moved to disillusion her, then just as quickly knowing that he had done it because he could not bear to hear Scammon praised, not even by this foolish and ignorant girl, Johnny moved on. "It does not matter. You would not be expected to know. It is not very wise, however, to judge until you know the facts."

"No."

Lightly he touched her arm and they went on up the hill, silent now.

Before the blacksmith shop Johnny busied himself with unstrapping his blanket. Judith stood uncertainly, and waited. Johnny looked over the back of the horse. "Stand away from his feet, Miss Lowell," he said, making his voice kind. He had been too hard on her. "I could answer for my own horse but this one is borrowed and I don't know what he might do."

Obediently she stepped back, the flush having now drained from her face leaving it a little pale, the freckles on her nose standing out clearly now. She was, he saw, watching the mustang carefully. "Can a woman learn to ride one of these little horses, Mr. Fowler?"

Johnny laughed. "Osage women have ridden them for years, Miss Lowell."

"But a white woman?" she persisted.

"Yes. My sister rides one. I gentled it especially for her. Do you ride, Miss Lowell?"

Her face suddenly lit and she broke into laughter. "No, but I think I would like to learn."

He brought the moccasins to her. She took them and examined them curiously. "How soft they are. As soft as gloves. And what a pretty pattern of beadwork. It's so delicate, so neatly done. Why, they're really beautiful, aren't they? How do they get the skins so white? Where do they get the beads? And what are these quills?"

"They bleach the skins by leaving them exposed to the weather, and they work them and rub them until they are soft. The quills are porcupine, and I guess they get the beads from me. Me and the other traders."

"I see." Her head bent, she continued to examine the moccasins. She rubbed their soft toes lightly. They would just about fit, Johnny thought, stealing a look at her feet. "My sister," he said casually, "wears them around the house."

"Does she? I expect they are very comfortable." She looked at his feet. "You wear them all the time, don't you?"

"Mostly. They are the most comfortable footgear ever made. Only trouble with them is they don't turn water. But then," he added lightly, "you wouldn't be wading water in them, would you?"

Her hand, caressing the shaped, thong-drawn toe, hovered motionlessly. She did not reply.

Johnny changed the subject. "Mr. Vaill was just telling me that you have had a wedding lately."

"Oh, yes. Mr. Redfield and Miss Beach. They were engaged before we left New York."

"So he said." Noncommittally he added, "He said another romance was blooming, too, but no wedding in sight yet." He glanced at her out of the corners of his eyes.

She held up the moccasins, looking at the stitching closely. "He must have meant Mary Foster and Mr. Woodruff. How do they get the size right?"

Feeling a relief which was unexpected in both its extent and its suddenness, Johnny said, "Each woman makes them for her own family. I think they put the foot on the skin and draw around it with a piece of charcoal."

"They're very ingenious, aren't they?"

"Yes." Quickly he added, "If you would like that pair, Miss Lowell, I would be happy for you to have them."

Abruptly Judith Lowell held the moccasins out to him. "Oh, no. I couldn't take them. But I thank you for showing them to me, Mr. Fowler."

"Why couldn't you take them?"

"Well — it wouldn't be proper."

"In Connecticut, maybe?"

"In Connecticut or Arkansas Territory, Mr. Fowler. A lady does not accept valuable gifts from a man."

"Stuff and nonsense. I can get these things by the hundreds. They are worth a cake of vermilion or a handful of beads, or if you're feeling generous, both."

"They should be worth more," she flashed at him. "Some Indian woman spent much time over them."

"And some Indian woman set her own price on them and thought me a fool for trading for them at all. The skin is free, and the quills. She bartered fifty beads sewed on the toes for something much more valuable to her."

Judith looked at him awkwardly, wavering. "They are really lovely. Will you let me pay you for them?"

Johnny swung up into the saddle. "With my compliments, Miss Lowell, or not at all. I don't sell them."

He rode quickly away, leaving her holding the moccasins which he had intended her to have all the time, and bereft of a woman's privilege of the last word.

Chapter 9

Will Bradford was still smarting over the Osage raid and he received somewhat glumly the news that Claymore would restore all the stolen goods and horses. He sat slouched in his chair, his arms on the table in front of him, and played idly with a mica-glittered rock he used for a paperweight. He looked even more untidy and rumpled than usual, as if he had slept in his clothes. Clean-shaven habitually, he had a week's growth of beard which added to his generally disheveled appearance. He eyed Johnny sourly. "Reckon he knew we would take 'em anyhow, is the reason he is being so big-hearted," he growled.

"What would you take 'em with?" Johnny asked. "Seventy half-sick men?"

"*And* every injured settler in the territory," Bradford snapped. "I don't think we would have any trouble."

"I do. I think you would have plenty of trouble, and I don't think you would get the stuff. You ever try recovering stolen horses from an Indian?"

"No, but I was sure aiming to." Still grumpy and peevish, Bradford shot Johnny a glance. "How did you get the old man to agree to it?"

"I didn't," Johnny said shortly. He unsheathed his knife and sliced a splinter of wood off the log wall beside him and started shaving it slowly. Fine and dry, the pine shavings curled thinly when they dropped to the floor. Bradford watched them mood-ily. "My orderly is not going to enjoy sweeping that mess up," he said.

The razor-edged knife did not hesitate. "Is that something I'm supposed to worry about?"

Bradford dropped the glittering rock and leaned his hands flat on the table. "You wanting a fight, Johnny?"

"Appears to me you are, Brad."

Johnny raised his eyes and locked them with Bradford's. Both men held the look a long time. Bradford's eyes dropped first and he laughed, then. "Hell, Johnny, I feel like I was sitting on a keg of dynamite."

Johnny slid his knife down the pine splinter. "I can see you would. But you got an awful thick skull, Brad. Claymore is a clever Indian. Give him credit for that. Give him credit, too, for not wanting this war. Why would he, for God's sake? He has got no arms or ammunition, nor any way to get 'em. His people are hungry and they need to hunt. He had already done his thinking by the time I got there. Had his proposals ready to make. He knew what a stink this raid was going to raise and he is doing what he can to ease it off."

"They got such a record of lawlessness though, Johnny. You don't know whether to trust 'em or not."

"You can call it lawlessness if you want. There's plenty would call it self-defense. There is no easy answer to any of this mess, though, Brad. You just got to take the best you can get, day to day. Looks to me as though the government was riding a tiger, not knowing where it's headed, and no way to get off."

"Don't get started on that again, Johnny, for God's sake. I've heard government, government, government from you traders until I'm sick of it. What's the government but a bunch of men doing the best they can?"

"If they was doing the best they could, I wouldn't raise my voice," Johnny said flatly. "It's the suspicion they aren't and that somebody is putting a godawful lot of money in his pockets off these Indian deals that worries me."

"Aw, shut up, Johnny. I'm not going to argue with you today." Bradford stood up, shoving his chair back with a grating noise on the bare floor. He stretched and yawned. "Well, we'll circulate the news that those who have lost anything can go to the village and reclaim it. It won't stop their grumbling but it's better than nothing. You think he can make those young men give up the stuff?"

"I asked him the same thing and the way he looked I have no doubts about it. He'll quirt 'em into line if he has to."

"Pity he can't do a little more of that before they break loose."

Johnny looked up at Bradford gloomily. To Will Bradford it was a simple thing to control a company of men. The men were soldiers and he was an officer with authority vested in him by the government. When he gave an order there was no argument. It was obeyed immediately. Johnny started to speak, then stopped and shook his head. There was no use trying to explain again how limited, in many ways, was the authority of Claymore or any other Indian chief. There were dozens of times when he had no more authority than the youngest warrior — when the village went on a hunt, for instance, and came under the direction of the partisan elected; or when a war party was raised and chose a warrior to lead it; when any of the bands making up the village decided to have a ceremony and the Wah-kon-da-gis took over. It was a titular office, inherited, and it had prestige and to a certain extent, power. But the power was always limited and could be set easily aside. To Will Bradford, however, and others like him, a chief was a chief. If his young men got out of hand, he was to blame. "He does the best he can," Johnny said, finally.

He studied his whittling contemplatively, ran his thumb over a bulging spot and set to work to smooth it out. Puckering his lips he began whistling a dejected little tune which was decidedly off key. Bradford stood it as long as he could. "God, Johnny," he burst out, "where did you ever hear a tune as mournful as that?"

Surprised, Johnny looked up. He hadn't been thinking what

he was doing and he suddenly realized he had been whistling the low-noted love song the young Indian lover had played on his eagle-wing flute. He grinned crookedly and shook his head. "No tune," he said, "just whistling."

"Well, quit it. Sounds like a cat squalling."

"You're jumpy today, Brad. Claymore said tell you he would sign an armistice for three months."

Bradford jerked around to face him. "So you've had that up your sleeve all this time! Why are you so shut-mouthed, Johnny?"

"One thing at a time, Brad," Johnny smoothed, "one thing at a time."

"All right! He wants an armistice. Talk, now, Johnny."

Johnny slid his knife cleanly down the pine splinter. "He says the Osages will meet with anybody the Cherokees choose, and he guarantees that if any depredations are committed by his young men during the three months he, personally, will see that they are punished. He says if the Cherokees still want war when the three months is up, they can have it. He says he does not beg for peace, but he wishes it and he is willing to do the right thing. He says tell the Blade that he has a thousand warriors he can send against the Cherokees, so he isn't on his knees. But he will keep an armistice if they will."

"Now, he's talking business! He'll meet with anybody?"

"He said so."

"The Blade?"

"The message is directed to him."

"God, if we could get those two together!" Bradford ran his hand through his hair, leaving it standing on end. "What do you think, Johnny? You think Scammon will council?"

Johnny narrowed his eyes and studied his pine splinter. "If it suits his purpose." He raised his eyes and looked directly at Bradford, his mouth suddenly flat and grave. "But if it don't, I sure as God mean to see he takes the blame for carrying on this war, Brad."

Bradford nodded. "It will be his blame. Lord, I'd like to have

a breathing spell for three months. We have got to have reinforcements here. A show of cannon may stop the Osages, but
this fort is too weak to back it up and those halfbreed Cherokee
chiefs know it. There is no way under heaven, if they ever mean
business, I can stop 'em. When the time comes they'll pass me
like I wasn't even there. I've been pounding at Calhoun for six
months to send reinforcements and I'll keep on until he does.
He'll have to, to shut me up. But if we can bring off this armistice it would give some time I need mighty bad."

"Yes," Johnny said, "I can see it would." Seventy able-bodied
men was a poor garrison, but with half of them sick most of the
time, to call Fort Smith an army post was a joke. To expect it to
maintain peace in one of the most disturbed times the territory
had experienced was to ask the impossible.

"I'll have to see Brearly and get him to go with me to Dardanelle."

Johnny didn't much think David Brearly would be any help,
but procedure had to go through official channels and Brearly
was the government agent for the Cherokees. He was new to
the job, though, and as yet didn't know his way around. Just the
year before he had replaced Reuben Lewis, a brother of Meri-
wether Lewis who because of ill health had been forced to re-
sign. Brearly was just beginning to find his sea legs.

Bradford stood pulling at his big nose, ruminating. "Wish you
would go," he said.

The knife in Johnny's hand paused. A shaving curled round
its point. He flipped it off. "That's a hell of a thing to wish."

"You hate him that bad?"

"I couldn't sit in the same room with the bastard without cutting his craw out."

"Why do you hate him so bad, Johnny?"

The pine sliver, whittled now to a delicate thinness, suddenly
snapped. Watching the snapped end fall, Johnny let the sliver
left in his hand slide slowly out of his grasp. Slowly, also, he
put his knife back in its sheath. His hand was shaking.

"If it's on account of that raid on Claymore's village," Brad-

ford bungled on, "there were others there . . . they said the
Chisholms planned it — "

Johnny wheeled on Bradford, his face turned gray with a sick
pallor, his mouth distorted. "Shut up, Brad. You don't know
anything about it. And I don't want to talk about it."

Bradford stared at him a long moment, then he let his breath
out on a long, slow suspiration. "All right, Johnny. I'm sorry.
Whatever you say. Talk to me, now, about what's best to do.
Somebody ought to go for the Osages. Reckon Steve would go?"

Unable yet to speak, Johnny gripped the chair rung hard.
He shook his head. Wetting his lips he made an effort to control
his voice. He brought out a word or two grittily, thickly. "He
would . . ." he swallowed and wet his lips again, waited, then
continued slowly, "he would go, but I don't think he's your man,
Brad. Nathaniel Pryor would be the best, I think."

The major averted his eyes. He had never before witnessed
so hard a man's ordeal with his own emotions. It was not decent
to watch Johnny Fowler struggle with himself. He had sure lit
a match to a long fuse, he thought. "Will you tell him, then?
Tell him I'll wait here for him — how long would you say?"

The voice was stronger now, but dead and strained. "Four
days will be enough."

"All right." Bradford felt an enormous relief. Lord help me
to remember this man has got a side that's like powder to touch
off, he thought, and let me never touch it off again. "I'll wait
four days. If he can't come, I'll go on then and do the best I
can. Me and Brearly."

Johnny nodded. Bradford, standing in the doorway, idly
picked at the rusted hasp of the lock. "When are the Osages
going on their spring hunt?"

Behind him Johnny's chair grated back. "What makes you
think they're going on a spring hunt?"

"Because they always do."

Johnny joined him in the door. "Not this year. Not with the
Blade on their tails. They're afraid to. Afraid the village will
be raided while they're gone."

Bradford flushed at the implication he would not be able to stop the Cherokees, but he kept his temper. "What will they do?"

Johnny stepped down on the long stone doorstep. "Go hungry."

"They going hungry now?" Bradford stepped down too.

"Their bellies are getting pretty flat."

"Out of corn too?"

"The Wolf had some, but the stew tasted musty like the women had used their seed corn."

Will Bradford touched Johnny's arm. "Johnny, if I don't get any satisfaction out of the Blade, I swear I'll take this armistice to Graham in St. Louis, and to Calhoun in Washington, and if need be I'll take it the hell to the President himself. I'll *get* this armistice, so help me God, one way or another. Your people can go hunting in peace, then."

Johnny tipped his hat back, ran his hand through his hair and settled the hat back in place. "All right, Brad."

They walked slowly across the sunlit square, small dust wheels falling from their heels. Shadows slanted long from the west blockhouse and laid a rounded dome across the squatty cannon in the middle of the square. Johnny touched the warm iron as he passed. One cannon. Four six-pounders. Seventy half-sick men. It was a hell of an army post.

At the gate they stopped. Johnny's mustang was hitched to the tie rail and he was slowly, luxuriously, scratching his neck against it. Johnny pulled on his mane. Bradford, glancing briefly at the horse, directed his gaze to the long, level prairie which opened before the fort. Johnny followed his look. A small plume of dust rolled in the distance. Neither man spoke, but the eyes of each fixed on the dust, waiting until the riders came near enough to identify. Johnny recognized them first. "Pryor," he said, "and Mundy."

"Save you looking out Nathaniel to give him my message," Bradford said.

They waited by the tie rail until the riders came up. The men all nodded jerkily at each other, spoke, and Pryor and Mundy dismounted and hitched their animals. Nathaniel Pryor pushed his hat back on his head while Mundy took his off and slapped it against his thigh to rid it of dust. He sneezed in the cloud he created and complained mildly, "If it ain't one damned thing in this country it's another. Like to drowned out with rain during the winter and now we're smothering in dust."

Mordecai Mundy was a short, beefy man with heavy, big shoulders and thick-set legs. He rolled a little when he walked, like a duck waddling. He wore a spade beard which was a thick, luxuriant dark brown. His mouth showed through, pink and moist, small like a woman's and tender-lipped. He wore a soiled flowered waistcoat over a woolen shirt, which his big belly stretched tight. His dark pants were tucked into a pair of black cavalry boots, with long Spanish spurs on the heels. They were showy and cruel, but Johnny suspected that Mundy wore them for the show and the clank, for he had never heard of the man mistreating an animal. Same reason, he guessed, he affected the cavalry boots. So far as anyone knew, Mundy had never been in the cavalry, but the boots made a big show.

Beside Mundy, Nathaniel Pryor seemed tall, though he lacked several inches of matching Johnny's height. He also looked gaunt and thin. He wore a beard, too, but it was straggling and thatchy, the color of a rusted piece of iron. Above it deep lines were cut along his nostrils giving his face a clawed, haggard look.

He was a man for whom nothing had ever worked out quite right. He had been a sergeant with the Lewis and Clark expedition, later a regular soldier. Because he was not a West Point man promotions had never come to him, in spite of his great service on the expedition. He had eventually resigned. Then he had tried to operate a trading post in Illinois, but the Winnebagos had run him out and he had lost everything, barely escaping with his life. Re-enlisting then, he had served with gallantry in the 44th Infantry at the Battle of New Orleans, finally being made a captain, but when the war ended again there had been no future for him in the army. He took an honorable discharge and came to the Osage country. He was married to an Osage woman now and had several children by her. At forty-six he was still struggling for a bare living. Last year he had sold a partnership in his trading post to Mordecai Mundy and it was Mundy's sagacity that kept the post going.

Nathaniel Pryor was a good man, and a brave and honorable one. He was also from Kentucky originally, and Johnny had heard that on his mother's side he traced a direct descent from the Indian princess, Pocahontas. He was a man who now was deeply troubled by the events of the times and was doing his worried best for the Indians he had married into. But he was a man dogged by misfortune, the greatest of which, now, appeared to be his ill health. Never quite well any more, often shaken by chills and fever, Johnny thought he might have the lung consumption and he knew for a fact that he had a crippling, painful form of rheumatism which frequently incapacitated him. He felt a pity for the man, a wish that his services might be recognized. It would be a good thing, he thought, if Nathaniel Pryor could be made agent for the Osages so that he would have a small competence and quit his everlasting worry about finances.

The four men moved inside the stockade gate where the sun poured down and Pryor squatted on his heels against the fence, tilting his lean, lined face to the sun. He picked up a pebble and chucked it again and again into the dust, watching the dust plop up and drift away. He listened intently as Bradford told Johnny's news. Johnny leaned against the fence, saying nothing. Mundy planted himself, spread-legged, solid and thick, in front of Bradford and nodded now and then as Bradford talked. Vigorous, shrewd, always looking out for a good profit, Mordecai Mundy was a ruthless man to do business with. He drove the closest deals of any trader with the Osages and crucified Nathaniel Pryor doing it. Pryor hated to see them taken advantage of. But he had been rapidly going broke when Mundy came along and rescued him so he had little to say about how the post should be operated any more. He had a look of bleeding inside, though, most of the time nowadays. "Good," Mundy said, when Bradford had finished. "You will go, won't you, Nat?"

Slowly Pryor's head tilted down. "Sure," he said, "I'll go."

"They know you can be trusted, Nathaniel," Johnny said quietly. A little praise never hurt any man and Nathaniel needed a little praise once in a while. His trouble was his good heart. Pryor smiled at him, a surprisingly gentle smile. He nodded and Johnny jerked his own chin down.

The talk veered to other things and presently Mundy announced, rocking back on his heels importantly, "Well, gentlemen, I reckon I've got a little news of my own." Pryor did not raise his head, but Johnny and Bradford gave him their attention. "I'm beginning to outfit me a train to take west." He chopped his hat down against his thigh again, screwed his small black eyes and chuckled. "Yes, sir, I mean to see them Rocky Mountains Nat is always talking about."

Johnny glanced at Nathaniel. He had often heard him tell about the Lewis and Clark expedition, always Johnny had thought with nostalgia that that time of high adventure was over with. Once, hunting with Pryor on the Cimarron, they had sat beside a fire late at night while Pryor had talked. "We went," he had said slowly, in the way of a man remembering good things and savoring them over again, "we went up the Missouri. There was three boats of us at the start — a keelboat over fifty foot long and two pirogues. Thirty of us in the main party and Captain Clark's black boy, York. There was others, some boatmen and some more soldiers, went as far as the Mandan villages. But they went back to St. Louis from there. The rest of us went on.

"We went up the Missouri and we wintered at the Mandan villages up north. Built us a stockade and lived fat and snug. That's where we took on Charbonneau and his Shoshone woman, Sacajawea." His hands had twitched restlessly. "There is some that say she led the way through the mountains but that's not the truth. Captain Clark never needed a guide anywhere.

But I don't know as we could have got the horses we had to have without her to talk to her own people for us." His voice softened. "She was the best woman, outside my own mother, I ever knew. You take a *good* Indian woman and they can't be beat . . . for work or for holding by a man or for enduring."

Johnny wondered if, the only woman on the journey, most of the men hadn't been more than a little in love with her. Maybe that was one reason Nathaniel had married his Osage woman instead of just taking up with her. Maybe Sacajawea still sort of lived inside of him. "What are the mountains like, Nat?" he asked.

"Like nothing you ever saw before. Peaks that have got snow on them the year round. Shining in the sun. Rock falls and slides and rough, hard going underfoot. Clear, fast-running streams in the canyons. Big country, Johnny. Big country. Biggest in the world, I reckon."

Johnny knew the story well. They had reached the Pacific, had built another fort and had wintered there. Then they had returned. For a while they had all been heroes, for the country had thought them all perished on the journey. But within a year their great adventure was a thing of the past and the men involved had been forgotten, excepting William Clark. "You'd like to go back, Nat?" Johnny asked.

"Well," Pryor had hesitated, hunting for words, "well, a man don't forget it, Johnny. If it's the best he has ever had, it kind of stands out in his mind. Makes everything else seem little, in some ways. What I ought," he said, his voice stronger, "what I ought to have done was not *come* back. Done what John Colton done. Stayed out there and trapped."

Johnny nodded. He could see how a man would reason that way, and maybe it was what Pryor should have done. Maybe things would have been better for him.

Nathaniel was continuing. "Makes it seem kind of puny to be trading with tame Injuns when you've been clean across the country. But," he hesitated, "I don't know as it would be the same again."

"No," Johnny agreed, "there's just one time that is the first time."

"Yes. Well, I make out," Pryor said quietly. "I've got nothing to complain of. But you like to remember a time, sort of, when you seemed even to yourself to be a little bigger man."

There had been no more to say and they had wrapped themselves in their blankets and gone to sleep. The next day Pryor had put it out of his mind apparently, fixed his mind on the buffalo hunt and had brought down more meat than any of the rest of them.

But Johnny had never forgotten that night talk and he knew that Pryor's tales had now inspired Mordecai Mundy to try his hand at the west. He wished it was Nathaniel going instead. He guessed Nathaniel wished it too, though he kept quiet. Johnny moved restlessly. "Going to leave soon, Mundy?"

The man shook his head. "Not before fall, I guess. Takes a while to get an outfit together. Man don't want to go off half-cocked." He spat in the dust and the spittle bored a tiny round hole. "Been thinking," he went on, "some of going towards Santy Fee. Hear there's pretty good chances of making a pocketful in the Spanish trade there."

Bradford snorted. "Good chance of getting a skinful of lead, too. Those Spanish aren't wanting American traders coming in there, way I hear it. Look what happened to the McKnights."

One of the McKnight brothers had taken a train of American goods to Santa Fe several years before. His goods had been confiscated and he himself had been thrown into the Santa Fe jail where he had lain for seven years before his brother had been able to get him released.

"Times have changed," Mundy said. "I heard they won't put nothing in the way of American trade now."

"What do you think, Nat?" Johnny said.

Pryor dusted off his hands and stood, settling his hat on his head more firmly. "I don't know anything about the Santa Fee trade."

"Naw," Mundy put in, "he went to Oregon. Somebody," he

continued, "has got to open it up if it's ever going to be opened up. Figger I might as well give it a try."

Seeing the sick look in Pryor's eyes, Johnny rode Mundy a little. "Somebody," he said, "has got to make the first two hundred percent profits, don't they, Mordecai?"

Mundy grinned. "Thousand percent is a closer figure, Johnny."

Johnny grinned back at him. "You wouldn't settle for pickings, would you?"

"Not me." Mundy shook his head. "Not this trader. I can trade with Spanish same as Osages, I reckon."

"I expect you can," Johnny said. He moved back, where he could see the horses. "That gelding of yours," he said quietly, "is eating wood again, Mordecai."

"Oh, hell," Mundy said disgustedly. "I thought I had him broke of that."

Johnny untied the reins of his mustang. Mordecai Mundy would not ride a prairie pony. He wanted horseflesh under him, he said, when he rode. His big black gelding was a handsome piece of horseflesh all right, but it pleased Johnny to remind Mundy now, "You can't ever break one." He swung his leg over the saddle. "Pure worthless when they commence eating wood. Well . . . be easy, boys. Brad. Nat." He lifted his hand, the mustang reared and pawed the air, then straightened out, set himself a fast, jolting pace across the prairie. Johnny gave him his head, glad to leave the fort behind.

He forded the Arkansas north of the fort where the sand bars were flat and dry and wide. Cottonwoods marked the course of the river and their large white limbs branched like skeleton bones, not yet fleshed with leaves. Over the bluff, where the river curved into the Devil's Elbow, the sun hung red-gold before slipping down behind the bluff's edge. It looked swollen and surly, hazed by the dust raised from Johnny's horse. The water of the river was red, too, and shallow. The ford here was tricky with quicksand and Johnny guided his horse through cautiously. The animal splashed through patiently, coming finally to the narrow main channel which he had to swim for a hundred yards. Coming out on the high bank on the other side, he rippled his skin to rid it of water, tossed his head and whinnied. Johnny cut him over toward the timber and set him again at a trot. He held the pony to it for half an hour, then let him slow to a walk.

He leaned forward in the saddle, folding his hands on the pommel and resting his weight on them. He slumped his shoulders. He was tired, he realized, very tired. And that was a poor thing he had done with Will Bradford back there. He had thought he was quit of that kind of foolishness. He had thought he had sealed his feelings up better than that. He felt shame for it and an invading sense of disquiet. A man on the prod was of no use to himself, or to his friends either. He knew when the prickly, edgy feeling had begun in him — when he had listened to old Claymore tell of the young eagle chief. That was a long time ago, he told himself, that Cherokee raid. Put it away, as you have put it away before. That is a thing that is done and Will Bradford's way is best now. His eyes felt hot and gritty and he rubbed at them with the heel of his hand. He sighed deeply and kicked his heels into the mustang's sides.

On the north side of the river the hills began, blocking up to the big mountains beyond. The trail followed over the rounded hills and down in the narrow valleys between them. The sun went down and the air chilled. Johnny shivered in the slow wind that got up from the north, and watched the sky darken, the first stars come through. When he came to Frog Bayou he stopped. Under the starlight the little creek was a riffling sheet of pewter sliding between its banks with a sound like wind in the trees. Stiffly he dismounted and slung off his saddle. He freed the horse's mouth of the bit and let him roll half a dozen times. Then he hobbled him to keep him from roaming too far away.

He built a fire and spread his saddle blanket near it. He was not hungry, he discovered, and he let go the chore of eating. He sat on the saddle blanket and drew his legs up locking his arms about them and stared into the fire, his flesh warming, the chill down his spine slowly leaving. When he was warm all over he felt sleepy, and pulling his gun handy beside him he lay down.

The sky was as black as chimney soot, with the stars like chimney sparks flown up against it. The only sounds in the dark were the whiffling sniffs of the mustang as he cropped the new grass, and the sliding, slipping sound of the creek flowing between its banks.

Chapter 10

He DREAMED AGAIN.

He and Suard were hammering across the prairie, Suard like a man gone crazy, screaming and cursing and beating his horse. The sun was hot, and the wind was hot, and flecks of foam from Suard's lathered horse spun back into his face. Bent far forward over the neck of his pony, he knew they would be too late and in his mind's eye he saw, with the clarity and forevision of a dream, what they were racing toward, and in his mind's eye he saw himself shrinking away from it though his pony ran toward it as if the devils of hell were after him. The wind beat in his face and flapped his old hat brim down and he pulled on it and bent his head against the wind. His skin was blistered by the hot wind and his lips felt sore as if he had bitten them into shreds. The dust boiled up from Suard's horse ahead of him and boiled around him and mixed with the sweat on his face, settling like scum around his eyes and mouth. He had to keep wiping his eyes so he could see.

They raced on and he groaned as they neared the village, and he could see the groan escaping from his mouth, vast and mis-shapen and gross, a black thing like a cloud, ragged-edged and torn, streaming out on the wind behind him and mixing with the dust into a dark plume. Then it changed and became smoke. He was in two parts, able at once to rage across the prairie with Suard, to feel the jolting of his horse in his body, feel the mud on his face baking in the wind, feel the great, swelling fear in his heart and the flinty anger and the desperate hope, and to stand apart and watch himself racing, knowing it was futile, pitying that small, impotent thing on the back of a horse riding to horror.

They came to the village and it was still smoking, and there were the blackened timbers and the still-hot ashes, and the burnt-out cornfields, and the sweetish, sick smell of burned flesh. There were all the beautiful young boys, the kangas, slim and leggy yet, their skins sleek with oil. They lay where they had fallen, killed and murdered, their bodies maimed and disfigured. There were the withered old people, like brown, sun-dried raisins, wrinkled, full of age, now flung aside and struck down in their feebleness, their faces slack and the flesh hanging down in folds where they had been scalped. There were the women, more than forty of them, bloody, trampled, bestially mutilated . . . and the babies and small children . . . and Suard going among them, bent as if cramping in his gut, weeping so that tears runneled his cheeks and made more mud on his face, turning the heads, looking into the faces, searching, running, wringing his hands, crying, "Les pauvres, ah, les pauvres!"

And behind him there was Johnny Fowler turned to stone, his mind as vacant as if the brain itself had suddenly petrified, the soft tissues curdled and frozen, his eyes seeing nothing but a gray membranous curtain. All the slain bodies on the ground melted together and became a churned mass of gray, thick mud. There was Suard clutching his arm and weeping, bent over in pain, his face contorted with anguish, and Johnny Fowler licking his lips and tasting salt on them.

And then there were the mourning wails from the low hills as the people sifted back, the ones who had got away, and there was Suard crying again because his wife was among them, safe, telling how she had run so fast, herding the two children before her, dodging this way and that, keeping to the bushes and the gullies so she would not be seen and tracked down. There was Suard's woman, her hair falling around her face, the children clinging to her skirts and wailing, crying to Johnny Fowler, still frozen where he stood, "It was the Blade. It was the Blade."

There was Suard's woman, then, sitting on the ground holding the head of her sister in her lap, who had been too big with child to run fast, whose child had been cut from her belly and thrown aside, slit as if it had been a young pig.

There was nausea, then, and a bilious blackness pouring from his mouth, and Claymore saying, "His heart is on the ground . . . his flesh is eaten away . . . he does not sing the good songs." And Johnny Fowler's heart swelled and swelled until it burst and the freed blood clotted in his chest and he knew that Johnny Fowler was dying.

He waked with a jolt, a feeling of falling through space, from a great height, his voice screaming silently in his throat. The fire was dead. A rind of old, useless moon was pinned to the top of the trees and the night air was very cold. Johnny Fowler turned over and buried his head in his arms. A long shudder ran through him. He ought to have taken the Osage way. He ought to have ridden after the Blade . . . then.

Chapter 11

The BURKE & FOWLER establishment sprawled loosely on the bank of the Verdigris River. All about it were the tall, beautiful trees which grew over the point of land, all the trees which liked a well-watered soil — elm, pecan, ash, walnut, mulberry, wild cherry, sweet gum, and cottonwood. Grape vines as thick as a man's arm swung in twisted awkwardness from many, and in places the forest was a thicket of greenbriers, wild plums and persimmons. It was a lush soil here at Three Forks.

Stephen Burke, when he built here, had cut as few trees as possible for his clearing, and set down among the trees, hit or miss, there was little order in the settlement that had grown up around the stockade. The trading post, with its weathered, un-mended fence, was a solid block to itself, nearest the river. About it, the cabins of the trappers and hunters were set wher-ever the whim had struck the men, some jammed next to the sagging fence, others straggling off into the woods. The rutted road made a street of sorts which was always alive with children, dogs, the Indian wives of the men, and those Indians off the prairie who had happened to wander in. There were usually a dozen hanging about the blacksmith shop, the trappers' cabins or the store.

Riding slowly toward the post, Johnny surveyed it dispassion-ately, seeing it after an absence of several weeks with a stranger's eyes. Every cabin had a small porch in front which was stacked with hides and bridles and saddles, traps and odds and ends spilling over onto the ground. Blankets and mats hung over porch railings with an occasional buffalo robe stretched in the sun to warm and become pliable. Dogs lay in the sunny dust and scratched at their fleas; chickens wandered about stiff-legged, thrusting their heads forward, pecking in the dust, scratching occasionally. Some wild turkeys which Adam's wife had tamed and two of Rebecca's white geese were among the chickens, superior to them, more majestic, strutting a little.

At the far end of the street a fire smoked and three Indians sat about it roasting some meat. Outside the blacksmith shop their mustangs were tied, switching their tails from time to time, tossing their heads when the flies, already in thick swarms, settled on them. Osage women came and went with their loads of wood, their kettles of river water, their haunches of venison given them by the visiting Indians. And down the whole length of the street small brown children tumbled, playing, falling down, picking themselves up without wailing, running after their mothers, falling over the dogs, sneaking hot bites of the roasting deer meat.

It was slovenly, Johnny thought, jinked and racky and shiftless. But it was lively and interesting and strangely homelike. The bright sunlight streamed down through the trees and slanted off the silvered walls and roofs of the houses, off the old dilapidated fence, like warm honey. The blanketed Indians, the dogs, the children, even the dust of the road, were part of his way of life, a deep, profound part which was comfortably satisfying to him. His weariness and the sodden weight of his depression lifted from him and he straightened his shoulders as if a physical load had been taken from his back. He ripped off his hat and whacked the mustang on the rump. "Come on, hoss," he yipped suddenly, "get your tail up! Let's let 'em know who's come home!"

Stung, the horse jumped, then bowed his back and sunfished. The implacable reins straightened him out and, catching the spirit of the thing then, he stretched his legs. Dogs, chickens, turkeys, geese and children scattered. There was a great flapping of wings, indignant cackling and gobbling, high-noted yelping, a great scuttling of legs and heels, a great flying of dust as the horse came in on the run, Johnny bent low over his neck adding to the tumult with the short, barking yips of the Osage victory cry. The dust billowed up in a thick cloud behind him, pluming over the cabins and the post like smoke, as the mustang pounded down the street.

The Osages about the fire got to their feet and stood watching the crazy entry. Johnny rode his horse around the group at a run, then slid him to a dust-smothered halt only a few yards from them, vaulted from the saddle and landed standing. Settling his hat loosely, he threw his head back and whooped a long and shrill war cry, then went into a toe-and-heel stomp around the fire. The Indians, nudging each other, sat down again, laughing silently at his antics. "Johnny Osage," one said to another, "has too much whisky, I think."

Johnny let out another war whoop and postured, clowning. "Yah-hoo!" he yelled, howling like a prairie wolf, beating his chest. "I am the great chief of Three Forks! I am the finest warrior of the prairies! I am part timber wolf and part mountain lion! I spit fire when I talk and I breathe smoke out my ears! I chew up Osages for breakfast and Pawnees for my supper! I comb my hair with prickly pears and shave with a shin-oak tree! I use thunderbolts for arrows and carry lightning in both my hands! I am half alligator and half panther and I can shoot fifty Indians with one shot! I am the great bucko of the west! I am — "

"You are crazy," Stephen Burke interrupted him, grinning.

Johnny flopped to the ground. "Just feeling good, Steve. Here, Rabbit-tail, give me a hunk of that meat. I am also hungry."

"When you get through feeding that ugly face of yours," Steve said, "we have some work to do."

There followed a week of intensive activity getting the keelboat loaded with cargo for its trip downstream to New Orleans. Stephen was going to take it down and Parley Wade had been sent to recruit hands for a crew. Johnny and Stephen labored over baling and listing the pelts. "As big a shipment as we've ever had," Stephen said with satisfaction when they had finished. "We've got thirty-eight thousand seven hundred and fifty pounds of furs and skins."

"How do they figure out?" Johnny asked.

"There's three hundred packs of female bearskins, one hundred and sixty bear cubs, three hundred and eighty-seven beavers, sixty-seven otters, seven hundred and twenty cats, ninety-five fox, and three hundred and sixty-four bales of deer hides. Seventy-two packs of those deerskins belong to Nathaniel, though."

Johnny flexed his stiff arm muscles. "Not bad, is it?"

"Not bad at all. You've kept 'em moving all season, Johnny." Stephen paused reflectively. "Johnny, having this keelboat opens up some more business. The settlements along the river will have cargo we can pick up — pecans and wild honey and bear oil and tallow. We ought to buy all that stuff we can and haul it down the river. And those lower settlements are growing pretty fast. Now that there's a newspaper at Arkansas Post they are getting civilized, and Little Rock is becoming a handsome little village. All this talk of moving the territorial capital there sounds as if business would be good. Why don't we double our usual order of goods and spread it out a little — get more stuff white people can use. Plows and tools, and some things the women need, like Queensware, domestics, a few fancies and such. I expect we could make a good profit. I have even thought," he rubbed his chin slowly, "we might open a general store there."

"Where?"

"Little Rock."

"Open one if you want," Johnny said shortly, "but don't count on me spending any time in it."

"Why?"

"I like it here."

"You like the Osages, you mean," Stephen said, laughing.

"It's all the same — Osages and the Verdigris and prairie. It's my country."

Stephen glanced at him. "You wouldn't have any objections if we tried it, though?"

"None. Long as you took the care of it. Might even be a good idea."

"We'll think about it then. If it doesn't work out we can still spread our trade out and haul cargo for the settlements."

"Reckon this trip will pay us back for buying the boat?"

"And some left over, I'd say."

Johnny chuckled. "Wasn't such a harebrained notion I had after all, was it?"

Stephen pulled at his chin. "Did I ever say it was?"

"No, but you looked almighty gloomy when it took the last of our hard money to buy it. Well, come on. Let's get this stuff on the boat."

The next morning, in a chill thin mist which rose slowly from the river, the boat warped out into the current of the Verdigris. The sun was not yet up and the mist and the sky were both smoke-colored, while the river was like the metal of a gunbarrel. Rebecca stood beside Johnny on the landing and watched.

As the boat swung around and was taken swiftly by the water, she lifted her hand. From the deck Stephen waved, then the mist shrouded the boat and it disappeared. Unseen, Parley, who was going along as far as the fort, was swearing loudly and heartily. Johnny grinned and glanced at his sister. He was surprised to see a shine of tears in her eyes. She was so little given to any show of emotion that it touched him. She was thirteen years older than he and had always had something of a maternal attitude toward him, as if he were, instead of a younger brother, an older son. She also had a serenity of bearing which was comfortably like that of their mother and which he realized now he took pretty much for granted. It was easy to forget she was also a wife and that Stephen was still her lover. Of course she would feel his going away. Awkwardly, Johnny moved over and touched her arm. Trying to comfort her, he said, "It won't be long before he'll be back, Becky. By the middle of July he'll be here. 'Twon't be more than three months."

Solid, frankly well-fleshed, she stood on the log wharf, clutching an old shawl, which she had thrown over her head against the mist, under her chin. It framed her dark-skinned face like a nun's cowl, leaving it cleanly severe and unsoftened by the little short curls which usually sprang loose on her forehead and about her ears. Beads of mist had gathered on the shawl. They looked like small seed pearls sewn along its edge. She looked out over the river, into the mist which had swallowed the boat, into which it had disappeared as if going down the maw of some giant fish. She made no attempt to hide the tears in her eyes. "Three months can be a terrible long time, Johnny."

Penitently, he said, "I know. I would have gone instead, but we thought it was such an uneasy time in the country . . ."

"Yes. You might be needed. And you're better at that kind of thing than Steve is. Besides, he wanted to go." She smiled at Johnny a little wanly. She pulled the shawl tighter, wiped at her eyes with the end of it and turned away. "Let's go back to the house, Johnny. It's raw out here. I'll be all right. I'll keep busy and the time will pass. It's just that I miss him so when he is gone. He is mostly around, you know."

Johnny followed her. "Tell you what we'll do," he said, then. "I have been gentling a pony for one of the teachers at the mission. We'll ride up there with it pretty soon. I've been promising to take you, and I will. And we'll stay the night and you can get acquainted with the womenfolks up there."

He caught up with her and peered at her face, which brightened perceptibly. "Will you, Johnny? I would like that. I would enjoy it. And I can talk to them about taking the boys into their school."

Rebecca had been complaining ever since the boys had got old enough to read that they needed a more proper schooling than they were getting. She had spoken several times since the missionaries came of sending them there when the school opened. Stephen was not enthusiastic about it. He thought he and Rebecca could give the boys what they needed, but he seemed never to have the time to get down to it regularly. Rebecca did not feel competent, without his help. She had continued to remind him and had finally talked him around to agreeing that for a year or two it might be a good idea to let the mission teachers have the boys in their care. "They're growing up as wild as Osages," she said, "and that is not what I want for them."

The path from the landing to the post wound through the trees, and was wet now from the mist. Fog swirled through the woods like ghostly smoke and vision was limited to the twenty feet just ahead. Walking cautiously, peering at the path, Rebecca said now, "What horse have you sold them, Johnny?"

Johnny hesitated, uncomfortably. "I've not exactly sold it. It's more of a loan, I guess."

Rebecca glanced at him slyly, not turning her head, only her eyes moving. She broke into a laugh at the look of discomfort on his face. "Is that why you have been making me ride that pony you bought off Mark Bean? So it's not a man you've promised that horse to, Johnny. You've been making me ride him so he would get used to skirts."

Johnny yanked his hat brim down and his face colored. "You think you're sharp, don't you?"

"I know I am, and I'll bet I'm right. Which one is it, Johnny?"

He stepped over the root of a big tree which humped up across the path. "Miss Lowell." He was caught and he might as well own up.

"Oh. The one that was nursing the sick man on the boat that time. I remember. You said she was a teacher."

"Yes." He felt a need to explain though he didn't know why. "She said she would like to learn to ride. I thought if she had a horse of her own it might make it easier for her. They've got a few head of stock up there but the men use them pretty hard and I doubt if she could ever get the use of a pony for herself."

"I think it's a lovely idea."

"I just hope she thinks it's a lovely idea," Johnny muttered.

"Why wouldn't she?"

He raised an eyebrow. "We don't get along too good sometimes. She's about as full of needles as a porcupine and I sometimes don't know when she's going to shoot."

"You been seeing her right often?"

"A time or two."

"But you like her," Rebecca insisted, "enough to gentle a horse for her."

"I've not thought whether I like her or not," Johnny said. "She said she wished she had a horse. She's a spirited girl and horses are common around here. I figured she ought to have one. That's all." There was a long pause, then he added thoughtfully, "You can't get to liking anybody so quick."

Rebecca was airy. "Oh, I don't know. Sometimes it takes only one time."

"I'm not even thinking about her. One time or three or a dozen times of seeing her."

"You've not got any notion in your head that she's too good for you, have you?"

"Oh, hell, Becky, I've got no notions at all. How did we get started on this thing? Just put it out of your mind or I won't even take you up there."

"Oh, yes, you will." Rebecca laughed. "Just remember, though, Johnny, Mama saw to it we were all raised up right."

"Mama," Johnny said, grinning, "might think I had strayed pretty far from my raising."

"Mama," Rebecca said, looking him over deliberately and fondly, "would be pretty proud of her youngest boy."

They had reached the decrepit stockade gate and Johnny stopped. "You go on. I'm going to get Adam and fix this gate right now. It's been hanging here lop-eared long enough."

"Well." She gave him a parting shot, however. "You're getting no younger, you know. And nice girls are as scarce as hen's teeth in this country."

Johnny picked up a pebble and shied it at her. "Hush, now."

He watched her walk away, the dark skirt gathered in folds

over her ample hips. It swung with her steps. Judith, he remembered, was as slim as a candle. And what did it matter, he
reminded himself.

The gate repaired he was still in a mending mood so he
worked the rest of the day on the fence, replacing rotted poles,
straightening the leaning ones, tidying up the entire stockade.
Hearing him whistling as he worked, Rebecca, in the house,
smiled and nodded. It would be nice, she thought wistfully, if
Johnny married one of those mission girls — someone from a
good family back home, with schooling and manners and a decent sense of propriety. It would settle him down some and it
would be company for her to have a good sister-in-law. Hopefully she swept and cleaned her house. He was too much on the
prairie and it troubled her.

Before they could go to the mission, however, Johnny said he
wanted to take Suard and one or two other hunters and go out
on the prairie to find buffalo. "I can't feed the whole village," he
said, "but I'd like to know the Wolf and his family don't go
hungry."

"Isn't he Suard's father-in-law?" Rebecca asked.

"Yes."

"Isn't it Suard's job to help feed them?"

"One man can't do it," he said shortly.

"How long will you be gone?"

"Not more than three weeks, I'd think."

Rebecca was washing the dishes after supper. Methodically,
her mouth set, she washed, rinsed, and set the thick crockery to
drain. "If the Pawnees," she reminded him grimly, "don't lift
your hair."

"We'll take care. I'll leave Adam and Parley in charge here."

Her careful restraint snapped. "With Stephen gone, Johnny,
I don't think you should go. It's taking too big a chance. It's
taking a chance, goodness knows, when the whole Osage village
goes, and three or four men alone will be asking for trouble, in
my opinion."

Johnny traced a circle on the tabletop with his finger. "Not necessarily. Not if you're careful."

Rebecca sniffed. "I never saw a man yet didn't think he knew how to be careful. They usually get killed just as easy as the next."

Johnny stood and raised his arms over his head, stretching lengthily and yawning. "I feel like I've got to do it, Becky."

Rebecca wrung out her dishcloth and spread it on two pegs to dry. She lifted the kettle of dishwater. With the kettle in her hands she stopped to eye him angrily. "You think more of that old Osage than you do your own folks, looks like."

Stubbornly Johnny set his mouth. "It is a poor thing if a man can't help his friends."

"Open the door for me, will you?" As she sidled through she looked up at him. "There is a time for helping friends and a time for using sense, the way I see it."

Johnny held the door. She emptied the water with a great slosh and wiped out the pan with a dry cloth. Hanging the kettle up she dried her hands and looked around. Johnny had swung a chair around and was sitting straddled of it, his chin resting gloomily on his hands. "Well, say something!"

"Nothing to say, is there?"

She put her hands on her hips. "Are you going?"

He laughed suddenly. "You look just like Mama standing there, trying to jaw me out of doing something."

"And having no more luck than she had, I'll wager." She switched her skirt tail into the next room. "You'll go, in spite of me."

He followed her slowly. "Yes." Serious, now, he added, "I don't know, Becky . . . it's a thing I have to do. I can't explain it."

Suddenly giving in, knowing he had to do what he must, she settled herself in her rocking chair and picked up the inevitable mending. "No, I guess you don't know, and can't explain. Things make sense to me when they're told plain, but a man has always got reasons that aren't plain to a woman and I guess you've got 'em. Go on, then." She looked across at him, her eyes glinting now, and teasing. "Man-Not-Afraid-of-Pawnees," she said laughing. "Be afraid of them enough to take no chances, Johnny."

"I won't."

It turned out that a larger party went on the hunt than Johnny had foreseen. Some of the young men of the village wanted to go and, since a few would not weaken the warrior strength of the village seriously, they were allowed to join Johnny and Suard. At the last moment two hunters from Nathaniel Pryor's post went along, so that finally the party rounded up sixteen men. They took a string of pack horses to bring back the meat and left in high spirits and with a vast clatter of hooves and much confusion one morning the second week in May.

Rebecca watched them as they prepared to ride away. The young Indians were painted and were magnificent in their finery. As young as they were most of them wore the eagle feathers in their braids. They milled their horses about nervously, sweeping the pack horses before them. Osages, Rebecca thought, were the finest horsemen in the world. They rode a horse as if he were an extension of themselves, their blankets spreading behind them in the wind, their smooth coppery chests bare to the sun, their eagle feathers spinning, their coin-profile faces illuminated with excitement. It simply was not true, she reflected, watching them, what people who had never been around Indians said of them — that they were stolid, unfeeling, impassive, unhumorous. They could be all those things, and sometimes, provokingly, were. But she had lived among them too long now not to know that they were so emotionally sensitive that any happening out of the ordinary sent them into high, wild waves of excitement; that unaffectionate as they seemed except with their children, they could grieve themselves to death over the loss of a wife or husband, father or mother; that their humor was always just one step behind their sense of tragedy and it was both lusty and earthy, though never hilarious.

Watching the elegantly ornamented young men she thought how greatly they loved pageantry and color, how they dressed for every occasion, adapted their conduct to it, how conscious they were of its importance. Watching the young men wheel into line, Johnny at the head of it, she saw their faces become suddenly serious and knew they were forcibly quelling their excitement, sobering their outward appearance to match the strength of their intention, and she laughed silently, knowing each young man carried an image of himself in his part to be played, saw himself in his own particular role. Vanity? Or pride? She did not know. It sufficed to make an Osage a very great hunter, and a very great warrior.

Beside the young Indians the white men looked sloppy and careless. They were drab in their old buckskins, dressed for the work of the hunt. She felt torn between anxiety for them and a tenderness of understanding. Men were somehow veined with a current of restlessness which could not be too long pent up. When the long dark winter was over, when the south wind blew limpid and soft from the prairie, and the trees greened out and the sun was warm, they must be away and gone . . . Stephen to New Orleans, Johnny to the buffalo feeding grounds. It was their business, they said, which took them away, but she knew it was also their pleasure and their compulsion. Stephen restored something worn thin in himself by this isolated life when he returned to the city each year. And Johnny, for whatever reason he conjured up to himself, had an equal need to feed some lack in him which only the prairie and the Indians could feed.

She waved one last time and turned back. It was just as well, she thought with good humor, that she was a homebody, like her mother, content with four walls. She laughed to think how unsettling it would be if she had the same itching streak of adventure the men had. But her sense of adventure, small to begin with, had been amply satisfied too often in her life. She craved nothing more, now, than to live peaceably at home with her family around her.

Chapter 12

They were gone less than the three weeks Johnny had expected.

He rode in late one afternoon, blackly sunburned, his eyes red-rimmed from the wind and his lips tender from sun blisters. He was slack with weariness but the hard fever of the hunt was still on him. His eyes were bright with it and his face still compressed with it. He was caked with old dirt and sweat and so stinking that Rebecca made him strip and bathe before she would allow him in the house. "Why do you get so filthy?" she fumed at him, handing him clean clothing to take to the river with him.

He took the clothing and the crock of soft soap she gave him and looked down at the crusted, stained front of his buckskins. "Kind of gamy, isn't it?" He looked up at her and grinned crookedly. "You can't dress out meat without getting it all over you. Had to do it ourselves because we didn't take any women with us. And it dries and in time it stinks."

"Had good luck, did you?" she asked, standing in the door.

"Good luck." He propped a foot up on the step and hung the clean clothing over his leg. "And not too far away. That was the best of it. That's what made us get home sooner than I'd thought. Didn't have to go any farther than the Salt Fork before we come on a big herd. I brought along some hump meat and ribs for you." He was still so full of the hunt and so wound up that he talked more rapidly than usual for him, and at greater length. "Sent a dozen ponies loaded heavy to the Wolf. His women will have it jerked by this time tomorrow." He took off his hat and threw it in a corner of the porch, scoured his head with both hands. "God, it was fine, Becky. We come up on 'em about midday, I'd say. We'd been riding along not thinking about finding 'em so quick, and Walking Bear and Cut Leg was riding scout, when Suard suddenly held up his hand. They were signaling. So we crept up to a knoll, kind of, and kept downwind of 'em, and there they were — not as big a herd as I've seen on the Cimarron, or even on the North Fork, but big enough. Moving along slow, grazing, not even guessing we were anywhere about. And already fat on grass. It was . . ." He shook his head, unable to say how it had been, unable to put into words what it was like to come up on a fine herd of buffalo and suddenly go charging in among them, your horse running swiftly, needing no guidance, his feet pounding, crowding, parting the herd, taking you right into the middle, you yourself finding your fat cow, taking a rough aim, shooting, reloading, shooting again, reloading, until the air was thick with smoke and the gunbarrel was hot and the herd now scared and running, stampeded, off across the flat prairie and the dropped bulls and cows lying in dark spotted humps where they had fallen, the ground wet from their blood. A woman wouldn't know even if you could put it into words, he thought. If Steve was here, now, to tell it to. Or if he could have gone on to the village and told it to the Wolf. You needed a man to tell a hunt to. He gave it up, threw his hands out helplessly and strode off to the river.

When he sat down to the supper table later Rebecca looked at him approvingly. His thick straw-colored hair was still wet. It was combed and, for the time at least, lay smooth to his head. His grubby beard was gone and his face was scrubbed to a clean glaze. There was a line on his forehead where the brown of sunburn ended and the white skin, protected by his hat, began. His clean linen shirt was smooth and soft and he had put on dark trousers. "Now," she told him, "you look like a human being."

"Feel like one, too," he agreed good-humoredly. He piled his plate with food. "What's the news?"

"Not much." She sat down opposite him, brushing away crumb and leaning her arms on the table.

"Aren't you going to eat?"

"I ate with the boys, earlier. We weren't looking for you hom

He nodded. Rebecca was a good cook and he was suddenl ravenous. As she talked, he listened and shoveled the food in.

"I got my garden planted," she told him and, at length, in the way he had heard his mother talk of her own garden, she told what she had planted, row by row. "Now if it will only rain this spring."

She continued with the small news of the settlement. "Young Steve had a chill two days running, but I dosed him with Peruvian bark and it broke up the fever."

"Other boys well?"

"Yes. Adam's wife had her baby. A boy this time."

Johnny broke off a piece of bread from the fat, brown loaf at his elbow. He grinned. "That will please Adam, after . . . how many girls?"

"Four. It did. He got crazy drunk and shot all the windows out and then went down to the shop at four o'clock in the morning and made a set of horseshoes for the boy's first horse."

Johnny held his cup for more coffee and drank it down, black and scalding. He chuckled. "I'm glad he's got his boy." Finished eating, he got his pipe and filled it, tamped down the tobacco and lit it. He shoved his chair back against the wall and tilted it. "Adam don't go on a spree very often. Reckon he felt it was time."

Rebecca smiled. "It's a fine boy. I'd guess he weighed ten pounds." She leaned back in her chair and folded her hands on the edge of the table. "The missionaries' boat has come," she went on. "Some of them came down and met it here at the Forks."

"Here?"

"No. The point. Parley went over and talked to them. He said the boat was loaded with stores, food and clothing mostly, but there were some millstones they had been wanting. Their millwright was with them and he told Parley they couldn't find a good place for a water mill so they were going to make do with a treadmill worked by oxen."

Johnny sucked on his pipe. He tried to recall the streams that fed the Neosho near the mission station. "No," he said, talking around his pipestem, "I don't guess there is a fall of water close to them. A treadmill will be slower, but it will work."

"That's what they said. Captain Douglas called before they started up the Neosho and said he had met Stephen at Arkansas Post and he was well and everything in order. He brought me a letter from him."

"Well, now, that's fine."

Rebecca nodded. "Stephen said he had picked up a considerable cargo and got it pretty cheap. He said the Cherokees were still talking war and he sent word to you that he got past the Dardanelle all right. I don't know what he meant by that."

Johnny took the pipe out of his mouth and grinned. "Lot of gambling goes on there. There's a saying on the river that if you can get a dollar past the Dardanelle you'll make out all right. It's just a joke."

"Oh." She got up and began clearing away the food. She stopped, however, resting a hand on the table. "I knew there was one other thing. He said he saw Nathaniel Pryor."

Johnny looked up. "He did?"

She nodded. "Nathaniel told him the Blade wasn't talking very favorable."

"About what I expected," he said noncommittally. "Nathaniel come home yet?"

Rebecca took his plate from the table and scraped it clean before sliding it into the kettle of dishwater. "No. He's still gone."

"Did Stephen talk to Will Bradford, did he say?"

"He didn't say. I don't guess he did or he would have."

"Yes." His pipe had gone out. He lit it again, puffing slowly. "Well. Nothing to do but wait, I reckon. I look for them to talk most of the summer."

"You don't look for anything to come of it, do you?"

"No. They're trying to starve the Osages out. If they can drag out the talks and keep threatening, the Osages won't go on their hunt. Afraid to. It won't suit the Blade to make this armistice, I'm afraid." He rose abruptly. "Believe I'll go talk to Parley a while."

"Go ahead. If you see the boys tell them to come in. They've got to read their lessons to me yet."

At the door Johnny paused. "When would it suit you to ride up to the mission? We can go any time now."

Rebecca held the dishcloth suspended, thinking. "I ought to do a washing first, so as to leave the boys clean clothes . . . and see if Parley's woman will look after them while we're gone. What is today, Johnny?"

"Haven't got the least idea."

"Wednesday, I think. Well, say Saturday?"

Behind her back Johnny grinned. She was maneuvering so as to be there over Sunday. He guessed she meant to go to church. A woman, it occurred to him, was called on to do without many things in this frontier country, not the least of which was the homely habit of going to church. "Fine," he said heartily, "you can count on it."

Chapter 13

SATURDAY WAS HOT.

Johnny Fowler and his sister rode slowly up the neck of land which was made by the two rivers converging on the Arkansas. At its narrow, fingertip point it was not more than three miles wide. Ten miles upstream it had broadened to fifteen miles, and at the site of the Union Mission it had become a plain, some thirty miles in width. The heavy-leafed trees shut out the prairie wind and the heat beneath them was intense, a thing of weight and blanketing oppression. Rebecca led the way, her horse following the trail without help from her. Johnny rode behind, leading the pony he was taking to Judith Lowell. Rebecca mopped the sweat off her face with a white linen square. "You'd think," she said, "it was July instead of May."

"You always forget," Johnny said, "how early the heat comes on here."

"Yes. I do forget. Each year I forget and I expect it to be the way it is back home." She paused and then went on. "Johnny, do you remember how it is back home in May? Do you remember how the hill goes up so steeply back of the house and how it's covered over with sarvis berries and wild plums in May? And how the locust trees are in bloom and the bees swarm around them? Remember how green the valley is in May? And how it looks like plush — soft, soft — and how, when the wind blows through it and the sun shines on it the little seed flowers look blue. Remember how white the birch trees down by the creek are until the leaves are out? And how clear the water is in the Hanging Fork? Remember, Johnny?"

The pony he was leading hung back to nip at a sassafras shrub and Johnny jerked on the lead rein. "Yes, I remember."

"May. May in Kentucky. Johnny, everybody in the world ought to be in Kentucky in May. It's such a heavenly time!"

Troubled by the passion in her voice, by its quivering hint of tears, Johnny rode up alongside. "You should, at least," he said, looking at her. "I think you're homesick, Becky."

Her dark eyes fixed on his face, but she shook her head. "No. I don't think so. I don't really think so, Johnny. No more than . . . well, I expect everyone is always homesick for the past, and the past places. It wasn't really as good as I remember it, I know. And I know I have the best right here and right now. But one must always have a place in the heart to go back to, Johnny, and my place is Kentucky. It is my small heaven which stays forever the same to me. You know that little book Stephen has by that Frenchman — Voltaire? Somewhere in that book he says, 'the place where all is well, for there absolutely must be one such place.' The only place where all is well, Johnny, is in the past. For it's over with and can never be touched again. If I went back home it wouldn't be the same. But when I remember it, it is unchanging, a blue and green and shining place of tall trees and clear water and lovely hills — the place where all is well. The hills . . . Johnny, don't you ever get tired of this flatness and sameness? Don't you ever want to see a knob again?"

"There are hills here," Johnny said slowly, "and up near the Missouri line there are mountains."

"Not mountains. And not these small, separated mounds. But hills, Johnny, like the ones at home, folded and tumbled and close together. Friendly. And the little knobs sticking up like bones here and there. Sometimes I close my eyes and think ver hard about them and pretend if I open my eyes quickly and sud denly I can look out the door and see the hill back of Mama's, with the path going up to the meadow on top. But it doesn't really work. All I can ever see is the river and beyond it the prairie, and the little stunted trees on the prairie."

"The woods all around the post is as pretty a growth of trees as any back home," Johnny insisted.

"Cottonwoods," she said, "and hickories and walnuts and pecans. I want," her head went back and she looked up through the trees at the blue patches of sky, "I want great, tall copper beeches, and chestnuts, and the little clump of birches down by the Hanging Fork."

Slowly Johnny gathered in his thoughts, ordered them so that he might speak carefully. "Each place has its own kind of goodness, I expect, Becky. Kentucky has one kind. We grew up with it. Here, there is a different kind. The trees are smaller, maybe, and maybe, farther out on the prairie, they are stunted. But they are very tough trees. They are the kind that will stand strong winds and violent storms, and they don't take much water and they get along with hard rations and grow tough and rugged. I like them. They are like these little mustangs, shaggy and awkward looking, but as strong as iron.

"And the bluegrass back home is pretty, nothing prettier in the world, but there never was a better grass for grazing than this short grass that grows on the prairie, Becky. Ride out in April, not May, and see how it is all one great carpet of little flowers, and it is not stopped a mile away by a line of hills. It goes on and on and on as far as you can see. It's wide and it's open and you are either pretty big when you ride out across it, or pretty small. I have been both."

Rebecca nodded and they rode on silently for a while. Then she said, speculatively, "Do you think Mama ever got homesick for the mountains in the border country? Do you think she had to get used to Kentucky?"

"No," Johnny said. "Mama is not a looking-back sort of person. But I have heard her tell that *her* mother never got over missing the sea."

"It's best to be like Mama. I expect I am missing Stephen," she said simply.

"I expect you are."

By the time they stopped to eat, the trees were thinning out and there were short stretches of open space where the sun beat down intensely. The sky was metallic and clouds were forming and shadows raced swiftly across the glazed, yellow openings. "Do you think it's going to storm, Johnny?" Rebecca asked, looking at the clouds. She gathered up the bread and meat and packed it away.

"Scared?" Johnny said. He was saddling the horses again.

"No. I'm never frightened of storms. But I've got on my best dress and I don't want it to get wet."

Johnny led her horse up and lifted her on. "Not soon, I'd say. Maybe tonight. I think your dress is safe."

She straightened her skirt and settled her knee over the horn of the sidesaddle more comfortably. "How much farther is it?"

"We're more than halfway." He put his toe in the stirrup and swung himself up.

"We've been poking along pretty slow."

"Too hot to hurry the horses."

They rode on at the same slow, easy pace. Johnny felt sleepy with the heat. Only the occasional tug of the horse he was leading kept him from nodding in the saddle. He thought Rebecca must be dozing for she rode along silently, her body drooped a little, heavy in the shoulders, thick in the waist. His eyes feeling sandy with heat and sleepiness, Johnny studied her back. She was wearing a black dress, with a high collar and long sleeves, unrelieved by any touch of color. He wondered why so plain a dress could be called her best dress. It was some kind of silk, he knew, though he could not recall the name of the material, and so heavy that the skirt could stand alone. But black made Rebecca look sallow. He liked her best in one of her bright calicoes. She would have been horrified, he supposed, if he had suggested she wear one. And he supposed also that the women of the mission would be impressed by this dark silk dress. Women's styles were a thing he could not pretend to understand. He was himself more uncomfortable than he liked. The long wool pants and the heavy wool coat were scratchy and hot, but he knew Rebecca wanted him to wear them. He sighed and straightened his shoulders. It was no small sacrifice he had made to his sister's pride.

When they came to the low hill back of the mission station they stopped and Rebecca dampened the linen square with the lukewarm water carried in a skin bottle at her saddle horn. She wiped off her face, brushed her dress, set her bonnet on more firmly, and rode into the mission with her back erect and her head held high.

Johnny watched the women of the mission greet her kindly and welcome her courteously. She had brought them butter and eggs, of which they had none yet, and a dozen loaves of her good bread. She had also brought them six hens and some cured bacon. She had brought so much, in fact, that Johnny had complained she was making a pack horse of the pony he was loaning Judith Lowell. Unloading the gifts, Johnny listened to the women's cries of delight. "Butter!" they said. "And eggs!"

Mrs. Chapman, who was young and pretty and soft looking, said quietly, "We have some cows but only one is giving milk. This spring, however . . ."

Mrs. Vaill was fondling the eggs. "How we have missed them!"

Rebecca untied her bonnet strings. "I thought the children would like them. My boys can eat half a dozen each for breakfast."

With a quick glance at the other women Mrs. Vaill said, "Oh, they must go in the Family storehouse. We share everything alike here."

Rebecca's hands paused. Swiftly she was carried back to the time when she had been a member of the Shaker community. Everything was owned by the community. No one had any personal rights to even an article of clothing, or a bit of garden truck, or an egg, for instance. How she had longed for just one thing of her own, just one thing, a needle, a book, that did not belong to the community. Firmly she said, "Not the eggs. I brought them to the children. Growing children need them." She laughed, to remove the sting from her words. "Everything else into the storehouse if you like. But the eggs are my gift to the children."

Mrs. Vaill darted another glance at the women. "Brother Chapman will say," she said softly.

Johnny led the horses off and the women carried Rebecca into the house, a chattering ring surrounding her. He took note that Judith Lowell was not among them.

Feeling at loose ends and ill at ease in his unaccustomed best clothes, Johnny allowed himself to be guided around the station by Mr. Chapman. He spent some time looking at the finger-high corn in the new field. He inspected the treadmill. He cast an appraising eye on the foundations of another new building. He looked at the new boat landing on the river and at the pirogue the men were hewing out. He went with the missionary to look at the stock, the dozen or so cows and the small string of horses. "Three cows will freshen the latter part of the month," Mr. Chapman said.

They passed then up the easy slope of the knoll, to the left of the dwellings, where they came to a large enclosed plot. "This is the garden," the missionary said. "We have planted potatoes and beans here, and some other seeds which the women were pleased to bring with them. This will add to our store of food next winter." He explained that they wished to become self-supporting as soon as possible. "The Board," he said, "have not been mean with us, but we must be stingy with ourselves so as not to be a burden to them."

Johnny propped his boot on the middle rail of the fence and plucked a twig of sassafras. He peeled the aromatic shrub and stuck it between his teeth. He listened quietly as Epaphras Chapman told about the plans for further clearing and plowing and cultivating. The missionary's eyes were lit with a fever of concern and he fixed Johnny with an intense, concentrated blue stare. Above his beard the man's face was peeling from an old sunburn and it was scaly and patched with scars. His high forehead domed shinily above the deep-socketed eyes and he talked jerk-

ily, with emphasis, in a painfully rasping voice. On and on he
talked, in a spate of words that seemed to have no ending.
Johnny chewed on the sassafras twig.

At length the missionary threw his arms wide, as if overborne
by his own eloquence, as if overwhelmed suddenly by the distances about him and the weight of the burdens he carried.
"There is so much to be done," he cried, "and we are distraught
by so many problems. We are held back by these constant ill-
nesses, by the failure of the hands we have hired to arrive, by our
plows breaking, by lack of a proper mill, by our lack of an interpreter, by our own lack of knowledge of the Osage language. We
are thwarted on all sides and tried desperately by the hand of the
Lord. If we were a fainthearted people, sir, we should be dis-
mally discouraged. But we bow to the will of the Lord." His
own head sank, bowing, as he said, more softly, "We adore and
we do not murmur."

Johnny felt a queasy twist of discomfort. Such talk, such pious
and easy use of the name of the Lord always embarrassed him.
He didn't think he was a very religious man, but he didn't think
he was wholly irreligious either. It was something a man worked
out for himself and then kept to himself. If you did the best you
could, by your friends and neighbors and the rest of humanity,
he thought the Lord might consider you did the best you could
for Him, too. But what was the use forever talking about it? It
was too easy to lay everything at the Lord's door, the blame as
well as the virtue. No use bringing the Lord into most of it, the
way he saw it. Any man went a long way toward making his own
cares and burdens. Do the best you can. It looked to Johnny as
if the Lord had so much on His hands with the rest of the world
to see after he would be mighty thankful for a few that didn't
bother Him with prayers and cries for help. And it occurred
to him, too, that Mr. Chapman did a considerable amount of
murmuring, in spite of his denial. Aloud, however, he only said,
"It takes time, sir."

"Yes . . . time." The man seemed actually anguished. "But
time is wasting! Time is fleeting! Here are these children of God,

lost in the blackest night of the soul, waiting to be redeemed! And we are caught up in the puny problems of plows breaking, of stock straying, of cutting and sawing lumber! I cannot tell you, Mr. Fowler," he cried, a bony hand waving toward the distant prairie, "I can find no words with which to tell you how eagerly I look forward to the day when I can preach my first sermon to those poor, benighted heathen on the prairie there. When I have command of the language and can speak to them from my heart, it will be a glorious day. It will be a day which I am confident God will bless with the fullness of gratitude." He threw his head back, closed his eyes, and Johnny was appalled to see tears trickling from under the tightly clenched lids. "How long, O Lord," the man intoned, "how long must this Thy servant wait!"

God! The man should have been on the stage! Johnny spat out the twig and hitched his trousers up. "Well, sir, you are doing the best that can be done. Looks to me that way."

The missionary opened his eyes and blinked them, as if recalled from some far distance. "Yes, yes," he muttered. "We console ourselves. We are doing all in our power at present."

It seemed to Johnny they had made remarkable progress. He did not know what Epaphras Chapman expected of these men and women, but considering their number and their inexperience, the high percentage of sick, they had almost worked a miracle in his opinion. Since February they had built three houses; they had cleared, fenced, plowed and planted forty acres of corn; they had cut and rafted downriver one hundred and forty pine logs; they had begun a treadmill. They had a blacksmith shop in operation, and they had another permanent building under construction. It was true these things contributed nothing to the saving of souls, but they were necessary and first things had to come first. Johnny felt an ungrudging admiration for their stubborn persistence. Groan and flounder under their loads as they did, it looked to him as if their heartwood was sound. "Even the Lord," he murmured, "took seven days to make the world, Reverend."

"Six," Mr. Chapman corrected him. "He rested on the seventh. Oh, dear me!" He clapped a hand to his brow. "Tomorrow is the Sabbath. It is my turn to preach. I should be . . ." He looked at Johnny, distracted.

"Don't let me keep you, sir," Johnny said. "Go on about your affairs. I will visit around a little."

"I do not like to be unmannerly . . ." His mind had already moved on. His eyes were vague, his voice trailed off. He bent his steps to the cluster of houses.

Johnny watched him go, a tall, thin, black-clad figure, a little shambling in gait, stiff-legged as if his knees had trouble bending. It might be, he thought, that it took the singleness of purpose Epaphras Chapman had to lead a group of people into a new and untried world, but he doubted if he would be an easy man to serve, or an easy man to live with. He demanded so much of himself that inevitably he would demand as much of others, and not every man was as equipped as the reverend to fix his heart and his soul on one lofty, undeviating goal. The voice of God, speaking so authoritatively through one man, he felt, must be pretty terrible as a daily utterance.

He swung lazily about and leaned against the fence rail. Johnny Fowler had a reservoir of patience that was bottomless when he sat for hours and listened to a council of Indians. It was bottomless when he rode for days across the prairie tracking game. It was bottomless when he engaged in any of the duties or pleasures of his many-sided life. But it had a very shallow bottom when he found himself with nothing to do, as now, nothing to occupy either his hands or his mind, his time pointless except for standing about sticky and hot in his unnatural clothing. Idly he picked at the bark of the fence rail and chunked pieces of it at the weeds already sprouting in the trim rows of beans. Beans! He hoped Rebecca would appreciate this sacrifice of his time!

Then he laughed at himself. He was no better than Becky's youngest boy, finding someone to take the blame for his own foolishness. Rebecca had been simply a good excuse for coming to the mission himself to see Judith Lowell again. It was true he had promised to bring her, and it was true she was lonely for Stephen, but she had been lonely for Stephen before when he had gone away and in his absorption in his own affairs he had left it to her to handle as best she could. His concern for her now was not wholly unselfish and he had better not fool himself that it was. He had looked, he knew, for Judith Lowell all afternoon, kept an eye out for her as he went around the clearing with the reverend. She had pulled him here to this place, like a lodestone, or the polar star. He felt a fool admitting it, but he had better look at it straight. He chunked an especially big slab of bark at the weeds, then dusted off his hands. He would get his horse and ride out on the prairie a way. That would ease his restlessness.

He met her on the way to the pasture and he saw her before she saw him. She was walking along the path, a woven basket slung from one arm, her head bent as if she were thinking. Her dress was crimson today, a little shorter than she usually wore, and faded, as if it had been washed many times. The sleeves were rolled back from her wrists and the skirt was gathered in wide pleats about her slim waist. It swayed a little as she walked.

He went to meet her slowly. Whatever was occupying her mind was absorbing, for she did not hear him or look up until they were separated by only a few yards. He was afraid she would be startled, so he cleared his throat noisily. Her head went up and her eyes flashed open widely. "Why, Mr. Fowler."

"I was afraid I would scare you." The crimson dress made her eyes look lighter than he remembered them. They were brandy-colored today. He saw them move over his figure, taking in his black coat and trousers, and he flushed darkly. "I have brought my sister to visit the mission," he explained, hoping it *was* an explanation.

She took a step forward. "Then I must hurry and welcome her."

"She has been welcomed," Johnny said, barring the path.

"Mrs. Vaill and Mrs. Chapman have her in charge. I have been looking for you," he said then, simply.

Her eyes were steady on him. "Have you?"

His coat felt too tight and his muscles felt strained and bound inside the shoulders. He twitched them impatiently. "Yes." He blurted out the rest. "I have brought you a horse to ride." Hurrying on before she could protest, he said, "We have several extra horses at the post — don't use them all. This one my sister has ridden considerably. He's a good horse . . ." He felt himself stumbling but caught up his nerve and went on, "I'm sorry I can't make you an outright gift of him, but he is just a loan I'm afraid." He dropped his eyes. "For the summer, maybe. I might need him next fall."

Her laugh rang out and looking up he saw that she had set the basket on the ground. It was full of wild greens, dark and damp with the water she had sprinkled over them against the wilting heat. With a gesture she abandoned them. "Wild greens we have every day. A horse is very special. May I see him now? Where is he, Mr. Fowler?"

Johnny blew out a gusty breath in relief. He laughed shakily and swung into step beside her. "In the pasture. Lordy, I thought you might take the top of my head off."

She slanted a look at him. "Am I such an ogre then?"

"You made a right smart to-do about the moccasins."

"The *horse*," she reminded him, "is a loan." But she lifted her skirt a little and stuck out a foot. "And I do thank you for the moccasins. I wear them constantly."

He felt a sudden stricture in his throat and could not reply for a moment. Then all he found to say was "I'm glad."

"Where have you been *this* time?" she asked, swinging along beside him, he shortening his steps to accommodate her, her skirt brushing against his leg because the path was so narrow. "You're very brown. You must have been on the prairie."

He knew he should have fallen a little behind and given her the whole path but he was too conscious of her nearness and not willing to forfeit the brush of her skirt, or the swing of her

body toward him when she leaned under a hanging limb. He told
her he had been on the prairie and told her a little about the hunt.
She listened, her head bent a little, her eyes going from his
face to the path, then back to his face again, alive with interest.
"You love it, don't you?" she said, when he had finished.

"Yes."

He held back a branch and she stooped under it. He saw the
springy little curls on the back of her neck — drake tails his
mother used to call them — and the white line where the skin
had been protected by something, a collar, a bonnet, and looked
so tender and young. He felt an unexpected weakness in his
knees.

"I think I would love it too. Now that I have a horse perhaps — "

Johnny took her arm abruptly. "You must not ride out on the
prairie alone, Miss Lowell. Promise me, or I cannot leave the
horse for you."

"Why? Why must I not?" She looked up at him. Seeing him
very serious, her face sobered. "Is it dangerous?"

"For a woman alone, yes. It could be very dangerous. There
are young men among the Osages that sometimes . . . they
would not know you, and in a certain mood . . . besides," he
finished lamely, "the season for snakes is beginning. The prairie
is infested with rattlesnakes."

"Snakes!" She shuddered and began to walk on.

Following, he continued, "And the prairie is wide and almost
trackless. Few people can find their way on it. There are so few
landmarks once you are out of sight of the timber. I have known
hunters to get lost and perish on it. The Indians have a way of
saying that no white man can go a straight mile on it."

She looked back over her shoulder. "Can you?"

He laughed. "I am half Indian."

"Are you? Really?"

"No. But I have lived with them for a good many years."

"Well, I won't ride on it alone, Johnny. Snakes petrify me and
I have no wish to get lost and perish, either."

It was the first time she had called him Johnny. If it had slipped out, he thought, it meant she had thought about him enough that the name came naturally to her. If it was intentional . . . a gush of feeling rose in his chest . . . it meant, surely it meant, she liked him pretty well. She had been so careful to be formal. He was grateful she was not in a prickly mood today.

In the edge of the timber a small pasture had been enclosed for penning the mission stock at night. Johnny had put his horses there. They came out into the clearing and stood by the fence, Judith leaning her arms on the top rail, her chin resting on them. The sun, low in the west, red and bulging, lit up the dark clouds banked above it, its bright light reflecting on them and making them look purple and dense. Automatically Johnny assessed them and decided the rain was a few hours away yet.

"Which one is mine?" Judith asked.

Johnny pointed. "The one with the white stockings."

"Does he have a name?"

"Well, the man — " he shifted quickly — "*we* call him Socks."

She hitched herself up on the rail to see better and, giving her a boost, Johnny swung himself up to sit on the top rail. "He's a beautiful horse," she said, studying him admiringly, like a child.

"He's a mustang," Johnny said. "Rough-coated, a little rough to ride, not much change of gait, but he's tough. The only horseflesh most of us have out here."

"How do you catch them, Johnny?"

"Well, the Indians use a forked stick with a noose on the end of it, but I use a rope."

Braced with her hands spread on the fence railing, Judith swung her legs slowly, not taking her eyes off the horse. "Do you know, all my life I have wanted a horse."

"Have you? Well, at least you've got the use of one now. Would you like to try him out?"

"Could I?" Then her face fell. "But I have no saddle."

"Yes, you have. I thought of that." He swung himself down and went to the corner where he had piled the saddles under a tree. He whistled and the horses looked up, angled their ears, whiffled in answer and came toward him. From the corner of his eye he saw that Judith was getting down from the fence. "Stay where you are," he told her sharply. "Wait until he's saddled."

He saddled his own horse first and ground-tied him with the reins. Then he threw a sidesaddle on the white-stockinged horse. He slapped the rump of Rebecca's horse. "Not this time, Fanny. Go on and crop grass."

He led the two saddled ponies over to the fence, hung their reins through his elbow and helped Judith down. She looked curiously at the saddle with its queer bent horn for her knee and glanced down at her skirt. "How do I get on him?" she asked, helplessly.

"This way." Johnny encircled her waist with his hands, lifted, and sat her on the horse. "Crook your knee around the horn. That will balance you. That's what Becky says, anyhow. I don't know why women can't ride the sensible way . . ."

Judith arranged her skirt and Johnny handed her the reins. "Keep them tight. Don't let them hang loose on his neck. We'll just walk him around the pasture a little. Are you scared?"

Her face had gone a little white. She nodded. "He seems very tall and I'm a long way from the ground."

"Not really. There's nothing to be frightened of. Becky has ridden him every day for a month. He is used to women's skirts by now."

He turned to get on his own horse. Behind him he heard the mustang snort, then he heard a startled gasp, and as quickly as he swung around the mustang had taken off across the pasture, swinging his head wildly, snorting and blowing, sunfishing and curvetting. "Sonofabitch!" Johnny swore. He plunged toward the horse, saw it was useless, and yelled at the girl. "Grab the reins! Get hold of the reins! Pull his head up!"

But of course she could not hear him. He ran back to his own horse and leaped into the saddle, kicked his bootheels into the animal's flanks. Judith's horse had quit bucking and was

straightening out, pounding hard across the pasture. Johnny
could see her hair streaming behind her and her skirt blowing
crazily in the wind. She rode so loosely and her seat was so in-
secure that Johnny groaned.

The horse was headed for the fence on the other side of the
pasture. Johnny bent over his mustang's neck and beat his flank
with his hat, kept kicking his heels in. But Mark Bean's mustang
was pretty fast. He saw the animal gather himself for the leap
over the fence, and then there was the flash of his heels, the arch
of his body, and Judith was flung backward, then forward, like
a limp sack of meal. When the horse hit the ground on the far
side of the fence she went flying off over his head. "God,"
Johnny moaned, "her neck will be broken."

His horse vaulted the fence and Johnny pulled him up. He
was off at the same instant and running to the limp body that
lay in the piled leaves blown against the fence. It looked as
boneless and soft as a pile of crimson rags, huddled, spread
against the brown leaves.

Johnny flung himself down beside her and lifted her head, his
heart racing in his chest. He had one wild, desperate thought.
If he had killed her, he would shoot the mustang and then shoot
himself. "Judith," he begged, struggling with the wide skirt
which had been flung up, trying to pillow her head on his shoulder, "Judith."

Her face was dirty and there was one long grazed place with
leaf mold grimed into it and little separate drops of blood bead-
ing it, but there seemed to be no other cuts and bruises. Her
head, however, was dreadfully limp against him. Panicky with
fear he braced it against his chest and ran his hand down her
thigh and leg, not knowing exactly what he sought, a leg off, a
hip unjointed. She seemed all in one piece but there was no telling how many bones were broken. He squared himself around
and let her head down in the crook of his arm. She was very
pale. He smoothed her hair back from the wide brow and
picked leaves and twigs out of it. Suddenly he saw the bluish
vein of her temple beating. He put a finger against it and felt

the steady pulse. He took a deep breath. She was not killed, then. He watched the pulse a moment, smoothed the vein with his finger, then he laid his face against hers and rocked her a little, to and fro, in his arms.

He could not have said how long it was before she stirred — one minute, five, or ten. But then she lifted her arm, let it fall limply, and after another few seconds opened her eyes. At her first movement, Johnny raised his head and watched her face. When her eyes opened, he smiled at her. When she smiled back at him, he had a hysterical impulse to shout or whoop or burst into song, to do some outlandish thing in his relief. He choked. "You're all right," he assured her, shakily. Then, thinking she might be confused, he added, "The horse threw you."

She nodded and lay still a moment longer, staring at him, then she lifted her head from the crook of his arm and looked around at the horse now grazing peacefully nearby. "Just a little walk around the pasture," she murmured, wrinkling her nose at Johnny. He grinned fatuously. She dropped her head back against his arm and then as if realizing where she was, in what position she was being held, she struggled to sit up.

"Hadn't you better lie still a little longer?" Johnny asked anxiously.

"No." She shook her head. He helped her and kept his arm protectively about her waist. "I must look a sight." She picked at the leaves and twigs on her skirt, left off to reach up and pat her hair. Her hand touched her face and she winced.

"You skinned your face," Johnny told her. "It needs washing."

Her fingers probed the grazed place. "I don't doubt it does."

"I meant the skinned place needs cleaning," Johnny stammered.

She got to her feet and took a few steps, flexing her arms and knees. "Everything seems to work. I think I was just stunned." She eyed the pile of leaves. "I expect I have them to thank for coming to no more harm."

Johnny picked up his hat. "Yes. They broke your fall." His knees felt weak and quivery now that it was all over.

Speculatively she looked at the mustang. "If I were a man," she said, "there are some words I would like to address to that animal. There seem to be only a few choice things to say at a moment like this. Unfortunately a lady's vocabulary is not allowed to include them. What did I do wrong, Johnny?"

"I expect you forgot to keep the reins tight."

"Keep them tight! I never had a chance to keep them anything! That animal jerked them out of my hands the minute your back was turned and I never had hold of a rein from then on!"

Johnny kept his face straight. "Yes. Well, he took advantage of having his head."

"He will never do it again." She squared her shoulders back. "Bring him around, Johnny."

Johnny looked at her sharply. "No," he said, "I am not going to risk having you — "

"I am going to ride that horse, Johnny. He is going to learn who is the boss." Her voice was determined.

Johnny hesitated. She was spunky all right, but having succeeded once, the mustang might try the same thing again. Probably would. Johnny had been through too bad a time to repeat it. "Judith . . ." he said. His lips felt dry. He licked his tongue over them and cursed his inarticulateness. "I will lead him for you," he finished tamely.

"No. I am going to ride him."

She was right to insist on riding the horse now, if she ever meant to ride, but he was so scared for her he did not know whether he could muster the strength to set her up in the saddle. Reluctantly he brought the mustang around. "You'll keep the reins tight?"

She set her mouth sternly. "I'll keep them tight."

He looked at her, little and slim and fiercely determined, her mouth flat, her brows scowled. He laughed. "Well, here goes." He lifted her onto the horse and handed her the reins and watched until she gathered them up tautly. "That's fine. Now don't let him jerk them loose."

Without taking his eyes off her he swung up on his own horse and, keeping close, led the way around the fence. As gently and as peacefully as an old hack, as quietly as if he had never had an idea of doing anything but what the woman on his back wished, the mustang ambled along. They circled the fence and came to the gate. When they pulled up, Johnny met Judith's eyes and they both broke into laughter. "There, now, the worst is over. We'll have many good rides on the prairie this summer."

Before she could reply, a clap of thunder as sharp as the report of a cannon deafened them. Instinctively they both ducked, and looking up, startled, Johnny saw the gray curtain of rain sweeping across the prairie. He swung Judith off the horse. "Run for it! It's going to rain great guns!"

She gathered up her skirts, then hesitated. "You?"

He was uncinching the saddles. "I'll be along. Run, before you are drowned."

She ran, he thought, like a young antelope, as fleet and as un-awkwardly. The dark crimson of her dress on the path was like a bright flag for him to follow.

Chapter 14

THE STORM BLEW all evening, violent as all prairie thunderstorms were, with brilliant jags of lightning and great, rolling bellows of thunder. A high wind lashed the trees wildly and the rain, in weaving sheets, fell steadily.

Quartered with the unmarried men of the mission, Johnny stood for a long time at a window and watched the storm. He felt that it spoke for him. Full of an unnamable and strange turbulence, disturbed, he felt as if the wind and the rain, the thunder and lightning, were part of his own inner storm and in loosing themselves so wildly they loosed something of his own tempest of emotions. Shaken, he welcomed each blinding bolt of lightning, as if it shot from his own body, and when the thunder rumbled growlingly it was as if his mind shook and cleared itself. The beating rain was his own heavy pulse and the earth that received it his hot face, sluiced and cooled by the flood.

He forgot where he was, so wholly did he enter into the lashing storm. He did not remember there was a roof over him or a group of men in the room behind him. When someone spoke, calling him to eat, he had to withdraw himself slowly, as someone coming out of sleep, and turn almost blindly to awaken to the room, the men, and the food waiting. He flexed his fingers, still feeling the electric tingling in them, scrubbed them over his face and shook his head. "Yes," he said, "I'm coming."

He did not see her alone again, but he sat against the wall in the gathering for church the next morning and looked his fill at her back among the women toward the front.

He heard the reverend announce his text from the Book of Revelation and heard him begin to read. "Be watchful, and strengthen the things which remain, that are ready to die; for I have not found thy works perfect before God." Then he listened no longer. He did not hear another word the reverend said. All during the two hours the man preached Johnny sat with his head leaned back against the wall and watched Judith Lowell under his narrowed eyes.

She sat erectly, Rebecca beside her and sharing a hymnbook. She knelt at the proper times. She bent her head and lifted it. But she never once looked around. Johnny explored the little tentacles of feeling that reached out inside him. Deliberately he brought back into his mind every time he had seen her, all the things she had said and done. Her courage, he remembered, on the boat when the storm had struck; her directness of manner and the quickness with which she grasped and understood things; her censure when she did not approve of him; her quick temper, and then her readiness to forget it; her laughter, not silly or giggly, but rich with humor and enjoyment.

He tried out in his mind every tone of voice she had ever used to him. He had heard her angry, cold, eager, anxious, concerned, friendly, happy, gay. Loving, he thought, it would be warm and rich, tender and heartening.

He went over the way she looked, noting down everything about her as if for reference — the light, reddish brown hair, the light, brandy-colored eyes, the smooth, close-textured skin, the wide, full-lipped mouth, the white, crooked little tooth. Taken alone and separately her features were not beautiful, but put together they seemed to make a design especially right for her. He could not imagine her with darker hair, or with a smaller mouth, or without the small crooked tooth. He could not imagine her taller or shorter, plumper or much thinner. She was, he felt, rising with the congregation as the last hymn began, essentially right exactly as she was, temper leavened with humor, determination backed by courage, sinewy but wholly womanly.

He knew his own mind now. She could make him feel awkward and inarticulate, but he did not think she could ever make him feel humble. By the standards of manhood on the frontier, admittedly tougher than any she might know and be familiar with, he knew he measured up pretty well, and he took an honest pride in it. He could not bring her innocence, but he could bring her an unashamed strength and discipline and loyalty. His body was clean and his mind was clean, and his love was whole. There were things in his past she might not understand, but there was nothing of which he was ashamed.

He and Rebecca left immediately after the church service was over. The mission people stood on the steps of the dwelling in which the Chapmans and the Vaills lived and told them goodbye. They spoke of their pleasure in the visit and urged Rebecca to come again. "And when you bring your boys in September," Mr. Chapman said in his booming voice, "we will care for them as if they were our own."

As they rode away Johnny looked at Judith once more. She stood a little apart from the others, her hands clasped about her psalmbook. After the storm the air was very clear and the sun was bright. A brisk west wind was blowing and as Johnny looked at her, it caught her skirt and billowed it fully. She did not trouble to catch it but kept her eyes on him. He bent his head a little, as if promising something, and she lifted a hand, made a small gesture of goodbye, smiled, and turned away.

Chapter 15

NATHANIEL PRYOR had returned when they got home and Parley Wade brought Johnny a message from him. "He said ride up and see him. Said he wanted to talk to you."

"When did he come?"

"Yesterday. Little bit after you left. I told him you was at the mission and he could go past there and see you, but he wouldn't. Said he had to get on home. But he was some glum over the way things is going and said he wanted to talk to you soon as you got back."

It was only four miles to Pryor's post and there was an hour of sun yet. Johnny decided to go at once. "Get me a fresh horse, will you, Parley?"

He found Nathaniel as gloomy as Parley had said. The two men squatted on their heels against the wall of Pryor's house and in the warm, fading evening, talked. Nathaniel had a quid of tobacco in his cheek and from time to time he spat. Johnny whittled on a peeled twig. "We talked till we was talked out, Johnny, and got nowhere. They won't even talk about an armistice." Johnny said nothing. Pryor was tired and his voice sounded rusty and strained. Johnny looked at him and saw the cud of tobacco in his cheek like a great, swollen tooth. Nathaniel went on. "It took us a week to get a council together, but we finally got Takatoka and Jolly, the Black Fox and the Blade and some others to meet with us. Will had wrote out a good treaty. Both sides was to promise not to set foot on one another's land for three months, and both sides was to promise to punish their own people if they broke loose. He made it fair to all. He give it to Takatoka when he had finished reading it to 'em, and you know what the sonofabitch done with it? He spit on it and tore it up and ground it under his heel."

Johnny eased his weight onto his other leg and felt the gathering of too much saliva in his mouth. He spat and cleared his throat. "About then I would have lost my temper."

"Brad liked to. He turned red as a turkey's wattles and for a little he couldn't say anything. Just stood there trying to get hold of himself. It broke up the council, for Takatoka walked off and we never did get him back for another word. That's one Indian hates white men as bad as he hates Osages."

Johnny nodded. "Who did you council with after that?"

"Jolly and some of the others. The Blade was no help. He's aiming to go to war and no budging him."

"I expect he is."

Nathaniel Pryor shifted his tobacco. "I talked to him in private some. He said when they had evened up the score of killings he would talk armistice. Said the Osages was still way ahead."

"They will always be ahead by Cherokee count."

"Well, me and Dave Brearly stayed on in the village trying to talk up the armistice and Brad took a pirogue and went down to see the Governor. When he got back we all come on home. No use staying on. But Miller has wrote to the Secretary of War and to Richard Graham in St. Louis. He promised Brad he would urge Graham to call a council of both tribes and send someone official down here to act for the government. And Brad has wrote again to both of them and he took it on himself to write to General Gaines in Louisville."

"Who is General Gaines?"

"He is the commander of the Western Division of the Army. It would be in his power, Brad said, to send reinforcements. Brad wrote him the strongest letter he could. Said he would not answer for the peace of the country if reinforcements did not reach Fort Smith pretty soon. Said he could not control the Indians with his present strength and he needed two full companies sent as soon as possible." Pryor paused and Johnny heard him sigh. "The Cherokees are bringing on their relations from the east again. We saw Delawares and Creeks and Shawnees, and a few Choctaws, in the village. It won't be long, Johnny, till they have a big band of warriors ready. I don't like it."

Johnny sheathed his knife and stood. The air was very still. With his skin Johnny felt the silence and the coolness. It was the time of evening when nothing moved, not even the wind. It was the dead-quiet time, as if the earth, tired of movement, paused a moment, rested, breathed deeply before moving on into the night. The leaves hung as if the air was a vacuum and the only sounds were the croaking of the frogs from the river. Pryor groaned as he tried to unkink his back. Johnny gave him a hand. "Rheumatism bothering?"

"It's a mizry," Pryor said, "low down in my back. God, Johnny, I ain't half the man I was even five years ago. You wouldn't think this old crock had ever got to the Pacific and back, would you?"

"Been out in the weather all your life, Nathaniel. It's catching up with you."

"Maybe." A glow of light came through the window. "My old woman," Pryor said, "has lit the Betty lamp. Come in and set."

"No." Johnny said. "I'll get on home. You will take word to Claymore, I reckon."

"Well, that's another thing I wanted to talk to you about. How much to tell him."

Johnny leaned against the wall and thought. "Best tell it all, seems to me. He'd better know the worst so as to be ready. He would not want to be caught with his warriors out on the prairie."

"It's not entirely hopeless, though," Pryor said slowly, "and I'd not wish to discourage him too much. If the government will crack down and make 'em sign this armistice, there is some hope."

"Well, I'd tell him that. Tell what Brad has done and what Miller has done and what they are trying to get Washington to do. Make it as hopeful as you can without fooling him." He straightened up abruptly. "One thing is damned sure, Nathaniel. Don't either one of us want to see that village caught the way it was five years ago. It would be a damnfool thing for Claymore not to know the truth."

"Yes. Well, I'll tell him. It will be hard on them."

Johnny laughed. "They may come to eating fish yet."

Nathaniel's laughter joined his. Both men were remembering that Osages would not eat fish. "How," they said, "can anything be good that fills your mouth with little bones?"

Johnny blew out his breath. "Well, you can see that your wife's family don't go hungry and I guess Suard and me can take care of the Wolf's. Maybe we'll be lucky enough to keep a few others going. The corn will be in the ear next month and that will help. Like hopping from one little rock to another crossing a creek, Nat. We'll just have to keep hopping."

"I don't know as there is any other way right now," Pryor agreed. "I'll ride out to the village tomorrow, then."

"That's best. If there is any more word, let me know."

In the stalemate, with nothing to do but wait, Johnny spent most of his time hunting. He left Parley, disgruntled and unhappy, at the post with Adam and took Suard with him. A few of the young men from the village went occasionally but Claymore was too uneasy to allow more than a handful to be away from the village at a time.

There was no use going for buffalo. The herds had moved farther north and Pawnees would be all over the prairie now. It would be a foolish man who went out without the protection of warriors now. There would be no more buffalo hunting until the herds began their migration south again in the fall. Johnny kept to the timbers nearer home, going only as far as the Ouachita mountains southeast, and up the Kiamichi and Jack Fork rivers, along the crest of the Winding Stair, up the steep humps of Kavanal and the Sugar Loaf, and he hunted the bottoms of the Poteau and the Arkansas.

Sometimes he went north into Missouri, traversing the deep hollows of the great, flat-topped mountains called the Ozarks. When he went in that direction he always came back by the mission. He timed his arrivals so that it was necessary for him to stay the night there. He was always welcome because he shared the meat he had killed and because, out of his experience in the country, he could often give helpful advice. He often felt as if the whole mission knew the true reason for his visits. He did not know how they felt about it, but he sometimes caught a sly look between two women, as if they were nodding their heads, saying I-told-you-so. He did not know whether Mr. Chapman approved, or even if he noticed, and he doubted if he noticed. The missionary was too engrossed in the affairs of the mission and, for that matter, he was often not present when Johnny was there. The business of the mission fell on his shoulders and he made trips to Fort Smith, even to Arkansas Post, and to the Osage village, constantly. In fact, most of the men of the mission were usually far afield, felling timber, clearing new fields, fencing, plowing, and planting.

Each time he came Johnny took Judith out onto the prairie. Ostensibly he was teaching her to ride. Actually she was becoming a good horsewoman by now, sure of her seat and with a firm hand on the reins, and she needed no further teaching. But she said nothing of discontinuing their rides and Johnny was content to let the excuse stand. "I shouldn't, perhaps," she told him, "but I manage to steal a little time each day to ride."

It was now late in June and the heat was perishing the prairie grass. It was dry and brittle and already gold, only its roots a little green. The air was always hazed with heat and a hot wind always blew from the west. They had ridden out to a little gullied wash where a clump of shin-oaks grew and had got off the horses to sit in the shade. This had become a favorite place of theirs and though it was unspoken between them, each of them thought of it as especially theirs. Judith leaned against the bole of a tree, looking tired, her face waxed with perspiration, leaf-shadows dappling it. Johnny lay in the grass beside her teasing an ant with a brittle blade of grass. "When?" he said. "What time of day do you ride?"

"About this time — around sundown. We are too busy for me to get away any earlier, and it's too hot besides. Johnny, is it always this hot in the summer?"

"Mostly. It's a little worse this year probably on account of the drought. When it's droughty it's like a furnace." He gave up teasing the ant and turned over on his back, tilting his hat over his eyes against the glare. "Where do you ride?" he said.

"I've kept my promise," she said. "I ride in the woods near the pasture. Sometimes down in the meadow. But you know I only come out on the prairie with you."

He drew up a knee and wobbled it. "I've been meaning to ask. Anybody say anything about me giving you the horse?"

Judith laughed. "Of course. They all had something to say."

"What?"

"Why do you want to know? Only nice things."

But peering at her from under the brim of his hat Johnny saw her face color. They had teased her, he thought. And he had his answer. She knew his intentions, for women, teasing, would make them plain. And if she minded, she would not ride with him. "Who saddles the horse for you when I'm not here?"

"You're full of questions today, aren't you? I saddle him myself. I've watched you often enough."

That, too, gave him an answer. She did not ride with one of the other men. He slung a foot up and rested it on his knee. "I didn't know whether you could manage or not."

"He's getting very gentle. He comes when I whistle and I give him a lump of sugar. I save mine at the table for him. Then he stands. Well, nearly always," she amended, "he will stand for me."

Johnny grunted. "You're spoiling him. A mustang is a grazing animal. Don't start feeding him."

"I'll miss him when you take him back in the fall. I've grown very fond of him."

He had forgotten he had told her he might need the horse in the fall. Well, that bridge could be crossed when they got to it. He turned on his side and pushed his hat back. "When is the school going to open?"

"The first of September. We have three more pupils promised."

"Whose?"

"Charles Donne's children. I think he will keep his word and bring them."

Johnny nodded. "He's a good halfbreed. The kids have got no mother now and it will be a kindness to him to take them."

"With Rebecca's three boys and the Vaills' three oldest children that will make nine for a beginning. It isn't what we hoped for, of course, but it will be a school." She leaned back against the trunk of the tree and looked at his face. "Do you still believe the Osages won't send us theirs?"

Intuitively they had avoided any more talk about their differing points of view, but during their rides she had asked Johnny many questions and he had seen her face thoughtful and reflective at his answers. She had asked him about the religion of the Osages and, expansive for once, he had told her and she had listened attentively, saying nothing but her face looking a little troubled. She had asked about their customs, how they taught their children, and Johnny had told her. Though she never commented she had, through him, absorbed a considerable amount of knowledge she could have got no better way.

Now, Johnny felt he could not bear for her to be too disappointed. Her heart was still set on teaching the Osage children and she would not feel she had done what she came to do until a few, at least, had been entrusted to her. "Not this year," he said gently. "You must not expect it this year. They are too afraid this year. Maybe next. I will talk to some I know about it."

"Would you, Johnny?" Her voice was light and eager. "They trust you so much. They would listen to you, I'm sure."

"Maybe," he said. "No man can influence them on some things, but we will see. Will your schoolhouse be finished by the first of September?"

There was a small darned place in her skirt which was spread wide around her. Johnny's finger found it and rubbed over it. He studied the neat, even little stitches. She had done this. Her hands had taken those stitches. They were folded in her lap now, idle, but they were capable hands, slim, quick, and clever. They were brown from her work in the garden. He looked quickly away. The only times he ever touched her were when he lifted her on or off her horse. But her hands always rested on his shoulders to brace herself at those times. Afterward, it took him an hour to lose the feeling of them there. It was as if they burned their print into his flesh.

She was nodding. "We think it will be. But we propose to begin anyhow."

"I am going to be doing some building of my own about that time," he said, casually.

"You are? Are you going to enlarge the store?"

From time to time she had asked him about the trading post so that she had some idea of its buildings and extent. She also had a very good idea of how fair he tried to be in his dealings with the Osages, how protective he felt toward them and how he tried to guard them against their own weaknesses.

He shook his head and kept it bent so that he did not look directly at her. "No. Think I'll build me a house." He looked up quickly, then looked away just as quickly. "What kind would you say?"

"Why, I don't know, Johnny." She sounded confused. "Don't you live with Stephen and Rebecca?"

He nodded tautly. "Man needs his own place, in time." He sat up abruptly, drew his knees up within the circle of his arms and rested his chin on them. "Thought I might build a plank house. If your men get their mill to working right and start sawing out lumber." He talked rapidly now, hurrying on as if trying to get it all said before he ran out of time, or ran out of

courage, or ran out of words. "I would build of logs first, naturally, but board them over outside and in. Logs get wormy after
a while. There is room," he began drawing lines in a dusty place
between two clumps of grass, "right here, down by the river,
see? It's not too near the post. Be a nice place for a home. Lot
of shade there. And quiet."

Judith bent her head to look at his drawing. Her forehead
wrinkled a little as she frowned over it. "Isn't that too far away
from the store to be convenient? Shouldn't it be connected in
some way?"

"Stephen and Rebecca live in the store," he muttered, almost
inaudibly.

But she caught it and nodded. "Of course. You don't really
have to be near the post, do you? I had forgotten." She continued to study the drawing. "What about floods from the river?"

"It's pretty high land. The bank is sharp there and I've never
known it to flood. Higher than the post, for that matter."

"How big a house are you going to build?"

Now was the time for him to tell her, to say that the size of
the house depended on her wishes, that it was to be built for
her, to admit it would be inconvenient for him that far from
the post but that it was the best he could do to remove her from
the noisy, mixed and integrated life of the settlement. Rebecca
had never minded it, but neither she nor Stephen was very con-
ventional or given to sitting in judgment. Judith was different.
She was, he felt, tenderer and gentler. And there was this religion thing. The missionaries wouldn't even spend a night at a
trading post themselves, much less allow their women to. He
owed her, it seemed to him, if she could be persuaded to join her
life with his, the effort to protect her from those things her training and her background thought heathen and immoral. But the
words, formed in his mind for so long a time, stuck now that the
occasion had been carefully brought around to it, and refused
to come out. It was not right, somehow. He studied the drawing, then slowly he rubbed it out with his palm. "I don't know.
Maybe you're right. Maybe I won't build there at all."

He looked westward where the sun, as if plunging into the sea, was dropping behind the dark line of the horizon. Long rays of light shot upward from it and made separate bands of gold. Dust in the air, he knew, but the effect was beautiful. No. If she was to be persuaded to join her life with his, it would have to be on a full and complete acceptance of him and his way of life. He saw it clearly now. She would have to accept the post, the way it was, as Rebecca had done. No other way was possible. Any other way would lead to a dismal unhappiness in time. If she hadn't the courage for that, if she couldn't do it, then it would be better to forget her. This was the way, his stick floated, he thought, remembering the language of the fur trappers, and it was for a man to say what he should do with his life. He could not amend it and weaken it without amending and weakening himself in some inner and strong place. Johnny Fowler was a trader. His life lay in rough places. He could not, without corrupting himself, bribe her by offering to be different or to live differently from the way it had to be. Hard. Hard lines for any woman. And he didn't know. Right now he didn't know at all.

He looked at his hands clasped around his knees and breathed in deeply. He loved her and he wanted her. But this was no way to begin. Better never to have her than to have her on any terms except complete understanding and total commitment. What he owed her was not protection, but the expectancy of a full faith and strength. And this was not the time. He unclasped his hands and laid them flat against the earth. He shoved with them and pushed himself up. "I expect we had better be going," he said.

Silently they rode back to the mission and turned their horses loose in the pasture. As they started down the path to the settlement Judith said, a little timidly, "Johnny, I didn't mean to criticize."

He smiled at her. "It's best you did. Gave me a new idea to work on."

He held a branch back for her and she walked ahead. "Well,

in that case . . . but it is entirely your own affair, you know."

He did not reply.

Around a bend in the path, Mr. Vaill had come into view, running along at a half-trot. He waved when he saw them and called out. "Mr. Fowler! Mr. Fowler!"

"Something has happened," Judith said quickly, and they hurried their steps.

Mr. Vaill stopped where he was to wait for them. He was still breathing hard when they reached him, holding the stitch in his side with his hand, bending a little to the pain. "Mr. Fowler," he gasped, "Joseph Revoir's family — his wife and children — have come in. Brother Chapman sent me to find you. We cannot understand Mrs. Revoir very well and the children speak even less intelligibly. We can make out something about Cherokees. They are all very badly frightened."

Forgetting, Johnny swore.

Judith touched his arm. "Go on, Johnny. I'll come with Brother Vaill."

Joseph Revoir was the manager of the Chouteau trading post farther up the Neosho. He was part Osage, but he was also related to the Chouteau family. His wife was a full blood Osage. Johnny knew she had a smattering of French which the missionaries might have understood, but she was probably too frightened to remember it, and their knowledge of Osage was still fragmentary.

The woman was sitting on the ground before the Chapman house, the missionaries grouped around her, her children gathered near, huddled against her. When she saw Johnny she scrambled to her feet and ran toward him, moaning and weeping. Her black eyes glittered with fear and her dark skin had turned ashy and splotched. She flung herself at Johnny, wailing. He took her by the shoulders. "Be calm, now. You must tell me what has happened." He led her to the porch and she collapsed on the steps.

She held to his arm and the strong, rancid odor of her hair came up to him. She pushed it out of her face and then, overcome with weeping again, let it fall back to cover her eyes. She sobbed brokenly. Johnny waited. The women gathered about spoke quietly and pityingly. "Poor thing. Poor, poor woman."

Judith came up. She went directly to the Indian woman and sat down beside her, taking her hand. The touch of sympathy sent the woman into fresh wails and she buried her head in Judith's lap. "Must she talk now, Johnny?" Judith said. With one arm around the woman, the other hand stroking the black, stringing hair, she looked up at him.

"I think so," he said gravely. "We have to know what to do."

He stepped up and squatted in front of the woman and spoke softly to her. "We must find your man. We cannot look for him until we know what has happened. Control yourself now and help us."

Mr. Chapman interposed. "Mr. Fowler, would it not be better if she were given time to eat some hot food and rest a while? They came very hurriedly and she must be exhausted."

Johnny shook his head. "The mission may be in danger, too, Reverend. Let's hear what she knows right now." He took the Indian woman's hands in his. "Talk, now, my friend."

She lifted herself up heavily and broke off her sobbing forcibly. "My man — he went to the salt spring this morning — when the sun come up. He say he would not be gone long. He did not come. Cherokees came and they took all the horses. Put us," she motioned to the children, "put us in the house and say they burn it up. They rode over the corn and trampled it in the ground. They turned the cows out and they took all the horses and many kettles, and some salt and hides. My man . . . he not come home all day. When Cherokees leave, we come here. We do not know what to do. We afraid to stay alone." She wailed again and tore her hands loose, scrabbling with them through her hair, tearing at her face with them. Johnny caught them again and said, sternly, "Wait. How many? How many Cherokees?"

She held up one hand and the thumb of the other.

Johnny nodded. "Six. Did you recognize them? Did you know any of them?"

Her eyes grew wide as she remembered. Her voice was a whisper when she spoke. "The Blade. Only him. The others I did not know."

Johnny felt the muscles of his face thicken and grow heavy on their bones. The long nerves in his thighs ached and his haunches felt cramped. His mouth drew down and flattened, and he felt the old sickness in his stomach. He glanced quickly at Judith and saw the horror in her eyes. He stood. "Take her inside now," he told Judith.

When they had gone in the house, the other women following quickly, Johnny turned to Mr. Chapman. "Her husband has been murdered very likely, sir. Will three of your men go with me to search for him?"

"You are going to their place?"

"Yes, sir."

The missionary did not hesitate. "I will go." He looked over the group of men standing near. "Mr. Fowler needs two more men. Will you volunteer?"

Every man in the group stepped forward and Johnny felt a quick admiration for them. It was a dangerous thing they were asked to do. No one could know whether the Cherokees were still around the Revoir place or not. It might be walking into a trap. But as quickly as their leader they had decided. By God, he thought, they had guts! Mr. Chapman's face flushed with pride in his men. "Choose them yourself, sir."

Johnny pointed out the blacksmith and one other man whose name he did not remember. "Eat first," he told them, "then we'll leave."

He spoke to the others with grim earnestness. "Until we return it would be wise for you men to stay near the dwellings and the women. I don't think they will bother the mission. But you can't be sure. Keep your guns loaded and ready, and don't stray far. Remember that one man alone is always a sitting duck for an Indian. Keep together above all things. If we have not returned within three days get word to the trading posts."

Mr. Chapman took Johnny into his own house to eat. Judith had the Revoir children at a table and was putting food before them. He watched her move quickly about the room, from the fireplace to the table, back to the pots hanging above the fire. Moving gracefully among them, she stooped to speak to the children, laughed at things they said, touched them, encouraged them to eat. She was very good with children — any kind of children, these little Revoirs or the Vaills, he thought. He guessed she would be an excellent teacher.

He took his own place at the table and she set a thick crockery plate in front of him. "Judith," he said, keeping his voice low, "don't let any of the women or children go far from the houses. Your lives may depend on your staying close by. Don't go to the river, or down in the meadow. Don't ride while we're gone. Don't even go to the pasture."

There was a small spot of soot high on one cheek and her hair had loosened with her bending. She brushed it aside with the back of her hand and spread the sooty spot. "Johnny, where are you — "

"Do you understand about staying near the houses?" He was stern with her.

The fire had flushed her cheeks. She put up her hand and touched her mouth. "I understand, yes. We will do as you say." She hesitated, her eyes traveling quickly over his face. She smiled and the crooked tooth flashed briefly. Her hand went out, paused as if to touch his hair, then dropped very lightly and only for the shortest moment to his shoulder. "Take care of yourself."

He nodded. She moved behind him and he ate. Then it was time to go.

Two days later, just after dark, they were back with Revoir's mutilated body. "We didn't find him until this afternoon,"

Johnny told Judith as she fed him again. "Don't know whether they had captured him and taken him so far from home, or whether they had come up on him where we found him. He was ten miles from home."

She sat beside him on the long bench in the Chapman kitchen. He was stopping only long enough to eat before going home. "You didn't see the Indians?" she asked.

"No. They had gone. We found Revoir by tracking them. The house is still standing. Plundered, though. Everything else about like his woman told it."

A long shudder ran through her. "Why? Why, Johnny?"

"Revoir was part Osage. That was reason enough. And that is another reason why you should have no Osage children here at the mission until the times are more settled. Their presence might endanger the mission and it isn't certain you could guarantee their safety."

"He is a dreadful man," she said, slowly, "a dreadful man, this Scammon. It is terrible for an Indian to murder and loot but when a man who is part white, who is what we call civilized, does it — "

Quickly Johnny cut in. "Don't. Put him out of your mind." He added, "I am troubled about Revoir's woman. She ought not to go back up to the place for a time."

"She doesn't want to go back at all. She seemed to know he had been killed. She says she wants to go to her own home in Missouri."

"Yes. She is a Gross Côte woman. Natural she would want to go back there. Chouteau will have to send another man here to run the post and there wouldn't be any place for her then. It's just as well."

She watched him eat. He looked at her from the corners of his eyes. "You make me feel awkward," he said finally.

"Shall I turn my back?"

"No."

She folded her hands and laid them on the table, looked at them. "Are you going home? Or to the fort?"

"Home first. But Major Bradford has to know about this. Not that it will do any good, but he ought to know."

There was a silence, then, and Johnny sensed her tension. "You worrying?" he asked.

Swiftly she answered. "This was murder, Johnny, not war. Isn't there any law in this land? What is the territorial government for? What is the court at Arkansas Post for? Can't a murderer be brought to trial?"

Johnny slid around on the bench and rose. He picked up his hat. "An eye for an eye and a tooth for a tooth is the best law here, yet."

Judith gazed up at him. "Johnny, when we were coming up the river last year Dr. Palmer shot and killed one of the boat hands. You've heard of it?"

Johnny nodded, his eyes on his hat.

"It was an accident, of course. A most unfortunate accident and poor Dr. Palmer was distracted. But it was reported properly to the justice of the peace at Billingsley's settlement and an examining trial was held. The correct procedure was followed and it was settled in a lawful manner. Mr. Scammon ought to stand trial for murder."

Johnny laughed shortly. "Judith, Blackstone was right. The best law is the vindictive law. We have to deal out our own punishment. Someone, sometime," he said slowly, "will deal with Scammon."

Looking down at her he saw the pupils of her eyes widen until they were all dark. She shook her head. "No . . . no, Johnny. That's not the way."

"You don't know anything about it. I must go."

She walked outside with him to the blacksmith shop where he had tied his horse and stood beside him in the warm, dark night. The stars looked yellow and hot. Without speaking they stood together for a little while and then Johnny moved away. Judith sighed. Johnny untied his horse and thrust the reins through his arm. He came back to Judith. "I'm very glad," she said, softly, "you are safe."

He took her hands and swung them slowly. "Yes. Well . . . there wasn't any danger. You'll have to put up with a lot of wailing from the Indian woman. It's their way when there has been a death."

He heard Judith take in her breath quickly. "I don't blame her," she said fiercely, "I don't blame her at all."

"Judith . . ."

He thought he might have kissed her, and he thought she might have let him, but a door opened, candlelight showed through and Mrs. Chapman called. "Judith? These children are going to sleep on the floor! Judith!"

"I'm coming."

Johnny squeezed her hands. "I will be back."

She gasped suddenly, freed her hands, and fled. In the darkness he heard her footsteps quick and rushing on the gravel, then quiet and lost in the soft padded grass. He waited until he saw her against the candlelight of the opened door. When the door closed, he rode away.

Chapter 16

"Why did he pick on Revoir, Johnny?" Major Bradford leaned against the tie rail. He was tired. They had been talking all morning and before that he had been in the saddle for a week. Tomorrow he would be in the saddle again. His shoulders sloped down heavily and his big, broad-featured face was hot and burned and dirty with sweat and dust. He wiped at it distractedly. He was a man who sweated a lot and heat was a torment to him. The baking, intense glare of the sun at this moment was a stabbing pain in his eyes. His eyeballs felt ready to burst.

Johnny was probing for a stone in the hoof of his horse. He did not look up at Bradford's question, nor did he answer immediately. Cautiously, delicately, with forefinger and point of knife blade he hunted for the pebble. He moved a little when the horse shifted uneasily. "At a guess," he said, then, "I'd say it was because Revoir was a Chouteau man. In the Blade's mind that might figure. Be easy for him to say to himself the Chouteaus back the Osages to be troublesome. Be easy for him to figure if he hurt the Chouteaus by killing one of their men it would be a blow against the Osages. Might be, though, something nobody knows about. Bad blood between the two, though I've not heard of it. Might even be it was just a chance they run up on him."

"They don't think so at Dwight," Bradford said. He rubbed his gritty, bloodshot eyes. Dwight was the mission to the Cherokees which had forestalled Epaphras Chapman. "At Dwight

they say he went purposely, riding two hundred miles, hunting
for Revoir."

Johnny's knife poised, then swiftly flipped a small pebble from
the mustang's hoof. He remained bent a moment, smoothing his
hand down the horse's foreleg, then he straightened. He studied
the strong-bladed knife, ran his thumb down its edge. Taking
it by the point he flipped it into the dirt at his feet where it stuck
upright, quivering, the sun flashing fire from the bright blade.
He recovered it and spun it down again, his wrist barely moving,
all the strength in his long fingers. Bradford watched him dully,
the heat soaking into him sweatingly. Johnny pulled the knife
out of the ground and sheathed it. "What else do they say at
Dwight?"

"They say he bragged he was going after Revoir. They say
there was a big celebration when he came back with the scalp
and Revoir's horses. Said the hollering and whooping and dancing could be heard for miles, and the big fires burned all night."

Johnny nodded tightly.

Bradford twisted his neck from side to side and rubbed at an
aching spot at the base of his skull. "They say there are twenty-
four new Delawares come in, and all the horses are being shod
for an expedition."

Johnny gazed reflectively at the big, tired soldier. "You look
all in, Brad."

"I am all in." The major heaved himself away from the tie rail
and struck a fist against it helplessly. "God damn it to hell,
Johnny! What is a man to do? I ride my rump off and talk till
my throat is raw, and all the time I have to wait and wait and
wait. Wait and see if Graham is going to make the armistice
stick. Wait and see if the army is going to send reinforcements.
Wait and see what the Cherokees are going to do. It's enough to
drive a man crazy!" He hawked and spat. "I never was much of
a hand to wait."

Johnny untied his horse. "You're in the wrong business then.
Best I recall, waiting is what you do the most of in the army."

Bradford snorted. "Look out for yourself, Johnny. You have

got a bad name among the Cherokees. If they went for Revoir they might go for you."

Johnny heaved himself into the saddle. "I'll watch out."

The uneasy days dragged on.

In July the drought was broken by a week of rain and the clearwater rivers, the Verdigris and the Neosho, both quick to rise, were swollen to flood stage again. The missionaries' keelboat was washed away and was recovered a week later on a sand bar in the Arkansas fifteen miles downstream. Also in July Captain Douglas arrived at Three Forks with another cargo for the mission. This shipment had been sent by the Board and it contained flour and pork and bacon, beans, vinegar, shoes, mill iron, medicines and, finally, a wagon which the missionaries badly needed. Captain Douglas could not get up the Neosho immediately. The missionaries sent their pirogue down to take some of the stores up. They were surfeited, they told Johnny, with game. They could not wait for the river to go down to taste salt pork and beans again.

In July, Stephen came home from New Orleans and Rebecca was lifted from the doldrums to sudden and excited happiness. The trip had gone well. Success had attended him in every way. "Even," Stephen said happily, "the old Arkansas helped out. We weren't hauled up on the shoals a single time. She was full of water."

Stephen brought gifts — shoes, clothing, a new gun each for the boys; dresses, bonnets, a tortoise-shell comb for Rebecca; a new suit for Johnny. Johnny eyed it dubiously and fingered the heavy, excellent cloth. "What am I supposed to do with it? I've not worn my old one a dozen times."

"You might," Rebecca said tartly, "use it to get married in."

Johnny rolled it into a bundle and shot it across the table at her. "Keep it till the day," he said shortly.

After the house was quiet for the night the two men talked long and soberly. Stephen had much news of the journey but nothing new to report on the situation on the lower Arkansas.

He had stopped at the Cherokee towns but he could only verify what Johnny already knew. They were still preparing for war.

They talked about whether the time was right to open the general store in Little Rock, and eventually Stephen agreed they should wait a while. "I couldn't even help with it right now," Johnny said. "It would all be on your shoulders."

Over his pipe, Stephen nodded. "I understand, Johnny. Next year will be soon enough. They've not moved the capital yet. But it's the place to be, Johnny. Steam is coming up the river. I heard it all over New Orleans. Talked to men that know. By next year, they say, steamboats will be coming up the Arkansas."

"This far?"

Stephen shook his head. "Not generally. Maybe as far as Fort Smith. But they'll have no trouble coming up as far as Little Rock regularly. That's where the low water begins to be a problem, however. And that's where commerce is going to center."

Johnny fingered the bowl of his pipe nervously. "I don't know, Steve."

"You don't like the idea of change, do you?" Stephen said. He laughed. "It has to come." He waved his hand sweepingly. "A trading post like this will soon be out of date. With steamers coming upriver, the territory settling up rapidly, the trade and commerce is going to be with white people. I wouldn't give an establishment like ours another twenty years, Johnny. Maybe not more than ten. And if we mean to stay in business we had better get ready for it."

Johnny nodded. "You're right, of course." He grinned crookedly. "Don't make me like it any better though."

Stephen shrugged. "We've had the best of this. It's sensible to change with the times. Next year will be soon enough, though, and we can run the post also — as long as we can. Depends on how soon they push the Osages out. But it's as clear as the handwriting on the wall, Johnny, and unless you want to get into the fur trade farther west, or the Santa Fe trade, you'll have to settle for general merchandising in some town. That village Moses Austin started at the *petit roche* would do fine."

Johnny squinted his eyes against the smoke from his pipe. "I expect you're right," he said. He scrubbed a hand down his thigh. "I just hate to turn my face back east is all. I'll run the post as long as it's profitable and I'll venture the cash on the store there, but you'll have to operate it."

"Yes. I think Rebecca would like it there. We can run that end of the business." Stephen puffed meditatively. In the silence the night sounds of crickets, cicadas, jar flies, frogs, were loud in the room. The candle flame flickered and a great white moth hovered about it. The heat was stifling. Stephen wiped the sweat off his face and yawned. "Lord, it's hot. And I'm tired. Had to push a pole from Fort Smith. Paid off three hands there." He knocked out his pipe. "What's this," he said quietly, "about you getting married?"

"A notion of Becky's," Johnny said. He knocked out his own pipe.

Stephen lifted an eyebrow. "She doesn't get notions without some foundation. One of the mission women, Johnny?"

"Judith Lowell . . . the teacher."

Stephen whistled softly. His chair was tilted back against the wall and he let it down easily. "I see."

Johnny laughed briefly. "Becky wants a sister-in-law pretty bad."

"The important thing is, do you want a wife?"

Johnny rubbed his mouth. "I've not asked her yet. May not work out at all."

"No. I can see it might not." Stephen ran his long, slender hand through his hair. "You know what you're doing — but a *mission-ary*, Johnny!"

Johnny looked directly at Stephen. "She's different." Then quickly he added, "but whether she's enough different to marry a trader and live on a post, I don't know." He shoved his chair back and stood. "Like I said, it probably won't come to anything."

"You're fond of her?"

From the doorway, Johnny nodded.

"Any reason to think it's mutual?"

"Maybe."

"Well." Stephen rose and joined Johnny in the door. He laid his arm across his brother-in-law's shoulder. "Well, at least she has not got a husband living, son."

Johnny's face twisted. "I don't know how you and Becky stood it."

"You can stand a whole lot more than you think you can," Stephen said quietly. "Don't forget that, Johnny. And don't let her forget it." He lifted his arm and turned on his heel. "It's late. I'm going to bed."

"Who is guarding the boat?"

"Suard. We'll unload tomorrow."

Johnny stepped out into the dark. "Think I'll walk down there a minute."

Stephen Burke stood a moment listening to Johnny's muffled footsteps dying away. He didn't know. Maybe if Johnny married it would be a good thing. Rebecca thought so. But women always wanted to see a man married and settled down. He pinched out the candle and felt his way in the quick dark across the room. Any woman married to Johnny, he thought, would have some things to live with which most women wouldn't like. He didn't much think Johnny would ever be a simple and easy person to live with. It would take a very great love to leave him as free as he liked to be — as free, Stephen was convinced, as he had to be. And it would take a very great love to penetrate that wall of inarticulateness which was Johnny's nature. It might even be it could not be penetrated. It might simply have to be accepted.

Undressing, Stephen laid his clothing neatly on a chair. Women, even a woman like Rebecca, did not like to be held off. Something in a woman's nature made her want to be enclosed in the warmest circle of love, and made her want to probe into the most intimate folds of a man's mind and soul. Few women, Stephen was convinced, could stop short of making both themselves and their men unhappy if this was denied them. The woman Johnny Fowler loved would have to stop short, if he knew Johnny Fowler right, for certainly there would be many areas of his heart into which he would admit no one else.

He slid into the big double bed beside his wife. Rebecca turned a little, murmured and touched him. He smiled. There were compensations, though, for a man as well as for a woman and he wished them, now, for Johnny Fowler.

When the rains stopped, the heat set in with a fierce intensity again and August was a time of misery and a plague of sickness. At the fort, half the roster was dragging about with chills and fever, and over the country generally the same was true. Every family had its share of fever. At the mission, new to the heat, with no resistance to the intermittent, the people suffered greatly. It seemed to Johnny, riding the country regularly now, that more of the mission people were sick than well, and many of their hands quit because of the heat and because of the illness and because of their continued fear of being caught in Osage country if the war began.

Doggedly, however, those who could work made progress. The hay was cut and the yield was good, two tons to an acre. Work on a permanent mill was continued, work on the school building went on, fencing was done, and the corn was laid by. Having watched these people working for months under every adversity, Johnny gave them an ungrudging respect. He disagreed with their purpose in being here, but he had never seen a group of people hold more tenaciously to their goal. The country thought them tender and green and they were objects of derision everywhere, but what the country failed to see and understand, Johnny thought, was that saplings were the toughest of trees in their fight to live and grow. These missionaries were tough. Nothing stopped them. Everything they tried to do went wrong in some manner. They learned everything in the hardest possible way. But they learned, and they refused to be discouraged. Their men, green with inexperience, attacked every difficulty, not with confidence, but with determination. Their women were soft, but they somehow hardened themselves. Led by a fanatic, they had all become fanatics themselves. It was a hard country, but they would conquer it. They would get a foothold here, they would put down roots, they would grow and they would live and they would do what they had come to do. In Johnny's mind, differing as he did from them, they were due credit for plain guts and he gave it without stint.

He worried about Judith. Almost singlehanded she tended the big garden patch. Few of the other women could stand the hot sun, but bonneted against it Judith picked the beans, hilled up the potatoes, gathered the corn. She had slowly browned until she was almost as dark as Rebecca. She seemed well. At least the fever did not attack her. Marcus Palmer had an ample supply of Peruvian bark finally and she told Johnny that she dosed regularly with it. She was thinner, though. Such hard work in such terrible heat was stripping her down. But she was impatient with Johnny's worry. "I am well," she told him. "It is nothing. Just the heat."

Along toward the last of the month, however, when it seemed to Johnny that between the heat and the stalemated war the tension had stretched just about as far as it would stretch without snapping, there came good news, real good news, news that was like a life-saving rain.

Mordecai Mundy, who had been in St. Louis making final arrangements for taking his pack train across the prairies to Santa Fe, came home over the Osage Trail, and he brought with him a letter for Major Bradford. Johnny, who was at Nathaniel Pryor's establishment when Mundy arrived, offered to deliver it. "What's it say?" he asked.

"Good news. Graham says they'll make the armistice stick. Says enforce it whether the Cherokees like it or not. Says for 'em to call a council at the fort and tell 'em so."

Johnny gazed across the heat-shimmered prairie. "Who's going to make it stick?"

"There's talk of reinforcing the fort," Mundy said.

"They'll have to if they want to enforce this armistice," Johnny said, tucking the letter in his hat. He looked over the string of mules Mundy had driven from St. Louis. "When do you aim to leave?"

"Pretty soon. Next three or four weeks, I'd say."

Johnny looked at Nathaniel. Pryor was just out of bed from a siege of the intermittent and looked more gaunt than ever. Johnny thought again it ought to be Nathaniel that was going. A trip across the prairies would do him good. But he said nothing. The arrangement between the partners was none of his affair.

Johnny delivered the letter to Bradford and watched as he read it, then tossed it aside. " 'Major Bradford's troops will enforce the armistice,' " he quoted, then he added with deep irony, "What troops?"

But within the week he came riding over to Three Forks with even better news. "Reinforcements! On the way!" he shouted, riding up in a cloud of dust, waving a letter in his hands. The worry-cut lines of his face had smoothed out and a broad grin stretched his mouth. He slid the mustang to a stop and leaped out of the saddle, throwing the reins to Parley Wade. "Turn him out to graze," he said, "I don't even want to see a horse till morning. I'm going to sleep in Johnny Fowler's bed tonight and sleep easy for the first time in six months!"

Johnny led him inside and gave him the whisky jug. Bradford tilted it expertly. "God, Johnny, this is the best news we could have." He smoothed out the letter. "Calhoun has finally woken up and prodded General Gaines to take action." He tilted the jug again, then peered at the letter. "Four companies coming!" He slapped Johnny thunderingly on the back. "Ain't that good news, hoss?"

Johnny rubbed his own gaunted face. "God, yes!" It came too suddenly now. It was hard to take in. "When do they report?"

Bradford waved the letter airily. "He don't say. But the letter was wrote in July. Likely, orders went direct to Arbuckle and he's on the way."

"Any reason why I can't see the letter?"

Bradford handed it over. "None. Nothing secret in it."

It was dated July 16. Johnny read it carefully. The military wording was precise and succinct. Major Bradford was advised that Colonel Matthew Arbuckle, now stationed at New Orleans, was being ordered to hold the entire 7th Infantry Regiment in readiness to proceed up the Mississippi River, to occupy Natchitoches on the Red River with six companies and Fort Smith on the Arkansas with four. "Well, that's clear enough," Johnny said, handing the letter back to Bradford.

"We'll have something to hold these Injuns with now," Bradford crowed jubilantly. "There's not a better outfit in the army than the 7th."

"Reckon Arbuckle will come on to Fort Smith himself?" Johnny said, reflectively.

"I don't know," Bradford said, throwing himself into a chair, loosening his collar and easing his neck. "And I don't care. Four companies of infantry is twice as many as I asked for, and four times as many as I expected to get." He blinked owlishly at Johnny. "You worrying about me being outranked?"

"Some," Johnny admitted. He grinned. "We've got used to you."

"Arbuckle is a good man. You'll like him." He reached for the jug again, laid his face against the cool neck and chuckled. "You know something, Johnny? You know what? This just *might* mean old Will Bradford is going to be transferred. This just might mean old Will Bradford is going back to civilization. Where there's no Osages or Cherokees to worry about. Where it ain't as hot as hell in the summer and where they never heard of the intermittent." He tilted the jug and drank deeply. Lowering it he nodded solemnly. "Yep. This just might mean old Will Bradford is being pardoned for his sins and is going to live like a white man again." He closed his eyes and sucked in his breath. "God, Johnny, pray for it! I've done my time on this god-forsaken frontier."

Johnny laughed. "Ten to one, Brad, if you're transferred out of here you'll be asking for duty on the frontier again within a year."

Bradford leaped out of his chair. "You think I'm a lunatic?" He swayed, caught his balance and flailed his arms wildly. "All I ask of the good Lord is to let me see the last of this hell-hole. Just let me live long enough to take a boat downriver and never see it again."

"That's what you say now," Johnny said, rescuing the jug which was within reach of the waving arms. "But it's got in your blood same as it's got in mine and Steve's and Nathaniel Pryor's."

Bradford shook his head positively. "Not in this coon's. You are wrong, my friend. The day Matthew Arbuckle takes over command of that damned stockade, that day, mind you, I'm getting on a boat if it is nothing but a pirogue and I'm leaving the Arkansas Territory."

"If," Johnny reminded him, "he brings orders for you."

"Don't even whisper it he might not! Don't even think it! Give me the jug again, Johnny."

Johnny held it high, shook it against his ear. "If we're both going to get drunk tonight," he said, "I'd better break out another keg."

The next morning, Bradford, with an aching head, went on to carry the word to Nathaniel Pryor and to Claymore at the village. He had a talking point now for bringing both tribes together in a council at the fort. "And we'll get 'em, too," he said, "by September."

Johnny laughed, watching Bradford gingerly mount his horse, trying not to jog the pain behind his temples. Bradford scowled down at him. "Ought not to let me get so sousing drunk, Johnny."

"Your idea," Johnny reminded him.

"Damn bad one." He gathered up the reins. "Well, be easy, Johnny." When the horse wheeled around, Bradford groaned. "Hell," he moaned, humped over in the saddle, a bowed bundle of misery, "the things I go through with for these damned Injuns."

Johnny watched him disappear in the woods and then he, himself, rode north to the mission.

Chapter 17

Hᴇ sʟᴏᴡʟʏ ᴡᴀʟᴋᴇᴅ out of the woods into the pasture clearing. It was an old arrangement. When Johnny came, they met at the pasture gate. Whoever got there first, waited. It was Johnny who usually waited. Today his feet were slow and his thoughts were far away, his eyes bent on the path. He did not see Judith until he almost reached the gate, then he looked up, startled, and hurried toward her. "You are early," he said.

She smiled. "You're late."

She was wearing a green-sprigged dress he had not seen before. It looked thin and cool and as fresh as a willow leaf. "New dress?" he asked, touching the sleeve band.

"From the missionary barrel on the last boat," she said. "We were each allowed one. I had to take it up a little, but it's very cool."

He studied her without replying. Though she was slimmer than she had been, she was not gaunt. The small loss of weight showed mostly in her face where the flesh had a more compact look, looked closer to the bone, more shaped and more closely textured. There was nothing left of the boat pallor of the early spring now — not even the freckles showed plainly any more. She was too brown. Gazing at her face, studying it, Johnny felt that the clearer lines of it had the queer effect of making her look a little older and, somehow, stronger — as if she had in some quiet but formulated way grown up a little. The cheekbones stood up more boldly and the soft, round chin was more plainly articulated. She was almost all one color now, as if poured, hair, eyes and skin, from one mold of thin, golden metal. The green-sprigged dress was like the calyx of a marsh lily, holding the golden flower.

She stirred under his look and fiddled restlessly with her hair. "What's the matter? Am I not put together right?"

Deliberately misunderstanding her, Johnny laughed and leaned an arm against the fence rail. "You couldn't be put together more right," he said. "I was just thinking how beautiful you are."

Her mouth quivered a little but she returned his look steadily. "It's the new dress," she said.

He shook his head, then he pushed away from the fence. "Well, shall we go?"

"Phoebe and Abraham Redfield are going with us," she said. "They will be here soon."

"But, why —" Johnny began, objecting.

"Have you looked at the sun?"

He glanced up and saw, to his chagrin, that the sun was almost down. "I lost track of the time," he confessed, "talking to the reverend."

"It doesn't matter, except — do you want us just to ride around the pasture?"

"No." He was positive about that.

"Then we have to be chaperoned. It will soon be dark. Besides, they need it too. It's cooler on the prairie, and Phoebe is . . . well, she isn't well."

Remembering the Redfields had been married early in March, Johnny grinned. Phoebe was starting a baby with no delay. "All right," he said, "but I hope they have sense enough to stay to themselves."

"Why, Johnny," she teased, giving him a wide, disarming look, "don't you like the Redfields?"

Johnny met her eyes without confusion. "Sure, I like 'em. But I don't come up here to see the Redfields."

The blood rose in her face but she refused confusion too. She had got back better than she had given, and she set aside her teasing manner and met his meaning honestly. "Just this once, Johnny. They have all been very good about your visits. I cannot fly in the face of the conventions. A lady would not ride alone with a gentleman after dark. In fact," she grimaced wryly, "I have trimmed pretty close to the edge riding with you alone at any time. I wouldn't have, you know, back home."

Johnny's mouth quirked in a one-sided smile. Back home, many things could have been done differently. "I think you are absolutely right," he said. "The Redfields are necessary tonight. But I still hope they have got sense enough to make themselves scarce."

At first it looked as if they did not, for when the group reached the little clump of shin-oaks on the bank of the dry wash, the Redfields dismounted and settled themselves gratefully in the grass and Phoebe, at least, began a voluble conversation with Judith. Abraham sat quietly beside his wife and listened as she rattled on. He was not given to conversation at any time, but around his wife he rarely had an opportunity of saying anything. Judith, in her favorite place against the bole of a tree, listened also, replying occasionally with a monosyllable. After a time, tiring, Johnny wandered a little apart and sat down with his legs swinging over the shallow lip of the gully.

He listened to the prairie sounds. Across the wash a meadowlark called and farther up, in another little clump of trees, a wood phoebe sent up a plaintive question. Nearer, a dickcissel piped a tiny note, and in the dried grasses the cicadas kept up a constant, shrilly metallic rasping. The leaves of the shin-oaks rattled dryly in the slow breeze, the sound dying away as the breeze faded. The horses cropped and there was the sound of grass being torn loose jerkily, the occasional blowing out of dust with its rubbling of their loose-flapped lips, and the clomp of a hoof against the earth.

Far, far out on the prairie the air was hazy, and in the puffs and starts of breeze which still moved Johnny caught, once in a while but not steadily, the smell of burnt grass. Prairie fire. Started by some Indians to flush small game from the grass. But it was very far away. The twilight deepened and the heat-devils died away. Johnny could hear the chattering voice of Phoebe Redfield behind him, enthusiastic about the afterglow of the sunset, about the opening distances of the prairie, about the cooling breeze.

Idly he wondered why some people needed to talk so much about things, as if it needed exclamations and descriptions to make them real. As if they did not exist unless put into words. What could words add? To be on the prairie at dusk, at this exact moment, he thought, was like being in the heart of an enormous jewel, the rays of the sundown color still lingering overhead, pale but still radiant, the dark advancing, swallowing the color, the earth holding, till the last, the gold and the heat and the essence. It was enough to be there, at the heart of the jewel. It would sound foolish to put it into words.

His mind ran on. Before these golden days were gone the Osages would fan out across the plains in their fall hunt. With the armistice enforced and reinforcements on the way to the fort, they were free to go. Soon the partisan would be chosen, the lodgepoles would be struck, the wayfinders would be appointed. In his mind's eye he saw the long, colorful caravan winding across the prairie, fording the wide, shallow rivers, making their night camps in the scattered groves along the washes, moving on and on, ever westward. He saw the night fires and the young men in their finery and the old men folded in their blankets by the fires, and he felt the good feeling of sleeping on the ground again, the stars far, far above, the little night wind brushing his face. He moved restlessly, scraping his heel against the dried-mud side of the gully. It had been too long a time and it could not come soon enough again for him.

He was startled when Judith came to sit beside him, clumsy a little in the full dark which now enveloped them. He steadied her and helped her arrange herself. "Did she finally run down?"

"Abraham took her in hand. She was nervous. I think she is asleep."

"Good."

They sat side by side in the close, warm darkness, a comfortable silence between them. There was silence in the night now, too, except for a night-twittering of a few birds not yet settled down, and the chirping sounds from the grass across the gully. Johnny felt caught in a kind of trance of comfort and peace and a deeply sunk feeling of tranquillity and well-being. Content without talking, when he reached for Judith's hand and, uncomplaining, she let him have it, it was as if he had simply extended himself, spread to her his own pool of peace.

They sat a long time thus, not talking, not moving, then Judith stirred and whispered, "What is that queer light in the north?"

The whole northern horizon was brightening with a pale green light which was rising rapidly toward the zenith. As it rose, nearer the earth the color deepened to an almost emerald green, and the band of color wavered and spread, like curtains drawn by an invisible hand. "Is it the moon? I never saw — "

"Northern lights," Johnny said.

"This far south?"

"Sh-sh-sh," Johnny whispered, as if their voices might disturb the lights. "Watch."

Rippling and weaving, the green hues changed constantly, licking darkly at the line of the horizon, fading toward the zenith to the paleness of the sea. Gauzy, webby, the curtains of light moved and shifted, drawn together, then parted, swaying gracefully, sinuous and ropy, intense one second, faded the next, a half-sky full of reflected arctic ice, thousands of miles from the ice bed which caused it. Then slowly the curtain descended, sank as it had risen, and the stars blinked out again, gold and hot in the inky sky. Judith took a long, slow breath. In a hushed and awed voice she said, "It was so beautiful, wasn't it? It almost

frightened me. It was weird, Johnny . . . and uncanny. Too
lovely. It was like," she laughed a little shakily, "it was like
standing before the throne of grace. I wonder if the Redfields
saw it." She twisted around.

Johnny held her. "Don't. Leave them alone, Judith."

"Well. But it was so lovely. I hope they saw it . . . weren't
asleep. Do they occur often, Johnny?"

"No. Once before I saw them. Six years ago. The oldest Indians could not remember having seen them before. They were
frightened. They said it was Wah-kon-tah speaking and they
did not know whether he was pleased with them or angry. We
were on the prairie then, too. We were on a long hunt." Almost
dreamily he spoke, as if speaking from sleep. "We had good
luck. I killed fourteen cows that day myself, and we had eaten
the livers and roasted the humps. The young men were dancing
and the fires burned high and crackled and sparked. No one was
hungry, and the Wolf told such tales as I never heard him tell
before — about when he was a young man and when he counted
coup on the Pawnee chief. I never felt so good in my life. The
stars were a mile high and we were camped in a long draw near
the Cimarron. I felt like my skin would burst, I felt so fine. It
was a big herd and there was plenty of buffalo for everyone, for
even the poorest man who did not have a pony to hunt with.
The women skinned so many buffalo they worked until the sun
went down and some had to be left where they had fallen because there were so many. We felt good, and the Wolf was
proud, and Suard played his little concertina and sang. We sang
and the young men danced and I danced with them, and when
the fires had died away the northern lights came and we watched
them."

Beside him Judith moved and murmured, "Johnny, are you
sad?"

When the northern lights had begun that time and all the
Indians had been afraid and the wailing had started and the
Wah-kon-da-gis had brought out their bundles and rattles and

the singers had gathered and the plangent chants had risen over
the long, shallow draw, they had scrambled up the sandy side of
the tumulus together. They were not afraid because he knew
what the lights were and he told her and, trustful, she believed
him. Laughing, she followed when he ran up the gritty flank
of the hill, holding his hand which pulled her over the roughest
places. Bull cactus and chokecherries had grown thick over the
hillside and they had fled, swaying around the cactus, crushing
the chokecherries under their feet. Slipping in the sand, they felt
the small drupes burst beneath their moccasins, popping with a
little hissing, liquid sound.

At the top of the little hill, no more actually than a swell, a
parting of the land made by the draw, they stood and watched
the arching, weaving, raying lights. His blanket was folded
about them and she stood within the circle of his arm, so small
her head came no higher than his shoulder, so delicately boned
and so slim that his two hands could span her waist.

Behind them the wind sighed down the shallow draw and the
singers sang and the Wah-kon-da-gis shook their rattles and
the people, wailing and afraid, hid their eyes. A few brave young
men stood forth boldly, arms folded over their chests, their eyes
defiantly raised to the gleaming sky. And the wise elders sat, an
example before their people, about the dying fires, their faces
brooding and inscrutable, showing no fear.

Before them the great lights flamed and swayed and the shadows disappeared over all the wide land and the darkness was
made silvery bright. In the silver brightness she who stood beside him was all silver too. Her hair was gleaming with silver
and her skin and mouth were glazed with it. Her eyes glittered
with silver.

When the curtain of light reached the zenith and the earth
was plated with the green-silver brilliance, he threw his blanket
down and in the great brightness, every shadow banished, in an
insupportable and transporting ecstasy, born of the good hunt
and the red, dripping meat, and the crackling, sparking fires, and

the young men dances, and the songs, and the howl of the coyotes around the buffalo carrion, born of the sensuous, sinuous lights, the silver girl, for whom he had that day paid Sho-mo-kah-se twelve good horses, laughing sweetly, her mouth as ripe as the chokecherries they had burst under their feet, became his wife.

Until the dawn they had lain wrapped in his blanket, and when they had wakened the dew on her hair was as silvery as the northern lights had been.

Once in a man's entire life, he thought, curiously, it may be that he commits his whole self and he is the most beautiful and the unquestioned best it is in him to be. For that length of time, drunk on the wine of life, he is keyed to the greatest deeds, the greatest emotions, the greatest exultation, it is in him to do or feel. Bloodstream, nerves, and flesh are wonderfully tuned and in harmony with their total environment. For him, that was a time of being unbelievably young, being one of the Osage young men, riding over the prairie, being part of the Wolf's band, going on the long hunts, killing buffalo, dancing the young men dances, fighting Pawnees, and always coming in the dusky evenings to the lodge of Sho-mo-kah-se and the dark-wrapped hours with the daughter of Sho-mo-kah-se. It was being alive to the end of every nerve, in every vein and blood cell, with no day dawning that was not crammed with joy and fullness and excitement and all things good and fine. And she, the girl, was part of it — not the essence, for there was no essence — part of the whole . . . the wide, sandy plains and the young men and the shallow, silty rivers, and the lodge fires and the high, blue sky, and the willow islands, and the love flutes calling in the night hours.

A year — he had had one fine, lucky year of it. Then it was gone and he would never have it entirely that way again, for it was gone like the innocence of childhood or the fresh, green strength of youth. But out of what he had been that year, and out of what he had done, he had come like tempered metal, burned strong and incorruptible by the heat of the long fires. And the goodness was part of him forever.

He turned slowly to the girl who sat beside him in the warm, close darkness now. "No," he said quietly, "I am not sad. It was a long, long time ago." He gathered her hands to his mouth. "I love you, Judith." With great gentleness he drew her to him. "I love you very much."

Chapter 18

IT WAS NOT altogether as simple as that, however, nor had Johnny expected it to be. He knew exactly what he was asking of Judith, and with more sensitivity than he might have been credited with he knew that, freely and honestly as she admitted her love, it could not be wholly untroubled for her. But with the simplicity of a man who always went straightforwardly to an objective, he felt that the first big hurdle had been taken. They loved each other and they had said so.

The next day, talking about it, she had misgivings. "There are so many difficulties."

"Which can all be worked out," Johnny told her. They had met, as usual, at the pasture, but with an unspoken agreement they did not ride. Instead they stood against the fence and talked. "The thing," Johnny went on, "is not to make too much of them. Just take one thing at a time. If we know our own minds — for instance," he plunged on, "if you are willing to live at the post, as Rebecca does . . ."

She winced. "It would be so much easier if that were not necessary. Brother Chapman is going to be horrified."

"The question is," Johnny said firmly, "are you going to be horrified. That's where I work, you know. That's where my wife has to live."

Not touching her, Johnny stood beside her, and he heard her sigh. "Life is very queer, isn't it?" she said, wistfully. "When I came here, and it was such a short time ago, I had such **very**

clear and definite ideas. I could draw a line down the middle
and everything went very simply to one side or the other. It was
all either black or white, plain and direct, no gray or in between.
But that's not the way it is, is it? I've learned that much from
you. Brother Chapman is so certain . . . and I am not any
more." The tree shadows dappled her face, already shadowed
with her thoughts. "I do not mean to be harsh, Johnny . . . but
you know, I expect, that he thinks the trading posts are immoral
places and he does not believe you have a good influence on
the Indians. He believes you give them whisky and some of
your men live immorally with the Indian women."

He knew this was the missionaries' position. He refused, however, to defend it, or to give her any help. Instead he said,
slowly, "What is your opinion?"

Judith looked from the long switch of ironweed she had been
idly stripping of its leaves to his face. There was a little worried
frown between her eyes, but as she looked steadily at him, it
smoothed away. The troubled eyes became serene. "My opinion," she said lovingly, "is that whatever you do, or allow to be
done, is not bad. How can it be bad when you are so good a
man?" She dropped the switch and took his face between her
hands. With one finger she traced his brows, his temples, his
eyes, and finally his mouth. "So dear a face," she said softly.
She pulled him forward and kissed him. "So strong . . . so
good."

He held her for a long time and they were quiet. Then she
moved. "Phoebe married Mr. Redfield," she said, laughing shakily, "and Mary Foster is going to marry Mr. Woodruff . . ."

"And they have none of your problems, because you are going
to marry Johnny Fowler, Indian trader," he finished for her.

"It would be nice," she said, stirring in his arms, "if you were a
missionary."

"Heaven forbid!" he said, laughing and turning her so he could
see her face. "You don't really wish that, do you? If you wanted
a missionary there is Dr. Palmer, and Stephen Fuller, and Mr.
Spaulding, and — "

"Hush," she said, putting up her hand.

He brushed it with his lips. "You did not have to fall in love with me."

"Did I not?"

"Did you?"

The impasse amused them and they fell to laughing. Then Judith became serious again. "We must be practical."

"Let me be practical now, then," Johnny said. "I think I should speak immediately to the reverend."

"Oh, no. No, not yet, please."

"Why?"

"Let's just leave things the way they are for a while longer. When everyone knows it will . . . well, it won't any longer belong just to us. Let's keep it to ourselves."

"I don't want to keep it to ourselves," Johnny said flatly. "I don't want everyone here at the station wondering about us any longer and talking. I want it open and understood that we are going to be married. Are you afraid to face up to it?"

"Oh, dear." She leaned against him and knotted and reknotted the fringe on his buckskin shirt. "It's going to sound so silly. I do dread it, Johnny. I come all the way from Connecticut to be a missionary and within six months I am in love and asking to be released. How shocked they are going to be."

"They'll live," Johnny said. "I want to talk to the reverend before I leave."

She pushed away from him. "Well, speak to him if you must, Johnny, but there is one thing about which I am going to be firm. I must help with the school this first year. I owe the Board that much."

Johnny nodded. Though he didn't like waiting, he agreed that she did owe the Board that much. "How long will the school term last?"

"Johnny, I really think . . . this time next year?"

"No."

"June?"

"How long," he asked again, "will the school term last?"

"I don't know," she said plainly, then. "Brother Chapman talks of not breaking it into terms. We will be boarding the pupils, you know and I suppose he means to run continuously."

"Very well," Johnny said firmly. "Then we ask for your release in May, and we get married the first of June. Is that fair?"

"I suppose it is," she said, slowly. "Yes, if any of this is at all fair, I suppose it is."

"What do you mean?" Johnny said quickly. "What do you mean if any of this is at all fair?"

Her face was troubled again. "Well, they couldn't have expected . . . I was chosen, you see, Johnny. Brother Chapman came to North Guilford after he made his journey to this country and he recruited each of us for special reasons. We were all from New England, or New York, so that we should have a harmonious background and work willingly together. And Brother Vaill was my minister. He recommended me because, in his opinion, I was a good teacher, and because I had some knowledge of nursing. I came in the full knowledge it was a dedication — "

"And now you are undedicating yourself, is that it?" He laughed gently. "How old are you, Judith?"

"Twenty-one."

"And you really meant never to love or to marry? At twenty-one you could be certain of that?"

"Yes, I could be certain," she said spiritedly. Then, realizing she had been anything but certain she added, ruefully, "Well, in Connecticut I was certain."

"Of course," he went on, teasing her, "they thought they had taken care of the ways of nature by bringing an equal number of unmarried men and women. Did they expect you to pair off like the animals in the ark?"

Suspiciously she looked at him, but his face was solemn. "What would have been wrong with that?"

"Nothing," he said innocently, "except that people aren't animals. They don't pair off according to plan sometimes."

"You needn't joke about it, Johnny," she retorted. "The last thing, the very *last* thing they could have expected was that one of us would — "

"Would fall from grace," he supplied.

Shocked, she looked at him, her mouth trembling, her eyes filling with tears. "Oh, Johnny!" she mourned, collapsing against him. "Don't say such things!"

He held her and smoothed her hair. "My darling, I won't. You are being very good about all of it. And I know it is hard for you. But don't let that terrible conscience of yours trouble you so much. This is good, too. This is the best, really. Don't put such a premium on yourself. The best of us isn't indispensable. The mission isn't going to fall apart because you marry and leave it."

"I never thought it would," she said, wiping her eyes, "but I do feel a little as if I am deserting."

"I can see how you would," Johnny said, and he could not make it easier for her. "But I think that is something you must get used to. It's something no one else can take on for you. There are few things in life that come to you free, without cost. Maybe that's your cost. Let me tell you what Rebecca and Stephen paid for their love."

This was a thing Johnny knew she must know. There would be no living near Rebecca and Stephen without knowing it, for they sometimes, not often but occasionally, spoke of their days in the Shaker community. This was one more thing Judith must accept, the knowledge that Rebecca had been married before and that, so far as she knew, her first husband, Richard Cooper, still lived in the Shaker village. Telling it, he did not look at her. He kept his eyes, instead, on the ground, speaking slowly but telling it all to the end. He wondered as he told it if any woman could be expected to meet so many new and different things. All of it, leaving the mission, making a new life in a place which all her friends and associates held to be immoral, marrying a man who was in a business they considered not only worldly but grasping, taking as a sister a woman divorced . . . all of it, if it could be done at all, required so very much cour-

age, and she was, after all, very young to be called on to have
it. He knew, however, she *must* have it, if they had any future
together. But he was grateful she knew Rebecca.

When he had finished, however, and looked at her, instead of
being shocked as he had expected her to be, she was ablaze with
indignation. "What a terribly, terribly cruel man Richard
Cooper was!"

Johnny slumped against the fence, an inner amusement mixed
with a draining sense of relief. Who could ever tell how a
woman was going to react? In her shoes a man, especially a man
of a strict religious persuasion, would probably have held to a
rigid adherence to the ideas of the times. He would have shaken
his head and said it was a woman's duty to follow where her
husband led. Instead, Judith had immediately and emotionally
identified herself with Rebecca. Her whole reaction was blessedly feminine, personal, and uncritical. The *man* was at fault.

It occurred to Johnny, belatedly, that in his own way he was
asking Judith to follow as blindly where he led as ever Richard
Cooper had asked Rebecca. But into life, he defended himself,
not into a living death. He shook his head. "No. He wasn't
cruel, really. He was a fanatic. But," he said, more slowly, "I
suppose all fanatics are a little cruel. Remember that," he told
her, "if the reverend gives you a bad time over this."

"You think he is a fanatic?"

"Any man obsessed with a dream is a fanatic," he replied.
More thoughtfully he added, "I suppose I am a fanatic about the
Osages."

She made a little halfhearted joke. "I just go from one fanatic
to another."

They turned about, then, and went back to the house.

Johnny had his brief talk with Epaphras Chapman that night.
Catching the missionary off balance he exploited the element of
surprise by using the good army tactics of moving in swiftly,
striking, and retreating. He did not plead his case, nor sue for
Judith's hand. He simply told the missionary in plain terms that
they loved each other, that Judith asked to be released in May

of the following year and that they were to be married in June.

In a daze, astonished into disbelief, Mr. Chapman began, "I am not sure the Board will allow — "

"Reverend," Johnny interposed swiftly and more than a little arrogantly, "we are not asking the Board's permission. We are telling you our plans far enough ahead that you may know our intentions honorably. But that is all. We are not asking anything." He left the missionary still blinking his eyes and looking bewildered.

Leaving, the next morning, Johnny said to Judith, "If he does any thundering at you, let me know."

"Oh, Johnny, he doesn't thunder at people. He is going to be dreadfully disappointed in me, however, and that will be harder to bear."

"You will not let him change your mind, though?"

Stoutly she replied, "Of course not. No one can make me change my mind about you."

The next time he came it was to bring Rebecca's sons and enter them in the school.

He was proud of the little boys who, at six, seven and eight years, were both tall and heavy for their ages. They looked older than they were, and they had a fine mannerly bearing. They were intelligent boys and inquisitive and they had not been suppressed. Rebecca had taught them gentlemanly ways and they made their small bows to Judith properly. All three looked more like Stephen than Rebecca, with fair skins and Stephen's pale hair, but the youngest had got Rebecca's dark eyes, and seeing them round, a little uncertain, Judith kept him by her side a little while.

The schoolhouse was finished, she told Johnny. "And Charles Donne has brought his children. We have given them proper names."

"They didn't have names of their own?"

"Unpronounceable," she said stoutly. "We call them Joseph, Abigail and Charles now."

Johnny threw his head back and laughed.

"And what," Judith said tartly, "is funny about it?"

"Joseph and Charles," he said, "are all right. But a little girl half French and half Osage named Abigail is about as odd as anything I ever heard." He touched her hand. "Don't mind, dearest. You will probably teach her to be a good little Abigail."

"I have that intention," she said firmly. "They were very dirty, Johnny, and they are so thin and little. We gave them a good bath the very first thing and dressed them in clean clothing. But they are also very intelligent. I hope," she said wistfully, "their father will leave them with us long enough for them to learn a little, and for them to grow a little flesh on their bones."

"He probably will. All the Osage children are pretty hungry right now, but that's about over. Soon there will be meat again."

He studied the school building, so new that the pine lumber still oozed resin and smelled pungent and raw and clean. "The first school," he said, bemused, "west of the Osage line. I think you are making history, Judith."

"Not I," she denied. "Brother Spaulding is to be head of the school. But he is ill of the intermittent and Brother Chapman says we must proceed without further delays. Johnny," her eyes shone with her excitement, "it *is* a great day for us."

He took his youngest nephew by the hand. "I am very glad. Now, let's get these boys settled in their room."

The second week of September Johnny went to Fort Smith to attend the council. Major Bradford had been able to persuade the Cherokees to send a delegation, and the Osages, willing all along to council, sent their own delegation, headed by Claymore, far ahead of time. The government's representative, from St. Louis, had also arrived.

What Richard Graham wanted, the delegations were told, was for each tribe to agree to the armistice and, during the interim, he asked that they send their delegates to him in St. Louis to make a treaty of permanent peace.

Much talking followed the government agent's proposal, and

each side had speakers who rose and talked droningly for hours.
The Cherokees claimed that the Osages said all the time they
wanted peace but in their hearts they did not want peace or they
would stop their young men from killing and stealing horses.
Osage speakers retaliated by calling the Cherokees men of bad
hearts because for years they had been promising to return
the prisoners they had taken five years before but had never
done so. For three days they sat about, the Osages to one side,
the Cherokees to the other, the interpreters and white men between them, and the talks went on.

Johnny watched Claymore who sat apart, regal in his finery,
the new shirt his women had made him speckless, his silver ornaments polished until they gleamed, his eagle-wing fan fluttering, his dark, handsome face impassive. With a twinkle of
amusement Johnny thought how hard the principal chief's wives
had worked to get him ready for this occasion, how proudly they
had attired him and sent him on his way. He could imagine the
chattering, scolding scene, the new shirt held out, the fresh,
fringed buckskin leggins slid on, the vermilion stripe painted
carefully down the part on his head, around his eyesockets and
his ears. There would be the last anxious search for one small
hair on his face overlooked, the frowning rubbing of a speck on
one of the silver armbands, the haranguing discussion over
which blanket to drape about him, and the handing over, by his
oldest wife, of the last things: the eagle-wing fan, the wampum-
edged breastplate, the sacred bundle. Their man should reflect
their labors with honor and go forth to represent his people with
pride. This was a woman's duty and her greatest pleasure.

Claymore seemed to take no notice of the speakers. He
seemed above the contention, but Johnny knew he was biding his time; that he was listening carefully, weighing and bal-
ancing, and that when the time came he would speak and not
before.

The talks went on endlessly and the heat bore down oppres-
sively. The white men grew wearier and wearier, their patience strained, sweating, itching, uncomfortable in the heat and

tired enough of Indians to throw them all out of the stockade. Then at the close of the third day, when it seemed that nothing could break the stalemate, Claymore suddenly rose. He drew himself up proudly and waited for the full attention of the gathering, then he began speaking in his slow, careful way. He was a great orator and even the Cherokees present acknowledged this by listening courteously. He always spoke plainly, his words unadorned by any dramatics, their importance stressed by the strength of his voice and the sense of what he had to say. He sometimes spoke bluntly. On occasion he had been known to lash out, when deeply moved. But usually he spoke as he did today, straight to the point, his words coming like sharp, hard-tapped hammer blows. "Cherokees," he said, scorn dripping from the word, "will not see the tracks of Osages on their soil if they will keep off Osage land and out of our town. Osages don't want Cherokees to steal what game there is on our land. We want it for ourselves. We want it for our women and children. We do not farm like Cherokees. We have not yet learned how to raise hogs and cattle and other things like Cherokees. When we want meat for our women and children our dependence is in the woods. If we do not get it there we must go hungry and naked . . .

"When the President . . . sent the Cherokees on this side of the Great River and gave them land we had sold him he did not give to the Cherokees all the beavers, buffaloes and deer on our lands. We sold him land but not the game on our land. When Cherokees hunt on our land and kill our game we will always have trouble. This has always been the principal cause of all our difficulties. We made a peace with the Cherokees at St. Louis. That peace has been broken." The fine, deep voice went on and on, and then it summed up with a declaration of what the Osages were willing to do. "I am willing that the President, our Great White Father at Washington, shall settle all the difficulties that have happened since the Treaty of St. Louis and make another peace between us and the Cherokees. We will not disturb the Cherokees between now and the time peace may be made if they will not disturb us."

As he sat down, his people murmured their approval of his speech with their soft, hand-flattened "Hoo-ooos," but Claymore, as impervious to their approval as he was to the scowls of the Cherokees, fluttered his eagle-wing fan and gazed steadily at the wall in front of him.

There was no answering willingness from the Cherokees, but that night, dismissing the council, Major Bradford told Claymore, in Johnny's hearing, "You can depend on it, Claymore. The government will enforce the armistice. We gave them an opportunity to agree willingly, but they have not. Reinforcements are on their way now and we shall not let the Cherokees pass the fort. Go on your hunt in peace. You will not be molested."

Riding back with the Osage delegation, Johnny learned that Claymore meant to go to St. Louis himself. "Sho-mo-kah-se," he told Johnny, "will stay behind. As soon as the partisan is chosen the village will leave on the hunt."

Chapter 19

For three days the women had been singing, trilling the fine, happy songs of the hunt, the heart-lifting, proud songs of wives of warriors.

> *Ah-hoooooooooooeeeeeeeeee!*
> He is the fine one.
> He is the great buffalo,
> We will spread our hearts on the land
> We will ride swiftly
> With our swift arrows
> Our men will strike.

"Meat!" the people said to each other, the smiles of happiness lighting their faces.

"We go on the long hunt again," they said.

"The time of leaving is soon."

The fires in the lodges burned brighter and the women cooked the dried jerky, boiling it in the salted water, and the children and the warriors ate it as if already tasting the good, juicy red meat of a fine fat cow.

The Wah-kon-da-gis painted their faces and fasted. They chanted and shook their rattles. They danced until the sweat poured from their bodies, working very hard to see the signs and to hear the voice of Wah-kon-tah. The young men cheerfully danced all night one night, certain Wah-kon-tah would be pleased.

For three days the women had been singing and for three days the candidates for partisan had been soliciting the people. Fasting, their faces masked with clay, their hair torn and hanging forward about their eyes, lamenting, each promising success, each calling attention to his special prowess, those warriors wishing to lead the hunt and those wishing to lead the war party went about the village, stopping before the lodges, crying and abasing themselves. Two must be chosen, one to lead the hunt, one to lead the warriors against the Pawnees should there be war on the plains.

The choices had been made and tonight, in the old man lodge, the warriors had come together to hear the words of the council.

On a buffalo robe spread on the ground, Johnny Fowler sat and listened. The lodge was cool and dim, the smoke from the pipes circling toward the roof and hanging there below the smoke holes in blue, hazy layers. The good traditions had been honored; the pipes had been offered so that Wah-kon-tah might know their hearts were good. The walls of the old man lodge were hung with reed mats, all made with the beautiful geometrical design the women liked, with the light and dark stripes alternating. The earth floor was covered with buffalo skins, the hair left on and turned up, a carpet on which the warrior circle sat, immobile.

Cut Leg, Johnny's friend, had been chosen the partisan, and the Striker had been elected the war chief. These were wise choices. A partisan, either of the hunt or the war party, had need to be clever, crafty, prudent, and wealthy. He promised many things. He assumed many responsibilities. He must have the means to take care of his obligations. Cut Leg was one of the richest warriors. He owned two lodges, forty horses, and five wives worked for him. He was a good hunter, he had a nose for buffalo, and he always took many skins. If lives were lost and it became necessary to pay the relatives of the dead, he could pay. Likewise, the Striker was a good choice to lead the war party. He had got his adult name because boldly he had ridden up to the fire of a Pawnee war party and before they could gather their wits he had struck the chief himself on the chest. The Striker was a brave man and he was also a lucky one. This mattered. An unlucky man could lose warriors.

But Cut Leg now became the highest chief in the entire village. All band chiefs, all lodge chiefs, the war leader, all came under his orders. For the whole journey, for as long as the hunt lasted, his was the greatest power in the village. No one was compelled to follow him, but those who did not must leave or stay behind. Cut Leg was now responsible for the entire village. He would decide the direction the long journey took; he would call the councils when he thought it necessary; he would preside over the council from now on; he would be responsible for the safety of the lodges; he would appoint the heralds and the wayfinders. He would determine the location for every camp, the length of each day's journey, where to cross the rivers. He would order and direct the buffalo hunt; in fairness and impartiality he would see that each hunter had an equal chance. He would decide when the hunt should end and the return to the village be made. To be partisan of a hunt was one of the greatest ambitions of any warrior but few could ever afford it. For if a partisan profited, by taking as his right a piece of all the game killed, and if the hunt were successful, the merit was all his; if things did not turn out well, the blame was all his. If hunters were killed, if horses were lost, it was his duty to pay the relatives of the killed, to replace the horses lost. The onus of a poorly conducted hunt would be his to carry the rest of his life and the disgrace would be handed down to his children. The risks were high. The rewards were many.

In like manner the leader of a war party must bear the responsibilities. He asked warriors to follow him. He promised victory and glory. The warriors would have the chance of brilliantly exploiting their efforts, of earning great esteem, of returning as heroes to the village. But the greatest glory belonged to the leader. To him was attributed all the shrewdness, all the planning, all the cleverness of the execution, and whatever scalps were taken, whatever horses stolen, whatever prisoners taken, all belonged to him. But if braves were killed, if their own horses were stolen, if the war party was defeated, to him belonged the shame, and the obligation of repaying and replacing. To be chosen a war leader was a great, fine thing. Once chosen, however, to fail was to hang one's head forever.

These were the Osage ways. Much honor, balanced by the risk of much shame. It was fair.

Johnny watched Cut Leg presiding over the old men council. His face was now washed, his fast was broken and he had eaten. Carefully he had dressed for the honor that was his. The part in his hair, his eyesockets, his ears were freshly painted. The silver loops that hung from his ears were glossy with new polishing, and his famous necklace, made from the small backbones of badgers, hung to his waist about his neck. His chest glistened with its recent oiling and his sacred bundle, tied in a cougar skin with the tail left on, hung so that it was held pressed against his side under his arm. With the humility of a man honored so greatly, he sat in his place at the head of the circle, saying little, listening much.

Johnny in his place in the circle sat watching and listened also. Legs crossed, blankets folded under their armpits, the warriors counciled, perfectly courteous, each man speaking in his turn. No one interrupted. Each man was heard out. No man ever raised his voice in argument or discussion. These things were known to be good. Each man must talk his own way and be heard. When a speaker had finished, heads were nodded, the soft "hoo-ooo" of commendation was given, a short silence of pondering his words followed, and then another speaker found his voice. Johnny thought how well they did these things. There was none of the wrangling so common when white men met together to discuss a thing. There were no rude interruptions or quarrels. To be sure, there was not perfect accord, but each man had the right to give his opinion, to be heard, and he had a voice in the discussion. Patiently the partisan, Cut Leg, would hear all opinions. He would then reach his conclusion as to the way to take. He would announce what he had decided, and the matter would be settled.

They were nearly all tall men, with lean, wiry arms and legs, with broad, big chests, with narrow, slim waists, and with hard stomachs. Johnny noticed again and thought it remarkable how small their feet and hands were, and how finely boned were their wrists and knees and ankles.

He studied their faces as if seeing them for the first time. The racial characteristics were very strong. There were not so many differences as among men of mixed blood. They all had high foreheads with wide temples, and though their eyes were deeply socketed and looked small, they were intensely bright and black. All had the strong, aquiline nose, a little curved and beaked. All had the flat upper lip and the more protuberant lower one. All had the rather wide mouths and below them the usual cleft chin. Their faces were calm and serious, dignified and, he thought, almost soldierly looking. The lack of expression, to which they trained themselves from childhood, gave them all a mature look. They were gorgeous men, beautiful men, magnificent men.

He brought his woolgathering thoughts back to the council. Cut Leg was speaking. The way had been decided. They would go, he said, by way of the Black Bear, bearing north, and from there they would go straight across until they reached Turkey Creek. If buffaloes were not to be found between Turkey Creek and the Cimarron, they would angle toward the Great Bend of the Arkansas farther north. The Wah-kon-da-gis believed, however, he said, that the great herds would be sighted between the Grand Saline and the Cimarron. It was the month of Ton-ni-pa-hon-gthe-kse, the month all yellow flowers bloom. It was late for the herds to be as far north as the Great Bend. If Wah-kon-tah pleased, the herds would be sighted on the great plain beyond the Grand Saline. In two days would be the time of leaving.

When Cut Leg finished speaking the warriors patted their

mouths, uttered their soft "hoo-ooo," and the council broke up. Tomorrow Cut Leg would call another council to assign the duties. It was enough tonight to have determined the way.

Within minutes the voice of Ho-lah-go-ne, the crier, was lifted. All down the long street he went, stopping before each lodge and calling in the strong voice which had given him his name. "In two days will be the time of leaving. Make the preparations. Take down the lodges. Bury the valuable things. Make the arrangements for the old and the sick and the poor who cannot go. In two days will be the time of leaving. Make the preparations."

Suard went away on some errand and Johnny and the Wolf went to his lodge. Alone in the lodge, now, with Johnny, the Wolf dropped his band chief formality and allowed himself the luxury of stretching. "Hooooo," he said, squinting at Johnny, "it is good, my friend. It is good to be going on the hunt again."

"It is good," Johnny agreed.

Suard's daughter, the slim young girl whose name was Star That Travels, because on the night she was born a star fell at the exact moment of birth, brought the bed robes and unrolled them. She was taut with excitement and her black eyes were beady and bright. "You are going?" Johnny asked.

She giggled and ducked her head and without replying fled to the rear of the lodge.

"He goes," the Wolf said. "It will be his first hunt. He is afraid he cannot skin buffalo very quick."

"She will learn."

The men lit their pipes and fell to talking. They spoke of many things, quietly, meditatively. They talked of the armistice and of the new soldiers that were coming, of the prospects for peace. They spoke of the direction Cut Leg had decided to follow on the hunt and of the chances of finding buffalo near the Cimarron. "They will be there, I think," the Wolf said, grinning at Johnny in the glimmering firelight. "Cut Leg, he got a good nose for buffalo."

Johnny thought the buffalo would be there too. He liked the

choice of place for another reason equally as well, though. Wild mustangs ranged in the red canyons of the country beyond the Cimarron. There would be an opportunity to catch many and replenish his stock.

There was a lengthy silence, then, unexpectedly the old man spoke of the mission people. "The preacher chief," he said, "comes here and he talks much about happiness. From his black book he says happiness will come. And from cutting down trees and making fences and plowing." The old man chuckled and shifted adventurously to English. "The preacher chief say cut down trees and make the fences and plow the earth, but I do not think I like this kind of happy. When I go to St. Louis to see Chouteau or Clark, he say hello and someone come in with food and wine. He say eat — drink. He have two, three, four people to do what he want. He no plow. He no work. He no cut wood." The Wolf leaned forward and tapped Johnny on the knee. "I tell the preacher chief these things. I tell him what I call happy. To have gun. To have wide plains. To hunt. To kill buffalo. To have plenty to eat. To eat and drink till full. To smoke. To beat my chest and sing. To lie down with woman. These I call happy."

"These," Johnny said, grinning appreciatively, "any man would call happy."

"Preacher chief talk about sin, too. Say I sin, I go to hell. Burn all time in hot fires. I say I not know about sin. He say he tell me. I say if I not know about sin, have I got to go to hell. He say no. You not know, not go. I say, not tell me then." The old man's chuckle came from deep in his belly.

Johnny laughed with him. He was a very wise old man. "The preacher chief," Johnny said, "believes differently. But he is a good man, my friend."

The old man nodded and said politely, "He is my brother." Then he squinted at Johnny surreptitiously and added slyly, "Sommabitch got guts, ain't it?"

Johnny wondered if the reverend would appreciate the compliment.

When the old man had gone to bed, Johnny walked down the shadowy street of the village. A new moon, thin, horned, very pale, was hung free of clouds and high in the evening sky. The stars were thick. The air was still and the heat of the day was gone. And the excitement of the hunt was everywhere. Lodges usually quiet by this time were still noisy and from each of them came a happy chatter of voices. The time of waiting was over. The long uneasiness of the summer was past. The time of leaving would be in two days and there was much to be done. He caught the words over and over again, the hunt . . . the hunt . . . the plains . . . buffalo . . . meat. The words hung in the air and echoed all down the long street, passed and repassed, like the round balls the Indian boys threw back and forth in their game. The hunt . . . the hunt.

He went beyond the limits of the village. He walked out onto the open prairie where the sky seemed as big as the land and the little night wind blew. For a long time he sat alone, his back against the bole of a shin-oak tree. His thoughts followed the long trail that would be taken two days from now, his mind's eye seeing the network of streams, the roll and swell of the land, the slowly opening plains, the timber of Turkey Creek. It was a good way to go, a little south of the usual hunting places of the Pawnees, though the Osage young men would feel cheated if they did not have at least one brush with their ancient enemies.

Wandering then, his thoughts went to Judith and he felt already a wrenching kind of loneliness for her. She had clung to him a little, when he had said goodbye, in the way he had seen Rebecca cling to Stephen, and as full as he was of this hunt, as glad as he was to be going, he had found himself hating to leave her. Love, it occurred to him now, without trying in the least, making no effort at all, simply by its existence, put curbs on a man and partitioned him. With its pity and its enlargement and its helplessness it tugged at him and narrowed the places he could inhabit with singleness of heart. Wherever Johnny Fowler went now, whatever he did, his love given, he was no longer a

whole man. This two months he would be gone now, something of his mind would keep running back all the time to
Judith, and even in the intensity of the hunt itself something of
himself would be absent. He twisted the bowl of his pipe in his
hand and grinned in the dark at himself. One paid a price for
everything. For love, one put on chains.

He went to the horse corral and he found Suard there. "All
well?" he asked.

"All well," the halfbreed said. "Two days," he added happily.

They stood silently, listening to the horses and the small chittering noises of the insects, beginning to slow now as the first
cool nights of fall came on. Johnny lit his pipe. "How old is your
girl, Suard?"

"Twelve . . . fourteen. I dunno. His mother, he know."

"She remembers the raid?"

"He remember. Yes."

"Why didn't you leave her in St. Louis, Suard?"

"The mother. He say bring him home. Say time he come
home. Marry. No good in St. Louis too long."

Johnny drew on his pipe and the small glow lit his face a moment. It was sober and grave. "Better than here, I think."

"I dunno."

From the prairie, from the little clump of shin-oaks where
Johnny had been sitting perhaps, out of the dark, there came the
eerie, quavering voice of a screech owl, beginning high, shivering, wavering, fading down, dying away, waiting, then beginning again. Johnny felt Suard swing around, and he felt the
silence between them grow more intense. Then he muttered,
"Me, I do not like that scritch owl."

"Just an owl," Johnny said quietly.

"An ill omen," the halfbreed said, his voice tight, "a bad sign."

"Superstition," Johnny said.

"Indians say scritch owl means death."

"Indians also say an old squaw who was left alone when her
party had gone hunting prayed to Wah-kon-tah to make something to amuse her, and he made the mosquito."

His effort at lightness did not avail. The halfbreed did not reply but when the owl remained silent he breathed out a deep sigh. "Is good. He has gone away."

Johnny yawned. "Let's sleep, Suard. Tomorrow will be a busy day."

The village was stripped and only the skeleton bones of the lodges remained. Caches had been dug and all the mats and even the bark roofs of the lodges had been buried. Each family had its own secret cache besides, where it buried those things not necessary on the journey but which were valuable and would be needed upon the return. Two lodges were left intact to house the old, the sick, the poor, all those who for any reason could not go on the hunt, and provisions were left for them.

On the morning of departure the daybreak chant was sung earlier than usual, the men beginning with their deep, mournful voices, the women raising their lighter, higher songs when the men had finished. The chant was different this morning. There was a special reason for the prayers today. Alone in the Wolf's lodge, tying up his own belongings, Johnny heard over and over again a single phrase — tseht-hou-ka . . . tseht-hou-ka. Buffalo. Buffalo. Wah-kon-tah, our hearts are good. Lead us where the buffalo are. Spread your spirit on the land. Let us have a good hunt. Let there be many fat cows. Guard us from the Evil Spirit.

When the people returned to the village there was a great activity as they made ready for the departure. The whole village seemed in a frenzy, warriors dashing about on their horses, the little bells tied to the manes ringing shrilly, eagle feathers tied to manes and tails of those whose owners had the right to wear them, blankets flying like curtains in the wind, children tumbling about in the dust, naked, brown, yelling, dogs yelping and yipping, women scolding and hurrying, horses getting loose and having to be caught again.

Johnny mounted and pulled away. He always had a feeling at this time that any crazy thing could happen and the safest

place was somewhere out on the edge of things. They were all
so beside themselves.

Then Ho-lah-go-ne, the crier, came down the street calling,
"All people make ready to leave now. The time for leaving has
come." And out of the unbelievable disorder, order came swiftly.
Immediately the crude, forked saddles for the women's horses
were in place, loads were tied onto the pack horses, and children were caught up and tucked into the safe, secure places
among the bundles. Babies in their hooped, belled cradleboards
were tied on, and puppies too small to walk were stuffed into
nooks and crannies.

In a long file the people formed, the horses of each lodge following that of another. The women were dressed with great
care. The girls wore red bits of wool in their hair and their
brightest shirts, their newest skirts. Johnny saw Suard's daughter, laughing happily when mounted on her pony, with the part
in her hair painted and her ears gleaming with silver. Beside
her were her mother and her aunt, One-Eye's woman, as gaunt
and stringy as the pony she rode. She was grumbling as usual.
"Look at my foolish old man riding that pole-legged horse as if
it were a fine animal. He is so fat it is a wonder the horse doesn't
fall down of his weight. He is so lazy he did not trouble to paint
his hair-part this morning. Look at him. He is a shame to us
all!"

Suard's girl, too excited to be critical, said, "Aunt, for this day
do not quarrel with him. He is happy. Let him be happy."

"He is always happy, that one," the woman grumbled. "He
has not the brains to be unhappy." But she kept her voice low
and when One-Eye rode grandly by on his rangy old horse,
bouncing bonelessly to the animal's stiff gait, she held her
tongue.

Watching, Johnny grinned. One-Eye had made few conces-
sions to the occasion. His hair was lank and stringy, the last
paint he had put on smeared with the grease from many meals
all over his face. The horse had burrs in its mane and tail, was

ribby from leanness and was so sway-backed that One-Eye rode
in a saddle of nature's making. "Hou, One-Eye," Johnny greeted
him when he came up. "This is a good day, is it not?"

The man's one eye glistened with excitement. "It is a very
good day," he agreed, his mouth twitching. "Soon we will reach
the buffalo. I will show you then, my friend, how a great buffalo hunter kills the fat cows."

"I will wait to see," Johnny said politely. "How many arrows
do you have, my friend?"

"Enough," the lardy warrior replied nonchalantly. "You will
see."

"I see only five in your quiver," Johnny said, keeping his face
straight.

One-Eye glanced at him, then his good humor overflowed his
dignity and he laughed delightedly. "Four of them are not very
good," he admitted, "but I shall need only one to kill the fattest cow on the prairie. I am a very great hunter and a good
hunter never needs but one arrow."

"Why haven't you sharpened your arrows?" Johnny asked.
"There has been time."

"I meant to," One-Eye said without embarrassment, "but I
have been very busy. There were two feasts to attend and a
dancing which the eagle band gave one night. And then I was
too tired and I had to rest."

Johnny's eyes wrinkled with his enjoyment of the fat, lazy
man. You could not help liking him. He was so honest about his
laziness. He never troubled to lie well about it. He was also so
very good-humored. Nothing ever angered him. He accepted
everything with good nature and smiled broadly when any blame
was attached to him. He lived pleasantly, Johnny thought, easily, happily, even joyfully.

"My friend will loan me his gun, doubtless," he said slyly now,
looking sideways at Johnny.

"Don't count on it," Johnny told him, grinning. "I expect to use
it myself."

"When you are not hunting, naturally," the man said, meeting Johnny's grin with one of his own.

"The signal will be made soon," Johnny warned him and he rode away, jolting easily with his horse's walk.

The warriors, stiff with self-consciousness, rode up and down the long rank. Each warrior rode his best horse, for the departure was full of ceremony. The bridles were gay with scarlet cloth and the little tinkling bells. The richest warriors had adorned the necks of their mustangs with bright bands of cloth and bells were hung from them also. The silver armbands shone and the long ear ornaments shook and dangled.

At each beaded belt hung a knife in its painted skin case, a waist axe, sharp and wicked looking, the warrior's pipe case and his tobacco pouch, and across the knees of some, but only a few, a gun was held. On the back of each was slung his war-shield, some in their painted skin covers, some uncovered showing their intricate designs and their fringe of crane feathers. Some carried their sacred bundles on their backs, the bundles made of rattle-snake skin, or cougar skins, or deer skins beaded and worked with color. The quiver of arrows was also slung on the back, and the feathered bows. Brilliant, colorful, gay, the warriors of the Osages were an honor to their wives, each of whom watched her own man slyly, trilled softly to him when he passed her, took pride in his handsome maleness, took pride in her care of him.

At a signal the warriors designated as wayfinders and scouts wheeled away and trotted their horses out ahead of the long file, the wayfinders keeping together, the scouts fanning out in twos and threes across the prairie to either side. They were the lookouts and warners. Each man carried a polished mirror with which he could signal for miles. These men held the safety of the entire party in their hands, for only on their warning could the people, traveling in so large a party, halt and make their preparations should enemies threaten.

The long line began to move, dogs running along beside the horses, nipping at their heels, yelping, the people solemn now, but excited. With the family of the Wolf Johnny took his place. Later he might shift, ride ahead with the wayfinders, swerve aside with the scouts, but at the departure his place was with the lodge to which he belonged.

One group of warriors stayed behind until the last family had passed. These were the men of the Dog Society, the soldiers, the rearguard, the men who watched to see that in the passing no one was forgotten, no one fell behind and was left, no danger threatened from the rear.

As the last soldier fell into place and the long caravan wound out of the village, the solemnity of the leave-taking disappeared and the women began to sing, their light high voices coming back from the head of the line, the song taken up finally by all the women. And the children, spilling over with excitement, bursting with it, howled and squalled and young kangas kicked their horses and broke from the line and dashed from one end of it to the other. There were some falls but the fallen lad picked himself up and mounted again, went pelting headlong down the string of horses again. No one forbade them. Lenient, indulgent, the elders looked on, uttered their soft, hand-flattened "hoo-ooo," and looked approvingly at the children and at each other. It was a very good world when Osages went on a hunt.

All day the long, slow, but steadily moving line proceeded, the dust rising and hanging over it until the air was milky and choking with it. The sun streamed down hotly and the skies stayed cloudless and all the land about them, as far as they could see, ahead, on either side, behind, was golden under the bright light. September — the month when all yellow flowers bloom. The month of golden grass and air and skies. The good month when meat would be found.

The kangas grew weary of their sport and fell into line again. Small children nodded and slept. The women hushed their singing and rode quietly; the heads of the horses swayed and the dust plumed and billowed and then settled in a fine veil on everything exposed. There were no signals from the scouts, no hurrying rides up from the rear by the Dog soldiers. Once an old woman, recognizing in the distance the burial mound of one of her people, rode out away from the line, her face twisted with old, remembered grief, her voice lifted in the lamenting song. No one rode with her. In the good, mannerly way, no one noticed. She went alone and the line moved on. No one noticed when she came back. She came back alone, her face composed now, her song silenced, and she joined her lodge group with a querulous complaint at her daughter-in-law who had crowded up into her place. Uncomplaining, the daughter-in-law fell back and, muttering and scolding, the old grandmother nudged into the line.

Johnny rode ahead now with Cut Leg. In front of them the wayfinders jogged slowly, and immediately behind the heralds rode. "How far today?" Johnny asked the partisan.

"The people will be tired the first day," the Indian said. "We go no farther than Bird Creek."

It was no great piece from the village, but it was not a bad day's travel, and it was a good place to camp. The little creek was in a narrow, woodsy valley. It was a pleasant place and the people would be happy with good water and plenty of wood for their fires. A good partisan selected the camping places carefully, the needs of the people kept in mind.

When the sun was half a hand high in the west the wayfinders broke their group and rode in a circle, signaling that the camp was just ahead. Cut Leg spoke to the heralds who rode back down the long line. "Make ready to camp. The day's journey is finished. The camp is just ahead. Make ready to camp."

Drawing up, the warriors dismounted and threw themselves at once on their blankets, lighting their pipes. Their women rode up and took the horses and went immediately into the woman's work of making camp. Swiftly, accustomed to the routine, they worked. They went into the woods and brought back long, pliant branches, ten, twelve feet long, which they set into the ground. Having tied the tops together they then stretched over them blankets and robes in a conical shape and soon there were two hundred camp lodges made. The opening of every lodge faced east. This was the custom. Rains came from the west. Each woman in a family had her appointed task. Some built the lodges. Others unpacked the cooking kettles. Still others laid open the packs of provisions and got out what was to be prepared. Others laid out the bed robes and floored the lodge. The young girls helped. The children and dogs tumbled about. Within an hour the camp had the look of having always been there.

One group of women, led by the Wolf's grumbling old woman, worked on two larger lodges outside the camp. One of these was for the old warriors. It was the Fire of the Old Men. The other was for the younger men and was called the Fire of the Braves.

Ho-lah-go-ne went among the people and told them it had been a good day's journey. No danger threatened. They could be at peace. They could cook the food and the women could bathe and the young men could have their games when the food was eaten. The dances could be held. The crier told the warriors that the partisan called a council. "In the Fire of the Old Men, all warriors will meet. A matter is to be discussed. A matter of the journey tomorrow is to be talked about."

Johnny did not attend the council. He went to the small, limpid-watered creek where the young men were already bathing and plunged his own salt-sweated, dust-covered body into the cool water. Like young brown seals the young men swam about. They watched Johnny dive, head foremost, into the water, calling out to him, "Han-hai!" Good. They did not dive so, though some, watching him, tried it. With their legs spread they jumped into the water, but awkward as it looked, once in the water they swam twice as rapidly as he, much less noisily, and much more gracefully. They rarely used their feet, their powerful, lean young arms pulling them through the water instead.

The call to eat came and the group left the creek, wound their bright loincloths about them and ran, shouting and crowding and tripping each other, back to the lodges. A few, older, stayed behind. Ostentatiously they made an effort to seem casual. Dressing, Johnny grinned. They would hide behind the screen of bushes to watch the girls when they came to bathe. Later, the girls sweetly clean, they would try to entice them into the woods and unless the mothers were very alert, some of the girls would go.

Little Beaver, the son of Handsome Bird, was among those who stayed behind. Slim, as gleaming as a new copper in the clear water, he was one of the handsomest of the young men and he was also one of the sweetest singers. He sat on a rock near the bank as Johnny dressed. "This is not a good thing," Johnny told him, "to watch the girls when they bathe."

The boy hung his head and his full lower lip pouted out. "The mother," he muttered, "is too watchful. I am not allowed near."

"You are in love, then?" Johnny said. "Who is the girl?"

"The daughter of Suard. Star That Travels."

"She is very young," Johnny said. "It is good that the mother is watchful."

"Old enough," the young man said. But he flung himself off the rock abruptly and seized his loincloth, frowning and ashamed. "I am not a boy to hide in the bushes."

"Maybe she will choose you in the dance tonight," Johnny said.

"No. That one chooses only the old men and laughs at all the young ones."

Johnny quelled his laughter. The boy's dignity was not to be affronted. "Then sing her one of your songs."

Proudly the young man lifted his chin. "I do not waste my love songs on one who does not hear."

Johnny put his hand on the young man's shoulder. "My friend, she will never hear if you do not sing. Tonight when the moon is high and the lodges are quiet, play your flute and sing your best song to her."

As the twilight came on, the kangas played a game with their knives, throwing them at targets, and some of the young men played a game of round ball. Others shot their arrows. An arrow was stuck upright in the ground for a target. Smoking, lying on his blanket, Johnny looked on. They had been practicing since they were old enough to stretch a bow. Some of these young men, when the herd of buffalo was sighted, when the hunters were given the word to go in, would shoot an arrow so straight and so hard that it would completely pierce the broad, thick chest of the animal.

When the dark fell and the fires were built up, the families gathered in groups. From where he lay Johnny watched as the young men formed themselves and the girls, now shy and giggling, waited. When the drums started, the girls moved forward, each choosing a young man, and the dancing about the fire began in a weaving, circling movement. Johnny watched Suard's daughter. Slim, beautiful, laughing, with a red flower stuck in the black braids coiled about her ears, she refused to choose. She stood instead and looked on until her own father leaped from the watching warriors and took her hand and led her into the dance. Johnny saw the Little Beaver scowl and stride away. He laughed, knowing it was not a laughing matter to the lovesick young man. It was a tragedy. Everyone knew that he loved Star That Travels. Such things could not be kept hidden. And everyone was witness to her refusal of him. If it was mischief, she would relent some day. But if she did not love him, his chances would never improve. It was not a matter for a young man to be humorous about.

Johnny moved his blanket away from the fire, into the edge of the woods. The lodge was too crowded and he did not wish to sleep under a roof. Always on a hunt he slept better with nothing but the skies over him. The dancing and the singing continued until Ho-lah-go-ne, bearing the word of the partisan, came crying that the dancing should now cease, all should go to their lodges, all should rest. He called the order in which the families would leave in the morning and at the last he begged them to sleep well, to rest peacefully. "Your men," he told the women, "are here. Your men will protect you."

When the camp was quiet, the fires faded, only the trickling waters of the little creek noisy in the night, the love flute of the Little Beaver came from far up Bird Creek where lonely and lovesick, unhappy and forlorn, the young man played a thin, sweet love song, a little sad, a little hopeless.

There was no sound from the lodge of the Wolf and Johnny wondered if Star That Travels slept or listened, smiling, in the dark.

Chapter 20

THIS WAS the pattern of the days as the Osages traveled toward the grazing lands of the buffalo herds. Across Bird Creek and the Sagamité, over the Arkansas at the Crazy Horse ford, and up the cottonwood-girt course of the Black Bear they moved, like a great snake bellying over the sun-drenched land, its head and its tail out of sight of each other. The days were brilliant with sun, and the nights, the moon waxing, were radiant with moonlight.

Twice it rained in the night, but it was a gentle rain, whimpering featherily on the skin coverings of the conical lodges. The Indians, who never snored, who slept more quietly than any people Johnny had ever known, smiled and said they were good sleeping rains.

Once there was a small fright, not lasting long, that the Pawnees were on their track. On the seventh morning, as they prepared to break camp Suard, who had been hunting the evening before, missed his butchering knife. He struck his forehead with his hand in mortification. "In that little thicket . . . from which the young antelope sprang. It is there, on the ground, where I skinned him."

He leaped on his horse and went to recover it, but he returned with a grave face, going straight to Cut Leg to report what he had discovered. "Horses — enough to mark the ground all around, and moccasin tracks, four, five, men."

Before even the crier went through the camp to say that the departure would not yet take place, the news sped through the people that it was possible Pawnees were following them, spying on them, and the women grew excited and frightened and ran about gathering their children together. Some stopped their work and wailed, but Ho-lah-go-ne assured them they need not fear. "Your men are here," he went among them saying, "there is nothing to be afraid of. Sing the good songs to your children, but do not spread your hearts on the ground. Do not be afraid."

Cut Leg called a council of the warriors and it was decided to send searchers to look over the thicket. Johnny and Suard, also the Wolf, went with the searchers.

There were, as Suard had said, the plain signs of horses, of more than one or two, and there were moccasin marks of, the trackers finally determined, four men. The small party had been hidden in the thicket for a number of hours. This could be told by the milling of the tracks and by the droppings of the horses. The last droppings were still humid and odorous.

The moccasin tracks were not clear. They were blurred and overstepped by the horse prints, lost in the dust which the hooves of the animals had churned up. For two hours the trackers bent over the muddled ground, studying it closely and intently. The Wolf, aloof, taking no part in the search but watching silently, went after a while a little apart to relieve himself. He motioned to Johnny, who went to him. The old man pointed to one clean, clear print in the soft soil, laughing silently. "No Pawnees," he said.

Johnny squatted over the print. The Pawnees wrapped the thong that tied their moccasins under the sole of the foot and a distinct track was thus made. But this was a smooth print, and it was a slight man who had made it, one who did not weigh heavily, and his foot was small. Johnny looked up at the Wolf. The old man's eyes glinted with humor. "Osage young men," he said.

Johnny nodded. It was likely. Four, slipping away from the camp for whatever reason, to gamble a little, to talk, might have spent the most of the night here. Neither man mentioned the print to the trackers. It would be found. Nothing, no possibility of a sign would be overlooked. It was not the place of any other man to show the trackers their business and shame them.

The close scrutiny continued in a widening circle and eventually, perhaps an hour later, the clean print was discovered. There were grunts of satisfaction and a huddled conference, then it was announced that the usual Pawnee moccasin had not made the tracks in the thicket. Cautiously, however, it was suggested that the Pawnees might be trying a ruse — they might be wearing other moccasins. Perhaps they had made a raid. Perhaps their own moccasins were worn. Perhaps they were wearing the moccasins of their victims. No danger was overlooked. It was not yet determined that the small party hiding in the thicket had not been Pawnees.

Leaving the thicket, now, the trackers followed the trail across the prairie. It went circling about, purposelessly, for a time, as if the men were lost or aimless, then, oddly, it went straight for the Osage camp and ended at the horse pickets. Quiet laughter ran through the group of trackers. "Osage young men," they said to each other, and went to report the matter to the partisan.

No young man spoke up, and no blame was attached to these four who had caused a quicksilver stream of fear to run through the entire village and who had delayed them for a whole morning. Johnny, mounting to ride on, felt a little impatience with the Osage way that excused this conduct, that even attributed wisdom to the young men for keeping silent and allowing the long delay. But Osages said, who were young men to say there were not enemies lurking in the thicket? Who were young men to decide? It was prudent, wise of them to hold their tongues. There *might* have been enemies about. It was best to search. It did not matter that the whole village had been delayed and frightened. What mattered was that a few Osage young men had shown they knew the proper way to behave. They had, properly, let a search discover who had been in the thicket. A little core of anger fed in Johnny. For once he disagreed with the Osage way. He would rather have discovered, for a certainty, that Osage young men had been there and who they were. But on a great hunt he had no more authority than the youngest and most inexperienced warrior. It would be presumptuous of him to speak out.

They camped only five miles farther on, and it was that night, in the dancing, that Star That Travels chose the Little Beaver for the first time and, later, under the now fulling moon, his love flute grew so lyrical with joy, and the trills he executed were so difficult and so numerous that, smiling, the elders said the moon had gone to his head.

It was in the darkness that followed, when the moon had gone down and only the stars were thick overhead, when the Little Beaver's flute was silent, that the horses were alarmed. Waking alertly at the first nicker and whiffled snort, Johnny was quick to get to the herd. Almost instantly Suard was with him, and a shadowy, quiet stream of warriors were among the horses. Running feet on the prairie sounded loud. Talking to his own horses, soothing them, Johnny listened. Not many, he thought. A few, on the far side of the herd, had broken their tethers and were running away. Slowly the horses quieted, though they remained restless, and Johnny settled himself to watch and keep awake the balance of the night. Suard came up to him. "They were frightened by something. What?"

A little sarcastically Johnny said, "Same little bunch of Osage young men, maybe."

"I think not."

"I think not, too. Maybe the moon. Maybe dogs. Maybe anything. Horses get the wind up pretty easy."

Suard settled beside him. "I no like," he muttered.

A close guard was kept and men walked among the horses the rest of the night. No tracks could be found in the morning. There was nothing. It was impossible, however, to lay completely the uneasiness that the horses could have been alarmed by enemies. It meant little that no tracks could be found. It would have been too simple for an enemy to follow the well-marked, many-horse-printed trail of the Osages, and to disappear back over it. But when two days went by and there was no further disturbance the Osages dismissed the affair from their minds. Many things alarmed horses. They even alarmed each other. A wolf skulking near had probably set off the horses on the far side and the contagion of fear had spread. It had happened many times. Johnny put it out of his mind also.

When they left the Black Bear and came out on the prairie again Johnny felt once more the swelling and sad loneliness which the great plain always raised in him. It was so empty. There was nothing but the majestic distance, the perceptible curve of the earth, and the vastest sky that ever hung over any land. There was only the stark granitic essence of beauty, the stripped and unclothed, naked heart of it. Man was puny upon its bosom and the Indians felt it and it was evidenced when the women began to sing, softly but wailingly, an old grief threaded through the singing, an old awe and fear and loneliness. It was the land as much as the fear of Pawnees which threatened them, and in their souls they felt it.

Now, the long file had a different look. Ahead of the great serpent body now rode a solid rank of warriors and very close in the rear came the men of the Dog Society. There was now allowed no straggling or distance between the lodge families. Close-ranked they rode, and there was an alertness in every eye, even those of the children, which had not been there before. They had come, now, into the dangerous country, the country which always held Pawnees whom, on nearly every hunt, they had to fight.

At Turkey Creek the prairie was marked with long, slow swells and it was gullied by shallow dry washes, with small rounded hills and little thickety clumps of trees scattered here and there. The people, seeing the cottonwoods again, seeing the good grass which was still a little green, cried their excitement and relief and hurried their horses to the place of encampment.

The creek was very low and the crossing was made with dry

feet. Only a few pools still held shallow water, but these were enlarged and new ones made by digging in the sand. This would be the permanent camp. From here the scouts would circle out toward the Cimarron to find the buffalo and the hunt would be organized. Here was timber and water and grazing for the horse herd.

It was October now and the nights were colder but the days were still sunlit and warm. The cottonwood leaves were yellowing and each day a few turned loose of the limb and fell, slowly swirling, to the ground. It was a good camp, and happiness, which came with the comfort of ending travel and fixing a lodge to remain more than one night, showed on the faces of the women. Quickly the camp took on the look of a village and the work became the slower, more routine, work of the village.

Each morning the scouts rode out and the people said to each other, "Today they will find the buffalo. Today the herds will come south." Johnny and Suard rode with the scouts but the Wolf, an old man of many hunts and wise in the ways of buffalo, sat in the sun and smoked. Something in the wind told him, Johnny thought, that the herds were not near yet. But Johnny was too restless to sit in the sun and wait. Better to be riding.

The sixth day after the camp on Turkey Creek had been made, in the middle of the morning, Johnny, riding with Suard, saw the circling movement of the scouts to their left. They had seen something. Swiftly they rode to join them and topping a rise they saw with their own eyes the small herd which moved slowly and ponderously down the flat and level and richly grassed trough between the slopes. Signaling to the other scouts they sat their horses and watched. "Cows," Suard said, with satisfaction. In the fall of the year the flesh of the bulls was too musky for good eating, though the village was hungry enough now to relish even the meat of tough old bulls.

Johnny looked at the great, humped, shaggy beasts with their half-grown calves beside them, estimating their number. "Around a hundred, I'd guess," he said. He grinned at Suard. "Osages will eat tonight."

Suard laughed, covering his mouth to make no noise. "Fat hump and ribs! Good!"

Johnny pushed down a little disappointment. This small herd was only the van. Tonight, or tomorrow, the greater herds would begin to come into sight. But the smallness of this herd meant that Cut Leg would allow no shooting. The warriors would use their arrows to avoid making noise and frightening off, perhaps sending into another direction even, the larger herds. He would have to look on today. But Osages would eat tonight.

The scouts wheeled and rode back toward Turkey Creek. To alert the camp, to give them the good news at once, they followed a crooked path, running their horses from side to side, so that all the people would know, as soon as they came into sight, that the buffalo had come.

Tremendously excited but containing it firmly, only their eyes flashing their emotions, the council of warriors sat and soon the heralds went among the people spreading the word, telling the size of the herd and its position. "Make ready for the hunt," they cried, their voices sternly controlled but rising with the emphasis of happiness, "make ready to kill. All women sharpen the butchering knives. Get the horses ready for your men. All children, be quiet. Nobody to shoot a gun now. Nobody to walk on the prairie. Nobody to sing or dance or make loud talk or laughter. Buffalo have good ears. Sounds carry on the wind. Soldiers are now in charge and their long whips will punish. All people make ready for the hunt."

The Dog soldiers now became the police of the camp. With their long whips they stationed themselves about, and excited children watched them, wide-eyed, and crept carefully around them. The women, trilling under their breath, made ready the horses and sharpened their skinning knives. Warriors put away their guns and took up their quivers of arrows, tensed their feathered bows, threw off their blankets. Cut Leg, coming to Johnny, said, "My friend, you have no arrows. It is not good that you should not hunt. One gun shooting will perhaps not alarm the buffalo."

"There will be plenty of shooting tomorrow," Johnny told him, refusing the courtesy, "and if not tomorrow, another day. The herds are moving. The hunting will be good."

The partisan's eyes glinted approvingly. This man knew the right thing to do. This man knew the good Osage ways and did not go apart from them. "My friend thinks straight," he murmured.

The hunt was organized now. Not all the warriors could participate. Showing no disappointment at being left out today, those who would not kill prepared to go along to watch, to head off, if necessary, any stampede. The scouts were sent ahead and Cut Leg led out the line of warriors, the women and the pack horses following in the rear. The entire party proceeded very quietly, slowly so that so many horses would not start a trembling in the earth which would alarm the buffalo.

As they topped each swelling rise the partisan halted the party, waiting to move on until the scouts signaled, until they came finally to the last swell. Here, at its foot, the women were told to camp, to wait until they were sent for. Here, the partisan dispersed his warriors, sending them on a far circle about the herd, keeping with him only a few. The excitement was growing almost beyond containment, but not quite. The discipline held.

Waiting for the signals, Johnny looked among the women for Suard's daughter. She was with her mother and the other women of the Wolf's lodge. He went to her. "Soon," he told her, "within an hour you will be skinning a fat cow."

She was restless with an excitement that could not be controlled. She moved her hands quickly, laughed softly. "I do not know . . . my mother has taught me well. May I not shame my mother today."

"You won't," Johnny told her, smiling down from the height of his saddle. "You will do well what you have been taught."

"Wah-kon-tah grant it," she said, her face becoming serious.

Thinking to relieve her nervousness, Johnny teased her. "Next year perhaps you will skin the Little Beaver's meat."

Mischief made her eyes merry. "Perhaps," she agreed, non-committally. But the skin of her face darkened a little.

Johnny rode away. The signal had come.

The warriors with Cut Leg moved slowly, cautiously, to the top of the swell. Reaching it, they halted again until the other warriors should make known they were in place. The herd of cows had not moved, Johnny thought, a hundred yards. Dull-minded, stupid beasts, they grazed unaware of any danger, un-frightened, ponderous and shaggy, following an instinct which moved them, when the days became shorter and the nights be-came colder, southward toward a warmer sun, feeding easily, un-troubled, on the clumpy prairie grass.

Cut Leg raised his hand, then he uttered one far-reaching, long-sustained cry and the hunters from all sides plunged down the slope, converging on the herd, the horses running hard, heels drumming their flanks, the hunters as they neared the herd reaching for an arrow, stretching the bow, riding headlong into the herd, scattering it. The dust rose and hid the scene, but from the rise Johnny knew that each hunter had picked his cow, was riding it down furiously, his bow tensed by now and his arrow ready, riding until he came up alongside the beast he had chosen, when the deadly arrow would be released, would pierce with hard certainty through the big chest of the animal and it would run on a little way, blood pouring from its nostrils, blinded by the dust, not knowing or understanding this quick pain which had overtaken it, pounding its hooves swiftly at first, twitching at the great pain, vomiting the blood, until finally, legs grown weak, it would stop and stand, legs spread now widely apart, great head hanging, blood pouring, eyes slowly dulling until, in the end, it would fall, the blood still snorting from its nostrils, the red foam still spurting from its mouth.

The dust rose a little and the wide grassy trough was dotted with the dead cows, but the hunters pursued those still running over the next rise and disappeared; and the dust rose in a plume and hung over the trough of the swell. The women were now motioned forward and they came leading the pack horses. Quickly they came and rode about on the field, hunting the arrows of their men. Johnny rode down with them, joining the women of the Wolf's lodge. With them he hunted for Suard's arrow, for Suard was the man of their lodge who had been designated to kill meat today.

Each family of women claimed the cow their man had killed and they flung themselves off their horses, quickly slit the skin of the beast's belly and ripped it down, spread it on each side, then turned the great animal until it rested on its now stiffening legs, the hide a blanket for the meat which would now be butchered off.

Suard's wife found his arrow, and the wives of the Wolf, and Star That Travels, joined her hurriedly. Johnny rode away. The girl would be nervous. It would make her more nervous for him to watch.

The hunt was over. Slowly the hunters rode back over the rise, gabbling a little but not noisily, still curbing their desire to yell their success. What was left now was woman's work and the hunters, flushed with glory, would ride back to the camp now, rest and smoke, and the women and the children in the camp would build up the fires in readiness for the fine feast, would cut the sharp sticks for roasting and whittle the ends into points. What remained now was the good eating and the fine, tight feeling of the belly filled.

Joining Suard, Johnny rode back to camp with him. The short, voluble little man told him about his chase. "He run way across the prairie and up the hill. Way down that little gully over there. My horse, he no good. He stumble in a prairie dog hole. Nearly break his leg. I go off, over his head." Suard blew his nose loudly to indicate his disgust. "I think I am killed. But no. I pick myself up and get back on that sommabitch horse. My cow, he not scared now. He stand in the thicket. He think he safe. I ride up and shoot him hard. Third rib under. He not even run no more. He fall right where he stand. Good," the halfbreed finished, "much good."

"Any get away?" Johnny asked.

"Maybe," the halfbreed said. "Some. Run too fast. Too far. Go down the wash. No matter."

The hunter who had killed had his glory, but the meat was divided among all. To be a donor, to give food away, was to reach the peak of honor among the Osages. With grand, generous gestures, the women cut great hunks of the meat and went about urging it on those whose men had not that day been chosen. Truly, no one reserved the best for himself. The best was the first to be given. To give the best was to amount to much, to be praised highly, to hear, with alert ears, the fine words said, "He kept only the tough for himself. He gave away the liver and the hump meat and even the ribs. He is very fine to give so much away."

But there was enough for all and the feast was fine. The meat crackled on the spit sticks and fried in the fires, and the faces of the people glistened greasily with the good juices and fat which ran out of the meat.

Star That Travels was flushed as much from happiness as from the heat of the fire. She had done well. She whispered to Johnny that she had been allowed to make the first cut in the buffalo. "I think an evil spirit breathes on my knife. It does not go deep enough at first. I am scared. But I press down very hard and the blade bites the tough hide and soon — " she made a quick flashing movement with her hand — "it is over. Next time," she nodded, "I will have no fear."

"Good," Johnny said, "you have done well."

Between gobbles, Suard told again the story of his cow for the benefit of his wife and the Wolf. One-Eye, who had not been chosen to hunt that day, his fat, squinted face dejected, made a show of being busy, but as the talk shifted to the big hunt tomorrow, the hunt in which everybody could join, and in which those who had guns could shoot, his face brightened. "Tomorrow," he said, "I will choose the biggest cow in the herd and I will ride up beside him on my horse and if Johnny will loan me his gun I will shoot him with one shot."

His woman, overhearing, scoffed. "You don't know how to shoot a gun! You can never do anything right. You would shoot your own head off!"

One-Eye quarreled back at her. "I have shot Johnny's gun many times." It was a lie but Johnny let it stand. In a quarrel between a husband and wife he was on the husband's side. "You will see, old woman. I will kill the fattest cow in the herd tomorrow. I have a good buffalo horse and he will take me fast and he will run down the finest cow. You will see."

"What!" the wife screeched. "You have a good buffalo horse! You have a carrion, that is what you have! It is a wonder the buzzards have not picked his eyes out. He will fall dead if you ride him among the cows tomorrow."

"You will see," One-Eye continued to mutter, "you will see."

The Wolf eyed him humorously. "My son," he said, "more better to be quiet. A man cannot argue with a woman, for a woman never knows when to cease talking, as a man in his greater wisdom does. Keep your tongue in silence."

Chapter 21

THE BUFFALO CAME down from the upper plains now in greater and greater herds, their numbers seeming endless, the whole prairie black with them for days. Never had the Osages had a better hunt. They killed and killed and killed until they were satiated with killing, and the drying racks hung heavy with the stripped meat and the women fell to the ground in their exhaustion. More and more drying racks were built until the camp was ringed with them and the whole village was invaded with the insects and flies which swarmed over the hot, bloody strips.

The praise for Cut Leg was long and extravagant. Never had there been a finer hunter. He was the greatest partisan they had ever followed. His was the glory for having led them to this particular place, straight in the midstream of the huge migration. "He has the good nose for buffalo," it was said, a hundred times a day. "He did not lead us wrong."

No one had more meat than the women of the Wolf's lodge. Good shots, with good horses, Johnny and Suard were always among those who killed the most any one day. The women built more drying racks and lifted their voices to praise the men of their lodge. "Fourteen cows today," they said, loudly, so everyone could hear. "Never have there been such hunters as our men. There will be no hunger in the lodge of the Wolf this winter. Nor will there be any with cold backs. They will lie on the warmest robes. The finest skins will cover the Wolf's family now." They sang their songs of triumph and praise, their pride running high, nothing too good for the men who had made them so proud.

It was inevitable that there should be jealousy. The very pride of the women made it inevitable and it was inevitable that some-one would turn and say the bitter word, the ugly word that would lower the pride of the women. It was the old grand-mother, in the next lodge, who grew weary of the praises and the great piles of meat and the proud ways of the Wolf's women. Where everyone could hear, one day, she raised her voice in scorn. "Not every man in the Wolf's lodge is a great hunter. There is one who is worse than a kanga on his first hunt. There is one that is only a pouch of tallow and cannot manage to kill even one cow. There is one, perhaps, who is not a man, but a fat woman in a man's trousers. The women of the Wolf's lodge have perhaps overlooked him because he is so much like them. He wears forked leggins, it is true. But perhaps it would be better if he wore a skirt."

The wife of One-Eye who, truly, had not yet killed any meat at all, heard, as she was meant to do, and looked darkly at the old woman. "Hold your tongue, grandmother," she said sharply, "or I will forget what I have been taught and pull your hair out."

"Then hold your own tongue," the grandmother retorted, "un-til you have something to be proud of."

That night One-Eye was berated shrewishly, shame and anger lending his woman's tongue a keener and more cutting edge. "You are a disgrace to the entire family. You are a laughter in the eyes of all men. You should be ashamed to enter this lodge where real men live. Why have you not killed at least one cow?"

One-Eye was full of excuses. One day his horse stumbled just as he found his cow and was ready to ride up beside her. "My bow was drawn tight," he explained, "then my horse, he stepped in a prairie dog hole."

"And what happened all the other times?"

But he had many reasons for his failures. His arrows were not sharp. His bowstring snapped. His horse was blinded by dust. He felt a sickness in his stomach. "Bah!" his wife cried. "If you hunted as well as you lie there would be no end to the meat piled in front of this lodge. The old grandmother is right. You are perhaps a woman in forked leggins."

Laughter rumbled out of the fat man's great belly, and he said slyly, "You know better whether I am a woman or not. Do you not have many children? Are you not used enough to be satisfied?"

The woman reached for a fire stick and clouted him over the head. "Better to be good on the hunt than in the bed! You are a piece of buffalo dung. You are useless and worthless and one day I will put you out of the lodge!"

Sternly the Wolf intervened now. "There is too much noise in this house. Be still, both of you."

The edge was gone from the hunting now. The winter meat was assured so that its seriousness was not now pressing. Cut Leg, who had led the hunt magnificently with fine discipline and organization, now relaxed the rules and let the men hunt as they would. The soldiers were given other duties and the men went out in small parties, riding with their chosen companions, for their own pleasure.

Johnny rode with One-Eye the next morning. The great herds were gone but there still were small straggling droves of ten or twenty buffalo drifting down the long shallow trough which had become beaten into a fine sift of sand by the thousands and thousands of sharp hooves. The buffalo moved along faster now, for there was little grass left and they kept more sharply to the little gullies which rutted the eroded sides of the slopes.

Going north and away from the largest party hunting that day, Johnny and One-Eye came to a narrower and deeper canyon and in the bottom, feeding on a meager stand of grass, were three fine cows with calves beside them. Drawing up before alarming them, Johnny handed One-Eye his gun. "My friend," he said, "it is yours. Now let's see if you can kill a cow."

One-Eye took the gun awkwardly but his broad, fat face beamed with pleasure. "You will see," he said, drawing himself as erect as his bulge of flesh would allow. "I will show that old woman of mine that I am as great a hunter as any man in the village. I will kill all three of those cows."

"With one shot?" Johnny laughed. "Here." He handed the Indian his shot pouch. "I think you will have to reload."

"Perhaps," One-Eye replied carelessly.

He kicked his gaunt old rack of bones in the flanks and the animal went humping stiffly down the steep side of the canyon, clattering the gravel and sand, sliding and slipping. Johnny groaned at the noise. One-Eye did everything wrong.

The cows, hearing the clattering, threw up their heads and wheeled about, facing the horseman. Loosely, bounced by his horse's pole-legged gait, One-Eye threw up the gun and fired. He appeared to take no aim at all. Where the bullet went Johnny had no idea. Instinctively he ducked, for the shot could as easily have come back toward him as gone in any other direction. "You stupid blundering lunatic," he yelled at the fat man, "watch where you're shooting. Your gun is empty now. Reload."

If One-Eye heard him he paid no heed. He brandished the gun and yelled at the buffalo and kicked his shambling-gaited old horse into what passed for a run.

Johnny was first to see the enormous old bull, as he broke from a thicket of bushes, and he drove his heels into his mustang's flanks instantly, yelling at the same time, "The bull, One-Eye! Watch the bull!"

One-Eye saw the bull just as he charged. He managed to turn his horse but as the bull, blowing and snorting, sped past him, missing the horse only by inches, One-Eye dropped the gun and reached for his spear. There was no room to maneuver. The sides of the canyon made a narrow box. The bull, puzzled, recovered himself and stood with his forelegs spread widely apart, his head lowered, his small eyes hidden by the shaggy hair that grew long over them. The Indian's nag came humping down the floor of the canyon and One-Eye, watching the bull over his shoulder, did not see Johnny racing toward him. Johnny tried to pull aside, but the horses collided with a hard, rib-cracking jolt.

One-Eye, riding bareback and as loosely seated as a sack of fresh-ground meal, was thrown off and piled in a heap on the sandy side of the canyon. Johnny felt his teeth jar together and heard his mustang's wind jolt out of him gustily, but his saddle helped him to stay on his horse. The buffalo bull was pawing the ground and blowing noisily. Weaponless, Johnny eyed him nervously. An angry bull could gore and kill a horse in a matter of seconds. One-Eye, looking dazed, was trying to push his fat bulk up off the ground. He still held his spear tightly gripped in one hand. "On your horse, you idiot," Johnny shouted at him. "That bull is making no jokes. On your horse and get out of this canyon!"

One-Eye pulled himself onto his horse. Instead of heading down the canyon toward safety, however, he turned the mustang to face the bull. "Now," he said, with great dignity, "I will kill that bull." He poised his long spear.

Johnny scrambled his horse up the bank of the canyon. "Get up out of that gully," he yelled at the Indian. "Don't be a fool!"

The bull moved a few steps forward but did not charge. Steadily the paunchy, blubbery, one-eyed Indian advanced his horse toward the bull. Johnny said no more. It was just possible that the man knew how to handle a spear. He had never seen him shoot an arrow hard enough or straight enough to hit what he was aiming at, and it was manifest he knew nothing about guns, but a spear was a heavy weapon, and it was possible to get a very good, a very sure grip on it. There must be strength under all that fat, Johnny thought. There was nothing he could do, anyhow.

In the sunlight the spear glinted. One-Eye kept his horse moving slowly until he faced the bull at no more than twenty feet. Then, all across the broad, naked back of the Indian, Johnny saw the shoulder muscles tighten. The spear flew. Johnny leaned forward, no plan in mind if the throw was too weak, save to rush down the bank again. The spear thudded home into the bull's chest and stood, erect and quivering, buried a third of the way up the shaft. It had been a mighty thrust. Blood gushed from the huge animal's nostrils and mouth. He shook his big head angrily and took two more steps before, drowning in his own blood, he coughed and went down on his knees. One-Eye was off his horse instantly. He ran to the animal and placing his hand on the shaft of his spear, his foot against the buffalo's head, he threw his head back and roared out his triumph, beating the other fist against his fat chest as if it had been a drum.

Johnny sucked in his breath and threw his own head back and roared. By God the man was entitled to roar! This was the way to kill a buffalo — the old, good way before ever there were guns. Matching strength against strength — man against beast — and winning in great personal triumph. They filled the small canyon with their mighty bellows and Johnny vaulted off his horse and scrabbled down to the floor of the gully, yelping and whooping like a lunatic. He pounded One-Eye on the back and leaped on the bull's big shoulders, gone as crazy as the Osage, spending the fear and the excitement and the triumph as urgently and as primitively.

The old bull was gray with age and his flesh would have been too tough for even the strongest pair of jaws to chew, but they ripped his hide off, took his tongue and his hump and tail and loaded them onto One-Eye's wheezing horse. They could ride double back to the camp.

Johnny recovered his gun, cursed at the sand in it, and One-Eye grandly hoisted his spear. He patted its shaft affectionately. "Good," he said, "it is a good spear. Straight home to the heart it went. Not like that crazy gun of yours which does not shoot straight."

"Nothing wrong with this gun," Johnny said. "I've shot plenty of meat with it. You didn't aim the damned thing. Just pulled the trigger and let 'er go."

Loftily the Indian replied. "If gun has not sense enough to send bullet where it should go, it is no affair of mine. I pulled the trigger, yes. Bull does not die. Bullet does not go straight. Spear goes straight. Spear knows where bull's heart is. Spear is better than gun."

Johnny laughed. "Oh, hell. But your wife is right, One-Eye. A gun is a dangerous weapon in your hands."

Returned, One-Eye for once was a hero. Over and over he told how bravely and fearlessly he had faced the mad bull and how he had advanced so magnificently to plant his spear in its heart. Each time he told the story something new was added. He was just about to kill a fat cow. He had fired one shot which, unfortunately, had gone astray, due no doubt to some evil spirit breathing on the bullet. But he had not been discouraged. He had swiftly reloaded and was taking aim to fire again. His horse had performed nobly. He himself had behaved with great courage. The bull had come charging from the thicket of bushes and he, One-Eye, the great hunter, had saved the life of his friend, Johnny Osage. Doubtless, at this moment, Johnny would be dead, trampled under the feet of the great bull but for him. It was undoubtedly the biggest bull that had ever been seen. Did not the tongue and the tail and its big hide prove how big an animal it had been? Alone, of himself, with only his spear in his hand he had faced that great bull and killed him.

Johnny grinned when he heard that his life had been saved but he said nothing. One-Eye was having his moment of fame and glory. He would not detract from it. Even the man's wife was impressed. She was proud of him at last. She brought his food and lit his pipe for him. She sang a victory song for him and she said, loudly enough that the old grandmother in the next lodge could hear, "My man is a great warrior. He has a big heart. He has killed the biggest bull on the prairie. He has no need of skirts."

The hunting over, the warriors were restless now, eager to make a war party and skirmish northward into the home of the Pawnees. It was impossible to persuade or contain them. It didn't matter that Pawnees had not bothered them. Pawnees were their ancient enemy. No excuse was needed to kill Pawnees.

Councils were held nightly to determine how they should go and when they should go, and whether the village should wait at this place or travel, still under Cut Leg's leadership, back across the prairie to the Black Bear. Johnny wanted no part of the war party. He meant, instead, to head up a band to look for horses. A dozen men, needing new horses, agreed to join him, but they waited to hear the decision of the council as to the disposition of the camp.

It was finally decided the village should remain where it was. No one knew what the situation would be on the Black Bear. Pawnees might be near. On Turkey Creek there had been no sign of the enemy. It was safer, they thought, for the women and children, protected by the old men and the kangas and a handful of warriors to stay where they were. The Wolf was named head chief and Suard and One-Eye were both told off for duty in the village.

The men of the war party fasted and danced and the Wah-kon-da-gis made their sacred signs, chanted, shook their rattles, went apart to fast and seek their visions and returned to report that there were no ill omens.

On the last night before leaving, the warriors broke their fast and danced the grave and grimly purposeful war dance. The women sang the death songs wailingly, but each woman dressed her husband in his finest clothing and plucked his face hairs out and painted his hair part and his eyesockets and ears carefully.

Among the warriors now was Little Beaver. He looked very slender and young, very solemn and brave, as he danced with them. It would be his first war party and he was filled with exultation and the high hope of gaining honor and glory. He had fasted rigorously and he had been rewarded with a good vision. His young face reflected his dedication.

When the dance was finished, given boldness perhaps by his inclusion in the war party, by its purpose and its demands on his courage, by dreams of greatness, he strode across the dust and drew his blanket about the shoulder of Star That Travels. Johnny watched, wondering if she would accept him. This was the singling out, the proposal. She had encouraged him by choosing him in the young men dances, but that did not mean that when he drew her under his blanket she would come. This, now, was the testing of her love.

Disconcerted, shy, laughing softly before all the people, she ducked her head, but she allowed the blanket to stay about her shoulders, and the tall, slender boy, frightened, Johnny knew, until he could hardly breathe, drew himself up proudly when she did not move away, stood beside her, the blanket covering them both. Star That Travels had said she would be his wife.

They were beautiful together in their untired youth, in the grace of their adolescence, and the people laughed and made jokes and the women sang advising songs to the girl, who was embarrassed by them but suffered them bravely, and the men said their rough earthy counseling things to the boy who withstood them nobly.

After a time they went apart together to sit and talk. He could not yet make her his wife. Only warriors could marry — men who had gone against the enemy. When he returned, his strength and his bravery tested, he could claim her. If he could return with the right to wear the war hatchet and bells, and with a string of stolen horses, his honor would be great. He would be a great warrior, and Star That Travels would be able to sing proudly of his exploits.

Johnny had his own feelings of restlessness. He was eager, now, to wind up this hunting trip and get back home. It was nearing the end of October and he was impatient to be returning. He wanted to see Judith again. It had been six weeks since they left the village. It would be another four before he could expect to see her again. Time suddenly lengthened for him and four weeks seemed interminable. Here among sweaty and salt-crusted Indians, odorous with rancid grease and dirt, he could smell her, her fresh, clean, skin-scented smell; and with nothing but gritty sand under his hands he could feel her, the tender softness of her face, the live, crisp feel of her hair, the curving firmness of her waist. Love was a sad, sweet imprisonment.

He cursed the Striker and the restless warriors. The only reason for this war party was the wish to add more glory to the journey, to push their luck to its limit and go home with nothing they might have done to add to their triumph undone. There was no necessity for it. He had talked against it, but the warriors would not listen. They were too near the Pawnee villages to pass by the opportunity to deal them a hard blow.

They left on the same morning, the war party going north, the party going to hunt wild horses going south by west.

Johnny led his little band of men fast across the prairie toward the broken, tumbled lands of the North Fork of the Canadian. Here, in the terraced, red-gullied canyons they would find the droves of wild horses.

But they never reached the canyons and they never saw a wild mustang. On the night of their second camp Little Feather, the young boy grandson of the Wolf, came pounding up with the terrible, disastrous news that the Cherokees had struck again.

Chapter 22

ONCE MORE, as five years before, they had planned craftily.

Beyond Turkey Creek, safe from the eyes of the scouts or hunters or trackers, the Cherokees had waited patiently, spying on the Osages, biding their time, knowing their ways and that their chance would come. In his mind's eye Johnny could see them, counciling, saying, "When the hunting is finished they will ride north to the Pawnees. It is their way. It is what they always do. We will wait. We will be patient." Then, truly, when all the warriors save a handful had gone north to the Pawnee country, or with him to the southwest, they struck, as before, on a camp of defenseless women and children.

They left a shambles, and the awful mourning wails of the women filled it with the noises of hell. The dead had been laid out ceremoniously, lovingly painted, and now the women sat with their long hair pulled over their eyes, their faces torn by their nails and with bleeding arms and legs where they had gashed themselves with their sharp knives. The lodges had been overrun. The drying racks were destroyed and the bundles of dried meat, already packed for the journey home, had been taken away or broken open and ruthlessly trampled in the ground. Many horses had been driven off, and more than one hundred women and children and young kangas had been taken prisoner. Stricken and beaten the whole camp mourned.

Grieving, his old proud face gullied with his weeping, the blood crusted on a deep scalp wound, the Wolf told the tale.

Early in the morning, the frost smoke of dawn just rising, the Cherokees had struck without warning. The camp was peaceful, the women just beginning to sing their morning songs, the children, many of them, still asleep. From across the river the Cherokees had poured, yelping their war cries. "Many," the Wolf said, making a wide, enlarging motion, "very many." He guessed there were three hundred warriors, and among them were Delawares, Shawnees, and Choctaws. "White men also," he added, holding up both hands. "I could not count, but there were ten . . . perhaps more."

Dully, Johnny listened. The disaster had numbed him and his sense of guilt brought the sour coppery taste in his mouth again. He, as much as any man, was to blame. Had he not from the first counseled the Osages to listen to the white men? Had he not insisted they could trust Bradford? He knew. He did not have to be told who had led the Cherokees. But how had Bradford failed? Why had he not stopped them?

He waited, sickly, for the old man to continue. "We fought as well as we could. We ordered the women to run away onto the prairie with the children, and some of them hid in the gullies and draws. Some of them were not found, but many were taken as they ran. Some were killed as they ran. Four warriors were killed." In a flattened monotone he told who they were. "The Bear. Man-Who-Runs-Swiftly. Suard. One-Eye."

Johnny felt a swift twist of pain. Suard had not liked the quavering screech owl, and he had not liked the restless alarm of the horses that night. Oh, there had been many signs and omens, if they had not been so blind, if they had not trusted . . .

"The one-eyed one," the Wolf was saying, "he fought bravely, my son. His hair flies from the war spear of an enemy but there is a Cherokee also who will never see the sun again."

Johnny was fiercely glad the lazy, good-humored fat man had had his moment of glory, and proud that he had taken an enemy with him when he died. You couldn't ask for more than that. You could only die once but it counted twice if you could take an

enemy with you. "How did Suard die?" he asked. He would miss
the halfbreed very much.

"Under their horses. They rode him down. You will see. His
body is like the jelly which the old women make from the hooves
of animals to glue their quills on the war shields." The old man's
voice droned on. "All my women, all of them were taken. My
oldest wife is sick, my son. There is something growing inside
that hurts all the time. He will die, driven by the Cherokees
across the land."

"Suard's wife?" Johnny asked quickly.

"Suard's woman — Suard's girl. The young one fought like a
cougar but it was not any good." The old man breathed deeply.
"The Blade put a rope about the neck of Star That Travels and
tied the child's hands and led the child away."

Johnny lifted his own hands slowly, examined them as if he
had never seen them before, turned the palms out, then turned
them in, curiously, widening the fingers, flexing them. They were
shaking like the hands of a man afflicted with the palsy. He
dropped them and got to his feet. He felt no great surging of
anger. He felt no hurrying beat of his blood. Instead it was as
if the blood had hardened inside the veins and stood still, too
thick, too cold, to flow. His hands felt numb with the thick,
slowed blood and his ribs ached with it. He was tired. He had
been traveling toward this moment a long, long time.

The Wolf stood also, more bent than Johnny had ever seen
him, burdened, defeated, beaten. Slowly, so slowly it was as if
every muscle hurt to move, he lifted his shoulders up until he
stood straight once more and he faced Johnny, fixing him with a
long, questioning look. Johnny met the look steadily. He was
the only son left to the old man. Then he nodded tightly, once.
"This time I will take the Osage way."

The old man's eyes glinted and his breath hissed out, his
mouth bent a little at the corners. "It is good," he said. "The old
ways are best. The old ways are best."

Not a warrior had been left unhurt. All were shot or cut or

slashed, but one of the less dangerously wounded had been sent to overtake the Striker and the war party. A more murderous enemy than the Pawnees had now to be tracked down and dealt with.

At the camp they waited and when the warriors returned, quickly, the council was held at once. Rapidly the war plans were made. No need now to work themselves up with fasting and dancing. No need to talk about which way to go or when to leave. Follow the Cherokees and strike. The way was plain before them. The only business before the council was how big a war party to send. The people were afraid now. They had rested their faith on the white man's word and they had been betrayed. Badly hurt, grieving, they huddled together under the cottonwood trees on Turkey Creek and counciled. The women wailed constantly until Cut Leg sent the crier among them. "Do not be afraid. The warriors will remain with the village. Fifty braves will go to find the Cherokees. You will be protected. Cut Leg and your men will lead you home. Your men will not leave you helpless again. Lift your hearts from the ground now and make the preparations to leave."

Johnny did not go to the council meeting. It was a matter for Cut Leg and the Striker to determine who the fifty braves should be. For himself, he knew where he was going.

He was saddling when the Little Beaver came to him, his hair still matted with the mourning clay, his face still stiff with it, his eyes swollen from his weeping. "There is a thing I wish to talk about," he said softly, his voice hoarse from crying.

"My ears are open," Johnny told him. He felt an enormous pity for the boy, an immense tenderness for him.

"If the Little Beaver is not chosen to go with the war party, will my friend allow him to ride with him?"

"I go with the war party," Johnny told him.

"That is true. But will Man-Not-Afraid-of-Pawnees allow the Little Beaver to ride beside him? Four hands are better than two when one goes against the Blade, is it not?"

"Four hands are better," Johnny agreed, his mouth jerking in the compulsive tic which the Cherokee's name caused now. The boy would go alone if not allowed to accompany him, he knew. He was a good Osage. His betrothed had been taken. It was his affair to try to avenge the wrong. Bitterly Johnny thought the lad would not wait five years as he had done. He turned back to his horse. "Wash your face, lad."

The boy bounded off and watching him go Johnny remembered he had no gun. He would ask the Wolf for Suard's gun for him, he thought. It was fitting that the boy who would have been Suard's son-in-law should inherit his gun.

Rapidly the war party rode away from the Turkey Creek encampment. The trail was broad and plain, for the Cherokee party had been a big one. Toward the end of the first day they came to the place where the Cherokees had camped while they waited. They stopped long enough to learn that the camp had been occupied for many days. All signs pointed to a stay of two or three weeks. Probably all during the time the Osages had been hunting, Cherokee spies had been watching. It would have been better, Johnny thought, climbing back on his horse, if they had taken the time to learn what had alarmed their horses that night so long ago. In his mind also there was now no doubt that Osage young men had not made the tracks in the little copse where Suard had lost his butchering knife. Cherokees, as well as Osages, did not wrap the tying thong under the foot.

The Cherokee tracks did not follow their own trail outward. They cut south when the encampment was left behind, bearing directly toward the crossing of the Cimarron and from there toward the head of the Deep Fork of the North Canadian. They were traveling the shortest and quickest way home.

Johnny, riding with the Striker, with Little Beaver beside him, set a steady, fast pace, one which would not kill the horses, but one which would eat up the distance. The Cherokees had a three-day start of them. But they had prisoners, women who would delay and demand to the limit of patience, and they could not travel as fast as the Osages. Also, they were not riding at night.

The war party of the Osages rode all day and all night the first night, then they rested briefly the next morning, each man throwing himself off his horse and onto his blanket, asleep almost instantly. They built no fire. They rested two hours then rode on. But they made a little camp at midnight that night. The signs showed they were catching up the Cherokees. They must restore their strength for the attack.

The next morning they came upon a place where the Cherokees had divided. One band had gone straight eastward, the other branching off more southerly. It required that the Osages halt and study the tracks and decide which band to follow. Impatient, Johnny followed each trail a little way, trying to divine which party had the prisoners. The band which went east was smaller, the larger band crossing the Deep Fork southward. In his mind's eye Johnny reconstructed the decision. The east tracks led the shortest and quickest way home. Johnny went to the Striker and talked to him. "The tracks going east are the ones we must follow. The Blade is taking the prisoners to the Cherokee towns the shortest and the fastest way. The largest party is going to hunt a little before going home."

Worried, the Striker listened, but he was not entirely convinced and he called a council. All the warriors gathered and, almost beside himself with impatience, driven hard by his conviction and by the knowledge that delay only increased the distance between them, Johnny told, carefully, his conclusions. There were murmurs of approval, but there were also arguments. There were crafty arguments. Wouldn't the Blade be clever enough to arrange it so the Osages would think just that? Would he be so obvious? He would know Osages were following. Was it not just a trick to throw them off?

Johnny did not think so. Had there been only Cherokees in the big war party he thought the Blade might have played such a trick, but there were Delawares and Shawnees and Choctaws. They would not be so concerned with the prisoners. They would be hard to control now that the attack had been made. They would be saying they had done what they had promised to do and now they meant to hunt a little. The Blade would not be able to command them so easily.

At length he persuaded the council to his way and the small band set off on the eastward trail. They had lost four hours, Johnny thought acidly, arguing, smoking, haranguing, talking. He was pushed and twisted by the need to overtake this man. The numbness of disaster had passed and a hard purpose now sustained him. He had eaten very little since leaving Turkey Creek camp and his stomach hurt all the time, as if pinched by tongs, and though he was thirsty constantly, the water he drank from his skin bottle did not quench the thirst. His throat felt swollen and his mouth was dry and hot as if he had a fever. He thought perhaps he did, for a chill ran over him occasionally like the ague and made him shake until he had to grip the saddle horn.

The Cherokees were only a little way ahead now. The horse droppings were still moist and as the sun slid down the sky toward the black line of the horizon, the Striker signaled a halt again. They were in a little timber belt and there was water in the Deep Fork here. "It is better we camp here," he said. He did not call a council. He gave orders instead. "We will eat and we will sleep a while. Scouts will go forward and find the Cherokee camp. When they return we will go forward ourselves and at the dawn we will attack."

"Why not tonight?" Johnny said, conscious of his rudeness but driven by his own necessity, hating this halt. His teeth chattered so that he could hardly speak between them. He clenched his jaw on them hard.

Calmly, taking no offense, the Striker answered him. "It is not good to fight at night. My friend knows this. There are evil spirits abroad in the dark. We would not have success if we offended them."

On foot, scouts circled out from the camp and the warriors rested on their blankets, chewing on dried meat. There was not much talking. The men replenished their war paint and plucked their face hairs with the little wire tweezers each man carried in his personal pouch along with his paint. Some, following Johnny's example, cleaned their guns. At least each man had a gun now. There were so pitifully few among the Osages. But the warriors remaining with the village had loaned their guns to those in the war party. Ammunition was short, too. But, Johnny thought, with the element of surprise now turned in their favor, each shot would count, and if there could not be more than two or three, they would send several Cherokees to face the Great Mystery. After it grew dark the men slept. Johnny made no effort to sleep. He lay on his blanket and waited.

One by one the scouts came in, appearing suddenly and with no noise out of the night, standing as if materialized from the earth itself beside Johnny and the Striker. The camp was ahead . . . ten miles perhaps . . . two hours' ride. The women and children were there. The Blade was there.

The Striker woke the warriors and gave them their positions. They would ride now to encircle the camp. They would make certain they were not heard. They would not ride too near the camp. Slowly, his eyes looking at each man as he named him, the Striker told off his warriors and each man slipped away to his horse, not more than half a dozen to ride away together. The signal would be his own war cry, his, the Striker's. Not a sound until it was heard. Take care not to harm the women and children. Be watchful of them.

Hidden, with the Little Beaver beside him, shaking with his chill and his stomach tortured with pain, Johnny stood beside his horse in a small thicket of bushes. The Cherokee camp was ahead of them. The Striker was beyond, fifty feet perhaps, waiting for the pale light of the false dawn. Johnny could hear him intoning softly . . . a prayer, maybe, that Wah-kon-tah be with them, that they might strike hard at the enemy and recover their own people. Johnny spoke to the boy beside him. "The Blade is mine. Stay with me, but do not shoot unless I miss him. Then he is yours."

"My ears have heard," the boy said quietly, "I will not shoot."

The thicket was very dark and the time seemed to pass very

slowly, to creep on cold feet, as if the sun had delayed somewhere in its passage. The horses stood quietly, only occasionally stomping a hoof, swinging their heads. Watchful lest they nicker, Johnny and the Little Beaver stood at their heads. At the first sound a hand would be clamped over the betraying mouth.

There was no sign of the Cherokee camp ahead and a little below them. All was darkness and all was silence. There was not even the smallest glow of a fire to betray the camp. Not even the smallest sound.

Johnny bent his head against the shoulder of his horse and retched. He was sick. He was sick with the long years of guilt and he was sick of the waiting and of the night and of the fever which burned his face. With an immense effort he controlled the ague which shivered down his back and through his legs. The Little Beaver touched his shoulder. "It is time."

As quietly as a breath they moved forward together. The Striker led the way, Johnny and the Little Beaver flanking him. The pain in his stomach almost bent him double now, and the bilious saliva kept rising in his mouth. He spat and forced himself to sit erectly. The pain would keep. Pain would not serve him today. Pain would have to wait until this man who caused a greater pain was dealt with.

They came to the rim of a small, shallow depression, and here the Striker stopped. The light was milky now, very slight, barely enough to see the Striker's hand as he pointed. "It is here." He looked at Johnny and beyond him at the Little Beaver, and then he lifted his hand, drew himself up, raised his head and shattered the stillness with the long, piercing, ululating, terror-striking Osage war cry.

At the same moment, the cry still streaming forth, Johnny kicked his horse forward. The cry was taken up by all the other warriors and its sound filled the dawn and shook the timber all about the saucered depression. Down the slopes on all sides the Osages rode, yelling now, whooping, fierce and exultant and warpainted. They converged on the camp, encircling it, trapping it within their circling ride.

Frosty cold dust billowed thickly from the feet of the horses and, cursing his blindness, Johnny broke from the circle, the Little Beaver sticking at his side like a burr, and charged across the center of the camp. All was milling confusion, the Cherokees fleeing, shooting wildly, racing for their horses, the Osages chasing and shooting just as wildly. Johnny, saving his fire for one man, drummed his mustang about the camp hunting for him. Around the camp, to its farthest edges, to its fringes, across its center, again and again he rode and rode, driven by his fear the man would escape him, and then he came to his senses, noticing a thing which he should have noticed immediately, and he pulled the lathered horse up.

The man was not here. The women and children were not here. There were only those few Cherokee warriors they had startled from their sleep. Dulled by this knowledge he sat the heaving mustang and tried to think what could have happened, but his mind could not work it out. He had been too keyed up. The wits that usually were so nimble, that could so flexibly shift to an altered position and make the most of it, had failed him because his purpose had been too wholly fixed and too tightly held. The dust settled slowly and he looked about the camp, shaking his head to clear it. The Little Beaver was rigid beside him. "They are not here," he said.

"No. Something has happened."

The Osages rode back into the camp. Two Cherokees had been killed and the warriors fell on them triumphantly. An enormous fire was built up and hunters were sent to bring in meat for a feast. The Cherokee scalps were hung on two war spears and were fixed in the ground and the Osages danced their victory dance about them.

Johnny avoided the fire and the dancing. It had been no victory. He went to the scouts and questioned them. Steadily and unshaken they held to the reports they had made the night before. The entire party had been in the camp. They had seen them. The women and children had been there. They had seen them. The Blade had been there. They had seen him. Then what had happened? Where had they gone? When had they left? No one knew. Mystified, the scouts only shook their heads.

"We will look for the trail," Johnny told the Little Beaver and the two of them slipped away from the yelping, whooping circle about the fire.

But it was impossible to find any trail. Cherokees had fled in all directions and Osages had followed them. Horse prints were everywhere. They searched for a long time, treading out and quartering and circling, trying to find any place at all where there would be the signs that a larger party, traveling together, had passed. Johnny knew finally that he was too tired, his eyes too blurred from lack of sleep and exhaustion, to be tracking well, and the Little Beaver was too inexperienced. They might be missing signs that would be plain later. "Let's eat and sleep now," he said. "We are only wasting time."

Reluctant but obedient, the boy returned with him. The hunters had brought in meat and Johnny and the boy ate. Weary, his head against his knees drawn up in the circle of his arms, Johnny tried to think. The Blade had reached some sort of decision after the camp had been made the night before. One scout might be wrong, but five would not be, and five insisted the entire party had been in the camp. But what had the man decided? What had made him leave, in the night, with the women and children? There could not have been any knowledge that the Osages were close behind, or the warriors would not have been surprised this morning. Or had he deliberately sacrificed them? He was capable of it. Certainly the Cherokees this morning had been caught unready. How had the man's mind worked?

The pain in his stomach was easy now. It was hot food he had needed. The fever was cooled and the chill was gone. He felt only a dreadful draining weakness. They would never know what had occurred, he thought. It was perhaps only the sheerest and unluckiest accident . . . nothing more, perhaps, than a whim that had sent the Blade off in the darkness. There had been a sign, maybe, a personal omen. Perhaps these young warriors had quarreled with him and he had removed himself from them. They would never know, he thought, but the Blade had got away and with him the Osage women and children. The chance was gone, now. For this party of Osages would not follow any farther. Two scalps would satisfy them for the time being. They would go home now. Nothing would tempt them to follow the Blade. They would parley for the captives later, but they would make no further attempt to rescue them. Philosophically they would accept their failure, temper it with the meager success of the two slain Cherokees. Wah-kon-tah had not meant them to find the women and children. His own personal vengeance was now in his own hands. Satisfied, Johnny unrolled his blanket and fell instantly into a dead and stuporous sleep.

The sun was down when the Little Beaver awakened him and the air had grown cold. The boy had daubed his face with mud again and he was bleeding from a dozen wounds he had inflicted on his arms and shoulders. He plucked, without speaking, at Johnny's sleeve and sluggishly Johnny sat up and reached for his gun. The Little Beaver shook his head. "No. I have found Star That Travels."

Johnny went with him. They crossed the Deep Fork and rode in a heavy silence through the timbered belt and beyond it, onto the prairie. Five miles, perhaps, from the camp there was another small stream, only a trickle of water in the steep little ravine it floored. Back home, Johnny thought dully, they would have called it a branch, and he guessed Judith would have called it a brook. No matter.

Beside it lay Star That Travels, having traveled as far as she ever would now in this mortal world. She had been ravished and then killed, and with the ingenuity of the man who knew so fiendishly well how to use his knife, she had then been mutilated. Her breasts were cut away. Her flat, firm little belly had been slit. Her sweet, tender mouth had been widened grotesquely so that she seemed to be grinning hugely and perversely, and the long black braids that had coiled so virginally about her ears were gone, and with them the crown of her head.

A long, anguished shudder passed down Johnny's limbs. He

had stood and looked down on one other so treated by this man, but he had been frozen with his own grief then. The other bleeding head had been pillowed in the lap of her sister, Suard's woman. And his own child had been ripped from the belly of the other girl. This girl here had hidden in her mother's skirts then, frightened, crying, never knowing, never thinking, that her own end would be the same.

The death song welled from the throat of Little Beaver and Johnny turned on him. "Take her home," he said harshly, and he rode quickly away, not looking back, leaving the mourning boy beside the body of his unmoving dead.

Chapter 23

H E WENT HOME.

He slept fourteen solid hours and when he woke he ate enormously and went back to sleep for eight more hours. Slept out then he got up and bathed. He soaped himself over and over and over to get rid of the greasy, meaty, smoky, rancid, musky smell which seemed to have soaked through his flesh into the bone itself. When he was clean all over, when even his hair was clean, when he was rinsed and shaved and toweled and dried, with meticulous care he dressed himself in clean clothing. Finished, and not until then, he told Stephen what had happened and what he intended to do. Stephen said only one thing when he had heard him out. "Does it have to be with a knife?"

"With his own weapon. Yes."

Then he went to see Judith.

He went to the house in which she lived with the other unmarried women. Mary Foster opened the door to his knock and stood goggling at him. Her mouth opened and closed several times like that of a feeding carp. At length she gulped it shut and cried, "Why, Mr. Fowler! We didn't know . . . we didn't know you were back!"

It was a strange way for her to act; an odd thing for her to say. Why should they have known he was back? He closed the door behind him and leaned against it. "Yes, ma'am. Is Judith here?"

He heard his answer as she came flying down the dog-trot

stairs and he flung the door open again, took two steps into the hall and received her as she hurled herself into his arms. "Johnny! Johnny! You're back! You're safe home again!" Joyfully, laughing and crying at the same time, murmuring small broken things he could not hear, she twisted her arms about his neck and wiggled her nose under his chin. He felt the brush of her eyelashes as she blinked away the warm moistness. With his eyes closed, feeling her, smelling her, loving her, he held her tightly. She smelled just the way he remembered — fresh and tonic, with the little fragrance of herbs always lingering. He wished he need never let her go. He wished they were married now and had not the long wait until June. He needed her now.

She leaned a little away and looked up at him, smudging the tears away with a sooty hand. "You don't know," she said, tremulously, trying to laugh, "you have no idea what it's been like — just sitting here, waiting . . . Dear God, Johnny."

He took her hands. They knew, then. Here at the mission they had heard something. He turned her hands, showing her the soot. "What have you been doing?"

She blinked her eyes again and looked at her hands as if they did not belong to her. "This? The soot? Oh. I was building a fire. Trying to. Johnny, come make it burn for me. The wood is all green or something . . ." She led him upstairs to her own room.

In her room, furnished so barely but so neat, she closed the door and rested against him a moment, sighing deeply. "You're here," she said, a child's disbelief in Christmas finally come in her voice. "Let me feel you. I don't believe it." She slid her hands up his arms, squeezing hard the bunched force of his shoulders. She touched his face then and drew it down, kissed him lingeringly. "I have imagined everything in the world. I have seen you dead and scalped and lying stiff and cold on the prairie. I have seen you being tortured . . . I have seen you wounded and alone and dying of fever —"

"Hush," he said, stopping her with his hand light across her mouth. "I have come to no harm." She shivered and he put her gently away. "You're cold. Let me build the fire now."

He laughed at the way her logs lay, jinked and whichaway, and set them right and got them to blazing. "You're not much of a hand with a fire, are you?" he teased.

"Never," she said, warming her hands, hunching her shoulders, "never have I been able to lay a fire properly. I get splinters, the wind blows the smoke down the chimney, or the bewitched fire won't burn."

Johnny moved a log with the poker. "How have you kept warm all your life?"

Her eyes flew wide. "But there were always men. The hired hand. My brother . . ."

This was a nicety with which Johnny was not familiar. As far back as he could remember his mother had tended the fire, and Rebecca asked no help from any man now. He grinned humorously. It was one more thing Judith would have to learn. He could not be forever underfoot to tend a fire for her.

Standing before the blaze he looked more consciously at the room. He rarely noticed rooms or furnishings. He knew if they were comfortable; if they felt spacious and large, or small and packed, if they were hot or cold, smelly or clean, but any room was simply a place to be and, for himself, a place to put things. He felt only a mild curiosity now. It was more that, waiting for the fire to burn up hotly, there was a little time of awkwardness. So he took notice of the narrow cot bed with its white cover, and the floor, bare except for a small round rug beside the cot, and the thick crockery wash bowl on the plain stand. He came to no conclusion about the room. He got no feeling of Judith in it, for it was almost anonymous. He did absorb a small feeling of discomfort. It was not a room in which a man could be very easy, though he did not probe the feeling further. It did as well as any other place to talk. It was too cold for the pasture gate in November.

Because the room was still chilly, Judith drew two chairs up where they could sit with their feet on the hearth. He saw that she was still nervous. There was an abrupt, jerky feverishness in her movements. "Now, tell me," she said, when they sat.

"How long have you known?" he asked.

He was not comfortable. The chair was too narrow in the seat and the back was too straight.

"Since yesterday." She pushed at her hair. "Not very long," she smiled, "but it seemed a thousand years." Her hands shook a little.

"How did you learn?"

"Major Bradford sent a messenger. The Cherokees reached their towns two days ago and he had just heard the news from the people at Dwight."

Johnny's mouth twisted down. "He didn't say, did he, why he let them get by him? Why he let it happen?"

Judith looked at him quickly, catching the bitterness which invaded his voice. "The reinforcements have not come yet, Johnny." She paused, then continued hesitantly. "He couldn't help it."

"It was his job to help it. He had orders to help it."

"Johnny! Major Bradford tried to stop them. The messenger said he talked to them for two days trying to stop them."

Making no reply, Johnny eased his hips on the uncomfortable chair.

"There were three hundred in the war party, Johnny."

"So we learned," he said, "when it was too late. The orders were that the armistice was to be enforced. Brad himself told the Osages — ah," he broke off, "what's the use. Brad's a good man. He did what he could, I guess. The blame goes farther up." He moved again in the chair and drew his feet away from the blaze. He stared at the leaping flames broodingly. "Arbuckle hasn't come then."

"They have left New Orleans. They are on the way. They were delayed by sickness. The soldier the major sent said he was nearly crazy with worry."

Johnny nodded. "Brad's a good man. But it's poor luck about Arbuckle."

Without thinking he drew his pipe from his pocket and slowly, absent-mindedly, tamped it full. He bent for a coal and then he looked apologetically at Judith. "It's all right," she said, on an indrawn breath, "I don't mind. If you only knew how glad I am . . ." Her voice hung with a catch in it.

Johnny looked at her. "I am sorry you had to know," he said gravely, "before I got here. I'm sorry you had any time of worry. I would have come straight here but I was too dirty and smelly. You would not have wanted me to touch you. But I came as soon as I could. I didn't think about Brad sending word here. He had not at the post . . . yet. It was a piece of bad luck, Brad's sending the messenger when he did. I would have saved you if I could."

"I know. I know." She lifted her hands in the graceful, bending way she had. "But if he hadn't sent we would have known this morning at the latest. Charles Donne came very early, riding like a madman. He was so afraid — he had a great fear that they had attacked here also and his children might have been taken. He thought because they were part Osage, they might not have been safe here. Were you frightened about us too, Johnny?"

"Why, no," he smiled at her. "Though perhaps I ought to say I was. Scammon is too smart to do a thing like that. He doesn't work that way. I knew the mission would be safe. But Donne would be afraid, naturally. He would think that no living thing with a trace of Osage blood would be safe." An involuntary shudder ran over Judith. "Are you still cold?" Johnny asked.

"No. It isn't the cold. Was it as bad as they say, Johnny?"

He watched the chimney drawing the wraithy blue pipe smoke toward it and sucking it up hungrily. "It's a good chimney," he commented. "How bad do they say it was?"

"The Dwight people say the Cherokees are claiming a dozen warriors killed, forty horses stolen, and over a hundred prisoners taken. They claim a great victory."

"They are right about the horses and the prisoners," Johnny said dryly. "But there were only four warriors killed." His voice lowered in pitch and became flatter. "And if attacking women and children again, as they did five years ago, is a great victory, then they are right about that too. So I guess you could say it wasn't as bad as they make it out."

When he looked at her all the color had drained away from her face and her mouth looked pinched and white. He watched the slow, sick horror rise in her eyes. "They didn't tell us that. That it was women and children again."

"Why," Johnny said, "I expect Charles was too excited and Brad wouldn't know the truth yet. What he heard would be the Cherokee story."

With both hands covering her mouth, she said, "Why? Why, Johnny?"

"You didn't think Scammon would risk fighting Osage warriors, did you? No. He doesn't fight men. They followed us, and they waited for at least three weeks, and watched, and when they were sure all the warriors had gone, they attacked. There were ten warriors in camp. All the rest were old men, boys, women, and children. That is Scammon's way."

"You were there?" The question came thickly.

He shook his head. "I was not there. A small party of us had left to go to the Canadian country to hunt wild horses. We were two camps away from Turkey Creek."

"Is that where it happened?"

"Turkey Creek? Yes. We had been camping there for several weeks killing meat. We had a good hunt. There was plenty of meat for the winter. But what Scammon's outlaws didn't steal they ruined. The Osages will be hungry again now. Which is mostly what Scammon wanted, of course. He satisfied the war party by killing a few Osages and taking horses and prisoners. He did a greater harm, though, and he is clever enough to plan it, by leaving them with no meat."

There was a long silence. Nervously Judith rubbed her face. She was losing the summer color on her hands and face. She was not as brown as she had been when he left. She had been, Johnny guessed, pretty well confined to the schoolhouse. He asked her about the school.

Absently she nodded. "All right. They are good students, Rebecca's boys. And the Vaill children. One doesn't expect Mr. Donne's children to learn very quickly — not just at first.

Johnny," she said, then, hesitating as if trying to find the right words, "are you sure it was him?"

She wasn't going to leave it alone then. He pushed a spasm of irritation down. It was natural, he supposed, for it to be difficult for her to believe the man could be anything but what they had seen the year before, the part-white man with enough education to speak in cultivated English, with enough money to live graciously, with enough polish to entertain well. You had to know him a long time to learn that the shrewd, clever mind planned craftily and cruelly, and that underneath the smooth, civilized front there lay a more savage man than any full blood of either tribe. It was the kind of mind that could assess terror and make the best possible use of it, deliberately invoke it, and the mind was twisted just enough that everything he planned gave him the chance he wanted to vent his own sadistic cruelty. You could only guess why this was a necessity for him. Perhaps he hated being an Indian at all. Perhaps he cherished an undying hatred of his own Cherokee blood, which he never allowed to show but which made him hate all the more the Osages which stood in the way of the people among whom his lot, not by his own choosing but by the accident of birth, had to be cast. But having seen the civilized, gracious host, not knowing him, not having any knowledge of the real man, it would be difficult to go beyond what was on the surface. "Yes," Johnny said, "we are sure. He was seen." He took the pipe from his mouth and rubbed the smooth, warm bowl.

"Were any of your friends . . . were any of the women taken the wives of your friends?"

"Do you mean the traders' wives? No. I was the only trader on the hunt. Mordecai Mundy has gone on the Santa Fe trail and Nathaniel went as far as the Pawnee country with him, to help out on the start. I don't suppose he has got back yet."

She moved jerkily. There was a flat, strained look on her face. "I didn't mean that. Your good friend, the Wolf? The one you like so well . . ."

She was going to have it all, then. "Yes. All of his women

were carried away. His wives. Suard's wife. Suard's daughter. One-Eye's wife and children. Suard was killed. One-Eye was killed. The Wolf's lodge is empty." He waited a moment, then continued. "We trailed the Cherokees for several days. Had a little skirmish at the Deep Fork but it didn't come to anything. He had got away with the prisoners."

Judith's head was bent so that he could not see her eyes, but her hands were clutched very tightly in her lap. "Were any of the women and children killed?"

"Some. Yes."

He could no longer bear his chair and he got up and went to the window. The trees had lost their leaves and a weak, watery sun shone through the thin clouds on the stripped, bare trunks and branches The wind scraped some upper limbs against the roof and their rubbing noise, not very loud, sounded like the feet of scampering mice overhead.

From behind him, Judith's question came unexpectedly. "Johnny, what do you intend to do?"

So. He had come now to the edge of the ordeal. Charles Donne and William Bradford between them had seen to that. He could not escape it then. He watched the sun swim slowly out from behind a cloud, as sluggish as if it were filled with water, heavy and unwieldy. He thought again what bad luck it was that she should have known about the raid before he came. That was not the way he had planned it. He had wanted to spare her and he had meant to say nothing at all of the attack. She would have heard of it, but not until he had been there and she would have known he was safe. Of the other thing, she need never have known. That was the way he had planned it. But that was not the way it was going to be now. Given as much knowledge as she now had, her mind was too perceptive. It had grasped at once, and perhaps caused her as much of horror and fear as the raid, what his necessity would be.

She had followed him to the window. He turned to look at her, his face sad because of the abyss across which they must now speak and look. "Why," he said, gently, taking her hands,

"I don't think that is a thing you need to worry about."

She left her hands in his, as if the touch gave her courage. "Do not treat me like a child, Johnny," she said. "I am a woman. And I love you. Whatever you do is something I need to know, and to worry about."

"I do not think so," he said quietly. "There are things that men must do, sometimes, which it is not right a woman should have to know. In everything else," he smiled at her sweetly, "I will let you worry as much as you please."

She freed her hands. "Do you think you can keep me from worrying by not telling me?" Her head went up proudly. "I have the right, Johnny."

"Can't you trust me?"

"You are going to kill him, aren't you?"

"Judith . . ."

"You are going to kill him, aren't you?" she insisted. "You are going to take the vengeance of all the Osages on yourself personally, aren't you?"

"He killed one of the women. After he had taken her captive he killed her in cold blood. He is — " his voice cracked a little but he made it strong again — "he is an outlaw and a murderer."

"So you, Johnny Fowler, you are going to kill him. Yourself. You won't wait — "

"You don't know anything about it," he said roughly.

"I know what I have seen. I have seen your hatred of him. I have known how you fed it. I have watched this coming and I have been afraid of it." She leaned toward him. "Say you are going to kill him. Admit it. Say it, Johnny!"

"It is a thing that must be done."

"Not by you!" She cried it passionately.

Goaded, his restraint broken, he said swiftly, "By who, then? By Major Bradford? By an old Indian man?"

"By the law!" She wheeled about and walked to the hearth, shaking so terribly she had to grasp the back of a chair to stand, but she stood, nevertheless, very straight. "Don't make yourself an outlaw and murderer too, Johnny. This is a territory now, not a wilderness, not a wild, lawless place. There are courts in this land. There is a governor. There is law. Bring him to trial for murder. I know he is a terrible man. I know he must be made to answer for his crimes. But let justice be done!"

Tiredly, Johnny passed his hand across his eyes. There were so many things she did not know. There was no law for these Indians. They were outside the jurisdiction of the law except their own tribal laws. They could not be indicted. They could not be tried in the government's courts.

Judith leaned a little forward over the chair back. "Johnny, have you ever killed a man?"

He said, "Why, yes. In the war I had to kill a few. And I have shot some Pawnees."

"But not this way."

How persistent she was!

"No. I have been lucky about that."

She stared at him. "*Lucky!* You have been lucky that you have not killed a man in cold blood. What a strange way to say it."

"Is it not luck?"

Her words tumbled out rapidly. "It could be compassion. It could be mercy. It could be righteousness. It could be conscience. Thou shalt not kill!" She turned loose of the chair and came to him, standing rigidly before him. "Johnny, this will be murder. You will go with murder in your heart. With a man's death your intention. Deliberately you will seek this man out and kill him."

"He did the seeking."

She flung her hands out. "Oh, I do not say he should not die for what he has done. But don't let his blood be on your hands. Let it be done the right way. Even let it be war, if it must be. But don't — "

Her hands went out to his arms and she leaned a little forward so that her face was very near. Without touching her, he searched the beloved face. It wore a begging look. He saw her lips quiver, and she tightened her teeth against them. The little crooked tooth was very plain. He felt such a pity for her, such a great, swelling, gentle pity. "I wish," he said, his voice very low, "you did not have to know."

In her urgency she shook his arms a little. "But why? Why must it be you? I do not understand why you are taking this thing on yourself."

A less strong man would have portioned out to her now his greater knowledge, would have laid on her the burden of confession — calling it honesty, he would have shriven his own soul at the cost of her further wounding. But it did not once occur to Johnny. The thing he must do was a part of the cost of the good year he had had, and it was a cost he alone must pay. In perfect selflessness he was able to keep her ignorant. He took her hands. They were very cold. "It is not a thing for you to know. It is a thing between him and me. He will know, when he sees me. Once before I ought to have gone after him. This would not have happened then. But I did not. And it has been a shame on me that I did not. He has grown bold in contempt. He is my enemy and I have let him live too long."

He winced away from the despairing look on her face. He reached out his arms to enclose her. "My darling . . ."

But she put his arms away stiffly. "You don't understand at all, do you? You don't see. Johnny, I have to tell you. If you do this thing I cannot marry you. This thing which you are bent on doing, this thing which I cannot understand and could not understand in a thousand years, it would always stand between us. There is not enough love in any marriage to live with murder. If you love me, Johnny . . ." Her voice was so full of anguish she could not go on. She could no longer stand and look at him. She bent and buried her face in her hands. "Love," she said brokenly, woundedly, "love ought to guide you."

Johnny did not move. So full of compassion for her, hurting so deeply for himself, he stood tiredly against the wall. All his muscles felt slack and burdened. It had come to this, then. Though a man did well what he knew he must do, he wondered where the virtue lay. There was no healing in it. He pushed himself away from the wall. It was safest in the long run to remember, simply, that the other face of happiness was misery. When he spoke his lips were as stiff as if he had been riding in a freezing wind all day. They would not work freely. "I am sorry," he said. "I wish I could do differently."

Judith flung her head up. Her eyes shone with the tears but she shook them away fiercely. "No, you don't. You don't truly wish it. You *could* do differently. You do not love me! Love could not do this cruel thing!"

He moved, then, away from the window and the wall, as slowly as if age had descended upon him. He went to the narrow, white-covered cot and got his hat. "You will not believe me, I expect, but I do love you. I love you very dearly. But I could not live with myself if I did not do this thing which has got to be done. And though you do not now think it, you could not live with me either. No woman can long love a coward and a man afraid of a fight."

She flung herself on him, clutching him possessively, her body shaking so hard that his body shook, too, with the impact. "What does that have to do with it? You don't have to show me. I know you are not a coward. I know you are not afraid of a fight. Johnny, I will not *let* you go!"

One by one he loosened her tight fingers, his face now gone stony and inexpressive, clamped in the impassivity which was his protection. Unbelieving she watched him, when he had put her entirely away, as he walked to the door.

At the door he turned and looked at her as if printing her on some vulnerable place inside himself so that he might remember her forever. She stood frozen, looking at him. He said something, in so low a voice she did not hear it all. She heard only the last of it, said too softly, ". . . 'which art my nearest and dearest enemy.'"

She took one step forward, a hand outreached. A spasm of pain crumpled his face, but he regained his control. "I will not come again," he said, and then he was gone.

Chapter 24

LIKE DUELISTS they faced each other.

There was even the slow, cold, dawn mist rising from the river, coiling about the slick, black trees which glistened and dripped with its beads. There was the dawn sky, as pearly as an onion. There was the dark river hissing between its banks. There was the bluff at their backs, the many-layered, dark, foreboding rock of the Dardanelle. The setting was right, made legendary through the literature of centuries. It went wrong because there were no seconds, and there were neither pistols nor swords. There was no one at all but two men stripped to breechclouts, armed with razored, pointed, butchering knives.

Four days of travel and four days of watching and waiting had brought Johnny Fowler to this clearing on the bank of the Arkansas. He had chosen it because it was free of roots and pebbles, the floor as level as a table top and as smooth. His intention fixed, he nevertheless knew, in a hard, cold recognition, that he had to have every advantage — of light, of ground, and of preparedness. He knew how to handle a knife, but it was not, as with the Indian, a weapon he used imaginatively. He had height and a little weight over the man, but he had not his expertness. Against the Blade's instinct for thrust and parry, he had a longer reach and, perhaps, a stronger plunge. They must be made to count.

For four days Johnny had hidden and studied the man's habits knowing that in their own natural environment, in their own homes, all men follow a pattern of regularity in their work and chores. He had watched the man coming and going about his place, marking those things he did daily the same way at the same hour. He had fixed on the early morning hour eventually because not ever did the Blade's habit of going to the barn to feed his stock vary by more than ten minutes in time. And it was a good hour, when the sun had not yet come up to get in a man's eyes and blind him, but when there was enough light to see clearly. It was an hour crisp with cold so that a man's senses would be alert, but not yet, at this time of year, paralyzingly cold.

Having decided on the hour, he then found the place and perfected his plan. One hour before the dawn he drove a cow and and her calf into the clearing and tied them. When the moment neared he loosed the calf and drove it away, leaving the cow tied. Inevitably her distraught bawling for the calf would bring the Blade to find her. He had found Johnny Fowler waiting for him.

There had been no need for talk, but there was one thing Johnny had to say. "I am giving you more of a chance than you have ever given to anyone. I am going to fight you fair. But one of us is not going to leave this clearing alive." They had stripped then, in silence, and got down to the deadly business for which Johnny had come and which the Indian accepted.

Now they breathed heavily and watched each other warily. The Blade held his knife waist-high, with his left hand stretched out to the side, the fingers a little spread, the hand weaving with a slowly circling movement. He balanced and shifted lightly, his feet shuffling constantly, moving sideways, then back, to the other side, then back. For an Indian, he was short and heavy, with powerful thighs and legs. He was an older man than Johnny and there was a small paunch of soft flesh overlaying his belly. He had a short, thick throat, and his face was round, fleshy, and cruel looking, his eyes heavily hooded with wrinkled lids that sagged at the corners. His eyes were small and set very close together, the temples flat beyond them and wide.

Johnny faced him. He crouched a little, balanced on the balls
of his feet, his own knife held in his right hand, thumb up, and
the other hand, like the Blade's, outstretched, blocking and waiting. When the Blade circled, Johnny moved, still a little
crouched, keeping turned to face the man. All the beginning
feints had been made and both men had drawn blood. The
Blade's arms were trickling with pricks and there was one long,
shallow gash across his chest. Johnny had a surface scratch on
the cheek and his left forearm bled where he had blocked a
thrust. They had felt each other out. What was to come now
was final.

The Blade circled and feinted, then he leaned in quickly, like
the tongue of a snake striking, his knife ripping up in a swift,
strong motion. Johnny knocked it down and heard the man
draw in his breath, and saw the obsidian, flesh-hooded eyes glow
suddenly with hatred. The Indian stepped back but immediately thrust again, and Johnny stepped inside the thrust and his
own knife darted out, found thigh flesh and entered. Johnny
pressed it home, warding with his left arm, and ripped and tore.
He heard the Blade grunt as the knife found flesh, but he jerked
back and the knife tore loose. The blood streamed from the
gashed thigh, but Johnny shook his head a little and the Indian
grinned. He knew, too, that Johnny had not aimed at the thigh.

Johnny feinted now, right and left, then thrust again. The
Indian's arm met the blow and their wrists clashed together and
the thrust was turned aside. Like steel the Indian clamped
Johnny's wrist and he felt the great sinewy strength of the man,
but he made his own muscles hard and slowly twisted until the
grip was broken. The Indian hissed a little, the breath leaking
out between his lips as if pressed slowly out of an air-filled blad-
der. He drew back, his knife circling rapidly in the air.

Johnny, weaving on his feet, swung in again, ducking under
the circling arm, blocking with his shoulder. He found the
Blade's bunched shoulder muscles and ripped, but he took the
point of the Indian's knife in his own shoulder, heard it tear loose
as he stepped back, and felt the warm slipperiness of his own

blood running down his arm. He let it go. He was carrying the attack now. He knew he must harry the man and give him no rest, end the fight quickly or be killed. In a long fight the Indian's experience and expertness would tell.

He thrust in once more and this time laid open the bone in the Indian's upper arm. He felt it grate against the edge of his knife. He had one faltering, forever-lasting moment when the knife hung and would not tear loose, then he wrenched, with a terrible twisting motion, and the knife came free, but it cost him another slashing wound in his shoulder. This time he felt the great, burning pain as the Indian's knife ripped down and loose.

But as the Indian's knife hung a moment, Johnny drove in hard with an upswinging motion, and found the soft belly flesh. His knife caught, but not deeply. He heard the man grunt with a soft, coughing sound, and he strove to press the knife more deeply, to begin the mortal upward ripping.

The Blade's free hand knocked down on Johnny's knife arm and cut it loose, leaving the knife in the belly flesh. Johnny grabbed the Indian's wrist, and with his left hand he knocked away the flashing knife that was swinging down on him. He grappled with the Indian, clutching his wrists, unable to free his hands to press home the knife still hanging in the belly wound. They wrestled, their faces so close together that Johnny could feel the Indian's heaving breath on his cheek and see his small, glittering eyes under the hooded lids. Suddenly the Indian tensed and then shoved with the strength of a mustang kicking, and freed himself of Johnny's grip. Thrown backward, Johnny stumbled. Recovering he saw the Blade pull the knife out of his belly and throw it aside. But the man was too hurt to move swiftly now. He had to bend a little to accommodate his dreadful wound, and he breathed, gaspingly, sucking the air in and out of his lungs.

With a twisting, rapid movement, Johnny scrambled to recover his knife, swiveling swiftly again to face the Indian, who was moving in slowly, his mouth open. Like a great wounded bear he was coming, slowly, heavily, massively, a section of gut

oozing from the slash in his belly, his left hand covering it, holding it in. But it did not stop him. Like a landslide or a flood, he
came on, placing his feet carefully, all his sinuous, snaky movements gone now, only the power of his intention carrying him,
and his great, powerful thighs and legs holding him to it.

Johnny felt the breath tearing in his lungs and he smelled the
stink of hot blood and sweat which smeared him, his own and
the Blade's mixed and intermingled, and he felt the great searing
pain in his mangled shoulder. He tried to flex the fingers of his
left hand, and though they responded they were sluggish and
almost useless. He gripped the handle of his knife and moved
in. He feinted, right and left, pressing in, thrusting, driving the
Indian back, the blade of his knife catching the light now and
shining silverily. He thrust and cut and parried, drove the
Indian back and back, the man's breath coming in great gulps
now, his left hand clutching the slash in his belly, holding the
oozing gut back in. Johnny drove him hard, taking the weak
thrust the man could still make, until, luring the Indian into
making a stab at his throat, he had the chance again of plunging
the knife into the belly. This time it went in full and deep, to
the haft, and though the Blade's knife was stuck in his own clav-
icle he leaned hard against the blade of his knife and slowly,
exerting all his strength, pulled it up and up and up, feeling the
flesh give before it, rip and tear and open wide the covering
layers over the vital organs, rip loose the yards of soft, snaky
colon, hang, and then pierce deeper still. The blood spouted and
gushed, pouring over Johnny's legs, and he took the fountain and
let it go. Until the Indian went to his knees, he let it go, and then
he unwrapped his fingers from the handle of his knife and
stepped back. The Blade's eyes, as he sank slowly to the ground,
were fixed on Johnny and they still glittered with hatred, and
his lips, parted, foamed now with blood, uttered no sound. He
died as his head touched the earth, leaning forward against it,
the soft rope of his guts spilled out over his knees.

Johnny stood over him, waiting for his breath to slow. He
felt no exultation, no sense of victory. He felt nothing at all ex-

cept tired, and his left shoulder, cut and slashed and ripped, hurt him terribly. He put up his hand to hold it. He touched the great thigh of the dead Indian with his toe. Having hated the man in life, he felt no compunction for him dead. He did not feel, as he often felt when hunting buffalo, as if he had killed a brave adversary. He did not feel that the man had fought a good fight. He did not honor him with respect. He felt instead that he had killed a coyote, a slavering, cruel, ravening beast.

He turned the man over with his foot and pulled his knife out of the flesh. Then, unemotionally and quite methodically, he slid it around the crown of the Indian's head, a place no larger than the palm of his hand, and ripped it loose from the skull. That was for the Little Beaver to hang from his war spear — the hair of his enemy.

He scooped up a handful of leaves and wiped the blade of his knife. He went to the river and washed himself clean, then he put on his clothes.

It was done.

Chapter 25

He took the south side of the river back and rested a day at Billingsley's settlement, where Billingsley's wife dressed his arm for him. It was inflamed and sore and stiff, but he did not think it had come to any permanent harm. As the woman laid open his makeshift bandages, Billingsley, looking on, said dryly, "Must have run into a bear, way that arm's clawed up."

"No bear," Johnny replied. "Just a varmint."

Nothing more was said and the woman washed the wounds and bound them with clean white rags. The next morning Johnny went on.

He crossed the river and bore north avoiding the fort. He did not want to talk with Bradford yet. He felt too much anger still that he had not stopped the Cherokees and he did not want to quarrel with the man. He could say to Judith, and mean it, that Bradford was a good man, that he probably had done the best he could. But he could not yet feel it. Until he could, he meant to stay away from him.

Slowly he made his way through the hilly land north of the Arkansas, his aching arm slung and inactive but hurting with every jounce of the horse and fever making his head a little light. It would pass, he told himself, hanging onto his saddle horn, it would pass.

He crossed Frog Bayou and Lee's Creek, and he crossed the Sallisaw well above Brushy Mountain. He forded the Illinois at Mark Bean's abandoned salt works. The man had never rebuilt

his furnaces. Instead he had taken his losses and left. Johnny
came to the Neosho and crossed south of the mission.

A little later, reaching the trail that went north, which he had
taken so often, the mustang turned in that direction. He had
gone a mile perhaps when Johnny roused and saw where he was
heading. A swift skittering pain which had nothing to do with
his slashed arm ran over him as he pulled the horse out of the
path and turned him west. It cleared his head of the numbness
which had muffled it as if it were wrapped in wool lint and reminded him that he had paid more than a slashed arm for his
victory over the Blade. "Not that way any more, fellow," he told
the horse, "not that way ever again. She is done with us now.
We won't be riding north to see her any more."

Realizing he was babbling he shut his mouth and clamped his
teeth down tight. You are a man, he told himself, trying to fix
his eyes on the way ahead of him. You are a grown man and the
days of your boyhood are well behind you, so play the part of a
man. Do not go out of your head and babble like a child. She
is right to let you go. She is too good for the rough ways of this
country. She is gentle and soft and tender and it is not to be expected that she could follow the . . . follow the . . . but his
mind closed off coherent thought and he could not remember
what it was she could not follow.

He could not think now where it was he was going, nor with
what urgency, nor where he had been, nor why. He rocked his
wounded shoulder from time to time trying to rid himself of its
pain, not remembering what caused the pain. He thought he
was a child again, trying to get home. It was a long way to the
Hanging Fork and he wondered where the hills were. There was
only this strange, unfamiliar flat land and the hills which should
have risen up around him avoided him and stayed in the far distance, never coming closer until it fretted him and he wrenched
at his big shoulder and mumbled and questioned and peered
ahead. "I have lost the hills," he told himself, "and I have lost
my home."

He was huddled in the saddle, still mumbling, when he rode

into the Osage village, and as the Wolf lifted him from the horse he turned his head toward him and looked at him strangely, saying with perfect courtesy, "Perhaps you can show me the way, sir. I have lost the hills and I have lost my home."

The Wolf, carrying him into his lodge as if he were a child, laid him on a pallet and then he sent for the medicine men.

There was a moment of lucidity when the Wah-kon-da-gi laid bare the swollen arm and put cool wet poultices on it and looking up, Johnny saw the wolf band chief watching with troubled eyes. He nodded. "It is all right, my friend. I have killed the Blade."

He tried to raise his head but quickly the old Osage bent over him. "Do not move, my son. Lie still."

But Johnny saw the gleam in his eyes, the quick, happy gleam of triumph, and he smiled. "In my blanket," he said, "there is a present for the Little Beaver."

The old man nodded. "I will tell him."

Johnny slept, then, and when he waked it was night. A woman brought hot stew and fed him and the Wah-kon-da-gi changed the poultices. The arm felt better and the fever was abating. Unlike white people the Indians did not bandage a wound. No Indian could bear to be bound up. It was left open except for the constantly changed, constantly dampened poultices. Even in his sleep Johnny knew that the Wah-kon-da-gi never left his side that night. In the good sleep he had, he still knew the poultices were being changed, and he felt the hot fever sweat leaving and knew his limbs were cooling.

In the morning when he had eaten, he asked for the Wolf and the old man came to him. "You are feeling better, ain't it?" he said, squatting near the pallet. "The arm is not so swollen today."

"Better," Johnny said, heaving himself up on the pallet and punching another buffalo skin behind him as a prop. "Send the Little Beaver to the post, my friend, so that my brother may know I am safe. He will be troubled by my long absence. He will grieve, thinking I am dead."

"I will send him," the Wolf promised, "on my own horse which is faster than his. It is a good thing, I think," he said gently, "this thing which you have done. The Little Beaver has lifted his heart from the ground. He has washed the mourning clay from his face."

But not from mine, Johnny thought, not from mine, and my heart is still spread on the ground.

He made no sign, however. He lay back against the buffalo robe and looked at the old man whose eyes had told him the way to take and whose calm, impassive face now rewarded him, its trouble erased, expunged by the act which had become the necessity. He was filled with a deep tenderness for the old man and he felt no regret, though it had cost him so much, for the act. He guessed he had done what men must do — made his peace with the undeniable necessity and with the irrecoverable deed. He felt, anyhow, a calm pool of peace inside him and knew that his first, unbearable grief had been borne and that having borne it he could bear the lingering dryness of the deserts to come.

That night the young men danced again and the mourning wails were hushed. Johnny Fowler, the man not afraid of Pawnees, had brought the Osages their release.

It was midday the next day when the Wolf came into the lodge and said, "People are coming, my son."

"Steve?" Johnny said eagerly, hunching himself up on the pallet.

The old man held up two fingers. "A woman comes with him."

"Oh. My sister. Lord, Lord, what a scolding I am going to get. Go away where you cannot hear, my friend. That woman knows how to scold much better than any Osage woman."

A grin broke over the Indian's face. "Sommabitch always scold, ain't it?"

Johnny laughed, then grabbed at the shoulder which the burst of laughter rippled through with a shaft of pain. "All right. All right." He looked down at his blood-crusted shirt and sniffed the stink of it. He brushed his hand over his stubbled chin. "Rebecca is going to have my hide for this," he groaned.

The Wolf went out to greet his guests. Johnny waited for what seemed a long time, then he heard the horses come up. He heard Stephen's voice. "Hou, my friend. Where is Johnny?"

"He is in the lodge of the Wolf," the old man replied formally, then Johnny heard him laugh quietly. "He is a great man now, your brother. He is the greatest warrior among the Osages. Osages love this man very much."

Johnny raised himself on his elbow. If he didn't stop him the old man would tell the whole thing in front of Rebecca. He shouted, "In here, Steve. Come on in."

"In a minute, you son-of-a-gun!"

He was facing the door so that when she entered, hesitating, outlined against the light, he saw her at once. He sucked in his breath feeling as if something had hit him very hard in the pit of his stomach. There was a quivering looseness of all his insides, a sensation of their slumping and slowly falling, lapping at his skin and raising the flesh on his arms and across his belly in a fine nettle of shivering prickles. He watched her, coming in from the bright sunlight, trying to accustom her eyes to the gloom of the lodge. She stood still, one hand against the frame of the door, leaning a little on it, her head moving slowly as she searched the big room. Then she saw him. For a moment she did not move. She simply stood and looked at him and he knew she was crying. He wet his lips and lifted his good arm. "Judith."

Swiftly she came to him and in one encompassing movement had knelt and gathered his head to her breast. Though she hurt him he did not know it and he turned his face into the soft rounded flesh and rested his mouth against it, her tears raining down on his wholly closed eyes. Her heart pumped so wildly that it lifted his head and he wondered in a quick panic how an organ could throb so heavily without bursting itself. "My darling, my darling . . . do not cry so. Ah, Judith, Judith, I had lost you. I had lost you." And the pain in his voice was like the Little Beaver's eagle-wing flute, singing of love and longing and yearning and loss. "I had lost you. It was that all the time. Not the hills, or my way home, but my love, my dear, dear love."

"Hush, oh, Johnny, hush. I cannot bear it." She tightened her

arms about him and her mouth traced his eyes and his temples
and the bones of his face, and the shallow scar which the
Blade's knife had made and which was not yet entirely healed.
"I cannot bear it."

For a long time they held tightly to each other and then, her
crying slowly ceasing, she let him go and sat beside him, still
holding his hand, clutching it as if she never meant to let it go
again. She searched his face as if seeing him new. She reached
out her hand and touched the scar on it, then she shuddered and
looked at the shoulder. "Thank God," she said, her voice shaking, "thank God you are safe."

They held to each other and talked a little, but not much, and
looked wonderingly at each other, and no one came and they
were entirely alone. How long it was neither of them could
say. "Did Stephen go by the mission for you?" Johnny asked,
finally, "is that how you knew?"

She shook her head. "Oh, no. I went to the post."

"You went to the post?"

She looked at him steadily and answered bravely. "The day
you left. The day you left I went straight to the post. It was
. . . it was where I belonged."

She would have had him innocent and molded in her own
instincts, but that not being possible she would have him on his
own terms. In weakness, which was made strong by acceptance,
she extended the capacity of love to an unlimited horizon and
set it the task of absorbing, without understanding, but with
enormous love and enormous tenderness, all his man's necessi-
ties. In the event, she examined her love and found it whole
enough to withstand the partition of herself. More valid than
the instinct which would have kept him innocent, which would
have trained and civilized him, was the instinct which moved
her to love, and so moving, provided her with the courage and
the strength to love wholly, nothing kept back, nothing reserved.

She lifted Johnny's hand and warmed it against her face.
"How much I love you," she said. "How very much I love you."

Epilogue

Colonel Matthew Arbuckle, with four companies of the 7th Infantry Regiment, had begun their long ascent of the Arkansas River in November of 1821. They were detained for several weeks at the mouth of the Arkansas by low water and were only able to reach Arkansas Post by the first of the year. Here, because of the great number of sick men, Colonel Arbuckle rested and waited, reaching Fort Smith, finally, on February 26, 1822. Major William Bradford turned over the command of the fort to him on that date and received his own orders. They were not, alas, directing him to the east again. He was ordered to the post at Natchitoches on the Red River. He never again served his country in a comfortable assignment. In 1824, he was made sutler to the post at Fort Towson, still farther west, and there he died, at the age of fifty-five, on October 20, 1826.

A greater concentration of Indians having been achieved farther west, the post at Fort Smith was closed in 1824 and the regiment was removed to a new station called Fort Gibson. The new stockade was located at the old trading settlement of Three Forks. Here, as the years went on, men who were to become famous in the annals of history served, among them Jefferson Davis, Robert E. Lee, Zachary Taylor, Henry Leavenworth, and Captain Nathan Boone, the son of Daniel Boone. Washington Irving visited Fort Gibson in 1832 and made his famous tour of the prairies with the fort as his base. George Catlin, the great artist of the west, made the fort his headquarters in 1834.

Nathaniel Pryor continued to live among the Osages and his services to the government were recognized when he was made sub-agent to them on May 7, 1831. Ironically, however, he died one month later.

At Union Mission, Epaphras Chapman died on June 7, 1825, of the intermittent fever. He was buried in the little graveyard of the mission station. It is marked by a headstone chiseled from native stone, upon which is the following inscription:

In Memory Of

EPAPHRAS CHAPMAN

Who died 7 June, 1825

Aged 32

First Missionary to the Osages

Say among the heathen the Lord Reigneth

Nearby are the tiny graves of four children, the children of Abraham and Phoebe Redfield. Small, rough, uncut, unchiseled sandstones stand at the head of each little grave, the last pathetic, loving thing that could be done for them.

The first printing press was brought into the country by Union Mission and the first book printed within the boundaries of the present state of Oklahoma was *The Child's Book*, printed in 1835. There were many firsts at Union Mission — the first church, the first school, the first wedding between white people, the first printing press, the first printed book. But the people the mission came to minister to were moved away and it was closed in 1836.

In the same month of the same year in which Epaphras Chapman died, June of 1825, the Osages ceded to the government all their lands in what is now the state of Oklahoma. By 1836 they were all removed and the prophecy of men of foresight was fulfilled.